Secret for a Nightingale

On the night before my wedding I had a
strange dream from which I awoke in
terror. I was in the church and Aubrey was
beside me. The scent of flowers was strong
upon the air – lilies, heavy, overpowering,
the odour of death. I heard my voice –
disembodied as though echoing in an
empty place: 'I, Susanna, take thee,
Aubrey, to my wedded husband . . .'
Aubrey was holding the ring. He took my
hand and his face was coming nearer and
nearer . . . and then the terror overtook
me. It was not Aubrey's face, and yet it
was . . .

VICTORIA HOLT

Secret for a Nightingale

FONTANA/Collins

First published by William Collins Sons & Co. Ltd 1986
This continental edition first issued in Fontana Paperbacks 1987

Copyright © Victoria Holt 1986

Made and printed in Great Britain by
William Collins Sons & Co. Ltd, Glasgow

To my dear friend
PATRICIA MYRER,
who first aroused my interest in Dr Damien
and the young woman who inevitably became involved
in the Crimean war.
In memory of many productive hours
we have spent discussing my 'people'.

CONTENTS

The Wedding

On the night before my wedding I had a strange dream from which I awoke in terror. I was in the church and Aubrey was beside me. The scent of flowers was strong upon the air – lilies, heavy, overpowering, the odour of death. Uncle James – the Reverend James Sandown – was standing before us. The church was that which had become so familiar to me during my schooldays when I had stayed at the rectory with Uncle James and Aunt Grace because I could not join my father at the Indian outpost where he might be stationed. I heard my voice – disembodied as though echoing in an empty place: 'I, Susanna, take thee, Aubrey, to my wedded husband . . .' Aubrey was holding the ring. He took my hand and his face was coming nearer and nearer . . . and then the terror overtook me. It was not Aubrey's face, and yet it was. It was not the face I knew. It was distorted . . . leering, strange, horrible, frightening. I heard a voice crying: No! No! And it was my own.

I was sitting up in bed, shivering, staring into darkness, my hands, clammy, clutching the sheets. The dream had been so vivid that it was some time before I recovered. Then I told myself that it was nonsense. I was going to be married in the morning. I *wanted* to be married. I was in love with Aubrey. What could have brought about that dream?

'Wedding eve nerves!' Aunt Grace, that most practical of women, would have said. And she would be right. I attempted to shake off the effects of that dream but they would not go. It had seemed so real.

I got out of bed and went to the window. There was the church with its Norman tower, visible in the starlight, standing there as it had stood for eight hundred years – impregnable, defiantly facing the wind, the rain and the centuries, marvelled at and visited by many, the pride of Uncle James's heart. 'It is a privilege to be married in such a church,' he said.

Tomorrow my father would lead me down the aisle and there I should stand beside Aubrey. I was shivering still. But it would not be anything like the dream.

I went to my wardrobe and looked at my dress – white satin trimmed with Honiton lace; and there was a wreath of orange blossom to go with it.

Beyond the church in the Black Boar – the only inn in Humberston – Aubrey would be sleeping. 'A bridegroom must not spend the night under the same roof as his bride,' said my Aunt Grace. Would he be disturbed by dreams of the day to come?

I went back to bed. I did not want to sleep. I was afraid that the dream would continue and that I should go on from that moment when I had shouted 'No! No!' while Aubrey stood there forcing the ring on my finger.

I lay in bed thinking about it all.

I met Aubrey for the first time in India where my father was stationed. I had just gone out to join him after seven years in England where I had been at school, spending my holidays at the rectory with my Uncle James and Aunt Grace, who had nobly stepped into the breach to look after a brother-in-law's daughter who must, like all English young ladies of good family, be educated in England. The necessity naturally caused the usual complications to people serving in the outposts of Empire and, as was generally the case, good-natured relatives came to the rescue.

I remembered the joy of reaching my seventeenth birthday. It was June and I was at school at the time, but I did know that would be my last term, and in August I should be returning to India where I had spent the first ten years of my life.

It was ungrateful perhaps to be so eager to go, even though I should be joining my father. Uncle James and Aunt Grace, together with my cousin Ellen, had been very kind to me and did all they could to make a home for me. But it must have been something of an intrusion – particularly at the beginning. They had their lives to lead and parish affairs were demanding. Cousin Ellen was twelve years older than I and deeply interested in her father's curate whom she would marry as soon as he found a living; Uncle James had his flock of devoted parishioners; Aunt Grace had innumerable activities – organizing sales of work, garden parties, carol singers – something for every occasion, including the Mothers' Union and sewing parties. I dare say I was trying. My heart was far across the seas, and because I was aware of being something of a burden, no doubt I assumed an attitude of indifference and arrogance mingled with critical comparisons between an ancient, draughty rectory with one cook, one maid and a tweeny, and a Colonel's residence with numerous native servants scurrying around to gratify our wishes.

I was not exactly an angelic child and my ayah and Mrs Fearnley, who had been my governess up to the time I was ten years old, had said they never knew what to expect of me. There were two sides to my nature. I could be sunny-tempered, amenable, gentle and affectionate. 'It is like the moon,' said Mrs Fearnley, who liked to make an educational point out of every situation. 'There is the bright side and the dark side.' Unlike the moon, I showed my dark side now and then. 'Not often, thank goodness,' said Mrs Fearnley; but it worried her that it was there. Then I could be obstinate. I could make up my mind and nothing would make me diverge from it. I would disobey orders to get my own way. I was really a most recalcitrant child on these occasions – quite different from the sunny-tempered one who was so pleasant to teach and be with. 'We must fight the dark side,' said Mrs Fearnley. 'Susanna, you are one of the most unpredictable children I ever met.'

My ayah – to whom I was devoted – put it differently. 'There are two spirits in this little body. They fight together – and we shall see which one is the victor. But not yet . . . not now while you are little more than a *baba* . . . but when you full grown-up lady.'

During those years in England memories of my Indian childhood stayed with me. I dare say they became more delightful the farther I grew away from them. Vivid pictures came into my mind as I lay in bed remembering, before I drifted off to sleep.

After the death of my mother my life had been dominated by my ayah. My father was there in the background, grand, important, second only to God. He was loving and tender but he could not be with me as much as he wished, and I know now that I was an anxiety to him. The hours we spent together were very precious. He would tell me about the regiment and how important it was; I was very proud of him because he was honoured wherever he went.

But it was my ayah, familiar, musk-scented, my constant companion, who was perhaps more important to me than anyone else at that time. I loved the thrill of going into the streets with her. She would hold my hand in hers and warn me never to let go. That gave me a sense of danger to the expeditions which rendered them doubly exciting. There was noise and colour everywhere as we wended our way among representatives from every tribe and caste. I came to know them all – the Buddhist priests because of their shaven heads, their saffron-coloured robes swishing as they hurried along without glancing at the crowds; the Parsees in their odd-shaped hats carrying umbrellas; the women who must not show their faces and whose black-rimmed eyes looked out through the slits in their veils. There was the fascination of the turbaned snake-charmer, who played his weird music while the sinuous and sinister cobra rose from the basket to writhe menacingly for the wonder of the watchers. I was always allowed to drop a rupee into the jar beside him, for which I received fulsome thanks and a promise of a happy life, blessed with many children, the firstborn a son.

The musky smell hung about the air; there were other smells less pleasant. If I had shut my eyes I should have known by the smell that I was in India. I was fascinated by the brilliantly coloured saris of the women who were unveiled because, said my ayah, they were of low caste. I said they were a lot prettier than the higher caste ones with their shapeless robes and veiled faces.

Mrs Fearnley told me that Bombay was called the 'Gateway to India' and that it was given to us when Charles the Second married Catherine of Braganza.

'What a lovely wedding present!' I exclaimed. 'When I get married I should like a present like that.'

'It is only kings who get them,' said Mrs Fearnley, 'and they are often more of a burden than a blessing.'

We would ride in the pony cart up Malabar Hill and I could see the Governor's house looking grand and imposing on Malabar Point; and around it were gardens and the clubs frequented by the officers and British residents. Mrs Fearnley was almost always with me on these jaunts and she made use of every opportunity to improve my education. But sometimes I was with my ayah who told me more of the things I liked to hear. I was far more interested in the burial grounds where the naked bodies of the dead were left out in the open to be stripped of their flesh by the vultures and their bones to whiten in the sun – which, said my ayah, was more dignified than leaving them to worms – than of accounts of how the Moguls had once dominated the country before the coming of the East India Company, and how fortunate the Indians were now because our great Queen was going to look after them.

Often in school holidays during those years in England I would sit in my bedroom in the rectory overlooking the grave-yard with its grey stones, the inscriptions on many of which had long since been half obliterated by time, and think of the hot sun, the blue sea, the chanting voices, the colourful saris and mysterious-looking eyes seen through the slits in veils. I would think of the servants who had looked after our needs – the boys in their long white shirts and white trousers; the shrewd and wily Khansamah, who ruled the kitchen and sallied forth each day to the markets like a maharajah, with his menials a few paces behind ready to rush forward at his command and bear off his purchases when the conference, which each transaction seemed to demand, was over.

I thought of the carts pulled by the patient-looking, long-suffering bullocks; the narrow streets; the vicious, persistent flies; the bales of brilliant coloured silks in the shops, water-carriers, hungry-looking dogs, goats with bells round their necks which tinkled as they walked, country women, come in from the nearby villages to sell their wares; coolies, peasants, Tamils, Pathans, Brahmins, all mingling in the colourful streets; and here and there would be a dignified gentleman in his beautifully arranged puggree with a smattering of brilliant jewels. And in contrast the beggars. Never would I forget the beggars . . . the diseased and the deformed, with their appealing dark eyes which I feared would haunt me forever and of which I dreamed after my ayah had tucked me in and left me under my protective net which kept me safe from the marauding insects of the night.

Vaguely I remembered my mother – tender, loving, gentle and beautiful. I was four years old when she died. Before that she seemed to be always with me. She used to talk to me about Home, which was England, and when she did so there would be a great longing in her voice and in her eyes which, young as I was, I was aware of. It told me that she wanted to be there. She talked of green fields, the buttercups and a special sort of English rain – soft and gentle – and a sun which was warm and benevolent and never – or hardly ever – fierce. I thought it was a sort of Heaven.

She would sing English songs to me. *Drink to me only with Thine Eyes, Sally in Our Alley* and *The Vicar of Bray*. She told me about the days when she was as little as I was. She had been in the Humberston rectory then, for her father had been the rector. Her brother James had taken on the living on his death, so when my turn came to go, it was not an entirely strange place, for I felt I had been there with my mother in those early days.

Then came the day when I did not see her and they would not let me go to her because she was suffering from some sort of fever which was infectious. I remembered how my father took me on his knee and told me that we had only each other now.

I was perhaps too young to understand the tragedy in our

14

household, but I was vaguely aware of loss and sadness, though the magnitude of the disaster did not strike me immediately. Well-meaning ladies – officers' wives mainly – invaded the nursery; they made much of me and told me my mother had gone to Heaven. I thought it was a trip to a land where there would be green fields and gentle rain, like going to the hills, only more exotic, and perhaps taking tea with God and the angels instead of officers' wives. I presumed that she would come back after a while and tell me all about it.

It was then that Mrs Fearnley came. The same fever which had killed my mother attacked her husband who had been one of the officers. He died during the same week as my mother. Mrs Fearnley, who had been a governess before her marriage, was very uncertain about her future and my father suggested that while she made up her mind what she wanted to do, she might act as governess to his motherless daughter.

It seemed a Heaven-sent opportunity both to my father and Mrs Fearnley and that was how she came to me.

She must have been thirty-five years old; she was well-meaning, conscientious and determined to do right by me. I was fond of her in a negative way. It was my ayah who was a source of excitement to me, alien, exotic, with soulful eyes and long dark hair which I liked to brush. I would lay aside the brush and rub my fingers through it. She would say: 'That soothes me, little Su-Su. There is goodness in your hands.' Then she would tell me about her childhood in the Punjab and how she had come to Bombay to be with a rich family, and how her good friend the Khansamah had brought her into the Colonel's household and that the great happiness of her life was to be with me.

When my mother died my father would be with me almost every day – just for an hour or more, and I grew to know him better. He always seemed sad. There were tea-parties with a number of people and they talked to me and asked me how I was getting on with my lessons. There were one or two children with the regiment and I would go to parties arranged by the parents and then Mrs Fearnley would arrange for me to return this hospitality.

The ayah used to come and watch us while we played games. *Poor Jenny is a-weeping* and *The Farmer's in-His Den* and musical chairs with Mrs Fearnley or one of the other ladies playing the piano. My ayah used to sing some of the songs afterwards. Her rendering of *Poor Jenny* was really quite pathetic and she made *The Farmer's in His Den* sound like martial music.

The officers' wives were sorry for me because I had no mother. I understood this as I grew older and realized that her journey to Heaven was not the temporary absence I had at first imagined it to be. Death was something irrevocable. It happened all around. One of the houseboys told me that many of the beggars I saw in the streets would be dead the next morning. 'They come with a cart to collect them,' he said. It was like the plague of London, I thought, when I heard that. 'Bring out your dead!' But the beggars on the streets of Bombay did not have to be brought out, for they had no homes to come out of.

It was a strange world of splendour and squalor, of bustling life and silent death; and memories of it would be with me forever. Flashes of it would come back to me throughout my life. I would see the Khansamah in the market-place, a smile of triumph on his face, and I knew later that meant he was making a profit on all his purchases. I had heard the wives talking about it and telling each other the sad tale of Emma Alderston who had thought she would outwit her dishonest Khansamah by doing the shopping herself, and how the market salesmen had conspired to charge her so much that she was paying far more than the Khansamah's 'commission'. 'It is a way of life,' said Grace Girling, a captain's wife. 'Better accept it.'

I liked to sit in the kitchen, watching our Khansamah at work. He was big and important; he sensed my admiration and he found it irresistible. He gave me little tasters and folding his hands across his large stomach watched me intently while I sampled them. I wanted to please him and forced my features into an expression of ecstasy. 'Nobody make Tandoori chicken like Colonel Sahib's Khansamah. Best Khansamah in India.

Here, Missee Su-Su, look! Ghostaba!' He would thrust a meat ball made of finely ground lamb at me. 'You find good, eh? Now drink. Ah good? Nimboo pani . . .'

I would drink the chilled juice of limes flavoured with rose syrup and listen to his chatter about his dishes and above all himself.

For ten years that was my life – the first impressionable years – so it was small wonder that these memories remained with me. There was one which was more vivid than any other. I can recall it in detail. The sun was already hot although it was morning and the real heat of the day was to come. With my ayah I had passed through the narrow streets of the market, pausing at the trinket stall to admire its contents while my ayah had a word with the owner, past the rows of saris which were hanging on a rail, past the cavern-like interior in which strange-looking tarts were being cooked, avoiding the goats which blundered past, skirting the occasional cow, looking out for the quick brown bodies of young boys who insinuated themselves between the people, and being even more watchful for their quicker brown fingers. So we came through the market-place to the wider street, and there it happened.

There was a great deal of traffic on that morning. Here and there a loaded camel made its ponderous and disdainful way towards the bazaar; the bullock carts came lumbering in. Just as my ayah was remarking that it was time we made our way home, a boy of about four or five ran out in front of one of the bullock carts. I stared in horror as he was kicked aside just before the cart would have run over him.

We rushed out to pick him up. He was white and very shaken. We laid him on the side of the road. A crowd gathered and there was a great deal of talk but it was in a dialect I did not understand. Someone went off to get help.

Meanwhile the boy lay on the ground. I knelt beside him and some impulse made me lay my hand on his brow. It was strange but I felt something – I am not sure what – but a feeling of exultation, I think. Simultaneously the boy's face changed. It was almost as though – for a moment – he had ceased to feel pain. My ayah was watching me.

I said to him in English: 'It will be all right. They will come soon. They will make you better.'

But it was not my words which soothed him. It was the touch of my hands.

It was all over very quickly. They came to take him away. They lifted him gently and put him in a cart which was soon moving off. When I had taken my hand from his brow, the last I saw of the boy was his dark eyes looking at me and the lines of pain beginning to re-form on his face.

It was a strange feeling, for when I had touched him it was as though some power had passed from me.

My ayah and I continued our walk in silence. We did not refer to the incident, but I knew it was uppermost in both our minds.

That night when she tucked me into my bed she took my hands and kissed them reverently.

She said: 'There is power in these hands, little Su-Su. It may be that you have the healing touch.'

I was excited. 'Do you mean that boy . . . this morning?' I asked.

'I saw,' she said.

'What did it mean?'

'It means that you have a gift. It is there in these beautiful little hands.'

'A gift? Do you mean to make people well?'

'To ease pain,' she said. 'I do not know. It is in higher hands than ours.'

Some evenings I went riding with my father. I had my own pony who was one of the delights of my life; and it was a very proud moment when, in my white shirt and riding skirt, I rode out by his side. The older I grew the closer we became. He was a little shy with very young children. I loved him dearly – the more because he was a little remote. I was at an age when familiarity could breed contempt. I wanted a father to look up to – and that was what I had.

He used to talk to me about the regiment and India and the task of the British. I would glow with pride in the regiment and the Empire and mostly in him. He talked to me about my mother and said she had never really liked India. She was constantly homesick, but bravely she had tried not to show it. He worried about me – a motherless child whose father could not give her the attention he wished.

I told him I was well and happy, that Mrs Fearnley was a good companion, that I was fond of her and loved my ayah.

He said: 'You're a good girl, Susanna.'

I told him about the incident with the boy in the road.

'It was so strange, Father. When I touched him I felt something pass from me, and he felt it too because when I laid my hand on his forehead he ceased to feel the pain. It was obvious that he did.'

My father smiled. 'Your good deed for the day,' he said.

'You don't really believe there was something, do you?' I said.

'You were the good Samaritan. I hope he received proper attention. The hospitals here are less than adequate. If he has broken bones, God help him. It's a matter of luck whether they will be reset as they should be.'

'You don't think then that I have . . . a special touch . . . or something. Ayah does.'

'Ayah!' His smile was kindly but faintly contemptuous. 'What would a native know about such things?'

'Well, she said something about a healing touch. Really, Father, it was miraculous.'

'I dare say the boy thought it was pleasant to have an English lady kneeling beside him.'

I was silent. I could see it was no use talking to him, any more than it would have been to Mrs Fearnley, of mystic matters. They were too practical, too civilized, they would say. But I could not dismiss the matter so lightly. I felt it was one of the most important things that had happened to me.

After my tenth birthday my father said to me during one of our rides: 'Susanna, you can't go on like this. You have to be educated, you know.'

'Mrs Fearnley says I am doing very well.'

'But, my dear, there must come a time when you will outgrow Mrs Fearnley. She tells me you are already outclassing her and, moreover, she has decided to go home.'

'Oh! Does that mean you will have to find someone else to take her place?'

'Not exactly. There is only one place where English young ladies should be educated and that is England.'

I was silent, contemplating the enormity of what he was suggesting.

'What about you?' I asked.

'I must stay here, of course.'

'You mean I must go to England . . . alone?'

'My dear Susanna, it is what happens to all young people here. You have seen that. The time will soon come when it will be your turn. In fact, some would say you should have gone before.'

He then started to outline his plans. Mrs Fearnley was being most accommodating. She had been a very good friend to us. She was making plans to return to England and when she went I should go with her. She would take me to my mother's brother James and his wife Grace at the Humberston rectory, and that would be my home until I could rejoin him in India when I was seventeen or eighteen.

'But that is seven years away! A lifetime!'

'Hardly that, my dear. I hate the thought of parting as much as you do . . . perhaps even more . . . but it is necessary. We cannot have you growing up without education.'

'But I am educated. I read a great deal. I have learned such a lot.'

'It is not only book learning, my dear child. It is the social graces . . . how to mix in society . . . real society, not what we have here. No, my dear, there is no way out. If there were I should have found it, for the last thing I want to do is lose you. You will write to me. We will be together through our letters. I shall want to know everything that happens to you. I may come to England for a long leave eventually. Then we shall be together. In the meantime you will go to school and the rectory will be your home during holidays. Time will soon pass. I shall miss you so much. As you know, since your mother died, you have been everything to me.'

He was looking straight ahead, afraid to look at me, afraid to show the emotion he felt. I was less restrained. One of the things I had to learn in England was to control my feelings.

I saw the sea, the hills, the white building through a haze of tears.

Life was changing. Everything was going to change . . . not slowly as life usually did, but drastically.

There had been more than a month to get used to the idea, and after the first shock I began to experience a glimmer of excitement. I had often watched the big ships coming into the harbour and seen them sail away. I had seen boys and girls take farewells of their parents and depart. It was a way of life – and now it was my turn.

Mrs Fearnley was busy with her arrangements and lessons were not so regular.

'There is little more I can teach you,' she said. 'You should be well up to others of your age. Read as much as you can. That is the best thing you can do.'

She was cheerful, looking forward to going home. She was to stay with a cousin until, as she said, she 'found her feet'.

It was different with my ayah. This was a sad parting for her and for me. We had been so close – closer than I had been to Mrs Fearnley. Ayah had known me from the time I was a baby. She had known my mother, and the bond between us had grown very strong since my mother's death.

She looked at me with the patient acceptance of her race and said: 'It is always so with the ayah. She must lose her little ones. They are not hers. They are only lent.'

I told her she would find another little one. My father would see that she did.

'To start again?' she said. 'And where is there another Su-Su?'

Then she took my hands and looked at them. 'They are like lotus blossoms,' she said.

'Slightly grubby ones,' I pointed out.

'They are beautiful.' She kissed them. 'There is power in these hands. It must be used. To waste what is given is not good. Your god . . . my gods . . . they do not like to see their gifts despised. It will be your task, little one, to use the gifts which have been given.'

'Oh no, ayah dear, you imagine there is something special about me because you love me. My father says that that little boy liked to have me kneel beside him and that was why he seemed to forget his pain. That was all it was, my father says.'

'The Colonel Sahib is a very great man, but great men do not know all . . . and sometimes the beggar of the lowest caste has certain knowledge which is denied the greatest rajah.'

'All right, ayah dear, I am wonderful. I am special. I will guard my beautiful hands.'

Then she kissed them solemnly and raised her soulful eyes to my face.

'I will think of you always and one day you will come back.'

'Of course I'll come back. As soon as I have finished with school I'll be here. And you will have to give up everything and come back to me.'

She shook her head. 'You will not want me then.'

'I shall always want you. I shall never forget you.'

She rose and left me.

I had said goodbye to all my friends. On the last night father and I dined alone. It was his wish. There was a hushed atmosphere in the house. The servants were subdued and watched me silently. The Khansamah had excelled himself with one of his favourite dishes which he called *yakhni* – a sort of spiced lamb which I had always particularly enjoyed. But I did not on that evening. We were too emotional to want to eat, and it was as much as we could do to make a show of eating and afterwards to tackle the mangoes, nectarines and grapes which were set before us.

It seemed that the entire household was in mourning for my departure.

Conversation was stilted on that last night. I knew that my father was trying hard to conceal his feelings, which he did admirably of course, and none would have realized how moved he was except that his voice was brittle and his laughter forced.

He talked to me a great deal about England and how different it was from India. I should have to expect a certain discipline at school, and I must remember, of course, that I was a guest of Uncle James and Aunt Grace, who had so kindly come to our rescue and offered us holiday hospitality.

I was rather glad when I could retire to my room and lie for the last time under the mosquito net, sleepless and wondering what the new life in England would be like.

The ship already lay in the bay. I had looked at it many times and tried to imagine what it would be like when that ship sailed away with me in it. But it is hard to imagine a place without oneself.

The day came. We said our goodbyes, and there we were on board, in the cabin Mrs Fearnley and I were going to share. The moment had come. We stood on deck waving. My father was standing very straight, watching. I threw a kiss to which he responded. And I saw my ayah. Her eyes were fixed on me. I waved to her and she lifted a hand.

I longed for the ship to go. This parting was too sad to be prolonged.

The excitement of the journey helped me over the sadness of saying farewell to those I loved. Mrs Fearnley was a brisk and quite pleasant companion. She was determined to carry out the promise she had made to my father to take great care of me and scarcely let me out of her sight.

I knew I was going to be desperately homesick for my father, for my ayah and for India. Going to a new home was not all I had to face. There was school as well. Perhaps it was good that there would be so much change, so many new experiences that I should have less time to brood. Everyone was kind, but in a remote sort of way.

Mrs Fearnley in due course delivered me to the rectory – before she departed with the cousin who had met us at the docks – with the air of a person who has performed an arduous task commendably; and I said goodbye to her without much emotion. It was only when I was alone in the room with the low ceiling, the heavy oak beams and the latticed window looking out on the churchyard that I realized the enormity of my aloneness. On the ship there had been too many experiences: the wonder of sailing on a sea which could be wildly turbulent or smooth as a lake; meeting my fellow passengers; seeing new places – Cape Town with its magnificent bay and mountains; Madeira with its colourful flowers: Lisbon with its beautiful harbour – such experiences had helped to banish fears of the future from my mind.

That little room was to become so familiar to me. Everyone tried to make me feel at home. Uncle James, who was very dedicated to his work and was so serious, tried so hard to be jolly that his attempts at lightness were always laboured and had quite the reverse effect of what he had intended. Every morning he would say: 'Hello, Susanna. Up with the lark?' And if I did a little work in the garden: 'Ha, ha, the labourer is worthy of his hire.' Such remarks were always accompanied by a funny little laugh which somehow did not belong to him. But I knew he was trying hard to help me settle in. Aunt Grace was rather brusque, not because she wanted to be but because she rarely showed her feelings, and faced with a lonely child she found the situation embarrassing. Ellen was kind in an absent-minded way, but she was twelve years older than I and completely absorbed in her father's curate, Mr Bonner, who would marry her as soon as he found a living.

For the first weeks I hated school and then I began to like it. I became something of a celebrity because I had lived in India and, in the dormitory after lights out, I was prevailed upon to tell stories of that exotic land. I revelled in the popularity this brought me and invented the most hair-raising adventures. That helped me a great deal during the first weeks. Then because I was up to the standard of my age group – thanks to the meticulous care of Mrs Fearnley – I was accepted. I was neither dull nor brilliant, which is a far more lovable attribute than being very good or very bad.

By the end of the first year I found school enjoyable and I

was, during the holiday, caught up in village activities – fêtes, bazaars, carol-singing and so on. I was part of what was happening about me. The servants took me to their hearts. 'Poor motherless mite,' I heard the cook say to the maid. 'Sent across the world like that to her uncle and aunt . . . strangers, you might say. And living in heathen parts. That's no life for a child. It's a good thing she's here. I never could abide foreigners.'

I smiled. They didn't understand. I missed my dear ayah so sadly.

My father wrote regularly – long letters about the regiment and the troubles out there.

> Sometimes I'm glad you're home [he wrote]. I want to hear all about it. How are you liking the rectory? Your mother talked about it a great deal. She was homesick for it. The Khansumah was married last week. There was quite a ceremony. He and his bride rode through the town in a flower-decked cart. There was a fine procession. You know what these weddings are like. The bride will be living here. She will do some sort of work in the place, I suppose. I only hope the marriage is not quite as fruitful as everyone seems to be wishing on them. Ayah is happy. She is with a very nice family. Time will soon pass and before long you will be making your plans to come back. You'll be a young lady, then . . . finished, as they say. There will be a great deal for you to do out here then, I hope you will like it. You will be the Colonel's Lady. You know what that means. You'll have to be with me on official occasions. Well, that's in the future and I am sure then you will perform your duties with the requisite grace and charm. After all, you'll be an English lady, nicely 'finished off' at an expensive school which you will have to go to for the last year. More of that anon.
>
> In the meantime, I send you my fondest love. I am thinking of you, longing to see you again, hating this separation and telling myself that it will soon pass.

What lovely letters he wrote! He was more revealing on paper than in person. Some people are like that . . .

I should be happy to have such a father. And I was. I was lucky to have good kind Uncle James and Aunt Grace and Cousin Ellen who made such efforts to make me feel one of the family.

A year passed – then two. There was trouble in India and my father was not able to come home for that promised leave. It was a great disappointment. Then it would seem terribly important whether or not I was chosen for the school play or how many marks I had in history and I did not think of India. One summer holiday I went to the home of one of my friends – a very pleasant Tudor manor with acres of land which they farmed. There was a haunted room which intrigued me, and my friend Marjorie and I slept in it one night. The ghost, disobligingly, did not show itself. Then Marjorie came to the rectory for a holiday. 'It is only right,' said Aunt Grace, 'that you should return hospitality.'

Yes, I could see they were trying hard to make me feel wanted. These were, on the whole, happy memories. Cousin Ellen's belated wedding caused a great deal of excited preparation; and after that there was her departure with Mr Bonner to the living in Somerset. I tried to supply a little of that help which Aunt Grace had had from her, for I wanted to show them that I was grateful for all they had done for me. I took a greater interest in church activities. I listened to Uncle James's sermons with assumed interest and I laughed at his little jokes.

Time was passing.

There was one incident which stands out in my mind. It happened just before Ellen's marriage. I was paying a call with her. I remember it was early autumn because the fruit was being gathered in.

As we came to the Jennings's farm we saw a group of people under one of the apple trees and Ellen said to me: 'There's been an accident.'

We hurried along, and lying on the ground was one of the Jennings's sons groaning in agony.

Mrs Jennings was in a state of great anxiety. 'Tom has fallen, Miss Sandown,' she said to Ellen. 'They've gone for the doctor. They've been a long time gone.'

'Has he broken something, do you think?' asked Ellen.

'That we don't know. It's why we're waiting for the doctor.'

Someone was kneeling by Tom Jennings and strapping his leg to a piece of wood. On impulse I knelt down on the other side of him. I watched the first aid being applied and I could see that Tom was in great pain.

I took out my handkerchief and wiped his brow, and as I did so I was aware of the feeling which I had experienced before in India when the young boy had fallen under the bullock cart.

Tom looked at me and his expression eased a little. He stopped moaning. I stroked his forehead.

Ellen was looking at me in surprise and I thought she was going to tell me to get up; but Tom was watching me intently as I went on stroking his forehead.

It must have been about ten minutes before the doctor came. He complimented the man who had bound the leg to the wood and said it was the best thing that could have been done. Now they would have to move him very carefully.

Ellen said: 'If there is anything we can do, Mrs Jennings . . .'

'Thank you, Miss,' replied Mrs Jennings. 'He'll be all right now doctor's here.'

Ellen was rather thoughtful as we walked back to the rectory.

'You seemed to soothe him,' she said.

'Yes. That sort of thing happened once before.' I told her about the boy in India. She listened in her kindly, rather absentminded way, and I guessed she was really thinking about what sort of house she would go to with Mr Bonner – for he had only just acquired it at that time.

But I remembered that incident; and I wondered what my ayah would have thought of it.

It was mentioned during the evening meal.

'He fell off the ladder,' said Aunt Grace. 'I don't know why there are not more accidents. They can be rather careless.'

'Susanna was very good,' said Ellen. 'She stroked his brow while George Grieves did a little first aid. The doctor said it was the right thing and George is very proud of himself. But I must say he did seem to find Susanna comforting.'

'Ministering angel,' put in Uncle James, smiling at me.

I thought about the incident later. I looked at my hands. It was just comforting to have someone stroke one's forehead when one was in pain. Anyone would have done.

Living in this calm prosaic world, I was beginning to think like those about me. My dear ayah had been full of fancies. Of course she was. She was a foreigner.

And then at last it was my seventeenth birthday.

It was all arranged. A Mrs Emery was taking out her daughter Constance to be married to one of the officers. She would be delighted to take me with them. My father was relieved and so were Aunt Grace and Uncle James. It would have been unseemly for a young girl of seventeen to travel alone.

The great day came. I said my goodbyes. I went down to Tilbury in the company of the Emerys and at last I was setting sail for India.

It was a smooth voyage; the Emerys were pleasant companions; Constance was obsessed by her coming marriage and could talk of little else but the perfections of her fiancé. I did not mind. I had my own obsession.

What an impressive sight Bombay harbour is with its mountainous island fringed with palm trees rising to the magnificent peaks of the Western Ghats.

My father was waiting for me. We embraced. Then he held me at arm's length, looking at me.

'I wouldn't have known you.'

'It's been a long time. You look the same, Father.'

'Old men don't change. It is only little girls who grow into beautiful ladies.'

'Are you in the same house?'

'Strangely enough, yes. We've had some troublous times

28

since you've been away, and I have moved round a bit, as you know. But here I am now . . . just as you left me.'

My father thanked the Emerys when I introduced them. The fiancé was waiting for them and he took them off after we had promised to see each other soon.

'You were happy at Humberston?' my father asked me.

'Oh yes. They were good to me. But it isn't home.'

He nodded.

'And the Emerys, they were good too?'

'Very good.'

'We shall have to see more of them. I shall have to thank them properly.'

'And what of everyone here? Ayah?'

'Oh, she is with the Freelings now. There are two children . . . quite young. Mrs Freeling is a rather frivolous young woman . . . attractive, they say.'

'I'm longing to see my ayah.'

'You will.'

'And the Khansamah?'

'A family man. He has two boys. He is very proud of himself. But come along. We must get home.'

And there I was, feeling as though I had never left.

But of course there were changes. I was no longer a child. I had my duties, and as the first days passed, I discovered that these could be demanding. I had come back, 'finished' as they say – a young English lady fitted to sit at the Colonel's table and fulfil the duties expected of me.

In a very short time I was caught up in the army life. It was like living in a little world of its own, surrounded by the strangeness of a foreign country. It was not quite the same as it had been, or perhaps I had lived in the imagination too long. I was more bothered by unsavoury detail than I had been in my childhood. I was more conscious of the poverty and disease; I was less enchanted; and there were times when I thought rather longingly of cool breezes which used to blow across the ancient church and the peace of the garden with the lavender and buddleia, tall sunflowers and hollyhocks; then I began to feel a nostalgia for the gentle rain, for the Easter and Harvest festivals. Of course my father was here; but I think that if I could have taken him with me I would have preferred to go to that place which had now become Home to me, as it was apparently to so many of those about me.

I took the first opportunity to go and see my ayah. Mrs Freeling was delighted that I wished to call. I had quickly realized that my father's position made everyone want to please him, and that meant pleasing his daughter also, and some of the wives were almost sycophantic, believing no doubt that to curry favour with the Colonel helped their husbands on the long road to higher rank.

The Freelings had a pleasant bungalow, surrounded by beautiful flowering shrubs whose names I did not know. Phyllis Freeling was young, very pretty, rather coquettish I thought, and I was sure I should not find her the most interesting of the wives. She fluttered round me as though I did her a great honour by visiting her. She gave me tea.

'We do try to keep up the English customs,' she told me. 'One must, mustn't one. One doesn't want to go native.'

I listened to her chatter, all the time wondering when I was going to see my ayah, which was the sole reason for my coming. She talked about the dance they were having soon. 'I dare say you will be on the committee. There are *such* preparations to be made. If you want a really good dressmaker, I can put you on to the very best.' She folded her hands and said in a voice with an Indian accent: '"The very best *durzi* in Bombay . . ." So he tells me and I have every reason to believe him.'

I accepted the tea and one of the little scented cakes.

'Khansamah is greatly honoured to make tea for the Colonel's daughter,' I was told.

I asked about the children and the ayah.

'She is very good. The children are *angels*. They love Ayah and she is so good with them. Sometimes I wonder whether it is wise to leave them with a native . . . but what can one do? One has so many responsibilities . . . to one's husband, to the regiment . . .'

At length I thought I could come to the reason for my visit. I reminded her that I wanted to see the ayah.

'But of course. She will be so honoured.'

I was taken to the nursery where the children were having their afternoon nap. She was sitting there waiting, for she knew I was coming.

We looked at each other; she had aged a little, which was natural in seven years.

I ran to her and threw my arms about her. I did not know what Mrs Freeling thought and I did not care.

'Ayah,' I said.

'Missee Su-Su.'

I felt deeply moved to hear the baby version of my name. I said: 'I have thought of you often.'

She nodded. A servant came up and said something in a quiet voice to Mrs Freeling.

'Well, I'll leave you,' she said. 'I expect you would like to have a little chat.'

I thought that was tactful of her.

We sat down still looking at each other. We talked in whispers because of the sleeping children in the next room. She told me how she had missed me. The *babalog* Freelings were nice but they were not Missee Su-Su. There would never be another like her.

I told her about life in England, but I could see she found it difficult to visualize. She said there had been troubles throughout India and dangers . . . and there was more to come. She shook her head. 'There are murmurings. There are dark secret things . . . not good.'

She saw changes in me. I was not the same as the little girl who had left Bombay all those years ago.

'Seven years is a long time,' I reminded her.

'It seems long when much happens, short when it does not. Time is in the head.'

It was wonderful to see her again. I said: 'I wish I could take you home with me.'

Her face was illumined by a dazzling smile. 'How I wish it. But you do not need an ayah now like the Freeling *babalog*.'

'Are you happy here, Ayah dear?'

She was silent and I felt a twinge of alarm as I saw the

shadow flit across her face. I was puzzled. Mrs Freeling had not given me the impression that she would interfere in the nursery. I should have thought her ayah would have a free hand; more so than she had had with me, for then there had been Mrs Fearnley to contend with.

She would be too loyal to tell tales of her mistress, I knew; but I did feel uneasy.

She sensed this and said: 'Nowhere could I be content as I was with you.'

I was deeply touched, and surprised that she could feel thus when I remembered how difficult I had been at times. Perhaps time was playing its old tricks in making what was past seem more rosy than it had actually been.

'I shall see you often now that I am here,' I said. 'I am sure Mrs Freeling won't mind my coming.'

She shook her head. 'You should not come here, Missee Su-Su. Not too much.'

'Why ever not?'

'Better not. We meet. Perhaps I come to you.' She lifted her shoulders. 'I am just Old Ayah . . . not yours any more.'

'What nonsense! You will always be mine. And why shouldn't I come to see you? I shall insist. I am the Colonel's Lady now. I shall make the rules.'

'Not here,' she said. 'No . . . no . . . that not good.'

I did not pursue the subject because I thought there might be some absurd notion in her mind about the propriety of the Colonel's daughter visiting her old nurse in another household.

Her dark eyes were soulful and prophetic. 'You will go away,' she said. 'I do not see you here . . . for long.'

'You're wrong. I shall stay with my father. I have not come all this way to go home again almost immediately. Do you realize how far it is, dear Ayah, right across the seas? I shall stay here, and we shall meet . . . often. It will be like the old days . . . or almost.'

She smiled. 'Yes . . . no sadness. Do not let us talk of partings. You have just come. It is a happy day.'

'That's better,' I said; and I plunged into conversation which was punctuated with 'Do you remember when . . .' And it was amazing how much of the past, which I thought I had forgotten, came back to me.

The children awoke and I was introduced to them. They were round-faced, chubby little creatures of about four and two, I guessed.

When I left them I went down to say goodbye to Mrs Freeling.

She was sitting on a sofa and beside her was a young man. They rose as I entered.

'Oh, there you are,' said Mrs Freeling. 'Miss Pleydell has been seeing her old ayah who happens to be mine now. Wasn't that gracious of her!'

'It wasn't,' I said. 'I happen to be very fond of her.'

'One is of one's nanny. But I'm forgetting you don't know each other. This is Aubrey St Clare. Aubrey, this is Miss Susanna Pleydell, the Colonel's daughter.'

That was the first time I saw Aubrey, and I was immediately struck by his charm and good looks. He was about my height – but then I was exceptionally tall. He had fair hair – almost golden, vivid blue eyes, and his features were clear-cut.

He took my hand and pressed it firmly.

'What a pleasure to meet you!' he said.

'Do sit down, Miss Pleydell,' said Mrs Freeling. 'You must have a drink. It's a little early. But no matter. It is never really too early.'

I sat down beside him.

'You have just come back to India, I believe,' he said.

I explained.

'Fresh from school!' said Phyllis Freeling with a rather shrill, trilling laugh. 'Isn't that exciting!'

'It must be,' he said, 'to come back to India. Strange, exciting country, is it not, Miss Pleydell?'

I agreed that it was.

'Do you notice any changes?'

'I was so young when I went away – ten years old, to be exact. I think I took a somewhat glamourized picture with me. Now I see it more as it really is.'

'Ah,' he said, 'one of the penalties of growing up.'

I noticed that he was regarding me intently and I was pleasantly stimulated by his interest. I had known few young men – only those who had lived in Humberston and friends of Uncle James and Aunt Grace. I had been very closely, though unobtrusively, guarded, I realized. Now I felt a certain freedom. Yes, I was now grown up. And it was exhilarating.

Aubrey St Clare talked rather knowledgeably about India, which he appeared to know very well. I gathered he was not connected with the regiment. I wondered what he was doing in India but felt it would be impertinent to ask. Mrs Freeling took charge of the conversation. I thought she was rather flirtatious with her visitor, and I wondered whether I thought so because I was still under the influence of the Humberston rectory where everything was conducted in a most conventional manner.

At length I said I must go and Aubrey St Clare immediately rose and asked if he might take me home.

It was only a short way, I told him.

'Nevertheless . . .' he began, and Mrs Freeling added: 'Oh yes, you should have an escort.'

I thanked her for her hospitality and left with Aubrey St Clare.

As I came out of the bungalow I looked back and saw a flutter of curtains. Ayah was standing at the window. Did I imagine it or did she really look disturbed?

After that I saw a great deal of Aubrey St Clare. I became fascinated and flattered because he paid so much attention to me. He was attentive to Phyllis Freeling, but that seemed different because she was married.

My father liked him and I think he was pleased for me to have an escort. I gathered that he would have preferred us to have been in England where I could have been launched into society in the conventional manner. He was eager for me to enjoy life and he regretted that he did not have more time to spend with me.

Aubrey was charming. He had a wonderful personality that

could change and be different according to the people he was with. With my father he was serious and talked about the problems of India; he told me about his travels round the world; he had been in Arabia; he had met people of many races; he found exploring different cultures fascinating and he had a vivid way of expressing himself; yet with Mrs Freeling he could be extremely frivolous, being exactly the sort of man whom I was sure she would find attractive. It was a great gift.

He was becoming my constant companion. My father was ready to let me go into the bazaars with him, although I should not have been allowed to go by myself. Things were not quite what they had been when I was a child here, he told me. There were undercurrents of unrest. The regiment was on the alert.

Oh, nothing serious, he insisted. But the natives were unpredictable. They did not reason in quite the same way as we did. Therefore he liked me to go where I wanted but in the company of a strong man.

They were pleasant days.

I saw my ayah several times, but she was always uneasy about my going to the Freeling bungalow. I suggested that she come to us. She did once or twice, but it was difficult for her to get away. I knew something was bothering her but I could not guess what; and to tell the truth I was so caught up in all that was going on, particularly with my new friend, that I did not pay as much attention to her as I would otherwise have done.

One day when we were in the garden under the apricot trees, one of the boys brought us a cooling drink and Aubrey said to me: 'I shall have to be thinking of going home soon.'

I was dismayed. I had never thought of his leaving and I suddenly realized how much I had begun to depend on his companionship. I felt vaguely depressed.

'I have had grave news from home,' he went on.

'I am sorry.'

'So am I. It's my brother – my elder brother. He's ill. In fact I believe he cannot live very long. It will make a great deal of difference to me.'

'You are very fond of him.'

'We have never been great friends. There are only two of us and we are so different. He inherited everything . . . quite a large estate. Since he has no children I shall take over everything if he dies, which it now seems certain that he will before very long. I doubt he can last another year.'

'How distressing for you.'

'So . . . I should be there. Soon I shall have to be making plans to leave.'

'We shall miss you.'

He leaned towards me and, taking my hand, pressed it.

'I shall miss everyone . . . everything here . . . and particularly you.'

I felt excited. He had always implied that he admired me and I was aware of an attraction between us; but I felt myself to be such a novice in these matters and I was very uncertain of myself. All I knew was that I should be very sad when he went away.

He talked to me about his home. The estate was in Buckinghamshire. It had been in the family for centuries. 'My brother is very proud of it,' he said. 'I never had the same feeling for houses. I wanted to travel, to see the world. He wanted to absorb himself in squiral duties. If he dies it will fall on my shoulders. I am rather hoping my sister-in-law, Amelia, will have a son before he dies.'

'Is that likely now that he is so ill?'

'One never knows.'

'When shall you be going?'

'Rest assured I shall stay as long as I possibly can.'

When I was dining alone with my father that evening I mentioned to him that Aubrey would be leaving us soon.

'I'm sorry about that. You'll miss him, won't you?'

He was watching me intently, and I said with faint hesitation: 'Oh yes, very much.'

'Well, he might not be the only one who is leaving.'

'What do you mean?'

'You know there has been a lot of unrest here lately. Nothing serious, but a kind of undercurrent. And there is something you don't know, Susanna. Two years ago I had an illness.'

'An illness! What sort of illness? You didn't tell me.'

'I didn't want to make a fuss. It passed. But it did not go unnoticed by HQ.'

'Father, what are you telling me?'

'That Anno Domini is catching up with me.'

'But you are amazingly fit. Look what you do.'

'The fact remains, I am getting old. There are hints, Susanna.'

'Hints?'

'I think that soon I shall be working at the War Office in London.'

'Do you really mean that? And what was this illness?'

'Some little trouble with the heart. It passed.'

'Oh, Father, and you didn't tell me!'

'There was no need to when it was all over.'

'I should have been told.'

'Quite unnecessary. But, as I say, there will be changes here.'

'When shall we go home?'

'You know HQ. When the decision is made there will be no delay. It will be a case of up and gone, and the new chap will be here to take my place.'

'Oh, Father, how will you like it?'

'As a matter of fact, I shan't be sorry.'

'But all the years you have been in India . . . and you let me come out.'

'I had a reason for that. I realized from your letters that you were building up a picture of the place. I believed that if you had not come you would have regretted it all your life. I wanted you to come back and see it with adult eyes. Besides, think how disappointed you would have been if you hadn't.'

'You are so good to me.'

'Dear child, I felt there was so much to make up for. That lonely childhood . . . sending you off to strangers, which they were, of course, although related.'

'You did your best and it is what happens to all children in our position.'

'True, but that does not make it easier. But never mind

motives. I am expecting orders at any moment and then it will be up and away.'

I was not entirely dismayed. I was already wondering whether I should see Aubrey in England.

That night in bed I thought about my ayah. I had neglected her somewhat. When I had come out I had thought with great pleasure of our reunion. But, as my father said, things change. I should never forget her and what we had been to each other in my childhood; but I was no longer a child. I was making exciting excursions into the adult world, and the feelings Aubrey inspired in me had so fascinated me that I had been inclined to forget other matters.

I promised myself that the very next day I would go to see her.

I chose a time when I knew Mrs Freeling would be at the Regimental Club. She was often there. I had seen her with some of the young officers. She invited Aubrey there, too. He told me he went quite frequently. Moreover, I had seen him there with her. I felt no jealousy. It did not occur to me that there could be any serious relationship between them, because she was a married woman. I was very naïve in those days.

My ayah was glad to see me and I felt ashamed because there had been too long a gap between our last meeting and this.

'The children are asleep,' she said.

We sat in the next room with the door ajar so that she could hear if they awoke.

She looked at me with her sad eyes and I said: 'You were right about my not staying long. My father has told me that any day he could be receiving orders from the War Office.'

'You will go away from here . . . yes. Perhaps it is best for you.'

'Ayah dear, I feel as though I have only just come.'

'There are bad things here. You are not a little girl any more.'

'There are bad things everywhere, I dare say.'

She shook her head. I took her hand and said: 'You have

38

something on your mind. Why don't you tell me? You are not happy here. I could ask my father to find you another place.'

She said: 'I love the little ones.'

'And Mrs Freeling and the Captain . . . they are not good to you? You can tell me, you know.'

'I am left with the children. The Captain loves them.'

'Then it is Mrs Freeling? Does she interfere? Does she complain?'

She shook her head. She hesitated for a few seconds, then she burst out: 'There are parties . . . meetings . . . they do strange things. I know what it is. They grow it in the villages. I have seen it . . . so much . . . when I was a little one. It grows well in India . . . so pretty it looks, with the poppies waving their heads . . . so innocent. You would not believe it. It flourishes if the soil is fine and loose and fed with manure and much water. I have seen the sowing in November, and in January it is ready when the flower seeds are the size of a hen's eggs.'

'What are you talking about?'

'They call it opium,' she told me. 'It is here . . . everywhere. Some sell it for money. Some grow it for themselves. They smoke it in their pipes, and they become strange . . . very strange.'

'Do you mean they are drugged? Tell me about it.'

'I must not. It is no concern of mine. I should not want my little one to be with such people.'

'You mean Mrs Freeling . . .'

'Please forget I speak.'

'You mean here . . . there are parties . . . orgies. I must tell my father.'

'Oh no, no. Please do not. I should not have speak. I am wrong. Forget. Please to forget.'

'How can I? They are smoking opium, you say. That should be stopped.'

She shook her head. 'No. No. It has always been. Here in the villages . . . it is so easy to grow. Please do not talk of it. Only do not go to these places. Do not let them tempt you to try.'

'Tempt me! Of course they never would. Ayah, are you sure?'

She shook her head. 'Not sure. Not all sure . . .'

'But you told me . . .'

She closed her eyes and shook her head. I believed that she was afraid and tried to soothe her.

'I have seen them here. They look strange. They seem strange. There is a man. He comes here often. He is the Devil Doctor. He wants opium. He buys it. He takes it away. He watches people and tempts them. I believe he is a devil.'

Oh, I thought with relief, she is romancing now.

'Tell me about this Devil Doctor,' I said.

'He is tall; his hair is black like the night. I saw him once. He wore a black cloak and a black hat.'

'He sounds satanic. Tell me, did he have cloven feet?'

'I believe so,' she said.

I breathed more easily. I remembered some of the stories with which she had beguiled me during my childhood: the exploits of the gods, Siva, Vishnu and Brahma in which she fervently believed. I did not take her stories seriously. Perhaps she had seen certain frivolous behaviour among Mrs Freeling's guests and had construed it as the manner in which people acted when they had been smoking opium; and her concern for me had made her exaggerate what she had seen. I did wonder whether I ought to mention to my father what she had said; but as she implored me not to, I put the matter from my mind. There was so much more to think of, because two weeks after my father had spoken to me, despatches came from London.

Colonel Bronsen-Grey was on his way to take over my father's duties and we were to make immediate preparations for our departure.

It seemed like fate. I could not help feeling very excited. This time I should not leave India with the same reluctance.

Aubrey St Clare was delighted, and when he heard that we were booked on the *Aurora Star*, he decided he would return home on the same ship. It proved the state of my feelings when I did not feel any great regret because we were going with him.

We had no home in England and my father decided that we should stay at an hotel while we looked for a temporary home and he ascertained from the War Office what his duties would be. When he knew we could set about finding a more permanent residence, which he expected would be in London.

My ayah took a tearful farewell of me. She was fatalistic and that helped her to overcome her sorrow at parting. It was ordained, she said and she had known that when I returned, I would not stay long in India.

'It is well that you go,' she said, 'even though those who love you suffer at the parting. There will be trouble here and I am happy to know that you will be safe. The monsoons have failed to bring the rain and the crops are bad. When there is famine people look round for those to blame, and they blame those they envy . . . those who may have what they would like themselves. Yes, I should rejoice. It is best for you. Do not be impulsive as you have always been, little Su-Su. Think first. Do not seize the dross in mistake for the gold.'

'I promise you, dear ayah, that I will curb my impulses. I will think of you always and try to be wise.'

Then she embraced me and kissed me solemnly.

As I stood on deck the last person I saw as we sailed away was my ayah, standing there, looking lonely and forlorn, her pale blue sari moving gently in the breeze.

It was a magic voyage. I felt very happy. How different from that time when I, a lonely little girl under the vigilance of Mrs Fearnley, had tried hard not to burst into noisy protestations at being dragged away from my father and my beloved India. This was quite different. My father seemed younger. Only now did I realize the strain under which he had been living. He had never talked to me about the fear of trouble; but it must have always been there – an undercurrent of apprehension. I remember moonlit nights, leaning over the rail, looking up to the rich velvety sky and the golden stars, listening to the gentle movement of the sea below. Aubrey was my constant companion; in the morning we paced the decks together; we played games; we indulged in lengthy discussions at meals with our table companions; we danced afterwards; and I wanted those days to go on and on. I tried not to look too far ahead when we should reach Tilbury and say goodbye, my father and I going to London and Aubrey to that stately home in Buckinghamshire.

There was something unreal about life on the ship. One felt that one was floating in a little world apart from the real one. There were no troubles here – nothing but long sunny days, lying on deck, watching the porpoises and the dolphins frolic, while the flying fish skimmed the water, and here and there the hump of a whale could be seen.

One day an albatross, and presumably his mate, followed the ship for three days. We marvelled at the beautiful creatures with their twelve-foot wing span; they circled above us and there were times when we thought they were going to land on deck. They were waiting for the food, left over from meals, to be thrown into the water.

They were magic days with calm seas and blue skies – and the ship sailing peacefully home.

Even so one was reminded of change. There was a day when we skirted a hurricane and the chairs slid across the deck and it was impossible to stand up. That was symbolic, I thought. Nothing lasts forever; and the most perfect peace can be quickly shattered.

We reached Cape Town, which I remembered from that other journey. This was different. My father, Aubrey and I went out in a flower-decorated carriage drawn by two horses in straw bonnets. It seemed far more exciting than on that previous occasion; perhaps that was due to the company.

It was the night after we left Cape Town. We had had a rough passage round the Cape and were now sailing northwards to the Canaries. We had left the tropical heat behind and the weather was bland with hardly any wind.

My father had gone to bed, which he often did after dinner, and that left me alone with Aubrey. We found our favourite spot on deck and sat side by side listening to the gentle swishing of the water against the side of the ship.

'It won't be long now,' said Aubrey. 'We shall soon be home.'

I agreed a little sombrely. 'It has been a wonderful voyage.'

'For a particular reason,' he replied.

I waited and he turned to me and, taking my hand, kissed it.

'You,' he said.

I laughed. 'You have contributed to the enjoyment. My father is delighted that you are here and he can go to bed with a free conscience and leave me in good hands.'

'So he thinks that of me, does he?'

'You know he does.'

'Susanna, I have been thinking. When we get to England . . . what?'

'What? It is all planned. Father and I will go to an hotel and look immediately for a house. And you . . . you have your arrangements.'

'We are not going to say "Goodbye, it was nice to have known you" when we get to England, are we?'

'I don't know what will happen when we get to England.'

'Doesn't that rather depend on us?'

'There is one theory which says that everything that happens depends on ourselves, while another believes in fate. What is to be, will be.'

'I think we are masters of our fates. Will you marry me?'

'Do you . . . mean that seriously?'

'I am deadly serious.'

'Aubrey . . .' I murmured.

'You are not going to say, "This is so sudden", are you?'

'No.'

'Then you will?'

'I . . . think I will.'

'You only think?'

'Well, I have never had a proposal of marriage before, and I don't quite know how to deal with it.'

He burst out laughing and, turning to me, took me in his arms and kissed me.

'I've been wanting to do that for a long time,' he said. 'Have you been wanting me to?'

'Yes, I think I have.'

'You think! Don't you know? You are so definite in your views on every other subject.'

'I feel such a novice . . . at love.'

'That is what I love about you. So young . . . so fresh . . . so innocent . . . so honest.'

'I would rather be more worldly like some of the wives . . . Mrs Freeling, for instance.'

For a moment he was silent. I thought he looked uncertain and was about to say something. He appeared to change his mind and I wondered if I had imagined it.

'Those people are not really worldly, you know,' he said at length. 'They are older than you and pose all the time as socialites. Don't be like they are, for Heaven's sake. Just be yourself, Susanna. That's what I want.'

He held my hand tightly and we looked out over the sea.

'What a perfect night,' he said. 'A calm sea, a gentle breeze and Susanna has promised to marry me.'

When I told my father he was faintly disturbed.

'You are very young,' he said.

'I am eighteen. That's a marriageable age.'

'In some cases . . . yes. But you have come straight from school. You haven't really met any people.'

'I don't have to. I know I love Aubrey.'

'Well . . . I suppose it is all right. There is that place in Buckinghamshire which I presume will be his one day. He seems fairly solid.'

'It's no use trying to play the mercenary Papa because you don't do it very well. You know that if I want it and I'm happy that will be all right with you.'

'That's about it,' he agreed. 'Trust you to sum up the situation in a few words. So you are engaged. It is amazing how many people become engaged on sea voyages. It must be something in the air.'

'Tropical seas . . . flying fishes . . . dolphins . . .'

'Hurricanes, rolling breakers and nausea.'

'Don't be unromantic, Father. It doesn't suit you. Say you are pleased and proud of your daughter who has managed to find a husband without the expensive London season you were planning, to launch her into society.'

'My dear child, all I want is your happiness. You chose this man and if he makes you happy that is all I ask.'

He kissed me.

'You'll have to help me choose a place in London,' he said. 'Even though doubtless you will be obsessed by your own affairs.'

'I shall indeed. Oh, Father, I was planning to look after *you!*'

'And now you will have a husband to look after instead. I am deeply hurt.'

I hugged him and felt a sudden twinge of apprehension. How ill had he been? And why had Head Quarters decided that he should leave India?

I was so happy. The future loomed ahead, so exciting that I had to warn myself that there was rarely complete perfection in life. I had to look for the worm in the wood, the flaw in the diamond. Nothing could be quite so perfect as it seemed that night when Aubrey asked me to marry him.

There was so much to talk of, so much to plan. Aubrey was to accompany us to London and see us into our hotel before going on to his home. Then it had been decided that my father and I should pay an early visit to Minster St Clare in Buckinghamshire.

I was looking forward to the arrival at Tilbury – not dreading it as I had anticipated when I had thought it might mean saying goodbye to Aubrey for ever. As for Aubrey himself, he was in a state of euphoria, and I was immensely gratified to know that I had created it.

So we said au revoir with promises to visit Aubrey's home in two weeks' time. Amelia, his sister-in-law, would be delighted to receive us, he was sure. As for his brother, he did not know how he would find him.

I wondered whether, as his brother was so ill, guests would be welcome in the house, but he assured me that it was a big house and there were plenty of people to look after everything and both his brother and his wife would surely want to meet me.

We had comfortable rooms in a somewhat old-fashioned hotel close to Piccadilly – recommended by Uncle James who used it on his brief visits to London; and on the following day I went house-hunting and my father presented himself at the War Office.

I found a small house in Albemarle Street which was to be let furnished, and I planned to take my father along to see it at the first opportunity.

When he came home he seemed quite excited. He was to have a job of some responsibility at the War Office, which he thought would be very demanding. He looked at the house and decided we should take it and move in at the beginning of the next week. I had a few very busy days engaging servants to start with and making arrangements to go into our new home, which we had taken on rental for three months.

I said: 'That will give us time to look round for a real home and if we haven't found it by then, we can no doubt stay here a little longer.'

My father said rather sadly, 'It will probably be a bachelor's apartment which I shall need, for you are bent on making a home with someone else.'

'Weddings take a long time to arrange and I shall be with you for a while. And in any case I shall be visiting you often. Buckinghamshire is not so very far away.'

I had found the search quite exciting. I had always been interested in houses. They seemed to have personalities of their own. Some seemed happy houses, others mysterious, some even mildly menacing. My father laughed at my fanciful ideas; but I really did feel atmospheric sensations quite vividly.

I was pleased, too, that my father was enjoying the War

Office. I had feared that after having been on active service he might find work in an office dull. Not so. He was absorbed and I could not help feeling that it had been a good move to bring him home. Sometimes he looked a little tired, but of course he was no longer a young man and that was natural. I wondered now and then about that illness he had had, but he was rather reticent about it and I fancied it disturbed him to talk about it so I did not mention it. He was well now and life was too exciting for me to want to cloud over the brightness, so I assured myself that there was nothing to worry about and that we were all going to be happy ever after.

We settled into the furnished house, which we found ideal; the two servants I had engaged, Jane and Polly, were very good, willing girls. They were sisters who were delighted to have found jobs together.

My father decided he must have a carriage to take him to and from the War Office and he acquired one and a coachman to go with it. Joe Tugg, a widower in his late forties, was glad to come to us for, as he boasted often, he had driven the mail coach from London to Bath for twenty years until as he said 'Steam took away me living,' by which he meant that the coming of the railroads had been the ruin of many of the old coachmen. There were two rooms over the stabling in the mews at the back of the house and Joe settled in. We were a very contented household.

I said: 'We must keep them all when we find the house.' And my father agreed.

I had a letter from Aubrey's sister-in-law signed Amelia St Clare. She wrote that she would be delighted to see me and congratulated me on my engagement. Her husband was very ill indeed but he wanted to meet me very much. They were not entertaining generally on account of her husband's illness, but they would regard me as one of the family.

It was a warm and welcoming letter.

Aubrey wrote that he was longing to see me and would meet us at the station.

Two days before the visit my father came home one evening looking very disturbed.

'I don't think I can possibly go,' he said. 'I can't leave the office. I shall have to be there . . . perhaps over the weekend. Something of vital importance has cropped up. It's India, and my special knowledge of the country makes my presence necessary.'

I felt hideously disappointed. Then I said: 'I can go without you, Father. Jane and Polly will look after you.'

He frowned.

'Oh come,' I said. 'I am not a child. I am a much travelled woman. And if you are thinking of chaperons, there is Mrs Amelia St Clare.'

He was hesitating.

'I shall go, Father,' I said firmly. 'You must, of course, stay. You could not leave your post – particularly as you have just taken it up. I'll go on ahead and perhaps you can come down afterwards. I must go. After all, I *am* engaged to be married.'

'Well . . .' he said. He was still hesitating. 'I suppose I could put you on the train. Aubrey could pick you up at the other end.'

'For Heaven's sake! You make me sound like a parcel.'

And so it happened that on that hot and sultry day I set out for Minster St Clare.

My father had, as he said, 'put me' in a first-class carriage, and as I waved goodbye to him I tried to set aside my anxieties. I did worry about his health and that mysterious illness he had had some time before, and I made up my mind that I was going to make him tell me all about it as soon as I was with him again.

But as I grew nearer and nearer to my destination I gave myself up to excited anticipation.

Aubrey was standing on the platform waiting for me.

He smiled as he hurried to me and took my hands.

'Welcome, Susanna. It is good to see you.' He put an arm round me and called to the porter, who was standing by watching us with interest: 'Here, Bates. Put the luggage in the carriage, will you?'

'Yes, sir,' said Bates; and Aubrey took me out of the station yard.

He led me to a carriage. I opened my eyes in amazement. It was so splendid. It was mulberry colour and drawn by two magnificent greys. I did not know much about horses but I could see that these two were very fine.

He noticed my admiration for the carriage.

'It's so grand,' I said.

'I've taken it over from my brother. He can't drive it now.'

'How is he?'

'Very, very ill.'

'Perhaps I shouldn't have come.'

'Nonsense. In there, Bates. That's right. Come, Susanna, up beside the driver.' He helped me into the carriage. Then he climbed in beside me and took the reins.

'Tell me about your brother,' I said.

'Poor Stephen. He has been dying for the last weeks. The doctors think he cannot last for more than three months . . . or he could go at any moment.'

'How very distressing.'

'You see why I had to come home. Amelia is most anxious to meet you.'

'She wrote me a very kind letter.'

'She would. It is hard for her, poor girl.'

'I am sorry Father could not come. You understand?'

'But of course, and as a matter of fact it was you whom I wanted to see. I hope you like the house. You have to, you know. It's going to be your home.'

'I am so excited.'

'These old houses take a bit of getting used to. For us who are brought up in them they seem like part of the family.'

'Yet you were away from home for quite a while. I know how much you've travelled. You must tell me all about it sometime.'

'Well, the house will be mine now. Things seem different when they belong to someone else. Oh, it was always my home, but my brother was master of it. I was afraid that I should feel like a guest.'

'I understand.'

'I think you'll find it interesting. There is little of the Minster left. The house was built by an ancestor of mine in the sixteenth century when a great deal of building and reconstruction was done on the site of old monasteries and abbeys. It's a real Tudor building – late Elizabethan – and there are only fragments of old ruined walls and a buttress or two about the place to remind you what it was before the Dissolution.'

'I had no idea it had such a history. I just imagined an old manor house.'

'Well, you will see for yourself.'

We had come to a stretch of road and the horses broke into a gallop. I was thrown against Aubrey and he laughed.

'They can really go, these greys,' he said. 'I'll show you one day what they can do.'

I laughed. It was exhilarating to be beside him and to contemplate arriving at this old house which was to be my home. I was struck by his masterly handling of the horses. He clearly enjoyed driving them.

We had come to a stone wall. Massive iron gates stood open and we passed into a drive. The horses were trotting now.

Then I saw the house. I caught my breath. I had not expected it to be so grand. The central keep with gateway and portcullis was flanked by two machicolated towers.

Aubrey glanced at me, well pleased by my obvious admiration.

'It's wonderful,' I stammered. 'How could you have left it for so long.'

'I told you. I did not know it was to be mine.'

We drove through a gateway into a courtyard where two grooms appeared. Aubrey threw the reins to one of them, leaped down and then helped me out.

'This is Miss Pleydell, Jim,' he said.

I smiled and the man touched his forelock.

'Have the baggage sent in at once,' commanded Aubrey. He turned to me and, taking my arm, said: 'Come along.'

He led me from the courtyard to a quadrangle. The walls

were creeper-covered and the latticed windows looked like eyes peering out from under shaggy brows. There was a table with some chairs on which were flame-coloured cushions; and a number of pots containing flowering shrubs added colour to the spot. It was very attractive, and yet I had a sense of claustrophobia, as though the walls were closing in on me.

There was a passage with moulded vaulting; we passed through this to a bigger courtyard. Before us was a door – heavy, iron-studded, with a panel in it which I presumed could be drawn back so that those who were inside could see who was without, before admitting them.

Aubrey pushed open the door, which creaked loudly. We were in a lofty hall. I glanced up at the hammerbeam roof and my eyes went to the whitewashed walls on which hung arms and trophies; two suits of armour stood at either end of the hall, like sentinels guarding the place. I looked with wonder at the heraldic panels on the windows and I noticed they all had the fleur-de-lys prominently displayed.

Aubrey was watching me with an almost childish joy which was very appealing.

'It's so . . . exciting,' I said.

'I see you are impressed. Most people are. At the same time you're a little alarmed. Don't be. This is the ancient part of the house. We leave it as it is. We have more comfortable quarters in which to live. I am sure you will agree that although we want to preserve antiquity it is more satisfying to allow a few modern comforts to creep in. Oh, here is Amelia. Amelia, come and meet Susanna. Susanna, this is Amelia, Mrs St Clare.'

She had descended the staircase which was at one end of the hall. She was elegant rather than beautiful and appeared to be in her early thirties. Her fair hair was piled high on her head to give her height, I supposed, for she was not very tall – or perhaps I thought this as I was well above the average in that respect. Her blue eyes were speculative. That was natural, of course, and she seemed pleasant.

She took my hand and clasped it. 'Welcome to the Minster,' she said. 'I am so pleased you came, even though your father could not. Would you like to go straight to your room? You probably want to rest after the journey.'

'It is not very far from London and I don't feel in the least tired. I am so impressed by this wonderful house. I had no idea it would be so . . . baronial.'

'Yes, it is fascinating. My husband made the care of this house and the estate which goes with it . . . his life.'

There was an infinite sadness in her voice and I warmed towards her.

'Do come this way,' she said. 'I'll have hot water sent up. I am sure you want to wash. They are taking up your luggage now.'

I followed her up the stairs. At the top I turned to look back. Aubrey was looking up at us with an expression I could not interpret.

We came to a gallery lined with portraits; there was a dais at one end on which was a piano.

'We call this the long gallery. Just above it is the solarium. Both rooms get the sun – and particularly the solarium.' We passed through the gallery and ascended a short spiral staircase. We were in a corridor. 'The main bedrooms are here. I have put you in the green room. It has pleasant views. Most of the rooms do.'

The green room was big with a high, vaulted ceiling and windows looking out on the drive. There was a walnut four-poster bed with a cover of green silk quilting. There was an escritoire in walnut and the chair seats had been worked in tapestry the predominant colour of which was green.

I said: 'It's beautiful.'

'There is an alcove here. Oh yes, there is the hot-water can. And here is your luggage. One of the maids will help you unpack.'

'I can do it myself,' I said. 'There is not very much.'

'I hope you will be comfortable.' She hesitated. 'My husband very much wants to see you.'

'I want to see him.'

'He is very ill.'

'Yes, I know.'

Her lips trembled. 'Well,' she went on with an attempt at brightness, 'I'll leave you. When you are ready ring the bell. I'll come for you . . . or maybe one of the maids will.'

'That's kind of you,' I said.

She went out. A tremendous excitement gripped me. I imagined myself living in this house . . . mistress of it. Then I thought of Amelia, who had been in that position and still was, and I wondered if she regarded me as a usurper.

I liked her. She had shown me a welcome which I believed to be genuine and she gave me the impression that she cared deeply for her husband.

I washed quickly, unpacked my bags and changed into a light afternoon dress. Then I rang the bell.

A maid appeared. She was young and I could see by her expression, very inquisitive; she could not take her eyes from me. I asked her her name and she said it was Emily. I told her that I was ready to join my host and hostess.

'Oh yes, Miss,' she said. 'Did you want me to unpack?'

I told her I had already done it and she looked disappointed. I guessed she wanted to give the servants' hall a description of my clothes.

'Just show me the way, please, Emily,' I said.

'Oh yes, Miss. There's tea in the winter parlour, Miss. If you'll follow me . . .'

I did so – down the spiral staircase and then down another. Emily knocked on a door and opened it. I went in. Amelia was presiding over a tea-tray. Aubrey rose as I entered.

It was a pleasant room – high-ceilinged like all of them, the walls lined with tapestries and the seats of the chairs were in needlepoint. It was a cosy room.

'You have been quick,' said Aubrey. 'I hope you find the room pleasant.'

'It's more than pleasant. It's splendid. I don't think I shall ever get used to being in such a house.'

'That is something you will have to do, nevertheless,' said Aubrey.

'How do you like your tea?' asked Amelia. 'Strong? Weak? Cream? Sugar?'

I told her and she handed me the cup. She said: 'After tea, you must come and see Stephen. He has heard you have arrived and is so eager to meet you.'

'I shall be delighted. Is he in bed?'

'At the moment, yes. Sometimes he gets up and sits in his chair in the window. That is on one of his good days.'

'I am ready whenever it is convenient.'

'Cook has made these cakes for you. You have to try them. She gets huffy if her food is not appreciated.'

'Thank you. They look delicious.'

'I want to show you the house,' said Aubrey.

'I'm longing to see it.'

I glanced through the windows.

'Those are the stables,' said Aubrey.

'They seem rather extensive.'

'My father kept a good stable and Stephen has been the same. We're a horsey family.'

'Do you like riding?' asked Amelia.

'I haven't ridden a great deal. I used to amble round on my pony in India and then when I went to school we didn't ride very much. I was with my uncle and aunt in the country and I rode a little then. I like it but I would not call myself a horsewoman.'

'We'll soon remedy that,' said Aubrey. 'You need a horse here. We're isolated.'

'The town is about two miles from us,' added Amelia. 'And then it is only a small one.'

She asked me about India and I told her of my childhood and how during the days in my uncle's rectory I had felt a longing to return. 'I saw it through rose-coloured glasses all those years when I was at school, and then when I went back . . .'

'You had taken off the glasses,' said Amelia, 'and you saw it in the cold light of day.'

'She had put them back when she saw me,' said Aubrey.

Amelia looked a little startled but Aubrey was laughing.

When tea was over Amelia said she would go and see how

Stephen was and if he was awake she thought it would be a good time for me to see him.

She left me with Aubrey for a few moments. He sat still, watching me intently.

'This is very sad for Amelia,' I said. 'She must be very worried about her husband.'

'He has been ill for some time. She has known for weeks that he cannot live.'

'She is very brave.'

He was silent. Then he said: 'Do you think you will like this house?'

'Y – yes, I think so.'

'You're hesitating.'

'At the moment it seems a little strange. Alien, perhaps.'

'Alien! What do you mean?'

'You said that houses are a part of the family. Families often resent newcomers. And I'm to be that.'

'Nonsense. Did you feel that Amelia resents you?'

'No. Certainly not.'

'The gatehouse? The portcullis? The winter parlour? Do they?'

'Well, it has taken me by surprise. I was not imagining such an *ancient* place. You didn't warn me enough.'

'I didn't want to overpraise and have you disappointed.'

'As if I could have been!'

The door opened.

'He's awake,' said Amelia. 'He wants very much to see you.'

'Come on, then,' said Aubrey.

Stephen St Clare was propped up in the big four-poster bed with its hanging of petit-point embroidery on a cream background. He was obviously very ill. His face was a yellowish grey, his dark eyes sunken; his clawlike hands lay on the counterpane.

'This is Susanna, Stephen,' said Aubrey.

The sunken eyes surveyed me with interest.

'I am delighted to meet you,' he said.

'And I you,' I replied.

Amelia placed a chair beside the bed and I sat down. She and Aubrey took chairs a little farther away.

Amelia said I would stay with them for a week and then go home to make arrangements for the wedding. 'I think that's what you intend, isn't it?'

I said it was.

'The wedding will take place at your home, I imagine,' said Stephen.

'My father and I have discussed it,' I replied. 'We thought it should be at my uncle's rectory. My uncle would like to officiate and I did pass a great deal of my childhood there.' I smiled at Aubrey. 'We haven't talked much about the arrangements yet.'

'I hope you will not delay too long,' said Stephen.

'There is no reason for any delay,' Aubrey put in, smiling at me, and added: 'I hope.'

Stephen nodded.

'I haven't been able to do very much for some time, have I, Amelia?' he said.

'No, but we have a good manager. Things run smoothly. And now that Aubrey is home . . .'

'Amelia has been a great help to me,' said Stephen. 'As you will be to Aubrey.'

'I shall do my best,' I said.

He nodded.

Amelia looked anxiously at her husband. 'I think you want to go to sleep, Stephen,' she said. 'There'll be plenty of time to see Susanna before she goes. I may call you Susanna, mayn't I?'

'Of course.'

'And we must be Amelia and Stephen. After all, you are coming into the family. Stephen, Susanna will come and see you tomorrow.'

Stephen nodded; his eyes were half closed.

Amelia rose and I did the same.

I leaned over the bed and said: 'I shall come to see you soon.'

The sunken eyes opened and he smiled at me.

We came out of the room and Amelia shut the door.

'He's feeble today,' said Aubrey.

'I know. But he did want to meet Susanna.'

Aubrey said he would take me for a walk round the gardens and show me the stables.

Amelia left us and we went out.

During the next days I became familiar with Minster St Clare and its occupants. I felt I knew Aubrey better than I had before. People often seem different against the background of their homes. I was amazed at his enthusiasm for the Minster. In India he had seemed something of a nomad, the man of the world, perhaps a little cynical. Now he was almost like a different person. Certain traits which I had not seen before were revealed to me. His passionate love of the house which seemed to have developed because it would shortly be his – and very soon, I could not help thinking, for his brother was undoubtedly very ill indeed. There was his love of horses. He delighted in the stables; he proudly drew my attention to the fine points of the horses. There was a recklessness about him which was apparent when he drove his carriage. He loved to control the magnificent greys and would have them galloping at a tremendous speed so that when I drove with him I was almost thrown out of the carriage – the faster he went, the better he liked it. I thought it was a little dangerous and told him so. 'Not with me,' he said proudly. 'I am in complete control.' It seemed to me that he loved danger for its own sake, and if he had not been such a superb horseman I should have feared for him. He was rather naïvely conceited about his prowess with the horses and that made him seem more vulnerable than before. I found that lovable.

When I rose each day I would go to the window and look out on the drive and I would say to myself: This great house will be my home. Shall I be happy here?

I was excited by the place. Every day new aspects were revealed; yet there was something about it which was a little repellent. I supposed that was the case with most old houses. The past was too close; it was as though it had been imprisoned within those walls and it continually intruded on the present. But I was too fanciful. I wished that my father had come with me. He would have laughed at my fancies.

Amelia – it was easy to think of her as Amelia for she had been so warm and friendly – had shown me the house, the various bedrooms, the solarium with its settees, chairs and long mirrors, its windows, its alcoves, in one of which was an ancient spinning-wheel. She had conducted me to the long gallery with its portraits and even to the kitchens where I was introduced to the cook – whom I did not forget to congratulate on her culinary excellence – and the kitchen court with its pots and querns which were still used for grinding grain and pease.

Each day I seemed to become more friendly with Amelia. There was a sadness about her which made me want to comfort her. She loved her husband; their life together had clearly been a happy one and now she was about to lose it. She was very interested in the house; she showed me certain improvements she had made; she told me how the roof had had to be renovated and how difficult it had been to find weatherproof medieval tiles; she showed me the furnishings she had chosen for some of the bedrooms because the original ones were too threadbare to be kept any longer. She loved the house and she was going to lose not only her husband but her home as well. But, I thought, perhaps she will stay here. After all, big families did go on living in the ancestral home; and she had been mistress of this one – so it would always be her home.

But I wondered. It was too indelicate a matter to speak of. Nor did I broach it with Aubrey. It was one of those situations which must be sorted out naturally.

Aubrey and I rode round the estate. I was a little fearful that I might prove inadequate on horseback; but he was most assiduous in his care for me. He constantly restrained himself and when we galloped he kept his eyes on me so that I felt I was being looked after. But when I rode with him in his carriage, he was very reckless – so eager was he to show me his skill; and he certainly had that. The horses responded to his lightest touch. I was falling more and more in love. I loved him the more for his vanity and his obsessive love of the house. I felt now, as I had not before, that he needed me to care for him; and that was very gratifying.

There were one or two dinner-parties – very small affairs because, as Aubrey said, there could be little entertaining at the Minster now that Stephen was so ill – just a few neighbours to meet me and some close friends of the family. I did meet Amelia's parents, Sir Henry and Lady Carberry, who were travelling back to their home in London after staying with friends in the country. They had just called for luncheon. I found them charming and they had a young woman with them who was introduced as the Honourable Henrietta Marlington. She was the daughter of some very old friends of theirs who had been staying with the people they had visited and was being taken to London to stay with them for a short while. I was struck with her; she was extraordinarily attractive and she owed this to her vitality even more than to her good looks, which were considerable. She talked a great deal about the season and amused us with her descriptions of being presented to the Queen at the Royal Drawing Room – and the solemnity of waiting in the queue with her train over her left arm until the magic moment when she entered, her train spread out in glory behind her. The Queen had given her a piercing look, she said, and extended her hand to be kissed, as though she were weighing her up and finding her wanting. 'She is very perceptive, they say,' she added.

Amelia's parents were obviously very fond of Henrietta and I could understand that. I was sorry their visit was so short.

I enjoyed my sessions alone with Amelia, which were quite frequent because Aubrey had so much to learn about the estate, having been abroad for so long, and he often spent the greater part of the morning with the estate manager.

One day Amelia talked to me more intimately than ever before.

She said: 'I don't know how I shall live without Stephen.'

'Perhaps,' I said rather falsely, for I knew this could not be, 'he will recover.'

'No,' she replied sadly. 'It is impossible. Right up to a month ago I went on hoping that he might get well. There were times when he was almost his old self. But really he was gradually getting worse. He has always talked to me a good deal about the estate. It is only recently that he realized it would pass to Aubrey, who has never till now shown much interest in it.'

'He certainly has a great deal now.'

'Yes, he's changed. I suppose it is because he knows it can't be long before it is his. We . . . Stephen and I . . . always thought that there could be children.'

We were silent for a few moments and then she burst out: 'Oh, Susanna, I can't tell you how much I have longed for children. Stephen did too. It was the one thing in which I failed him.'

'You can't blame yourself for fate.'

'I would have done anything. I had three miscarriages.'

'Oh, I'm sorry.'

'The first . . . I think was my own fault. In four months I should have had my child. I went riding and lost it. I was so fond of riding. We all were . . . Stephen, Aubrey and myself. We rode everywhere. It was folly. That was the first. And sometimes when that sort of thing starts it goes on.'

'How very sad.'

'I was so careful the next time. But after two months I had lost the child. I went to three the next time.'

'That must have been terrible.'

'A great disappointment to us both and I think particularly to me. I felt so strongly that I had failed Stephen. He desperately wanted a child . . . a boy whom he could train to look after things here.'

'I do understand.'

'Oh well . . . that's life, I suppose.'

'I suppose so.'

'Forgive my outburst. But you seem so sympathetic. I am sure you will be very good for Aubrey. He needs someone like you.'

'Oh, I think he is very well able to stand on his own feet.'

She did not answer. She just looked infinitely sad – thinking of those lost children, I supposed.

One day I was alone with Stephen. Aubrey had gone to one of the farms on the estate. I was in my room when Amelia came to me and said that Stephen would like to see me.

I went down to the sickroom. He was seated in a chair wrapped up in blankets. I thought he looked even more ill than he did in bed.

I sat beside him and after we had talked a little Amelia left us alone for a short while.

Stephen said to me: 'I am glad that you are marrying Aubrey.'

'I am so pleased you feel like that. Many families disapprove of newcomers to the circle. I had no idea when I met Aubrey that he lived in a place like this.'

He nodded. 'It's a responsibility. He will be the one to carry on. It is like a chain that has been forged over the centuries. One doesn't like to think of its being broken. If I had had a son . . .'

He shook his head sadly and I thought of what Amelia had told me.

'But now . . . I'm glad you're here. He needs someone . . . steady . . . someone who will look after him and prevent his . . .' He paused. I believe he was on the point of saying something important, but he changed his mind. He patted my hand and went on: 'I am sure since I have met you . . . that you are the one for him.'

'Thank you.'

'You will be strong. Strength is what he needs. You see . . .'

I looked at him steadily, but he was silent.

I prompted him. 'Yes . . . you were saying . . .'

The sunken eyes seemed to probe my mind. He was trying to tell me something. Or perhaps trying to make up his mind whether to or not. A great curiosity came to me. I was sure it was something I should know. And it concerned Aubrey.

Then he lay back in his chair and closed his eyes. Amelia came in.

We had tea together.

I wondered what it was he had been going to tell me.

It was late afternoon. There were dark clouds overhead and I thought there would be a storm before the day was out. I was in the long gallery looking at the portraits. I could see how like some of his ancestors Aubrey was. I studied the faces, some pensive, some smiling, some merry, some serious; and they all seemed to be looking out of their canvases assessing me!

It was quite an eerie feeling, standing there as it grew visibly darker. There were moments in this house when I fancied I was being watched, that unseen figures from the past were close to me – interested in this girl who had the temerity to attempt to intrude into the family circle.

There was one portrait which interested me particularly, perhaps because the face of the man reminded me of Aubrey's. His eyes followed me wherever I was, and the expression seemed to change as I watched. I fancied I could see the lips curl up in amusement because the subject of the picture knew that he both fascinated and repelled me. The white curls of his wig hung down almost to his shoulders and were crowned by a wide-brimmed hat which had just a touch of the military about it. His coat was mulberry-coloured velvet caught in at the waist; beneath it, his waistcoat was elaborately embroidered and almost as long as the coat. It was closely fitted to the waist and then flared out. The buttons were like jewels. His knee breeches were caught just below the knees with ornamental buckles. His legs were well shaped and the buckles on his shoes matched those at his knees. He was a very elegant gentleman.

'Hello!'

I started; and such was my mood that for a moment I thought it was the dandy in the picture who had spoken. I spun round. Aubrey must have come in very quietly and so absorbed was

I that I had not heard him. He slipped his arm through mine.

'I think you are rather fascinated by Harry St Clare,' he said. 'You wouldn't be the first one, I am sure.'

'So he is Harry St Clare, is he? He must be quite a distant relative. That must have been painted about a hundred years ago.'

'That's true. The hat gives it away. It's Dettingen . . . named after the battle. You ought to know the date. Somewhere in the 1740s, I believe.'

'Yes.'

'They were all the rage, those hats, after the battle. And you can imagine that Harry would always be in the height of fashion.'

'Do you know the history of all your ancestors?'

'Only those who distinguished themselves like Harry.'

'How did he distinguish himself? At Dettingen?'

'Not on your life! He was too clever for that. Harry was a Rake. Harry was the Devil Incarnate. He was involved in some fine old scandals and incurred the wrath of his father, grandfather and in fact the whole family.'

'What did he do?'

'Nothing that was good. If there was mischief, Harry was in it. He nearly lost the family fortunes. He died young. They said the Devil claimed Harry. I expect he is now having a riotous time in Hell. It would be just what he would revel in.'

'I think you rather like him.'

'Well, aren't villains always more exciting than saints? Not that we've had a great many of the latter in the family. Harry was a member of one of the Hell-Fire Clubs, which were a fashion in those days among the lazy good-for-nothing young men who had the inclination for dissipation and a certain amount of money which allowed them to indulge in it.'

'What did he do?'

'Evil. Dabbled in the black arts. Worshipped the Devil. Indulged in depravity generally. He was a member of Sir Francis Dashwood's club at Medmenham near West Wycombe. Dashwood built a place in the form of a monastery

63

and there the members worshipped the Devil. Black Mass . . . depravity . . . orgies. You could never imagine what practices they indulged in.' Aubrey's eyes shone with excitement. 'Harry wasn't content with that. The story is that he formed his own club and went one better than Dashwood.'

'A very clever artist painted the portrait,' I said. 'When you look at it, it seems to come alive.'

'That's Harry's character coming across to you. You can see, can't you, that he is no ordinary man. Now take a look at Joseph St Clare over here with his daughter Charity. They lived a hundred years before Harry. They are the virtuous St Clares. But don't you think Harry is more interesting?'

'I think his is a finer portrait.'

'Don't deceive yourself. That's Harry looking out at you. He's wondering how he can tempt you to folly. He'd like to make you a member of his Hell-Fire Club.'

'How dark it is. It seems to have got worse suddenly.'

He lighted one of the lamps which stood on a console table nearby. He held up the lamp. Harry St Clare looked malevolent in lamp light.

Aubrey laughed and as I turned and looked at him I thought that with that gleam in his eyes, he bore a strong resemblance to his ancestor.

I shivered and just then I heard the faint rumble of thunder in the distance. He put his arm round me and for a few moments we looked at the picture.

Then he put the lamp down on the table and, turning to me, took me in his arms and kissed me in a passionate and demanding manner. He had never held me quite in the same way before.

I felt faintly uneasy. I looked over my shoulder. It was as though Harry St Clare were laughing at me.

After dinner that evening Amelia delivered her astounding news.

We had eaten in the winter parlour which we did as there were only three of us. I had gathered that the main dining-room was used only when there were several guests as it was too big for so few.

There was a little ante-room leading from the winter parlour, like a comfortable sitting-room, and here we retired to have coffee.

Amelia had been abstracted during the meal and I thought she seemed nervous.

Then, as though bracing herself she said: 'I have something to tell you. I didn't want to mention it until I was absolutely sure. I am going to have a child.'

The silence was intense. I did not look at Aubrey but I was aware of him.

Amelia stumbled on: 'Of course . . . it will make a difference. Stephen is so pleased. I think it has done him a lot of good.'

I cried: 'Congratulations. You must be overjoyed. It is what you always wanted.'

She turned to me almost gratefully. 'I couldn't believe it at first. I thought I was imagining it. I didn't want to talk of it until I could be absolutely sure. But now the doctor has confirmed it.'

I got up and, going to her, embraced her. I was happy for her. She had moved me so deeply when she had told me of her longing for children and her disappointments. At the same time I guessed how Aubrey must be feeling. He seemed to have developed an obsession about the Minster since he had believed it was to be his. I wondered what was going on in his mind. For a few moments he appeared to be too stunned for speech.

I glanced at him expectantly and, as though with a great effort, he spoke. 'Well, I must add my congratulations to those of Susanna. When . . .?'

'It is only two months yet . . . I wanted to make absolutely sure before I mentioned it. There's quite a long time to go, of course. I intend to take the greatest care this time. It's like a miracle. After all my disappointments . . . and Stephen as he is . . . It will give me something to live for. I can't tell you how I am feeling . . . but, of course, this will make changes for you . . .'

'Yes, indeed,' said Aubrey wryly.

'I do understand,' said Amelia. 'I'm sorry . . . in a way . . . and yet I find it hard to be because more than anything that is possible . . . I want this . . .'

I could see that Aubrey was grappling with his feelings.

I said: 'We should drink to a happy outcome.'

'I shall not drink any alcohol,' insisted Amelia. 'I am going to be so careful.'

'Then we will drink, Susanna and I,' said Aubrey, 'to a happy outcome.'

Amelia could talk of nothing else.

'It's a miracle,' she insisted again. 'It's as though I have been compensated.'

'There are often compensations in life, I believe,' I agreed.

'It must have happened just before Stephen became so very ill, for there were occasions when he really was quite his old self. It is only recently that he has become so very ill.'

'I am so glad for you, Amelia.'

'I knew you would be. It's different for Aubrey. You see, this is his home. I know what he is feeling now . . . but Stephen is so happy because his son will be the next master of Minster St Clare . . . or his daughter its mistress.'

She said she was going to watch every step she took. She would consult the doctor and follow his advice in every way. There should not be another mishap.

Aubrey gave vent to his disappointment when we were alone. He was bitter.

'To think that this could happen! Do you believe that Stephen could conceive a child?'

'He has. Amelia says there have been periods when he has been quite well. It is only in the last month that he has been so very ill.'

'She would say that, wouldn't she?'

'What are you suggesting . . . that this child is not Stephen's? Oh, Aubrey!'

66

'Why not? It's a desperate situation. It's a way for her to keep her hold on everything.'

I looked at him in horror. 'How can you say such a thing . . . of Amelia!'

'Because it could very well be.'

'I don't believe it.'

'Do you realize what a difference this is going to make to us?'

'I hadn't thought much about that.'

His exasperation was apparent. 'My brother will want me to stay here. I'll be a sort of regent until the child is of age. A guardian to this infant who will one day wear the crown.'

'Well, why not?'

He looked at me almost with dislike. 'Don't you understand?'

'Of course I understand.'

'You won't be mistress of your own house. Amelia will be that. Can't you see?'

'If we stay here I shall be content. I am really fond of Amelia. We've become friends.'

He turned away impatiently. He looked peevish, as a child does who has had a toy snatched away from him. I felt tender towards him. I felt I had to soothe him.

I said: 'It will be all right, Aubrey. We'll be together. That's the important thing. It's relationships that count . . . not houses.'

He smiled at me faintly. 'You're a good girl, Susanna. I suppose I am lucky, aren't I?'

I said that I hoped he was – I hoped that we both were.

Aubrey seemed to have dismissed his disappointment from his mind. He hardly mentioned it. Instead we made plans for our wedding.

'It must be as soon as possible,' said Aubrey; and I was delighted by his impatience.

I had first fallen in love with him because he was good-looking, charming, and seemed so knowledgeable of the world, without really knowing much else about him. I suppose those were qualities which would appeal to a young girl who had had little experience of life and men. Now I saw him differently. I could imagine him as a little boy, growing up in this wonderful old house. I saw him as rather lazy, not wanting to be burdened with responsibilities and yet not caring to take second place. Had he been a little jealous of his elder brother? Perhaps. That would be natural. Then he had gone away, travelled extensively, trying to make a life for himself. Being called back, realizing that he would one day inherit the family estate had changed him, made him realize how much he loved his old home. Then, suddenly, when he had thought it was about to be his, another claimant was about to appear. I knew how deeply disappointed he was and that made him vulnerable and me very tender towards him.

I agreed that we should marry as soon as possible.

'This is hardly the place for a wedding,' he said. 'By the look of Stephen it seems more likely that we shall have a funeral.'

'Poor Stephen. I think he will now cling to life. He will want to see his child.'

'Perhaps.'

'My father says I should be married from the rectory. My uncle and aunt would like that and my uncle would officiate. After all, it was my home for a long time. I know my father would not want me to be married from a furnished house.'

'How soon?' asked Aubrey.

'Five weeks . . . six . . . two months.'

'The shorter period the better.'

'As soon as I return I will set everything in motion. I think I shall have to stay with Uncle James and Aunt Grace for a few weeks. They have to read the banns and so on. There will be a great deal to do and time will fly.'

'Then please set about it without delay.'

And that was what we arranged to do.

When I sat with Stephen again I thought he was much better. There was no doubt that the news of the coming child had acted like a tonic.

He spoke more clearly and there was a shine in his eyes.

'I'm glad you're getting married soon,' he said. 'Aubrey needs you. Look after him.'

I smiled and said I would. I guessed Stephen saw Aubrey as the young brother who had never been able to take care of himself.

It was the day before my departure. I had wandered out after luncheon. I was fascinated by the grounds which surrounded the Minster. In them one would come upon relics of the old monastery quite unexpectedly – a crumbling wall on which creeper was growing, paved stones among the grass – a stump of something which might have been a column.

I found it fascinating.

The Minster was already exerting its spell on me. I wondered if we should live there. If Stephen recovered we would surely not do so; and I could not imagine Aubrey enjoying his role of regent, as he called it.

But Stephen could not recover. The change in him was merely superficial. He looked better because he was happier, but happiness could not cure his malady.

It was hard to visualize the future, although only a few days before I had imagined I could do so. I had thought of our living here, having children, for my desire for them was as intense as Amelia's, and of loving the old house and having the portraits of my children hanging in the long gallery.

I had come to a copse. I had been as far as this before but not beyond. The fir trees grew close together, giving an atmosphere of darkness and secrecy to the little wood. I made my way through the tall straight trunks with their reddish bark, and as I did so, I felt as I often did at Minster St Clare that I was making a discovery. The copse was not large and when I came to the other side I saw that the ground sloped upwards forming a little hillock.

I climbed this and looked down. There was a sharp drop of about seven feet. I scrambled down through the mass of creeper which covered the drop and in doing so I disturbed the covering of plants. To my amazement I saw that it was not earth behind them but what could be a door.

I brushed aside the creeper. Yes, indeed, it *was* a door.

I felt a great excitement as I examined it, wondering where it led. It seemed a strange place for a door leading to what appeared to be a cave under the hillock.

There was a keyhole. I pushed the door but it did not budge.

I looked about me. There was silence everywhere. Again I had the feeling that someone was watching me and that there was something malevolent in the air.

I walked away from the door and stood back some distance looking at it. The creeper had fallen back and as the door was no longer visible the hillock looked like a feature of the landscape . . . rather unusual but not so very remarkable. It occurred to me then that the hillock was not a natural one and I wondered what was behind that door.

I skirted the hillock and made my way back to the copse. As soon as I entered it I felt I was being followed. It was an uneasy feeling. There was the sudden dislodging of a stone, and the crackle of undergrowth. It was foolish. It was broad daylight but my heart began to beat uncomfortably. I hurried on.

Then suddenly my arm was caught and held tightly.

I gasped and turned to face . . . Aubrey.

'Why, Susanna, what's the matter?' he demanded.

'Oh . . . you startled me. I thought I was being followed.'

'You were. Amelia told me you'd gone for a walk and I came to find you.'

'Why didn't you call out or let me know it was you?'

'I like to surprise you. Something's wrong, isn't it?'

'Not now you're here. It was silly of me. I had just seen a door.'

'A door!'

'Yes. Leading under the hillock.'

'What's strange about that? You'll find all sorts of odd things here, you know. It's the remains of the old Minster. There'd be an outcry if we attempted to move anything. Relics of the past, and all that.'

'Yes, I know. But this was a door. It must lead somewhere.'

His eyes were glinting. He was rather amused by my whimsical feelings. I supposed because he wanted to assure me that he was there to protect me.

He put his arm through mine. 'Were you going back to the house?'

'Yes.'

'Why should a door startle you?'

'I don't know. It was odd . . . standing there . . .'

'Did you expect it to open and the Devil to walk out?'

I laughed. 'It seemed so strange, and then coming through the wood and feeling that I was followed . . .'

'I'm sorry I scared you, dearest Susanna. I always thought you were so practical.'

'I don't think I am, really. I am a little fanciful.'

'And are you weaving fancies about that door? Well, houses like this are places where the most down-to-earth may be forgiven a few flights of fancy. I'll tell you, you are not the first to discover that door. We actually had it opened once . . . Oh, that was long ago, when I was a boy. There is nothing behind it. It's just a cave. It might have been a storage place for the monks. The door was put back and left.'

'Oh, I see. I thought there must be something . . . rather significant . . . behind such a strong-looking door.'

'Susanna, I'm sorry I startled you.'

'Oh, I was silly to be startled.'

As he walked back to the house he talked enthusiastically about the wedding.

Next day I left the Minster. Aubrey insisted on taking me home. On the journey back to London he seemed different. He had reverted now to the man I had known in India and on the ship – suave, carefree, confident; and he did not mention the coming baby who had blighted his hopes of inheritance.

My father was delighted to see me. He said that Jane and Polly had looked after him splendidly and as far as material comforts were concerned he had not missed me.

Aubrey returned to Buckinghamshire that day and when he had gone my father demanded a detailed account of the visit, watching me anxiously as I gave it. I told him everything. 'And you are still as eager to marry Aubrey as you were?' he asked.

I told him that I was.

'Well, we shall have to be practical. I think you should write off immediately to your Uncle James and we should get things in motion. You'll want to shop and you'll do that in London. You'll have to be with your aunt and uncle for a month before the wedding. I dare say you'll have plenty to do. Time will fly. I've decided that I like this house and Jane and Polly manage it and me very well. I have already written asking for an extension of the tenancy. There is no point in our getting a house which you are going to leave almost immediately. I can manage here very well. It will be your home whenever you want it.'

'I see you have everything in order. Military precision, I suppose you call it.'

'You might say that. My dear daughter, I shall be so glad to see you happily settled.'

'Poor Father! I must have been a great responsibility to you.'

'Well . . . away from home . . . a little girl to bring up. I did have a few anxious moments. But it worked out well and I always knew my daughter would know how to take care of herself.'

'I hope your confidence is not misplaced.'

He looked at me anxiously for a moment. 'Why do you say that? Has something happened?'

'No,' I said fervently. 'No.'

But I, too, was wondering why I had said that. Could it be that a certain uneasiness was beginning to creep in somewhere?

The next weeks flew by. I was fitted for my wedding-dress. I bought certain clothes which I thought I should need. We were going to Venice for the honeymoon. It was to last a whole month and some friends of the St Clare family had lent us their palazzo.

Uncle James and Aunt Grace were as helpful as I had known they would be. They were very gratified that the wedding was to take place in the old Norman church and that Uncle James would officiate. I was to go to them a month before the wedding. My father could come down for weekends or any time he could manage. It would be a rather quiet wedding because of the illness of the bridegroom's brother.

Aubrey was to come down to Humberston a few days before the ceremony and a room had been booked for him at the Black Boar.

Everything seemed to be working smoothly towards the desired goal.

In due course I arrived in Humberston. I felt very emotional as I sat in that bedroom looking out through the little window at the churchyard. Memories came back, the terrible loneliness, the homesickness, the longing for India, my father, my ayah.

I wondered what she was doing now. She had not been completely happy with the Freelings. She had become rather mystical, hinting at something. I was not sure what.

It was different now. Soon I should be leaving Humberston; my home would be at the Minster; but first there would be the magical honeymoon in Venice.

I was happy, I kept telling myself. I was contented.

Most young women would think they were indeed fortunate to be in my position. After all, I was not exactly a beauty. My reddish hair was startling in colour but it was thick and straight, and although it contained a wave or two it was not becomingly curly and was often unmanageable. And then my green eyes. They went with my hair, of course, but my lashes were fair and so were my eyebrows; and my skin was very white. It had given my poor ayah great anxiety. She had moaned about its delicacy and feared what the fierce Indian sun might do to it. I had never been allowed out without a big shady hat, even on dull days. But my height was what made me feel I lacked female attractiveness. I was too tall. I had looked down on quite a number of the young men of my acquaintance and I believed that was not an appealing trait. Men like to look down on their women – figuratively perhaps, but physically most certainly. And I, not exactly plain but definitely not greatly attractive in all eyes, had achieved what so many beautiful girls would have given a great deal for. I was lucky.

Cousin Ellen arrived with her two daughters the day before the wedding. She was so pleased that I was to be married; and she talked with less restraint than I remembered, recalling incidents of the past. It was rather pleasant. She remembered so much. She reminded me of one incident which I had not thought of for a long time.

'Do you remember Tom Jennings . . . the young man who fell from the ladder?'

'Oh yes. He broke his leg.'

'I shall never forget the sight of you, kneeling there beside him. All you did was stroke his forehead and speak soothingly to him and you seemed to comfort him.'

I spread my hands and looked at them. 'My ayah said I had healing hands.'

'They have those ideas out there, I suppose.'

'There was a boy in Bombay. I did the same for him. That was when she noticed.'

'Perhaps you should be a nurse.'

I was thoughtful. 'Do you know . . . I think I should rather like that.'

Ellen laughed. 'Thank goodness there is no question of it! You are going to marry . . . very well. We are ever so pleased. Nursing is considered hardly suitable for a lady . . . one of the lowest professions . . . like soldiering.'

'You are talking to a soldier's daughter.'

'Oh, of course I didn't mean men like your father. I mean the common soldier. Why do they go into it? Because they are unemployable at anything else . . . or they have been in trouble. And they say nurses are much the same.'

'That seems terrible,' I said. 'Isn't protecting one's country a noble thing. Isn't nursing the sick?'

'It should be, but so much which should be is not. But why waste time discussing such things when there is so much to be done, so much to arrange. You must be in a whirl.'

There was certainly a great deal to do but the conversation had brought back memories. I looked at my hands, well shaped, very white; there was a certain delicacy about the long tapering fingers, and yet they had a strength. I smiled at them. They were my only real beauty.

And so the time passed.

It was the night before my wedding. Everything was in order. My father had arrived at Humberston and was sleeping in one of the little bedrooms along the corridor. Ellen and her family were in two more. The rectory was full to overflowing. And beyond the churchyard, Aubrey was sleeping in the Black Boar.

I went to bed and then I had the dream . . . the dream which was to set me pondering on what could have conjured it up in my imagination.

Honeymoon in Venice

So Aubrey and I were married.

As soon as the ceremony was over I changed into my green gaberdine travelling suit and we set out on our honeymoon.

What a marvellous experience it was! My doubts and fears vanished. All my qualms disappeared. Aubrey was wonderful. He was such a man of the world and he understood that I was completely innocent – which of course means ignorant.

He was so much aware of my inexperience and he treated me with such gentleness and loving tenderness that, whatever happened afterwards, I would always remember it.

Gently he initiated me into the art of love-making and I have to admit that I took to it with relish, discovering in my nature traits which I had not before known existed.

This was love and it was wonderful. I saw a new Aubrey. He was a man who understood women – their feelings and their needs. He seemed to have forgotten the disappointment of the lost inheritance; he made me feel that the only thing that mattered was our love for each other and that everything around us should be perfect. And there was I indulging in the delights of married love in surely the most romantic setting in the world.

The Palazzo Tonaletti looked out on to the canal and we could sit on the veranda and watch the gondolas go past. How beautiful they were and especially so in the evenings when the gondoliers sang to their passengers as their craft shot under the bridges.

The Palazzo itself was splendid, with its tower at either end and its arches and long veranda. I was impressed by the mosaic patterns on the marble-paved floors. Servants had been donated with the house and we were looked after in very grand style. There was a solemn major-domo in charge of the household who told us we might call him Benedetto; there were numerous maids who giggled a great deal because, I think, they knew we were on our honeymoon. Our bedroom was a lovely apartment with walls and floor of mottled marble in an attractive shade of purple. There were lamps of alabaster; and the bed was large with a canopy of lavender and green silk.

In the mornings one of the maids would bring in our breakfast murmuring: '*Colazione, Signore, Signora.*' And then she would hurry away as though she could no longer suppress her mirth, I presumed, at the sight of us in bed together.

We walked through the streets lapped by the waters of the canals; we drank coffee and the occasional apéritif in St Mark's Square. We stood on the Rialto Bridge and watched the gondoliers on the Grand Canal. I had never seen such a beautiful city. I was completely fascinated. Aubrey knew Venice well and took a great delight in explaining everything to me. It all comes back to me in flashes – Aubrey standing beside me, pointing out the wonders of the Campanile which the people of Venice had begun to build as early as the year 902, although it had been completed much later. I marvelled at the Clock Tower and the two bronze figures on the dial of the clock which struck the hours. There was so much that was beautiful and yet even in those cloudless days I was aware of the contrasts. The beautiful palazzos with red porphyry, alabaster and coloured marble looking like coconut ice or some such confectionery; the Doges' Palace with all its grandeur, and close by, the Bridge of Sighs which conveyed the despair and hopelessness of those who passed over it knowing they would never set eyes on Venice again.

There was a gaiety in the streets near the canals, but there were narrow alleys, too, which could be dark and sinister. When I pointed this out to Aubrey, he said: 'That is life. Wouldn't it be dull if everything was good and sweet?'

'Why should it be?'

'Because you would never know how good it was if you did not have evil with which to compare it.'

'I think I should.'

'But the rest of the world is not as wise as my Susanna.'

Together we saw beautiful pictures – Titian, Tintoretto and the Bellinis. He was knowledgeable about art and he revealed so much to me. I was learning not only about love but the world.

They were strange dreamlike days; they cast a spell over me and I believed then that now I was married to Aubrey, life would go on like this always.

I was young; I was innocent; and all around me was evidence of life.

One morning, when we strolled along, we saw a crowd at the side of the canal; and when we investigated we discovered that a man's body had been brought out of the water that morning. I saw him lying there, his eyes open, staring in horror; his face was the colour of a grubby sheet and there was blood on his clothes from the knife wound in his back.

Aubrey drew me quickly away.

That incident coloured the whole morning. Aubrey said: 'It happens now and then. These are a hot-blooded people.'

But I knew I could never pass the spot without thinking of that man.

That was Venice. Dark, sinister alleyways where people met their enemies and knives flashed . . . and then the sound of a body falling into the water; the beautiful sunlit city with its confectionery palazzos and its singing gondoliers; the Doges' Palace and the Bridge of Sighs and the indescribable tortures which had been carried out in the prison adjoining them.

But this was my honeymoon. I would not think gloomy thoughts. This was being married to the man I loved. This was happiness.

I was fascinated by the little shops and would spend hours browsing in them. Sometimes I would leave Aubrey in the square where he might be sipping an apéritif while I lingered in the shops. He laughed at the fascination they had for me. They certainly did not appeal to him in the same way.

I loved the cleverly wrought bracelets and necklaces in

semi-precious stones, the embroidered handkerchiefs and slippers, the silk scarves and fichus.

I said I must take some gifts home – for my father, for Amelia and for Stephen.

'I shall leave all that to you,' said Aubrey. 'You are the shopper.'

I was going to enjoy searching for what I believed would please them.

The days were rushing past. We had only another week, I realized to my dismay.

We had taken our morning walk and come back to the square where we would sit in the sunshine and drink a cup of coffee which we had made a habit of doing in the mid-morning. We were making our way to a table under a blue-striped sunshade where we could watch the passers-by and the pigeons fluttering down, waiting for people to throw crumbs to them.

While we were drinking our coffee, a man and woman came by. I thought they looked vaguely familiar and then I recognized them.

The woman had stopped. 'Why, it's Aubrey,' she said. 'And . . . Miss Pleydell.'

Aubrey stood up. 'Phyllis. Willie . . .'

Phyllis and Willie! I had not heard their Christian names before as far as I remembered, but I knew them as Captain and Mrs Freeling.

Mrs Freeling talked breathlessly. 'What on earth . . . Well, fancy . . . and here of all places . . . and what are you doing in Venice?'

'We're having a honeymoon.'

'Oh Willie, isn't that just sweet! And Miss Pleydell . . . Oh, I'm sorry. You'll be Mrs St Clare now. What a lovely surprise.'

'You must have some coffee,' said Aubrey.

'I'd like something . . .'

There were two seats at the table and they sat down.

Mrs Freeling had changed; she looked much older than I remembered; her eyes were sunken and she seemed very thin. I had seen very little of her husband and could hardly remember what he had looked like before.

'What are you doing?' asked Aubrey. 'Having a holiday?'

'My dear, life is a constant holiday.'

'I suppose you are on leave, Captain Freeling,' I said.

Mrs Freeling leaned towards me and laid a hand on my arm. 'No more leaves. No more duties. No more regiment. We're free of all that, aren't we, Willie?'

Captain Freeling looked a little rueful. 'I've resigned my commission,' he said to me.

'Oh . . .'

He did not offer any explanation and I sensed that it would be tactless to pursue the matter.

'We're home now,' said Mrs Freeling, 'with Willie's people until we decide how things are going. It's so good for the children. We're having a holiday before we settle down to life at home, aren't we, Willie dear?'

'A very pleasant holiday, I imagine,' said Aubrey. 'How long have you been in Venice?'

'For three days.'

'Not long, which explains why we haven't run into you before. But Venice is not really big enough to lose oneself for long.'

'I'm glad of that. Wouldn't it have been a tragedy, Willie, if we had never found each other? And now we've done it . . . just in the nick of time. We're leaving in three days' time.'

'We're going at the end of the week,' said Aubrey.

'I could stay here for months,' said Mrs Freeling. She smiled at me. 'I dare say you could, too. And how are *you* liking life at home? An unnecessary question. You're revelling.'

'You must miss India,' I said.

'Not a bit of it. Glad to get away. Sometimes I used to get the shivers in the night. Those natives . . . They looked so sinister sometimes. You could never be quite sure what they were thinking . . . or what they would do next.'

'What happened to the children's ayah?'

'Oh . . . she was yours, wasn't she? She went off to one of the other families – the Laymon-Joneses, I believe. The children were fond of her. They made a fearful fuss about leaving her.'

'She was a very good ayah.'

'We've been to Florence and Rome, haven't we, Willie?'

Willie said they had.

'Marvellous! Those palaces! Those pictures! That lovely, lovely bridge . . . what was it called, Willie? Ponte Vecchio? The shops. Fascinating!'

Captain Freeling talked to me and Aubrey was occupied with Mrs Freeling. I heard scraps of their conversation as the Captain asked after my father and how he was liking being at the War Office after India. He said that he missed the army but he thought he would settle comfortably at home and the children had always been a worry. They would have had to be sent home to school sooner or later and that was always an anxiety and a disturbing experience for the children – as I probably remembered.

While the Captain was talking I heard Mrs Freeling say to Aubrey: 'Damien is in Venice.'

'My people live in Worcestershire,' the Captain was saying. 'We're at the family home for the present. It's a fine part of the country, really.'

I said I did not know it and he asked questions about the Palazzo Tonaletti and while I was describing that Mrs Freeling looked at her watch and said they must go.

They shook hands and we parted.

As we walked back to the palazzo, Aubrey said: 'It's a small world. Imagine meeting them.'

'I wonder why he resigned from the army.'

'Fancied some other way of life, no doubt.'

'People don't usually.'

'There speaks the soldier's daughter. There are some who might not find it such a glorious way of life.'

'I mean, I don't think it is easy to resign. I'll ask my father. I suppose we shall see them again.'

'Have to, I suppose. But they are going in a day or so.'

He sounded unenthusiastic, which pleased me.

'And so are we going very soon,' I said. 'Oh Aubrey, it has been so wonderful. Do you think anyone else ever had such a honeymoon?'

'Of course not,' he replied.

And we laughed and walked into the marble hall of our palazzo.

We did not speak of the Freelings after that. I fancied that Aubrey felt as I did, and that was that we could have done without the intrusion. The remark that we must meet before we left Venice was, I suspected, one of those vague statements which people make out of politeness rather than intention.

Two days after the encounter Aubrey asked me when I was going shopping for the gifts I intended to buy and why did I not do it that afternoon.

'I know you don't really care to have me around while you're doing it,' he said. 'So why don't you go and spend as much time as you like in those little shops and I'll wait for you. Oh . . . I know what I could do. I could look in at the Freelings' place and perhaps spend an hour or so with them. I know you are not very keen on seeing them. And I suppose it is only common politeness . . . having met them here.'

I said I thought it was a good idea.

I spent several hours in the shops making my decision. There was so much to choose from. I bought a bracelet for Amelia. It was gold, studded with lapis lazuli; and just as I was about to settle for a marble paperweight for my father, I saw some beautiful wall plates which I felt I had to buy. So I bought one with a picture of Raphael for Stephen and of Dante for my father. I was sure they would like them and they would remind me for ever of those magical days in Venice.

When I returned to the palazzo it was about six o'clock. Benedetto informed me that Aubrey was not yet home. I had a leisurely bath and lay on the bed reading for half an hour, expecting Aubrey to return at any moment.

As time passed, and he still had not come, I began to be alarmed.

Benedetto came to ask me if I would have dinner served, and I said I would wait.

He smiled sympathetically. I knew he was thinking that we had had a lovers' quarrel.

I began to be afraid. I thought of those dark alleys; memories came back to me of the man I had seen lying with blood on his clothes . . . dragged out of the canal. I had not heard the end of that story. Who had he been? A tourist who had been set upon by robbers – or was his death the result of some long-standing vendetta?

I sat on the veranda. I went back to my room and paced up and down.

Aubrey had gone to the Freelings. I had not heard the name of their hotel. Mrs Freeling must have told him but he had not mentioned it to me.

I felt inadequate. Here I was in a foreign country, not speaking the language, and I could not think how I should act. Surely Aubrey would not stay away so long unless something awful had happened. Suppose the Freelings had invited him to dine with them. Surely they would have asked me to join them – or perhaps sent word to me that he was with them. No. It could not be that. Something must have happened to him.

What should I do? Go round the hotels? Go to the British Consul? Where was that? Call a gondola and ask to be taken to the Embassy? Was I making a fuss? There had been times when Aubrey had made me feel a little naïve. Was I? Would he come in and say: 'The Freelings asked me to stay. I knew you'd be safe here.' Was that the way in which worldly husbands and wives behaved?

He would know how I was feeling. He would never worry me like this.

I must do something.

I went down to the servants' quarters. I could hear their voices. They were chattering as they normally did. They apparently did not think Aubrey's absence was unusual. I went back to my bedroom and stood on the veranda looking out at the darkening water.

He must come back. There must be news of him. How could I go through the night like this? I could hear the bronze figures striking on the bell in the Clock Tower. I must go and get help. I would find Benedetto and ask him to accompany me. We must find the Embassy and report Aubrey's disappearance.

But I remained standing on the veranda. Gondolas slipped by. I prayed for one of them to stop and for Aubrey to get out and come running to tell me what had happened.

Just as I was feeling I could endure it no longer and that I must go out in search of him without delay a gondola stopped at the palazzo. A man got out. He was very tall. He stood with his back to me; he was wearing a black cloak and a black hat.

Then both he and the gondolier were helping someone to alight.

I stared. It was Aubrey.

I gripped the rail of the veranda. I could not see the stranger's face because his hat hid it; and as I stood there as though petrified, for a moment floods of relief swept over me. Aubrey was safe.

I turned and ran out of the room to the stairs. He was coming up and he was alone. The man in black was no longer there.

'Aubrey,' I cried.

'Susanna . . . Oh, my dearest Susanna.'

I ran to him and was caught in his arms. He looked strange; his cravat was twisted, there was an almost wild look in his eyes and his hands were shaking.

'What happened?' I asked.

'Let me get in . . . I'll explain.'

I put my arm through his and unsteadily we went upstairs.

'Did someone attack you?' I asked.

He nodded, but he was clearly too weak to talk. He wanted to get to our room. When we reached it he sank into a chair.

'I'll get you some brandy,' I said. 'Or whatever you would like.'

He shook his head. 'Oh, Susanna, I'm sorry . . . so sorry this happened. Were you worried?'

'Desperately. I did not know what to do.'

'Oh my dear. That was my great anxiety. What would you be thinking . . . what would you be doing?'

'Are you hurt?' I asked.

'Dazed. Shaken a bit. No bones broken.'

'Can you tell me what happened?'

He nodded.

'I went to the Freelings. I left about six. I wanted to be home before you returned. I took a short cut through one of those alleys. It was a silly thing to do.'

'Oh no! I could not get the thought of that man lying by the canal out of my mind . . . the blood on his clothes . . .'

'Two men approached me. I did not like the look of them. I turned to retrace my steps, but there were two more behind me. I was hit on the head and I just passed out.'

'Oh my dear Aubrey, how terrible! I should have made enquiries. I should have gone to the Embassy.'

'It wouldn't have done any good. When I came to . . . I don't know how long after, I was alone . . . in some sort of hut. It was dark and I could see very little. But when my eyes grew accustomed to the darkness I explored a bit. I found a door. It was locked on the outside. I felt weak. I could scarcely stand. I shouted. But it seemed as if no one came that way.'

'They had robbed you, I suppose.'

'They took my purse. That was what they wanted.'

'But why did they lock you up?'

'Perhaps they didn't want the alarm given too soon.'

'Oh . . . the wickedness!'

He nodded and, taking my hand, kissed it.

'There was a man with you . . . in the gondola,' I said.

'Yes. He brought me home. What I should have done without him I can't imagine. I should still be in that hut.'

'I didn't know what to do. I felt so foolish . . . so inadequate . . . so helpless. I should have made Benedetto go with me to find someone to help.'

'You did the best thing by waiting. I don't know what I should have felt like if I had come back and found you gone.'

'What about this man?'

'While I was trying to find a means of getting out I heard footsteps. I called out. Someone answered. Fortunately it was an Englishman and I was able to explain. He said he would go and get help. But he found a window in the place. He broke it and came in. Then he got me out.'

'And brought you back. He should have stayed so that I could have thanked him.'

'He didn't want thanks. He was glad to help a fellow countryman in difficulties.'

'I have been afraid something like this would happen ever since I saw that man they brought out of the canal.'

'Some of the people here are so poor they would murder for a few lire.'

'Oh, Aubrey, I want to go home. I don't want to be here any more.'

'You're forgetting what a wonderful time we have had.'

'But this . . . this has spoilt everything.'

'No, my dearest, nothing can spoil what we have already had.'

He put his arm round me and I said: 'I am going to get you some brandy. I am sure you need it.'

'All right. Then we'll drink together.'

We sat talking of the night's events and the ordeal through which we had both passed. I had never felt so frustrated, so ashamed of myself for my ignorance and inability to cope with a situation. I kept saying, 'But I did not know what to do.'

He soothed me. I could see that he was very tired.

I said: 'I should like you to see a doctor in the morning. You don't know what harm has been done.'

He shook his head. 'No, no. I'm just a little shaken. I shall be all right after a night's sleep.'

'You are going to have that at once,' I said.

I helped him undress. I tucked him in as though he were a child. He shut his eyes and was asleep almost immediately.

I lay beside him going over the events of the evening: but finally I slept.

I was awakened suddenly. It was not yet light. One of the lamps had been lighted and it threw a dim glow over the room. A man was standing by the bed.

I sat up, startled.

It was Aubrey. But it was not the Aubrey I knew. There was something different about him. He advanced towards me.

'Aubrey . . . what's happened?' I cried.

'Wake up, Susanna. It's time you woke up.'

'But . . .'

He stripped back the bedclothes. He put his hands to my throat and at my nightdress. It was flimsy silk and I heard the sound of ripping cloth.

'What . . .' I cried. 'What . . . are you doing . . .?'

He laughed – a horrible jeering sort of laugh which I had never heard from him before. His hands were bruising me. I thought I was dreaming but I knew I was not. The nightmare of the eve of my wedding had become a reality.

I caught at the remains of my nightdress and tried to cover my nakedness.

'No,' he said. 'No, Susanna.' His hand shook as he seized me. 'You're growing up tonight. You have to learn . . . you have to learn all sorts of things. You're a big girl now. You always were, of course . . . but you are going to be especially big from now on . . . It's goodbye to innocent Susanna.' His speech was so strange and there was an odd glazed look in his eyes. I struggled but he held me down. I thought he was drunk or he was mad. Something had happened to him.

I felt sickened. I did not know this man he had become. He was a stranger to me. I wanted to run away. Where to? Could I lock myself in one of the rooms . . . run to the servants for protection?

I was helpless . . . as I had been early in the evening. It was as though I was being dragged into another world, a strange mad world where everything was different from what I had believed it to be.

But this was Aubrey – my husband, the man I had sworn to love and cherish . . . for better, for worse . . . in sickness and in health. He was ill. I must remember that.

He laughed at me. He laughed at my innocence – and I knew that he wanted to destroy it.

He did that night. I was shattered. I was limp with exhaustion, with fear and disgust.

The ordeal must have lasted for nearly two hours. I should never forget it. I should never be the same again. My body seemed unclean. I would never have that wide-eyed innocence, that belief in the world again. I who had been naturally passionate, with a delight in loving, had experienced the corruption of that loving.

Suddenly he seemed to be exhausted.

I thanked God for that. He lay down on the bed and was asleep almost immediately.

I sat by the window looking out into the veranda and beyond to the canal. I felt bewildered, lost. I did not know what I should do. Could I leave him? How could I explain – even to my father – what had happened? And why had it happened? What had turned the gentle, tender lover into a depraved monster? He had made me hate him and hate myself. I felt so frustrated, so young, so inexperienced. This day had been a revelation to me. I had always thought I had been self-sufficient, capable, but obviously I was not, for when I was faced with a situation which I could not understand, I was helpless, unimaginative, useless.

Something had happened to Aubrey that night. What? How could he have behaved as he did? Never before had I had an inkling of that side of his nature . . . sensual, determined that I should be a victim – and a despised victim. I was certain now that he did not love me. How could anyone behave as he had done towards a loved one? And yet how tender he had been, how considerate during the weeks of our honeymoon! How happy he had made me! And then that dreadful night! It was uncanny, supernatural, almost as though some wicked devil had come and transformed him overnight.

I wanted to get away. I wanted to hide myself. At dawn I bathed. I wanted to wash away all the impurities of that dreadful experience – as though soap and water could ever do that! It was marked indelibly on my mind. I dressed and left the palazzo. I walked along by the canal. The city was just coming to life. I was faced with a dilemma once more. What should I do?

I returned to the palazzo.

Aubrey was up. He smiled at me just like the man I had known during the first weeks of our honeymoon.

'Did you feel like an early morning walk?'

I nodded. I could not go on looking at him.

He said: 'I feel quite well this morning. I must have slept for hours.'

'You . . . you were awake in the night,' I said.

'Was I? I don't remember. What shall we do today? I forgot to ask you if you bought the gifts.'

I was astounded. I thought to myself: He doesn't remember! What can this mean?

'Aubrey,' I said, 'I think you should see a doctor.'

'Not on your life,' he replied. 'I feel perfectly all right this morning.' He smiled at me, the open, charming smile I knew so well. 'Now don't fuss. There's a good girl. Don't spoil the last days.'

I said: 'Aubrey, don't you remember? In the night . . . you behaved rather strangely.'

He looked bewildered and touched the back of his head. 'Did I? What did I say?'

'I didn't understand you. You were . . . different.'

'Did I have a nightmare?'

'Perhaps I did.'

'Poor Susanna. It was too bad you had to be worried. That's what I was so anxious about. My little adventure was nothing compared with what you had to put up with. Just my purse. "Who steals my purse, steals trash. 'Twas mine, 'tis his, and has been slave to thousands . . ." I'll tell you what, we'll go and have a last look at our favourite spots.'

I thought: He doesn't remember! What had happened to him? Some injury to his brain? He now looked so like the Aubrey I had always known . . . until last night.

Had I imagined it? How could I imagine things which I had never dreamed of? Besides the evidence was in my shamed and bruised body. He had been harmed in some way. The blow on his head? That could do strange things to people.

I must try not to shrink from him. I must remember what I had promised.

'In sickness and in health . . .'

There was a knock on the door. It was one of the little maids. *'Signore, Signora, colazione.'*

I don't know how I got through the day without betraying my feelings but I tried to behave as though nothing unusual had happened. Aubrey was just as he had been throughout our honeymoon until those hours of that night.

But I could not forget. Memories kept coming back to my mind. I never wanted to think of them again. He did not seem to notice my preoccupation. I dreaded the night. But when it came he was as gentle and solicitous as ever. It was just as though that nightmare experience had never happened.

I was beginning to feel a little better. I was even wondering whether I possibly could have imagined the whole thing. I had heard of some of the terrible tortures which had been inflicted on those who crossed the Bridge of Sighs and had been heard of no more. I had become obsessed by the memory of the dead man who had been brought out of the canal. Was it possible I had exaggerated what had happened? I was in a disturbed state. I had passed through an ordeal of terrible apprehension. But how could I invent practices which I had never known existed? Venice had had a strange effect on me. So much beauty – with so much which was sinister lurking behind it.

When I was home I should be able to assess this more easily. I would go and stay with my father for a while. I knew I should never bring myself to tell him of that night's experiences, but I could draw on his practical view of life, his common sense.

In the meantime there seemed nothing to be done but behave as though it had never happened.

Aubrey refused to see a doctor, but he promised that when we returned to the Minster he would do so; but he was sure no harm had been done.

I was glad when the last day came.

I declined Benedetto's suggestion to send one of the maids to help me pack. I said there was not a great deal and I would do it myself.

I took Aubrey's coat – the one he had been wearing when he had been attacked. It was dirty and he had not worn it since. As I folded it I felt something in the pocket. I put in my hand and drew it out.

I could not believe it. It was the purse for which he had been attacked. It was one of those leather ones, rather like a dolly-bag which are clipped and held together by a gold ring. It jingled as I drew it out. There was money in it.

I counted it. A fair sum – just about what one took out for a day's needs.

I could not understand it.

I went out to the veranda where Aubrey was sitting waiting for me to finish the packing. I held out the purse.

'What is it?' he said.

'Your purse. Those people didn't take it after all.'

'Where did you find it?'

'In the pocket of the coat you were wearing.'

'It couldn't be.'

'It was. Why should they have knocked you down and then not taken your purse?'

'I don't understand it.'

'Nor do I. Didn't you look to see if they had your purse?'

He wrinkled his brow. 'When I regained my senses . . . I don't know what I did. Perhaps I just presumed they had taken it. I felt very strange, Susanna . . . I have felt a little – odd – since.'

'Then you should see a doctor.'

'As soon as we get home.'

I gave him the purse.

'Why do you think they attacked you, if it was not robbery?' I asked.

'It must have been robbery.'

'Then why take nothing?'

'Perhaps they were surprised.'

'Then why take you to a hut and lock you in?'

'Who knows the motives of these villains? In any case I'm glad to have my purse back. I'm rather fond of this one.'

He took it from me and threw it into the chair. The coins

inside jingled and he laughed. 'So I'm richer than I thought,' he said.

'I am just going to finish the packing,' I told him.

As I did so I thought: This is all very mysterious. How glad I shall be to be home.

Satan's Temple

As we crossed the Channel and I caught a glimpse of the white cliffs, a feeling of reality seemed to return to me. What had happened that night had been due to a blow on the head which Aubrey had received. It had temporarily changed his character. I believed such things could happen. And the purse? The purse had worried me a little. The robbers must have been surprised and perhaps fearing they might have killed Aubrey dragged him away to that place, locked him in and made off. Wild conjectures, of course. But I had to try and find some solution if I was going to behave normally, if I was to delude myself into believing that nothing had changed between us. It had, of course. But I must consider my position calmly. I was married to Aubrey, bound to him; whatever he had done, I had to try to do my duty. I must not allow myself to despise him because of one incident which might have been an aberration on his part. Strange things did happen in people's minds in strange circumstances.

I had to go very carefully.

We stayed a night with my father before going on to the Minster. He was very pleased to see us and I would not worry him by letting him know that everything was less than perfect.

He was very contented. Polly and Jane had turned out to be treasures, and the house was conveniently near the War Office where everything was going smoothly, and it was clear that he was happier in London than he had been in India – even though he worked in an office instead of being on active service.

He was delighted with the plaque of Dante and we fixed it on the wall of his study where he could see it every day.

Then Aubrey and I went down to the Minster. Amelia was

delighted with her bracelet and looked well. She was sure everything was going well with her pregnancy and to crown her pleasure, Stephen was a little better. The news of the coming child, so said the doctors, had worked wonders.

I asked Amelia if they thought he might recover.

She became grave and shook her head. 'It is still there. It will grow and then suddenly that will be the end. But at least he is in no pain and I want to make his last months as happy as I can. I pray he will live long enough to see his child.'

'I'll pray for that, too,' I said.

Stephen was pleased that we had thought of him during our honeymoon. He professed himself delighted with the Raphael. 'How did you know I always had a special admiration for his work?' he asked.

'Inspiration,' I told him.

I was getting very fond of him and I believed he was of me. I used to look in for a brief visit every day, and Amelia said it did him good to see me. I discovered he had a great love of music, art, and literature. He was more serious-minded than Aubrey and it came out quite clearly that he had always regarded his young brother as the wayward one on whom he must keep an eye.

He implied that he had done this in the past and that now he was handing on that duty to me, in whom he had great confidence.

'I am glad you will live here,' he said. 'Take care of Amelia.'

'I think Amelia can look after herself.'

'I am glad you will live here. There is something strong about you.'

Strong! I thought of myself helplessly trying to decide what I should do when Aubrey had been missing, of that terrible ordeal through which he had forced me and with which I had no idea how to contend. I was weak . . . accepting life . . . shelving what I knew I should look more closely into – and I could not bring myself to do so for fear of what I should find.

And he called me strong! If he only knew. But how could I tell him? How could I ever tell anyone?

'And when the child comes,' he was saying, 'you will love

him. Perhaps you will have children of your own. I want you to regard ours – mine and Amelia's – as one of them.'

'Of course I will.'

We did talk about the attack on Aubrey. It was hardly likely that such an incident should not be discussed at length. Aubrey had been seen by the doctor as I insisted he should, and the verdict was that the blow on his head had done no harm.

One day Stephen told me how in his youth he had longed to travel.

'I never had the time,' he said. 'The Minster took it all. So I travelled . . . vicariously. I used to read at night when I could not sleep. Books were my magic carpet. India . . . Arabia . . . I was there. I have some fine books. A friend of mine has written one or two. You should read them. You know something of India.'

'Well, I spent my early years there . . . up to the time that I was ten. When I went back, it seemed different.'

'That's natural. Have you heard of the great Richard Burton?'

'Is he the explorer?'

'That's so. He has written a number of books about his adventures in India and Arabia. They are fascinating. He has lived among the people as one of them. I suppose that is the only way to get to know them. Imagine me, in my armchair, sharing such adventures. He writes so vividly one can imagine one is there. He disguised himself in various ways and wandered among the tribes. His studies are brilliant. You must read them. Go to the shelves and you'll see his books.'

I went across the room.

'I keep my favourites up here,' he went on, 'now that I am incapacitated.'

I saw several of Richard Burton's books but there was one which caught my attention. It was the name on the spine. Dr Damien. I had heard that name before.

'Dr Damien,' I said, picking up the book.

'Oh yes. An old friend of mine. He is a great admirer and friend of Burton. They've travelled together. Burton was a diplomat, Damien a doctor. His great interest is in methods of healing. He's an expert on drugs. They've had some adventures, those two. Their books make fascinating reading. Of course, one has to forget certain standards which are the accepted ones here in Victorian England. Burton lived as an Arab. He actually became a Moslem. He is dark . . . both men are . . . and that has helped them disguise themselves. It wouldn't have been so easy for golden-haired, blue-eyed fellows to go wandering through India or the deserts of Arabia! Burton started out as a soldier. That was one way of getting to India. There he took a native wife . . . a *bubu* they called them, as compared with a *bibi*, a white wife. But of course, not every wife found it convenient to go out with her husband, so a *bubu* was permissible. Burton went entirely native. Well, you read his book.'

'And what of this . . . Damien?'

'Read him too. He has travelled widely . . . disguised himself as a pedlar . . . his motive being that he could wander about unquestioned . . . or as a street vendor so that he could sit in market-places and listen. His great aim was to discover new drugs, new folk remedies, some of those which have never been heard of in this country . . . so that he can use them in his treatment of the sick.'

'That seems a very worthwhile project.'

'He is a man of purpose. I see very little of him now. He is hardly ever in this country. But when we meet we are the same old friends.'

'I seem to have heard the name somewhere. I can't remember where. I'll take the Burton and your Dr Damien.'

'Do. And when you've read them we'll talk about them. I'll look forward to that.'

I went off with the books and was completely fascinated by them. Both these men appeared to stop at nothing. They lived like natives; they practised customs of nomadic tribes and in some instances they were rather indelicately explicit. I read of the effects of certain drugs, of the sensual desires they aroused; and because of my experiences on that night with Aubrey, I could imagine much more than I should have done before.

I had grown up. I had been shaken out of a certain complacency. I had discovered there are things in the world of which I had been totally ignorant. I could read between the lines in these books. These men had had extraordinary adventures.

I was never able to discuss those books with Stephen, for soon after the day he had given them to me he took a turn for the worse.

It was as the doctor had said. There was no possibility of his recovery; and the best we could hope for was that his end, when it was in sight, should be swift and painless.

He had been more than usually unwell one day and during the night he died.

Amelia was very sad, but resigned. I think the prospect of having a child kept up her spirits and gave her courage to face the future.

There were several people staying in the house – among them Jack St Clare and his sister Dorothy. They were Stephen's first cousins, Amelia told me. Jack was a widower of some years standing and his sister Dorothy a spinster who kept house for him. They were clearly very fond of Amelia and she of them. I found them very pleasant and liked them immediately, but I fancied they were faintly critical of Aubrey.

Funerals are depressing occasions. The tolling of the bells is so dismal. The gathering of the mourners in the great hall afterwards seemed to go on far too long, and I was glad when they departed.

I stood at the door with Amelia bidding them goodbye. It was the first time many of them had met me and I am sure Amelia's obvious affection for me made them warm towards me.

Jack St Clare and his sister embraced Amelia tenderly and said that later she must go and stay with them for a while. She said she would.

Afterwards Aubrey discussed them with me.

'Both Jack and Dorothy spent a good deal of their childhood at the Minster,' he said. 'They have a proprietary feeling towards it and a little chagrin, I think. Jack would have liked it. And the fact that he had a chance of getting it, rankles.'

'I thought he seemed very fond of Amelia.'

'He always was. Well, she's a widow now . . . and he's a widower.'

'It is rather soon for matchmaking.'

'Of course, you are always so proper.'

I was startled. It was like an echo from that night.

But he was smiling at me tenderly and he put an arm round me and kissed my forehead.

I had to forget. It had been a momentary aberration due to a blow on the head.

It was not long after that when I discovered that I was pregnant. It must have happened during our honeymoon in Venice. I was overjoyed. More than anything, this could wipe from my memory the horror of what had happened on that night. I could become so absorbed that I would have no time for brooding on frightening possibilities. A child of my own! I was thrilled and delighted.

Shortly afterwards my expectations were confirmed.

Aubrey was delighted. But almost immediately he said: 'Ours won't be the heir to the Minster because of this child Amelia's carrying.'

'Two babies in the household. Won't that be wonderful!'

Amelia agreed with me and we became closer than ever. We spent long hours together talking constantly of babies. She was taking special care of herself, determined that this pregnancy was not going to end in miscarriage. The doctor told her she must take a little exercise but not too much. She must rest every afternoon.

She used to lie on her bed and I would sit with her and we would talk about the time when our babies came.

The nurseries were being refurbished. We discussed layettes and trimmings for the cots – two of them now.

This was just what Amelia needed to carry her over the loss of Stephen. I was so happy for her – and for myself. She liked to be with me more than anyone, for naturally I could understand and share her exhilaration.

I shall never forget that day.

In the morning we had all breakfasted together – Aubrey, Amelia and myself. I was beginning to feel a little queasy in the mornings. Amelia was very sympathetic. She said she had passed out of that stage.

She said the doctor wished to see her and she was going in to his surgery that morning. She was going to walk in and tell them at the stables to send the carriage to bring her back.

'I'll take you in,' said Aubrey.

'Thank you,' said Amelia, 'but I want the exercise. I'll be just right for the walk in as long as they bring me back. Are you feeling all right, Susanna?'

'I feel a little sick.'

'Go and lie down. It will pass.'

Aubrey came up to our room with me. He looked anxious.

'Don't fuss,' I said. 'It's normal.'

I lay down and felt better immediately. I read one of the fascinating books which Stephen had given me and the morning slipped away.

It must have been about midday when they brought Amelia home.

I heard the commotion and going to the window saw the doctor's carriage and Amelia being brought into the house on a stretcher.

I dashed downstairs.

'There's been an accident,' said the doctor. 'Let's get Mrs St Clare into the house at once.'

'An accident . . .'

'Your husband's all right. He's bringing his carriage back, so you see there is not much damage there.'

I was bewildered. I wanted to ask what had happened but the first thing to do was attend to Amelia.

She half smiled at me and I was thankful that she was alive.

I turned fearfully to the doctor.

'She's not badly hurt,' he said.

Amelia's expression was full of fear and I knew why. She was thinking of her baby.

'She should rest now,' said the doctor. 'I'll wait and see your husband. He insisted on bringing the carriage back himself.'

'I don't understand . . .' I began.

Aubrey was driving his mulberry-coloured carriage up the drive. I ran out to him.

'I'm all right,' he said. 'Nothing to worry about. We had a spill, that's all. The greys suddenly took fright and ran amok. I could handle them, though.'

'Amelia . . .'

'She'll be all right. It was nothing, really . . .'

'But . . . in her condition.'

'This sort of thing's happened before. It could have been a nasty accident, but I prevented that. They'll have to do some work on the carriage. We went right over. The side is badly scraped and the paint is scratched.'

'The carriage is not important,' I said sharply. 'It is Amelia.' Again I was reminded of that night. It was the expression in his eyes.

'I thought one of the grooms was going to take the trap to meet her after she had seen the doctor.'

'Yes, that was arranged. Then I said I would take the carriage and pick her up.'

'Oh!' I said blankly.

'Don't look so worried. It's all right. It was nothing, really. Just a little spill. We soon got the carriage up again, and I calmed down the greys.'

He was wrong.

Amelia lost her baby.

I sat beside her. There was little I could do to console her. She just lay there not caring whether she lived or died.

She said: 'I expected one of them to bring the pony trap. I should never have got into that carriage.'

'Aubrey is a very skilful driver. I think he prevented a worse accident.'

'There could not have been a worse accident. I have lost my baby.'

'Oh Amelia . . . my dear Amelia . . . how can I comfort you?'

'There is no comfort.'

'Except that I feel for you, that I understand completely. No one could understand more.'

'I know. But nothing can help. It is the end of all my hopes. I have lost Stephen. I have lost my baby. There is nothing left for me.'

I just sat beside her in silence.

When I was alone with Aubrey he could not conceal his feelings.

'Think what this means to *us*.'

I looked at him in horror. 'How can you talk like that? Do you realize what Amelia is suffering?'

'She'll get over it.'

'Aubrey, she has lost her child. The child meant everything to her.'

'She always lost children. It was to be expected.'

'But for that accident . . .'

'There would have been something else. The child is dead. It is no longer a menace.'

'A menace?'

'Dearest, don't be such an innocent. That child was standing between my and your child's inheritance. Well, that obstacle is removed.'

'I don't want to think about it like that.'

'There are times when you can be very unworldly, darling.'

'I expect there are, and if this is one of them, then I am glad. I wish with all my heart that this had not happened.'

He took me by the shoulders and shook me, half playfully, but I saw something else in his eyes. 'Of course I'm sorry for Amelia. It's a blow for the poor girl. But that doesn't alter the fact that it has made it easier for us. You must see that. Now I can make plans. I don't think you realize what this place entails. I can no longer be displaced by someone who has not yet been born. This is what was intended, what I came home for.'

'All the same, when you think of what it means to poor Amelia . . .'

'She'll get over it. She'll probably marry again and have a brood of children, then the loss of this one won't be so important to her. I know she won't get over it easily. She wanted this place. Of course she did. But it does seem wrong that when it was St Clare property for so long, it should go to someone outside the family. After all, *she* is not a St Clare . . . except by marriage. And the child . . . Well, it is hard to grieve because an unborn child has lost an inheritance simply because it is never going to be in a position to claim it.'

'You seem jubilant.'

Again he shook me with a kind of tender exasperation, and again I felt that shiver of fear. Would this go on? Would I always be watchful, waiting for the man I had seen emerge on that night?

'I am not jubilant, but I am not a hypocrite, and I should be if I told you that I hardly enjoyed seeing my inheritance snatched from under my nose. I would not be telling the truth if I said I was not glad it is coming back to me. I am sorry it had to happen this way, that's all.'

He was smiling at me gently, but the glitter in his eyes continued to alarm me. And a suspicion had come into my mind. He had gone to pick her up in the town. Why had he not let one of the men go with the trap? He was not all that eager for Amelia's company. But he had gone himself, and there had been an accident. I remembered how proud he was of his skilful handling of his horses and yet . . . there had been an accident . . . when Amelia was driving with him; and he knew, as we all did, that Amelia carried her children precariously and that the doctor had warned her of exerting herself in the slightest way.

No, I thought. I must not allow my thoughts to take that line . . . just because that night I had seen another side of him. He had had a blow on his head and he was not himself . . . on that night. I must not think the worst . . . if only for my own sake. But how can one prevent thoughts from coming into one's head?

In less than two weeks Amelia decided to pay a visit to Jack and Dorothy St Clare in Somerset. She told me that she felt the need to get away and I told her that I understood.

Sometimes I saw her looking rather oddly at Aubrey and I wondered whether the same thought which had come into my mind had occurred to her.

She was glad to get away and I think Aubrey was relieved to see her go. Perhaps I was, too. Her presence was a constant reminder of my suspicions, and I was trying hard to thrust them from my mind, to live normally, even to convince myself that I had imagined a good deal of what had happened on that night.

I did not want anything to intrude on my thoughts of the child I was carrying.

I went up to London to stay for a week with my father. He was delighted to see me and thrilled at the prospect of becoming a grandfather.

I thought he looked a little tired. Polly told me that he worked too hard. He brought papers home and long after she and Jane had retired he was shut up in his study.

I remonstrated with him about this and he replied that his reports and his work had become of great importance to him since he could no longer be active in the field, and a surfeit never hurt those who enjoyed it.

He wanted detailed accounts of everything that was happening. I told him of the pleasant part, but of course I had to mention the loss of Amelia's baby; and he referred again to the attack on Aubrey in Venice.

'It's an uneasy city,' he said. 'I don't think the Austrians will hold on to it much longer. In such conditions violence invariably simmers under the surface. You should have chosen somewhere else for your honeymoon – although I'll admit you would have been hard pressed to find a more romantic spot.'

'By the way,' I said, 'when I went shopping . . .'

'To good effect,' he said, glancing at the plaque on the wall, for we were in his study.

'Aubrey had called to see the Freelings – I was not eager to go – and it was when he was leaving that he was attacked.'

'The Freelings . . .' said my father slowly.

'Yes. They happened to be on holiday in Venice. Apparently Captain Freeling had resigned from the army. I thought that was rather strange.'

My father was silent for a few moments, then he said: 'Yes, I did hear something. There was some trouble.'

As he continued to hesitate I said impatiently: 'Yes? What?'

'Well, it was rather secret, it seems. They didn't want a fuss and scandal. Bad for the regiment and all that. He was forced to resign.'

'What had he done?'

'There was something about wild parties . . . taking native drugs and so on. Apparently there was a little community of participants. There was one other officer involved and some residents . . . not army personnel. So they couldn't be touched. In any case it was decided it should not be given any publicity . . . because of the army, you see. You know how these things get blown up in the press. We should have been hearing that the entire British army was taking drugs and indulging in orgies.'

'What a dreadful thing for Captain Freeling.'

'Secretly I think he was under the influence of his wife, a frivolous and rather silly woman, I always thought. Don't mention this to anyone. Keep it in the family. These things have a way of seeping out. Shouldn't have mentioned it to you, even. But I know I can trust you to keep quiet.'

'Of course you can. What drugs were they? And you say some people were involved . . . not in the army.'

'Oh yes. There was a little gang of them. It was largely opium, I think. There's some mysterious fellow, said to be writing a book about drugs or something. Interested in it all for research. He wasn't there at the time but his name was mentioned.'

'What was his name?'

'Oh . . . I forget.'

My thoughts had gone back to that conversation with my ayah. What had she said about a man? A devil, she had called him.

'It's dangerous to dabble in these things,' said my father. 'We couldn't have one of our men . . . and someone in a responsible position . . . not that they are not all in responsible positions . . . but these drugs it appears can make people act oddly and when they are under the influence of them they are capable of . . . just anything.'

I felt very uneasy and was almost on the point of telling my father of that nightmare experience when Aubrey had come home after the attack. He had been to see the Freelings. I had found the purse in his pocket – that purse for which the robbers were supposed to have attacked him.

Strange thoughts came into my mind – vague, disturbing.

Perhaps if I had not been pregnant I should have considered them more closely; but a pregnant woman can be obsessed by only one thing: her coming baby. And I was certainly obsessed.

I made many purchases. My father insisted that I take either Jane or Polly with me when I went shopping. They were Londoners, he reminded me; and they had the Londoner's shrewdness and knowledge of the dangers which could befall newcomers to the big city.

I quite enjoyed the company of both the girls and I had a good time getting together my layette.

I returned to Minster St Clare refreshed. Only occasionally did I remember what I had heard of the Freelings and reminded myself of that terrible night. I suppose I did not want to probe, which was unlike me. Normally I should not have rested until I had unravelled the strange coincidence of Aubrey's behaving so oddly after he had seen the Freelings who had been forced to leave India. But my thoughts were continually with the coming baby; and as Aubrey behaved impeccably as the devoted husband and the delighted father-to-be, it was easy to send all unpleasant thoughts to the back of my mind.

Aubrey was away from the Minster for most of the day and

I really saw little of him. I had taken to retiring early, for I was very tired at the end of the day and was often asleep by the time he came to bed.

Amelia came back from her visit to her cousins the St Clares, looking a great deal better.

'They were so kind to me,' she said. 'I always liked them. They used to visit us quite a lot. Stephen was fond of them.'

Later she said: 'Susanna, I think I shall move from here. After all, there is no real place for me at the Minster now.'

'My dear Amelia, this is your home. What do you mean?'

'Only when I married Stephen did it become my home. Now he is dead and there is a new master and mistress of the house. You see what I mean.'

'No,' I said firmly. 'This is your home and always will be as long as you want it.'

'I know you say that sincerely, and when I go away I shall miss you. We got on well from the beginning, didn't we? It is just that I feel I could be happier . . . right away. There are too many memories here. Stephen . . . all the children I've lost. I feel I should be wise to start afresh.'

'But where would you go?'

'I'm coming to that. There's a little cottage in Somerset . . . very close to Jack and Dorothy. I had a look at it. The lady who owns it is joining her son and his wife in a few months' time. She is going to live somewhere in the North, and she wants to sell it. Well, Susanna, I have offered to buy it.'

'Oh, Amelia, how I shall miss you!'

'You can come and stay. You and the child . . .'

A feeling of apprehension descended on me. I had not realized until that moment how very much I had missed her and had been looking forward to her return.

'Oh Susanna . . . I didn't think you would mind so much!'

'I look on you as my friend.'

'I am and shall still be. It's not so very far. We'll write and visit. Anyone would think I was going to the ends of the earth.'

'I liked to think of you . . . in the house.'

She smiled at me.

'I shall be here until the baby is born,' she said. 'I've promised myself that.'

'You shall be godmother.'

She nodded. I think she was too moved to speak.

The months passed serenely. The first three were the most uncomfortable, I think. I felt queasy so often and spent much of those days in my bedroom.

Aubrey was self-effacing and I saw little of him, which pleased me. I fancied he found illness rather distasteful and I was glad to be left alone. I did not want to think of that vague connection between him and the Freelings. I believed that unpleasant thoughts might harm the baby.

Amelia was often with me. We sewed together and talked; we went for little walks in the gardens and she was always watchful that I should not be over-tired. She was wonderful, taking a great delight in my condition, which was very noble of her, considering her own bitter disappointment.

By Christmas-time I was getting bulky and very easily tired.

Amelia took over what little entertaining we did. There was not a great deal as we were still in mourning for Stephen; but with a house such as the Minster there were certain obligations to the neighbourhood. It was a useful experience for me to see what must be done and to have an excuse for not taking a too active part in it.

Amelia had made another trip to Somerset – and how I missed her!

I was hoping she would return and say that something had happened to prevent her taking the cottage, which was wrong of me, for I knew she wanted to get away and make a new life for herself.

However, everything seemed to be going according to her plans; the owner of the house was making arrangements for her departure and by May of the new year Amelia believed she would be gone.

When we were alone Aubrey said it was for the best. He knew that Amelia and I were good friends but it was not wise to have two mistresses in the same house. I accepted it now because I was *hors de combat*. 'But wait until you are fighting fit,' he said. 'There could be little disagreements. "I am the mistress here," type of thing. I know you women.'

'It would not have been like that at all. If you think so, you don't know me and you don't know Amelia.'

'I know you very well, my love,' he said, smiling.

The thought came to me then: But how much do I know you, Aubrey?

The long-awaited time was coming nearer.

March blustered its way through the days in traditional fashion, coming in like a lion and going out like a lamb. April was the month of showers and flowers, so it was said. It was the month I had been waiting for ever since I knew how blessed I was to be.

Aubrey said: 'I'm going to send for Nanny Benson.'

'Is that your old nanny?'

'Yes.'

'She must be very old.'

'Old . . . but not too old.'

'I think perhaps we should choose someone younger.'

'Good Lord no! The heavens would fall if there was a baby at the Minster and Nanny Benson not in charge.'

'I will see her, then.'

He laughed. 'You'll not only see her, my darling, you'll engage her. She looked after Stephen and me and she always said she would come back and look after our children.'

'How old was she when she looked after you?'

'Quite young . . . as nannies go. Thirty-five perhaps . . . when she left us.'

'Well, she must be at least sixty now.'

'She's perennially young.'

'How long is it since you've seen her?'

'About a year or so. She comes to see us now and then. She was very upset about Stephen, although I believe I was always her favourite.'

I was not very pleased at the idea, but I thought that as Aubrey was so fond of his old nanny, it might be a good idea to have her. She had evidently been devoted to the family.

I talked to Amelia about her. 'Oh yes, Nanny Benson,' she said. 'She used to visit us now and then. Stephen thought that I should have her when . . .'

I said quickly: 'She is an old retainer. I know how important they are in families like this.'

And I left it at that.

Nanny Benson arrived a week before the birth. My fears receded, for she was so much the typical nanny. If she was sixty she did not look so old.

She was garrulous and immediately looked on me as one of her charges. She told me, in detail, anecdotes from the childhood of her boys, Aubrey and Stephen.

I thought her methods might be a little old-fashioned, but as Aubrey was so insistent that she should be in the nursery, I thought we might have a younger woman as well – who should be of my choosing. But I did not want to be too much encumbered by a nursery staff. I intended to do a great deal of the looking after of my baby myself.

Then the day came. My pains started in the early morning and before nightfall I was delivered of a fine healthy boy.

I had never been so happy as when I lay back exhausted in my bed and they put my son in my arms.

He might look like an old gentleman of ninety with a red and wrinkled face, but to me he was the most beautiful thing on Earth.

From that moment he was my life.

The weeks which followed were completely given to him. I could not bear him to be out of my sight. I wanted to do everything for him. I knew now what it was to love another person wholeheartedly. When he cried I was in an agony of fear that something might be wrong with him; when he crowed to show he was content, I was blissfully happy. As soon as I awoke in the morning I would go to his cradle to assure myself that he was still alive. When I fancied he knew me, I was ecstatically happy.

He was to be called Julian. It was a name which had been used quite frequently in the St Clare family.

Aubrey said: 'One day, all this will be his. So it is as well to make a proper St Clare of him.'

Aubrey was proud to have a son and heir, but apart from that, he did not show any particular interest in the boy. When I put him into his arms, he held him gingerly and Julian expressed his disapproval by screaming lustily until I took him, when he gurgled with contentment at the change.

Amelia planned to leave after the christening. I felt very sad about that, but I could not think about anything very much which did not concern my child.

The christening took place at the end of May. Little Julian behaved well and looked splendid in the St Clare christening robes which Nanny Benson knew all about and which had been laundered under her eyes.

She had settled in very cosily. 'Into my old room,' she said. There she had a spirit lamp on which she constantly made cups of tea. She had quite an addiction to tea; and I knew that on occasions she laced it with whisky. 'Just a little bit of old Scotland,' she called it. 'Nothing like it to put a bit of life into you.'

She was quite easy to get along with because she did not interfere too much. I think she liked her comforts and no doubt was too old to want to take on the entire charge of a new baby, but she was so delighted to be back in the St Clare nursery that I had not the heart to say her presence was not necessary – besides, I really did not want anyone else to be with my baby. I wanted him all to myself!

I hardly noticed how little I saw of Aubrey. Often he went visiting friends and spent a few days away from the Minster. I did not miss him. My life was tuned to that of my son.

The time came for Amelia's departure.

The night before she went she came to my room to say her last farewell, for neither of us wanted an emotional leave-taking in the morning.

It was late afternoon. Julian was asleep and so, I suspected, was Nanny Benson. She often dozed in the afternoon after partaking of tea augmented by 'a little bit of old Scotland'.

'I shall be off fairly early in the morning,' said Amelia.

'I am going to miss you so much.'

'You'll be all right. You have the boy . . . and Aubrey.'

'Yes.'

There was a silence and then she said: 'I have been wanting to say something for a long time. I don't know whether I should. It's been worrying me quite a bit. Perhaps I shouldn't . . . but somehow I think I ought.'

'What is it, Amelia?'

'It's about . . . Aubrey.'

'Yes?'

She bit her lips. 'At times . . . Stephen was very worried about him. There had been . . . trouble.'

My heart began to beat fast. 'Trouble? What trouble?'

'He was sometimes difficult. Well, not on the surface. He was very charming, really. It was just . . . Well, he became involved with some odd people. They did strange things.'

'What strange things?'

'I believe they lived rather wildly. He was sent down from the university. It may have been that he got into the habit there. Stephen had difficulty in hushing it up. Then he went abroad. I just think you ought to know. But perhaps you shouldn't. That is how it has been going on in my mind. I've been turning it over and over, asking myself whether I should tell you or not. But I think it is better to be prepared.'

'Yes,' I said, 'it is better to be prepared. Do you mean that he experimented in taking drugs?'

She looked at me in surprise. She did not reply for a moment but I knew that was what she did mean.

She avoided my eyes. 'People who do, can act very strangely when they are under the influence of them. Of course it was all long ago. Perhaps it is over now. There was that man. I always thought he was to blame in some way. He was here once or twice. Stephen thought the world of him. He was a doctor . . . an authority on drugs. He had done all sorts of odd things . . . going native and all that. He has written about it . . . so frankly. I always felt a little afraid of him. I suppose it was because of what I had read. I wondered if it was through him that Aubrey had begun to experiment. Stephen always insisted that the doctor's interest in drugs was to be able to use them for the good of mankind and that it was small-minded to regard other civilizations as backward because they differed from our own. In some ways they could be more advanced. Stephen and I almost quarrelled about the man. "Damien sounds like Demon," I said. And I thought of him as the Demon Doctor. Stephen said I was ridiculously prejudiced. Oh dear, perhaps I should not have spoken. Something just made me. I thought you ought to know. I – er – think you should be watchful of Aubrey . . . and if ever that Dr Damien should come here . . . be on your guard.'

She was looking at me fearfully and I said: 'You did right to tell me. I will be watchful. I hope I never have to see this man. Stephen gave me his book to read. It is mysterious and – er – sensual . . . and really rather disturbing. It has qualities like those I found in Sir Richard Burton's books. They both fascinate and repel.'

'Stephen admired both men so much. I read only one. I had no desire to read more. Stephen used to say that when he read them it was like taking a trip into those far-off countries. The writing was so vivid.'

'It's true,' I said. 'But I believe with you that the writers are dangerous men, even if remarkable. I believe they would stop at nothing to get what they wanted.'

'I always thought that it was because of this man that Aubrey began to experiment. He may have wanted to see what effect drugs would have on a man like Aubrey. I don't know. I'm only guessing. I don't suppose Aubrey would do such a thing now . . .'

She looked at me anxiously. I understood perfectly what she was trying to tell me. I was beginning to fit together a picture of what very likely happened on that never-to-be-forgotten night.

I almost told Amelia of it, but I could not bring myself to talk of it even to her. Of one thing I was sure: I would never endure that degradation again.

I thanked her for what she had told me, assuring her that she had been right to do so.

We did not say much more after that. We took a fond farewell and promised ourselves that we should meet again soon.

I suppose most unsatisfactory marriages break up gradually. The disintegration of mine certainly began on the night in Venice. True, I had made excuses for Aubrey, but I had always known that those impulses must have been in him somewhere, otherwise they would not have come out in any circumstances. I sensed that he was equally discontent with the marriage. I had failed him just as he had failed me. I was ready to believe that in these situations the blame cannot be all on one side.

I can say that when I married him it was with the intention of being a good wife. Perhaps he also first intended to be a good husband; but as his character was being revealed to me, I was realizing that I had made just about the biggest mistake a woman can make.

And yet . . . out of it had come Julian. And how could I regret anything that had brought me my child.

For the first two months after Julian's birth I was too absorbed in him to think about much else.

Aubrey did say: 'Aren't you getting rather absurd, darling? After all, old Nanny Benson is there. Must you always be dashing off to the nursery?'

'Nanny Benson is rather old.'

'She has looked after children all her life. She's more experienced than you are. You're so nervous about that child, you'll be upsetting him if you are not careful.'

There might be some truth in what he said; but I could not help it. I sensed the criticism in Aubrey's words and manner. I was so overwhelmed by motherhood that I was not bothering to be a good wife.

Through Julian I formed a relationship with Mrs Pollack, the housekeeper. Before, she had seemed to me a very formal woman, deeply conscious of her position in the household, humourless and something of a martinet. But since the coming of Julian she had changed. She looked completely different when she saw the baby; her face would be forced into a smile, which appeared to be most reluctant – and was all the more genuine for that.

'I have to tell you, Madam,' she said as though admitting to something sinful, 'I do like to see little babies.'

When I walked with him in the gardens, she would contrive to be there. When she thought he smiled at her, she was filled with delight. When he grabbed her finger, she marvelled at his intelligence; and Mrs Pollack's adoration of my baby brought us closer together.

I sometimes had a cup of tea with her in her sitting-room, and took Julian with me. I felt a certain pleasure in having a friend in the house – and such a stalwart, honest woman. She knew a little about babies too. She had had three of her own. 'All married and gone away now, Madam. But that's how it is.' She shook her head slowly. 'You remember them as little ones when they depended on you . . . and then they've gone to live lives of their own. Oh, mine are good enough to me. I could go and live with my Annie, but I don't think that's right for the young somehow. I wish they could stay little babies.'

I was so pleased to find that Mrs Pollack was quite human after all. I believed that she would have been a better nurse than Nanny Benson.

I asked her once why she had not found a post looking after children rather than keeping a household of servants in order.

She pondered that awhile and then she said that she thought madness lay that way. 'I should get too fond of them . . . and then they're too old to need you. It's like having a family all over again. I must say though, Madam, it's good to have a little one in the house.'

If I were going out, I used to tell Mrs Pollack. There was an unspoken agreement between us that I wanted her to keep an eye on Julian, for I did not want to leave him entirely in the care of Nanny Benson who might nod off at a moment when she should be looking after the child.

Mrs Pollack was the soul of tact. She understood and took

pride in the trust I placed in her. She was well repaid by Julian's obvious appreciation of her, when he grew old enough to express it.

One night, when Julian was only a few months old, I was worried about him as he had developed a cold. It was only a slight one but the smallest thing wrong with him sent me into a panic.

I awoke in the night. It must have been soon after three and I felt I must make sure that he was all right. I went into the nursery. He was restless, flushed and breathing heavily.

I could hear Nanny Benson's rhythmic snoring in the next room.

The door was open but she was in such a deep sleep that I was sure it would take a great deal to wake her.

I seized the baby and, wrapping him in a blanket, I sat cradling him in my arms. I stroked his hair back from his forehead and as I did so he ceased to whimper. I went on stroking his head for he seemed to derive much comfort from my touch, and from the back of my mind came memories of those other occasions when my hands had seemed to have a healing effect. I could see my old ayah's face clearly. What had she said? 'There is power in those hands.'

I had not believed her. Now I thought of what I had read in the books which Stephen had given me. It was true that in a society like ours we were apt to dismiss that which was not what we could call logical. But there could be other ways than ours, other cultures. Sir Richard Burton and the strange Dr Damien had hinted at that. It was to discover these things that they had set out on their wild journeys.

Now my thoughts were all for soothing my child, and I did so so satisfactorily that soon he was sleeping peacefully, his breathing normal, his face less flushed.

I sat with him through the night. I should not be able to sleep if I left him. So I just sat there happily holding him in my arms and becoming a little more certain that there was some power in my hands.

My ayah had said that it was a gift from the gods and such gifts should be used.

It would be a wonderful thing to save life. I could understand in a way why men like Dr Damien were ready to do anything in their thirst for knowledge. In his case, I read, it was to discover how certain substances could be used for the benefit of the sick. That sounded noble. But there was an arrogance about him which came through in his books, and I believed that he took an immense delight in the adventures which came his way – savouring a hundred sensual mysteries in the name of furthering medical science, which made me suspicious of the man – especially since Amelia had more or less warned me against him.

I wanted to learn more about this strange healing power which might be mine.

The next morning, when I returned to our bedroom, Aubrey said: 'You look worn out. What on earth happened?'

'Julian wasn't well in the night.'

'Couldn't Nanny B. look after him?'

'She was snoring all night. The child could be in convulsions and she would know nothing about it.'

'Well, I hope you are not going to make a habit of these nocturnal wanderings.'

'No. I am going to have the cradle moved into this room so that I can be near him.'

'That's absurd.'

'Indeed it is not. And I am going to do it.'

He shrugged his shoulders and it was done.

Julian was fretful in the night and Aubrey said it was an impossible situation, and either I moved out of the room with the cradle or he would.

I thought it was only fair that I should. There were plenty of rooms in the Minster.

So I had the cradle moved to one of them and there I slept.

I don't think either Aubrey or I was greatly disturbed by the fact that we now occupied separate rooms. I know I slept in peace knowing that my mother's instinct would wake me immediately if Julian needed me.

*

A year sped by. It was entirely taken up with Julian. Julian's first smile; Julian's first tooth; his first word, which I was delighted was Mama. There were cosy chats with Mrs Pollack when we discussed Julian at great length and he crawled about the floor playing with the empty cotton reels she found for him, rolling over the floor, clapping his hands when we clapped ours to show approval for his little achievements. He took his first tottering steps across the short space from her knees to mine, smiling up at us with triumph when he fell against us. They were wonderful moments which I would treasure for ever.

I was now and then aware of a certain exasperation in Aubrey's manner. Now that mourning for Stephen was officially over, he wanted to entertain his friends. I naturally had to take part in this; but I did so without much enthusiasm. They were not the sort of people who greatly appealed to me. Their main topic of conversation concerned hunting, fishing and outdoor sports with which I was not very well acquainted.

After those dinner-parties Aubrey now and then expressed his disappointment in my performance.

'You were scarcely the sparkling hostess.'

'They talk about such trivial things.'

'Trivial to you, perhaps.'

'They never talk politics for one thing . . . the change in the government, the *coup d'état* in France with Louis Napoleon making himself absolute head of the French government . . .'

'My dear girl, what has this to do with us?'

'Everything that happens in this country and those close to us must affect us.'

'You are a regular bluestocking, my dear. Do you know that is one of the less popular brands of woman?'

'I wasn't thinking of attractiveness, just a little interesting conversation.'

He looked at me with cool distaste.

'Of course,' he said, 'you have grown accustomed all your life to looking down on people.'

This was a reference to my height which he did not seem to like, for if I wore high heels I would stand above him. It was a symptom of his growing feelings against me, for when you dislike people you pick on certain points which normally would not be noticed. He thought my devotion to our child was unworthy of our class. We had servants to do what I insisted on doing myself. I believe he thought it showed a lack of breeding in taking so much on myself. Then there was my inability – or refusal – to form friendships with his friends; and now even my height.

I took Julian to see my father and we stayed with him for a week. That was a happy time. He delighted in the child and Jane and Polly revelled in having him to look after.

'Wouldn't it be nice if you came and lived here, Mrs St Clare,' they said.

And I knew my father agreed with them.

I heard from Amelia. She was happier in Somerset. 'Making a new life,' she said. It was pleasant to be near Jack and Dorothy. She obviously spent a great deal of time with them for they figured often in her letters – and perhaps particularly Jack.

On Julian's first birthday the cook made a cake with one candle on it. The servants came in to wish him a happy birthday and he thoroughly enjoyed that.

It was soon afterwards that Louie Lee arrived.

I had taken Julian for his outing in the gardens in his pushchair and when we came in I went up to the nursery. A young woman was there. She was opening the cupboard doors and looking into them as I came in.

I stared at her. 'What are you doing here?' I demanded.

She said: 'Oh, you're the mistress, are you? Thought so.'

'What are you doing here?' I repeated. 'Will you please explain?'

'I'm Louie. I've been took on for the nursery . . . to help Aunt Em.'

Aunt Em! That was, of course, Nanny Benson. I had discovered that her name was Emily.

'I have not engaged you.'

She shrugged her shoulders.

Nanny Benson came in. 'Oh, this is Louie,' she said. 'She's

come to give a hand. It's a bit much for me, as I was telling Mr Aubrey. I said there's our Louie and he said bring her.'

So Aubrey had engaged this young woman without consulting me! I looked at her intently. Her hair was bright gold – a little too bright for nature; her big blue eyes were bold – too bold for modesty; her nose was small and her long upper lip gave her a kittenish look. She did not appear to be the kind who would be an efficient nurse.

'My brother's son's girl,' said Nanny Benson. 'Well, there's too much for me in the nursery now our little man is growing up so fast . . . and there was Louie looking for something.'

I was dumbfounded. I wanted to tell the girl to pack her bags and go – taking Nanny Benson with her. I wanted to arrange my own nursery. It was for me the most vital part of the house and it was more than I could endure that it should be in the hands of a woman who was more often than not in a state of somnambulance brought on by lashings of whisky, taken in tea though it was – and now she had brought in this brazen-looking girl.

I waited for Aubrey to come in.

I said: 'What is this about engaging a nursery maid – Louie someone?'

'Oh, she's Nanny Benson's niece or grandniece or something.'

'She is unnecessary.'

He looked at me ironically. 'I thought it would relieve you a little.'

'Relieve me! I don't want to be relieved.'

'No. You enjoy playing nursemaid, I know. But as mistress of a house like this, you should realize your position. There are other duties.'

'My child is more important to me than anything else.'

He looked bitter. 'You make that abundantly clear.'

'He is your child as well.'

'One would hardly think so. You monopolize him. You hate anyone else to go near him.'

Was that true? I wondered. Julian *was* of paramount importance to me and I saw everything as it related to him.

'You are free to be with him when you want to,' I said. 'I imagine you do not like young children very much.'

'Well, I have engaged this girl.'

'But I won't have her.'

'And if I will . . . what then?'

'You can't . . .'

'My dear, I can do what I like in my own house. *You* have to change. What do you think my friends feel when they come here? You are not interested in them and you show it.'

'That girl must go,' I said.

'No,' he replied firmly. 'She stays.'

'What use do you think she will be in the nursery?'

'She will relieve you of the child.'

'I don't want to be relieved. Nothing is going to take my child from me.'

'Please dispense with the histrionics. What's the matter with you, Susanna? You married me, you know.'

'I am aware of that. But I thought I had a right to choose my own nursery maid.'

'You have no rights which do not come through me. Perhaps it would be as well for you to remember that. This is my house. I am the master here. Your authority comes through me and I say the girl stays.'

We regarded each other with cold dislike.

I knew that I was witnessing the disintegration of my marriage.

Very soon the last shreds of hope that we could ever be happy together were dispersed.

There was a truculence about the girl Louie Lee which gave me a clue as to what was going on. She had that air of insolence which can come from people who think they have a rather special place in the household. And how could Louie Lee be in such a position? Surely because she had found favour with the master of the house.

Her nursery duties were negligible; and I did not quarrel with that. If I must tolerate her in the household, I did not want her near my child. In fact Julian was hardly ever in the nursery and rarely if I were not there. I certainly would not have him left alone either with Nanny Benson or her distant relative.

I supposed Nanny Benson had been adequate enough when she had been Stephen's and Aubrey's nanny, but the years' growing addiction to whisky faintly camouflaged by very little tea, I imagined had scarcely improved her efficiency. As for Louie Lee, she had no talent for the post whatsoever.

I saw her once from my window. She was in the garden. Aubrey came into view and they were both laughing. Suddenly she gave him a little push and started to run off in the direction of the little wood; he followed her. It did not need much imagination to draw conclusions from that encounter.

The man whom I had seen once and so distressingly that night was never really far from the surface, I was sure. I wondered what he remembered of that night. I did not believe that he had been entirely unaware of it. He had tested me and found me unresponsive to bestiality, not love. Our relationship had changed from that night. I had shown him that I should never be the partner who would join in his depravities.

At this time I toyed with the idea of leaving the Minster. I could live with my father. In fact I did pay him another and more lengthy visit. Then I went to stay with Amelia for a while. My suspicions regarding her and Jack St Clare seemed to have some foundation. They were neither of them in their first youth; both had been married before; but if ever I saw a steady, though leisurely courtship, I believed I saw it there.

I was happy for Amelia. She was still young enough to bear children, and there was a glow about her which I had not noticed before.

When I returned to the Minster, the peace I had enjoyed in London and in Somerset seemed very desirable. I thought I must go to my father. He would welcome Julian and me. He loved his grandson and either Jane or Polly would be better nursery maids than Nanny Benson or Louie Lee. I could leave Aubrey to his nursery girl.

But one did not walk out of marriage lightly. There was too

much to consider. I wanted nothing from Aubrey, but there was Julian. He was heir to this fine estate; for it followed that in due course the Minster must be his. I owed it to him that he should be brought up there. I could not lightly take him away from his home and his inheritance.

After my visits I would feel more than ever withdrawn from Aubrey. There was no love between us now. I would lock myself in my bedroom with my baby; but there was no need to; he made no attempt to come to me.

I had suspected for some time that he had several mistresses and was rather glad of it. I did not want him with me.

Then one day I made a discovery.

I had long been aware of strange happenings in the house. Aubrey had taken to giving house parties which lasted from Friday afternoon until Sunday or Monday. I would receive the guests and arrange the meals. We used to dine at eight and by ten they would all have retired to their rooms, which seemed rather strange for they were by no means old people.

I was glad they did. I had no desire to sit up with them. I would retire to my room where Julian would be sleeping in his little bed; and on these occasions during the short time I was with Aubrey's guests, I always asked Mrs Pollack to look in at the child at intervals, so that we could be assured that he was all right – a duty which she was very happy to perform.

They were almost always the same set of people who came, although occasionally there were newcomers. I had grown accustomed to them and they did not bother me very much. They would make polite conversation about the house or the weather and ask perfunctory questions about Julian; but they gave me the impression that their thoughts were far away from the subjects of which they spoke.

One night when I could not sleep, I thought I heard people prowling about below and I went to my window and looked out. There were several people emerging from the little wood and coming towards the house. I drew back hastily. They were our guests.

I looked at the time. It was four o'clock.

I was very puzzled. Then I saw Aubrey among them. I could

not imagine what they had been doing. I went to my door and listened. I heard footsteps on the stairs – then silence. They were all sleeping in a different wing of the house and they had all gone to their rooms.

There was no moon that night and as it was cloudy it had been difficult to see them clearly.

I went to Julian's cot and looked at him; he was sleeping soundly. So I got into my own bed and lay there for a long time thinking about what I had seen.

It must have been five o'clock before I slept and then fitfully. I awoke just after six and the first thing I thought of was what I had seen the previous night.

Then Julian was clamouring to come into my bed, which he did every morning. I sang to him, as I did at the beginning of every day – old songs and ballads and hymns which he loved – with a repeat performance of his favourite *Cherry Ripe*. But that morning my heart was not in the singing.

Then I remembered that they had emerged from the little wood and there had been a day when I had gone through that wood and had come upon a mysterious door. I don't know what made me think of that – except that I had to find an explanation of where they had all been.

They slept late those weekends and often did not rise till luncheon-time. I had heard from the kitchen that they did not want to have breakfast.

The morning seemed a good time to test the notion that the mysterious door might have something to do with Aubrey's guests' nocturnal wanderings.

I told Mrs Pollack that I was going for a little walk. Julian was having a short nap which he took in the mornings. I asked her if she would look in and make sure he was all right while I was out.

Then I left the house. I went through the wood and came to the slight incline. I scrambled down, dislodging the creeper as I went.

There was the door.

Something like a warning came to me. I just had the feeling that I was in an evil place. I pushed the door and my heart leaped, because it was open. I stepped inside.

The thought immediately occurred to me that the door could swing back, shutting me in, and that I should be unable to escape. I came out at once into the open air. I looked for a large stone; I found one and propped it against the door so that it could not shut. Then, my heart beating violently, I stepped into what appeared to be a cave.

The floor was stone-flagged and as I advanced I was aware of an odour which I did not recognize. It pervaded the air and sickened me a little.

I saw that there were candles everywhere – some of them had burned out. I knew that they had been recently lighted and that confirmed my suspicions that it was to this place that those people had come.

The cave opened into a square room. There was a table which looked like an altar and I almost cried out in terror, for on it was a large figure – life-sized, and for one horrified moment I had thought that someone was sitting there.

The figure on the altar seemed to leer at me. It was evil. I saw then that it was meant to represent the Devil – the horns, the cloven feet were evidence of that; the red eyes seemed to be fixed on me.

There were drawings on the walls. I looked at them. At first they were incomprehensible – men and women in coupling groups in strange positions – and then the significance of this was brought home to me.

Now I had one desire and that was to get out of this place as quickly as I could. I ran. I kicked the stone away from the door and shut it behind me. I ran through the wood as though pursued by the Devil – and I really felt that I had come face to face with him.

My thoughts were in a turmoil. What had I stumbled on?

Mrs Pollack greeted me. 'He's still sleeping. I've looked in on him twice. Are you all right, Mrs St Clare?'

'Yes . . . thank you, Mrs Pollack. I'll just go up. I don't

want him to sleep too long, or he won't get his rest tonight.'

I went up to my room.

What did it mean? I had to know.

I don't know how I got through that day, but I was aware of what I had to do. I had to find out exactly what happened in that cave. This was my home . . . the home of my child. If what I feared was going on was true, I should have to take some action.

That evening I settled Julian in his bed and sat by the window. How silent the house was!

It was about fifteen minutes to midnight when I heard the first sound. I thought: This is why Aubrey gave orders that the guests were to be in the east wing. That is well away from the rest of the house and their comings and goings would not be heard.

I watched them emerge from the house. It was a dark night but I could make out the figures as they moved towards the wood. I sat there after they had disappeared, bracing myself. I was trembling, but I knew I had to be sure. I had to do this.

Images crept into my mind; I had heard whispers of strange sects when I was in India. There were rituals and secret meetings . . . there was worshipping of strange gods.

I thought of that figure of Satan on what could only have been a mock altar.

Don't go, said a voice within me. Go to London tomorrow. Take Julian with you. Say that you cannot live another day under this roof.

I could not do that. But I must have evidence of what was going on. I must see with my own eyes.

I put on my boots and a big cloak over my night things and crept downstairs. Out through the woods I went to what I had begun to think of as the unholy temple.

The door was shut.

I pushed it open and went in.

The sight which met my eyes was so shocking that although

I had been half prepared, I almost turned and fled. Candles were burning, many of them. There was a haze in the air. I saw people reclining on mats on the floor surrounding the hideous figure on the altar. Most of them were semi-nude or completely so. They were in groups of threes and fours and I turned my eyes from them because I did not want to see what was happening.

I saw Aubrey then and he saw me. He looked strange, wild-eyed, sneering at me. He lunged towards me and said in a slurred voice: 'I believe it is my little wife . . . no, no, no, my *big* wife . . . Come to join us, Susanna?'

I turned and fled.

Although I knew he had not followed me, I ran through the woods, scratching my hands on the tree-trunks, panic-stricken because the bracken caught at my clothes and I had a terrible fear it was attempting to hold me until someone came to catch me and carry me back to that scene of depravity.

I stumbled into the house and went up to my room, locking myself in. I threw myself on the bed, feeling sick; and for some minutes I lay there.

Then I rose and went to look at Julian. He was sleeping peacefully.

I thought: I will go to my father. I will tell him everything. I must take Julian away. He must not live here, where all this is going on.

I was making plans feverishly to get away . . . quickly.

That was the only thought which could give me any peace.

My father would help me. I thanked God for him. I was not alone. I would make my home with him. I could never see Aubrey again without thinking of him in that evil place.

Perhaps I had suspected something of this. Perhaps deep down in my mind I had, ever since that night. Yet he had been such a charming lover . . . in the beginning. I could not forget those weeks in Venice. His was indeed a dual personality. Something told me that the charming man was there . . . but being stifled by the man whose mind and body was being poisoned by the drugs he took.

So many thoughts turned themselves over in my mind. I

had a conviction that the mysterious Dr Damien had started him on this terrible road, that wicked man wanted to see the effect drugs could have on people, so that he could learn about them. He pursued knowledge with ruthlessness and did not care how many people he ruined on the way . . . as he had ruined Aubrey.

Amelia had hinted that I must be wary of him. I would, if ever he came here. But I should not be here . . . I should be with my father.

The night was over at last. There was Julian demanding his songs, including *Cherry Ripe*. I must have given a very poor performance on that morning.

I started getting a few things together. I would tell Aubrey what I intended to do and ask him not to attempt to get into touch with me. Not that I feared he would. I had seen contempt and hatred in his eyes when I confronted him. He must feel ashamed – as I was sure he did in his sane moments.

It was late in the morning when he came to me. I had packed a few necessities and planned to leave on the afternoon train. That was at four o'clock.

For a moment we just stood looking at each other. Then I saw his lips curl and my heart sank. He was in a truculent mood and that cold dislike in his eyes which always alarmed me, was apparent.

'Well,' he said, 'what have you to say?'

'I am leaving.'

He raised his eyebrows. 'Is that all?'

'It is enough.'

'You were not very polite. Bursting in like that . . . uninvited . . . and then making off without a word.'

'What words did you expect me to say?'

'Being you . . . so calm, so restrained . . . none, of course. Why don't you throw aside your inhibitions? Why don't you join us? I can promise you excitement . . . such as you have never dreamed of.'

'You must be mad.'

'It's the most thrilling thing I ever knew.'

'You are under the influence of drugs. You are not normal. I would rather not discuss that. I am leaving this afternoon.'

'But *I* want to discuss it. Do you know, when I married you I thought you were a woman of spirit . . . I didn't think you would be so afraid of life.'

'I am not afraid.'

'Oh yes you are. You are conventional, strait-laced, a prude. I knew my mistake very soon after I married you. I was going to make you enjoy what I enjoyed. I thought it would be interesting to watch you change. But I soon discovered that you could never throw off all the shibboleths of your upbringing.' He laughed wildly. 'There were times during those few weeks in Venice when I thought I might join you . . . become what you believed I was. I must have been crazy. I suppose I was really in love with you . . . then. But I need excitement. I couldn't live . . . conventionally . . . not since I knew what could be had . . .'

I said: 'Well, now we understand each other perfectly. We have both made the worst mistake two people can make. Still, even that is not irrevocable. You take opium . . . smoke it or take it in some other form. What does it matter how? Perhaps there are other pernicious drugs too. I know of your affair with the nursery maid. I know of what goes on in that appalling place and I want to put myself as far from all that as I possibly can.'

'If you were the virtuous woman you make yourself out to be, you would obey your husband. That is a wife's first duty.'

'In such circumstances? I do not think so. My duty is to get away from this place and take my child with me.'

He looked at me sardonically. 'Oh Susanna,' he said, 'I admire you in a way. So confident . . . so big. If you had only been prepared to make a little experiment . . .'

'Experiment? Do you mean become like you and your depraved friends?'

He said: 'I wonder . . .' His face softened a little and I think he was recalling those first weeks in Venice. I realize now that he had not been pretending then; he had genuinely shared my delight in them. I have grown older now and I understand what I did not at that time, that one cannot divide people neatly into categories – the good and the bad. The worst have good impulses sometimes; and the better ones act unworthily. But I was young; I was headstrong; and I was frightened. I was a mother whose first thought was for her child; and I saw Aubrey as a weak man who had formed dangerous, degrading habits and was ruining his life as well as ours because he had not the strength to fight against his obsession. I despised him. Any love I had had for him had died. It had begun to on that night in Venice. Perhaps it had always been a frail thing. Perhaps that is how young people often are. They fall in love – or think they are in love – with the first attractive man who is interested in them. They want to be loved; it is a delightful adventure: marriage, children, they are the foundation of the ideal existence. I was seeing it all clearly now. My love for Aubrey had been superficial; if it had been stronger I should have wanted to stay and help him fight this terrible affliction.

No, I did not love Aubrey; but at least I had learned the true meaning of one kind of love when my child was born.

The moment passed. 'At least,' said Aubrey, 'there is no longer need for secrecy.'

'That night,' I said, 'that terrible night in Venice . . .'

He laughed.

'The night of revelation . . . when I realized I had married a prude . . . a woman with fixed ideas, a woman steeped in conventionality, who would never come with me where I wanted to go. And you knew you had married a monster.'

'You were aware of everything,' I accused him. 'You pretended it was due to a blow on the head, that you had been attacked. You had been with the Freelings.'

'You are beginning to see a little daylight, aren't you? Of course I wasn't attacked. Seeing that man brought out of the canal gave me the idea. You found my purse, didn't you? That was careless of me. It was imperceptive of you not to realize then.'

'You met the Freelings. You went into one of your sessions with them. I understand all that clearly. You didn't care about my anxiety, waiting at the palazzo imagining all sorts of horrors which might have befallen you.'

'One doesn't think about anything at such times. You really should cast aside your inhibitions, you should try . . .'

I shook my head fiercely. 'And your devilish Dr Damien was present most likely. He brought you home, didn't he? That story about being in the hut and his rescuing you . . . False! All false! The Freelings had to leave India because of all this. My ayah tried to warn me. How I wish that she had never gone to the Freelings . . . and I had never met you.'

'I wonder how many disappointed wives have said that to their husbands, or vice versa come to that. You should have stayed last night. We would have initiated you into the mysteries and excitement of my Hell-Fire Club. What did you think of it? You stumbled across it before, didn't you? You found the door but it was locked. Do you remember that day in the gallery when I told you about Harry St Clare? I sometimes think I'm Harry born again. I'm just like him. You like stories of the past, don't you? You like to know the history of the house. Well, that temple under the hillock was built by Harry. I discovered it when I was a boy. There was a reference to it in some old document. I forced open the door. I had a new lock made for it when I was at the university. There was a circle of us there. Well, Sir Francis Dashwood built his temple at Medmenham. Harry saw no reason why he shouldn't build his here. Just imagine . . . a hundred years ago Harry and his circle were doing more or less what we are doing here now. History repeating itself. Always interesting, don't you think? You see, there is nothing new about all this. Perhaps we have advanced a little on the drugs. Harry had his, though. It's exciting. When you are under the influence, there is nothing, simply nothing, you cannot do. I could tell you . . .'

'Please don't. I have no desire to hear.' I looked at him intently. I said: 'And what of Amelia's baby?'

He stared at me.

'You said you met her in the town. Why? So that you could drive her back . . . and have a little upset . . . nothing to hurt the carriage much . . . but to destroy her baby . . . or try to.'

He was silent. I saw a glimpse then of the Aubrey I had known in the beginning. There was a look of contrition in his eyes.

'I might have known,' I said.

'It happened,' he said quickly. 'These things happen. I had no intention . . .'

'Why did you go to meet her? They were to take the trap. You must have arranged it.'

'She lost her babies . . . all of them . . . the least little thing.'

'So you decided to arrange . . . this little thing.'

'It happened, I tell you. It happened. Why bring it up? It's over.'

'There is only one thing more for me to say,' I went on. 'I am leaving here this afternoon.'

'Where will you go?'

'To my father, of course.'

'I see. You, who adhere so fondly to convention, should not take such a daring action.'

'It is not convention but decency which I want to adhere to. I will not have my child brought up in a house like this.'

'So you propose to take my son away from his home?'

'Of course he will come with me.'

He shook his head slowly. All trace of his old self had disappeared. A smile played about his lips and it was not a pleasant one, and a terrible fear struck me. His next words confirmed that fear. 'You are inclined to think that I have played no part in producing that boy. But that is not the case. Any court of law would tell you that.'

I stared at him in horror. He understood my feelings perfectly. He went on: 'You could leave here, of course. But you could not take my son with you.'

My mouth was suddenly parched. The air was full of menace.

'Yes,' he went on. 'You may leave. Of course, the world does not look too kindly on the married woman who deserts her husband, though there are some who take this unwise action. But you cannot take my son away with you.'

I cried out: 'Why do you keep calling him *your* son? He is mine, too.'

'Ours,' he said. 'But I am his father. This is a man's world, my dear Susanna. I am sure that fact has occurred to a strong-minded woman like you. If you went and took our son with you, I would soon have him back in his rightful place. The law would see to that.'

'You do not love him.'

'He is my son. This is his home. All this will be his one day. The house . . . the estate . . . even the temple. All his. He must be brought up in his own home. That is something I shall insist on.'

'You would not be so cruel as to take my child from me.'

'*I* do not propose to separate you. All you have to do is to remain. I shall not ask you to leave, but if you do, the child stays here.'

I was stunned. I could see that he had defeated me.

He went on: 'You have monopolized the child. You have taken him out of my care. He hardly knows his father.'

'Because his father has not had the time to spare for him, being so occupied with his drug-inspired orgies.'

'Who would believe that?'

'I do. I know it.'

'Your opinion would not count. If you want to go, if you want to create a scandal, if you want to bring disgrace on your father's grey hairs, and on the father of your son, then you must do so. I cannot make you a prisoner here. But let me tell you this: if you attempt to take my son from his rightful home, I shall see that he is brought back here. The law would demand it and you would have to obey the law.'

'You forget what I know of you. Surely no court of law would want a child brought up in a home where these evil practices are carried on, where the father indulges in intrigues with the servants . . .'

'That is no uncommon practice, my dear. And it would have to be proved. I could make sure that it was not. If you are prepared to lose your son . . . then go ahead and do so. I shall put no obstacle in the way of your going. But a court might well commit you as insane, a poor woman who has fantasies. I would see to it.'

He turned and left me.

I knew that I was a prisoner in this house. I was held here by the one thing which could prevent my escape.

What he had said about the law was true. If I went away I should lose my son; and that was the one thing I could never do.

I was in a state of wretched uncertainty. I knew that Aubrey meant he would not let me take Julian away with me. It was not that he wanted the boy himself; but he did want a son and heir to be brought up on the estate. I also thought that he wanted his revenge on me.

I knew now that his feelings towards me were mixed, and in the force of his hatred for me were the grains of love. He *had* been in love with me; there had been something very special about those days in Venice; it was just that the drug habit was too strong for him; he wanted me to share everything with him, and because I would not, because I despised him for what he was doing, he hated me.

My great desire was to get away. I had thought it would be so simple just to walk out of the place with Julian. How I had miscalculated!

It was hard to live through the days. Julian seemed more precious to me than ever – if that were possible. If we were separated he would be heartbroken, no less than I. There was one thing which was clear to me: I would endure anything rather than be separated from my child.

I should have liked to go and stay with my father, but I knew that after that scene between us, Aubrey would not allow me to take Julian with me. If I wanted to stay with Amelia – who had frequently asked me to visit her – I should have to leave Julian behind. It was clear to me that Aubrey would never allow me to take the boy from the Minster for fear I might not return with him.

Mrs Pollack was a little worried about my health.

'You're not looking yourself, if I may say so, Madam,' she said.

I assured her that I was all right. I tried to behave as though nothing had happened. I saw as little of Aubrey as I possibly could; but when I did he regarded me with a sardonic look, the triumphant look of a conqueror.

Two weeks passed, two of the most wretched weeks I had ever known till then. I would lie awake at night devising wild plans which seemed plausible then, but which I knew to be impossible in the light of the next day.

I could think of nothing else. When Mrs Pollack told me I should avoid going into the town I hardly listened.

'It's the linen-draper's daughter. They say it's cholera. That's frightened the life out of everyone. They all remember the epidemic two years ago.'

'Oh yes,' I said. 'I remember, of course. It was terrible.'

'They say that more than fifty-three thousand people died of it in England and Wales,' said Mrs Pollack. 'It's brought in by foreigners, that's what.'

I said I supposed so; and I wondered once more whether, if I gave Aubrey a solemn promise that I would return with Julian, he would allow me to go and see my father.

I could not go on like this. Yet what could I do? I longed to get away but I could not go without Julian. If necessary I should stay here until he was of age. I would never leave him.

It must have been about four weeks after that scene with Aubrey when I received a letter. I did not know the writing on the envelope and when I opened and read it my anxieties increased.

Dear Mrs St Clare [I read],

I am taking the liberty of writing to you because I am concerned about Colonel Pleydell's health. I think you should know that he had a mild stroke yesterday. It has impaired his speech a little and he is slightly paralysed. I am afraid that he could have another stroke and perhaps a major one at any time.

I thought you should know this.

Yours truly,
Edgar Corinth.

I read and re-read the letter. The words danced in front of my eyes. It was as though I felt that by staring at them hard enough I could change them.

I could not believe this. Not now . . . when I needed his help. I felt the need to lean on someone, to have someone to talk with me, plan with me, advise me. And when I thought of someone I meant my father. He was the one who cared most of all; he would make my troubles his own.

I must go to him at once and I must take Julian. Surely I could do that in these circumstances. I decided to talk to Aubrey.

He had come in from the estate and I watched him approach the house. It struck me afresh how he was changing. He looked considerably older than the Aubrey of our honeymoon; his eyes were sunken and his skin was an unhealthy colour.

I met him in the hall.

'I have to talk to you,' I said.

He raised his eyebrows and we went into one of the little rooms which led from the hall. I gave him the doctor's letter and he read it.

'I have to go to him,' I said.

'Of course.'

'I shall take Julian with me.'

'Take the child into a house of sickness?'

'It is certainly not communicable. It is a stroke. There are sevants there. They love to look after him. I can be with my father and Julian will be all right.'

He smiled at me slowly. 'No,' he said. 'You shall not take the child out of this house.'

'Why not?'

'Because you may decide not to bring him back.'

'I would give my solemn oath.'

'You are a very determined woman. Solemn oaths are not always kept by the ruthless and you could be ruthless where the boy is concerned.'

'You see how ill my father is.'

'How do I know that this is not a forgery . . . this doctor's letter? It's come at a rather opportune moment, hasn't it?'

'Aubrey, I am very worried about my father.'

'Go to him. Nurse him. You're good at that, I believe. Then when you have brought him back to health, come back. But you shall not take the boy.'

'How can I go without him?'

'Easily. You will go to the station, board a train and very soon you will be in London at your father's bedside.'

'Aubrey, will you try to understand.'

'I understand perfectly. You have told me of your intentions and, as I said, I know how resolute you can be. Go to your father. The boy remains here.'

He smiled at me as he turned and left me.

I went to Mrs Pollack's room. She was lying down.

'Just a bit off colour,' she said. 'Nothing that a little rest and a nice cup of tea won't put right. I'll make one now.'

'Not for me, Mrs Pollack. I am very worried.'

'Oh, what's wrong, Madam?'

'It's my father. He is very ill. I must go to him and I have to leave Julian behind.'

'He won't like that, Madam, will he? You've never been apart since he was born.'

'No, I don't like it . . . but his father points out that I can't travel with a child when there is sickness about. I . . . er . . . suppose there is something in that. I'll make a quick visit . . . just to see what I can do. I can go down often and just stay one night. I want to talk to you about Julian.'

'Yes, Madam?'

'You're so fond of him.'

'Who wouldn't be fond of the little darling?'

'I hardly like to say this . . . but Nanny Benson is rather old.'

'Past it if you were to ask me, Madam.'

'Of course, she is an old retainer. My husband's nanny. People feel sentimental about their old nannies. It's understandable.'

Mrs Pollack nodded. 'That girl,' she said, her lips curling, 'she's just about as good as a wooden leg would be to a soldier on the march.'

'That's why I'm anxious. I rely on you, Mrs Pollack.'

She bridled with pleasure. 'And you can, Madam. That little one will be as well looked after as if you were here, I promise you.'

'Thanks, Mrs Pollack, that means a lot to me.'

I set off for London early next morning.

When I arrived at the house I was met by a solemn-faced Polly.

'Oh, Mrs St Clare,' she said. 'The poor Colonel, he's so poorly.'

I went straight to see him and my heart sank. He gave me a one-sided smile and opened his lips but he could not speak. I bent over and kissed him. He closed his eyes and I knew what my coming meant to him. He could not speak so I just sat by his bed holding his hand.

When he slept I talked with Polly and Jane. They told me that he had been working very hard at the War Office and bringing work home.

'He was in his study until early morning,' said Jane.

'We were worried about him,' added Polly. 'I said to Jane, "He can't go on like this." Then it happened. One morning when I took in his hot water he was lying there in the bed and he couldn't move. Then we got the doctor. He asked us for your address and said he'd write to you. Yesterday the Colonel was worse again.'

Afterwards I saw the doctor. He was very grave. 'It sometimes happens like this,' he said. 'The first stroke was relatively minor. He would have been only slightly incapacitated, but he would have had to give up the War Office. But as I feared, a major attack followed.' He looked at me helplessly.

'I understand. Is he . . . dying?'

'If he survives he will be a complete invalid.'

'It is the worst thing that could happen to him.'

'I thought you should be prepared.'

'Thank you. I could arrange to take him home with me.'

'I believe you have a large estate in the country. That would be best. You would be able to have him well looked after. The two maids here are excellent but not trained nurses, of course.'

'No.'

'Well, leave it for a day or so to see how things go. I must tell you that I think his chances of survival are not very good.'

I bowed my head.

I was with my father when he died.

I had nursed him for three days, and although he took great comfort from my presence, I was well aware that there was little that could be done for him. In my heart I knew he would prefer to die. I could not imagine a man such as he was being inactive, not even able to speak.

I was numbed. Coming so soon after the revelations at the Minster and my need to get away, that I should lose my beloved father was so staggering a blow that I could not at first accept it.

Through the last weeks I had been thinking of him as my refuge. Now there would be no father to go to. I wrote a short note to Aubrey telling him what had happened and that I should stay in London for the funeral and then come straight back to the Minster.

There was so much to do that I got through the days somehow. I was very glad of Jane's and Polly's help. I sensed that they were a little anxious about their future although they were much too tactful to mention it to me. I was trying to come to some conclusion. The house had always been a symbol to me . . . of escape. If ever I got away from the Minster I should have somewhere to run to.

Now, of course, that had changed. I decided that, if I could afford to, I would keep it on . . . for at least a while. When I knew what my position was I would be able to assess the matter further. I knew that my father was not poor and that all he had – apart from a legacy or two – would come to me. I should be to some degree independent. Even if I could not live here, the house could be a refuge.

Uncle James and Aunt Grace with Ellen and her husband came for the funeral. They invited me to go back with them for a few days but I told them I was anxious to get home to my little boy. They understood perfectly and said that later I must bring him and my husband to see them.

The idea of Aubrey at the rectory almost made me smile, it was so incongruous; but I thanked them for their kindness and said I would remember it.

It was heartrending to see my father's coffin lowered into the grave and to listen to the clods falling on the polished wood and to face the awful reality that I should never see him again. I felt lost and alone.

Back at the house, the will was read. As I had guessed, the bulk of his money came to me. I was by no means rich, but independent. I could live – not extravagantly, but comfortably.

I decided, there and then, to keep on the house. That would allay Jane's and Polly's anxieties and those of Joe Tugg; and would provide a home for me when I was able to make my escape, for I did not entirely despair of doing so.

When I told them they were immensely relieved.

'We'll keep the place beautiful,' said Jane.

'And then you'll be coming on visits with the little boy,' added Polly. 'That'll be lovely.'

Joe said he would keep the carriage looking a treat and I'd be proud to ride in it.

So that was settled.

The day after the funeral, I left for the Minster.

As soon as I arrived at the station I sensed something unusual.

The station-master saluted me gravely, which was strange for he was generally rather garrulous. Jim, the porter, looked the other way. There was no conveyance to meet me as I had not told them the time of my arrival; but there was a station fly which took me to the house.

There was silence everywhere. No one was about. The door of the hall was never locked during the day so I went in.

There was silence everywhere.

I ran up the stairs to the nursery.

'Julian!' I cried. 'I'm back.'

Silence.

The blinds were drawn in the nursery. The cot was empty, but standing on trestles in one corner of the room was something which sent shivers down my spine.

It was a little coffin.

I went to it and looked inside.

I felt as though I were going to collapse, for lying there, an expression of serenity on his cold white face, was my son.

The door had opened and Nanny Benson stood there.

'Oh . . .' she said. 'We didn't know you was coming today.'

I just stared at her. Then I looked at the coffin.

'Two days ago,' she said.

I felt that the whole world was collapsing about me. I was dreaming. This was a nightmare.

Nanny Benson began to cry. 'Oh, the poor little mite. It happened so quick.'

'Mrs Pollack . . .' I cried. 'Where is Mrs Pollack?'

The old woman looked at me, her lips trembling. Louie appeared in the doorway. I had never seen her look so solemn.

'Terrible things has happened,' she said. 'Mrs Pollack went to the town and we never saw her again.'

'It's crazy . . .' I said. 'Everyone's gone crazy . . . the whole world . . . For God's sake tell me.'

'Mrs Pollack caught the cholera. There's been two cases in the town besides her. She went in to see to some shopping the day after you left, and she didn't come back. She collapsed in a shop there and they took her into the hospital. She died. It was the cholera.'

'I . . . can't believe it.'

'It's true. They're scared of the cholera. You have to be separated when you gets it. They're scared of another epidemic. They put her away in the hospital and she never come out.'

So she hadn't been here to look after him! That was my first thought. Good Mrs Pollack on whom I had relied had not been there. And he had died . . . my boy had died. They had let him die.

My anger was battling with my grief, which was too great to be borne. I knew that I was as yet too shocked to feel the enormity of it.

I could only stand there staring at those two who, I was sure, had failed to look after my precious child. He had been alone . . . without Mrs Pollack in this evil house . . . and they had let him die.

'And . . . my child . . .' I heard myself saying.

'Pneumonia. It was quick. Right as rain one day and fighting for his life the next.'

Why had I not taken him with me! I knew why. Yet why had fate played such a cruel trick as to call me away and then take Mrs Pollack when I most needed her!

'Was he in pain?'

'Fighting for his breath at the end,' Louie said.

'I want to see the doctor.'

'Dr Calliber didn't come till it was all over.'

'Why not? Why didn't you call the doctor?'

'There was a doctor here. One of Mr Aubrey's guests. He saw him and gave him something, didn't he, Aunt Em? But it was too late.'

'One of his guests!'

'Yes . . . one of them.'

'Was anyone with him when he died?'

Louie said: 'Yes . . . I was.'

I could have struck her. Oh no! I thought. Not Louie. No doubt she was thinking about assignations with her lovers while my child was dying!

'Mr Aubrey came up when he heard. He was here at the end.'

I could not bear the sight of them.

I cried: 'Leave me. Leave me alone with him. Get out.'

They crept away.

I stood over the coffin looking down at the dear face.

'Julian,' I whispered. 'Don't go away. Come back to me. I'm here now. My blessed boy. Come back and we'll never, never be parted again.'

I prayed for a miracle. 'Oh God, raise him from the dead.

You know what this child means to me. I do not want to live without him. Please . . . please . . . God.'

I pictured him, feverish, perhaps calling for me. Mrs Pollack was not there to soothe him. Cruel, malevolent fate had taken her. Death was implacable. Life was unbearable. Mrs Pollack, who had been so alive, to be stricken by the cholera which had claimed so many victims such a short time ago and might claim more. My dear father, that rock to which I had believed I could always cling, had been taken from me; and while I was making arrangements for his burial, my own child was dying.

It was too much to bear. I could not yet realize all that I had lost.

I felt bewildered and alone. I was desolate.

I do not know how long I stood there by the coffin.

Aubrey came in.

'Susanna,' he said gently. 'I heard you were back. My dear, this is terrible. And your father. I am so sorry. You can't stay here. Come away. Let me take you to your room.'

He would have taken my arm but I moved away. I could not bear that he should touch me.

I went to my bedroom. Julian's cot had been taken away. It looked so empty.

Aubrey followed me into the room.

'This is a terrible shock to you,' he said, 'and to happen while you were arranging your father's funeral . . .'

'I should have taken him with me,' I murmured, more to myself than to him. 'If I had, this would never have happened.'

'It couldn't be avoided. It came so swiftly. A cold one day . . . the next pneumonia.'

'When did Mrs Pollack go?'

'Poor woman, that was dreadful. It was the day after you left.'

'You should have told me. I would have come back and taken my baby had I known . . . no matter what you did. There was no one to look after him.'

'There was Nanny . . . and Louie.'

'A whisky-sodden old woman and a flighty girl whose thoughts are with her next meeting with the master of the house.'

'Oh come, Susanna, that doesn't help.'

'But there was no one looking after him. You didn't call in Dr Calliber.'

'There was no need. It was so sudden. There was a doctor in the house.'

I stared at him, fresh horror beginning to dawn on me. 'It was Damien,' I said.

'Yes, he was here for the night.'

'And my child was left to *him*!'

'He is one of the world's leading doctors. He is most highly thought of.'

'In your temples of sin, no doubt.'

'You are not being reasonable.'

'I am trying to understand why a perfectly healthy child should die so suddenly.'

'You talk as though children never die. They are dying all the time . . . from this ailment or that. It is not easy to rear children. In fact, child mortality is commonplace.'

'Among those who are not cared for, perhaps. My child has been neglected. I was not here. Mrs Pollack who cared for him wasn't here. I can see it all so clearly. His fever . . . his difficulty in breathing and Nanny Benson snoring in the next room and the delectable Louie cavorting in the Devil's Cave.'

'I was anxious about the child.'

'When have you ever cared for him?'

'I did care for him. I just didn't fuss over him and spoil him as you did.'

'Spoil him! He was not spoilt. He was perfect . . .' My voice broke.

'All right. He was a good child. He was my heir. I wanted the best for him. That was why –'

'That was why you took Amelia out in your carriage and arranged for a little spill . . . oh, not to do any damage to yourself or the carriage . . . but to be rid of Amelia's child who had blighted your hopes.'

He had turned very pale and I thought: He did it.

'I'm sorry you think I should be guilty of such a thing,' he said.

'I do think it,' I replied.

'Then you have a very poor opinion of me.'

'The lowest.'

He shook his head wearily. 'Susanna, I am trying to be gentle with you. I know what a shock you have had.'

'You do not. You are incapable of loving anyone as I loved my child . . . and my father. I have lost them both. I have no one now.'

'Suppose we tried . . . you and I . . . We could have another child. You would feel better then. Susanna, let's start again . . . Let's put all this behind us.'

I looked at him with loathing.

I know now that in his way he was stretching out a hand for help. This tragedy had sobered him, but I was too grief-stricken to see that then. I could only see my own tragedy and it soothed my grief a little to blame someone entirely and he was the obvious culprit.

He was aware where his addiction was leading him. I know now that by then he wanted me to help him fight that obsession; he wanted to try to get back to that time when we had been happy in the first weeks after our marriage. But I could only think of him as he had been on that terrible night in Venice and the sight of him when I had stumbled into that cave and had seen him with his friends.

I said: 'You killed my baby because you didn't take care of him. If I had taken him with me, he would have been well today. Do you think I would ever have allowed him to die?'

'You have no power over life and death, Susanna. None of us has.'

'We can fight against disaster. I left a healthy child and came back to a dead one. You were revelling with your friends while he was dying. You did not notice that he was ill. You ignored him. You hadn't time to look after your son. Why did you not send for Dr Calliber?'

'I tell you I had the best of all doctors on the spot.'

'That pornographer . . . that drug addict! He is a murderer. He murdered my child.'

'You are talking nonsense.'

'He gave him his drugs, didn't he?'

'He knew what he was doing.'

'I know that what he did resulted in Julian's death.'

'It was too late to do anything. He said it was too late.'

'Too late! And you did not call Dr Calliber. Oh, how I hate you and your precious friend. I shall never forget what you have done to my child . . . and to me.'

'Listen, Susanna. This has been too much of a shock. I understand that. I wanted to meet you at the station, to break it gently.'

'Do you think how it was broken would have made any difference to me!'

'No, of course not. But to come home and find him like that . . . must have been terrible.'

'How I found him is not relevant. I found him . . . dead . . . and that is what I hate you all for. Murderers, all of you! Your drunken nanny, your loose-living friends, you, with your hateful practices and your low living . . . and most of all that doctor, that so-called doctor. I have read his books. I know him through them. He wants sensation all the time. He is worse than you, for you are weak and he is strong. He hides his wickedness under a guise of benevolence. I hate you all . . . all your friends . . . everything to do with you . . . but most of all you . . . and him.'

'I'm going to have them send up something for you, and I am going to ask Dr Calliber to come and see you.'

I laughed bitterly. 'What a pity you were not as careful with your son. Then you might have called Dr Calliber to see him. Then he could have had the attention of a real doctor.'

I flung myself on my bed while abject misery descended on me.

*

I cannot remember the passing of the hours. Day slipped into night and it was day again; and there was no relief from my bitterness.

The day they buried my child I moved about as though in a trance. I stared in disbelief at the little coffin which carried the remains of the being who was all the world to me. I could have borne anything if he had been left to me.

The tolling of the bell proclaimed my grief; I did not listen to the words of the parson.

Julian was laid to rest in the St Clare mausoleum among his ancestors . . . Stephen who had so recently died, and that Harry St Clare who had made the temple, the cave, and there practised unholy rites.

I was still stunned; a numbing apathy had come to me; and I could think of nothing but that I had lost my child.

We came back to the house. I shut myself in my room and wanted to see no one.

Aubrey sent Dr Calliber to me. I came alive a little talking to him.

He said he understood my grief, but I must rouse myself or I should be ill.

'You will have more children, Mrs St Clare,' he said. 'And, believe me, in time the loss will be less painful.'

I did not want to hear about myself. I wanted to know about Julian.

'It was a virulent attack,' said Dr Calliber. 'There was little anyone could have done for him.'

'But had you come in time . . . had it been noticed . . .'

'Who can say? Mortality among young children is great. It amazes me how so many survive.'

'And when you came, Dr Calliber?'

'He was already dead.'

Already dead! The words echoed in my mind.

'There was another doctor who saw him . . . someone staying in the house.'

'Yes, so I heard. I did not see him.'

'If you had been called in time . . .' I insisted.

'Who knows? And now I am concerned with you. I am going

to send you a tonic. I want you to take it regularly, Mrs St Clare; and do try to eat. Remember this is not such an infrequent happening. You will have many more children, I'll predict, and then the loss of this one will not seem so great.'

When he had gone I sat at my window looking out on the wood, and fierce anger burned in my heart.

They had left him to die. That doctor was the one who saw him, not reasonable Dr Calliber but the Devil Doctor. I was sure he had given my precious child one of his experimental drugs and it had killed him. One day I would have my revenge on him.

The thought of revenge was, in an odd way, soothing. It took my mind away from that pale quiet face in the coffin, from the memory of my merry little boy, from the tolling bell: and there seemed to be a purpose in living.

What if I confronted the wicked doctor? What if I told him what I thought of him, what if I accused him of murdering my baby with his poisonous drugs . . . and of ruining my husband?

I do not think I had very much feeling for Aubrey now, except revulsion; but in a strange way I was sorry for him. There were occasions when he seemed to look out from his sophisticated exterior and ask for help. It was perhaps just a fancy. He had gone too far along the road to destruction to turn back. But he did know it and there might have been occasions when he looked back to what he might have been.

The doctor who had killed my child had made Aubrey what he was.

Why was it that he appeared at times of disaster? He was an omen of evil. He had been there in Venice. He had been at the Minster when Julian died.

He was like an evil spirit. I saw him with horns and cloven feet like the image in that sinister cave. He was a mysterious figure, a figure of ill omen.

There was born in me then an urgent desire to see this man. I think I was trying to assuage my misery and to brood on something other than my heartrending loss.

I would seek him out. I would confront him with what he

147

had done. I might be able to prevent his ruining other lives as he had Aubrey's . . . and mine. I was being melodramatic and absurd perhaps, but I had to have something to give me an interest in living; and the thought of revenge did that. It was all that assuaged my utter despair. It seemed that I had something to live for now: my quest for the Demon Doctor . . . the man who, I insisted, had killed my child.

I could speak to no one of this. It should be my secret. People would think I was crazy to suggest that the doctor had killed my child. Julian had been seriously ill when this doctor had seen him. That was true. But then I believed he had experimented on him with his dangerous drugs.

My fury against him was intense. I pictured myself coming face to face with him. I would tell him that I read between the lines in his books – those adventures in far places . . . India, Arabia. I would say: 'You indulged in native customs. You became a native. You spoke Urdu and Hindi and Arabic . . . like a native, you tell us. You are dark.' I pictured his flashing eyes deep-set and mysterious in a dark-skinned face. 'It was easy for you to disguise yourself.' I could imagine his following their customs, behaving as one of them, keeping a harem possibly. That would be much to his taste – all in the name of scientific research, of course.

And all this he did as the great doctor. He had made discoveries which no one else had; he had added to his knowledge of medicine. So much so that he had ruined my husband and murdered my son with his horrible drugs.

Hating had become part of my day. I re-read his books and saw more in them than I had before. I pictured his dark, satanic face, for although I had never seen it, it was vivid in my imagination. I brooded on him, nursing my fury, clinging to it as one drowning would cling to a raft, for I discovered that when I thought of this man I no longer wanted to die. I wanted to live and take my revenge on him.

Some weeks passed. I had become thin and my height made me look gaunt; my cheekbones, always inclined to be prominent, were now more so; my eyes looked large and mournful, and my lips as though they had forgotten how to smile.

Aubrey had given up trying to remonstrate with me. He shrugged his shoulders as though washing his hands of me. People began to come for weekends. I guessed what happened and I did not care.

There came a time when I awoke in the middle of the night. I sat up in bed and said to myself: You have to do something.

And suddenly in a flash of inspiration I knew what.

I was going to leave the Minster – not just for a visit to Amelia which she had suggested; not to Uncle James and Aunt Grace; but I was going away, never to come back.

I should not move away from my grief while I was here. There was too much to remind me. The Minster was, to me, a place of horror. I was haunted by memories of what I had seen in the cave; and I knew that Aubrey would grow worse, never better. Everywhere I went there were memories of Julian. They would come upon me suddenly. I had to go on living if I was to avenge his death, and I could not do so while I was here.

Moreover, I did not want to see Aubrey again. Every time I did my anger rose and threatened to choke me. I blamed him, for I believed his carelessness had caused Julian's death. I could not forgive him for that. And I must get away.

Then in the middle of the night, it seemed simple. I had the house in London. I had Polly and Jane and Joe to look after me.

I was not sure what I should do but I would do something. I would make a clean break. I would take nothing with me. I would call myself Miss Pleydell just as I had been before I married Aubrey.

When I arose next morning I was surprised that the plan was not merely a fantasy of the night. It was plausible. Moreover, I felt so much better.

I would pack my things and arrange to have them sent to London. And I myself would go at the earliest possible moment.

I told Aubrey what I intended to do.

'You mean you are leaving me?'

'I do.'

'Is that wise?'

'I think it will be one of the wisest things I ever did.'

'Are you sure of that?'

'I am more sure than I have ever been of anything.'

'Then it is no use my trying to persuade you. I must tell you, though, that you place yourself in a very difficult position. A woman who has left her husband . . .'

'I know women are not supposed to leave husbands. Husbands may behave as they will. They can have a hundred mistresses and that is acceptable . . . because they are men.'

'There is one condition,' he said. 'They must not be found out. So it is not so easy . . . even for them. But you have made up your mind and I know you are a very determined woman.'

'I have not been determined enough in the past.'

'And now you will make up for that.'

'I shall be better on my own. Nothing could be worse for me than staying here. There is nothing to hold me here now. You cannot blackmail me into staying as you could when Julian was alive.'

'You have taken all this too hardly,' he said.

'Goodbye, Aubrey.'

'I will say au revoir.'

'Whatever you say will make no difference.'

Determinedly I left him. I finished packing my last case. I slipped in the books Stephen had given me to read.

And then I returned to London.

An Accident in Oxford Street

My decision had been so sudden that I had not had time to warn them of my coming. I thought, with a sudden glow of comfort, that in future I should have Joe to meet me and to take me in my own carriage wherever I wanted to go. I felt a sense of freedom which I had never known before and which could not be anything else but agreeable.

I left the luggage at the station to be called for and took a jarvie to the house.

The door was opened by Polly who stared at me in wonderment. The smile of pleasure on her face warmed my heart.

'Well, if it ain't the mistress,' she cried. 'Jane . . . come here quick. The mistress has come.'

I found myself hugging them both and was faintly amused thinking what Aunt Grace would have said to see me behaving in such an unrestrained way with my servants. It was clear that mine was going to be a very unconventional household.

'I've come home to stay,' I said. 'I have left the Minster . . . forever.'

There was a stunned silence. Then Polly said: 'I know what you want and that's a nice cup of tea.'

I did not believe I wanted anything, but when the tea came I made them bring two more cups and sit with me – and it was amazing what comfort they brought me.

I found myself telling them what had happened, of Julian's death and my decision to leave my husband. They listened in awed silence but their sympathy was great. I did not, of course, tell them of the temple.

'Jane, Polly,' I said. 'I shall have to make a new life. You will have to help me.'

'There ain't nothing we wouldn't do – ain't that right, Poll?'

Polly said emphatically that it was.

'I want a complete break with the old life. I want to try to forget. I shall never forget my boy . . . but there are other things.'

I was amazed at their tact. They did not ask questions but waited for me to speak.

'I want to be an entirely different person. I am not Mrs St Clare any more. I want to forget I ever was.'

They nodded. I had made it clear to them in that brief statement that my marriage was no longer tolerable to me.

'I am going back to the name I had before I was married. I shall be known as Miss Pleydell.'

There were more nods.

'I am not even calling myself Susanna. I shall be Anna.'

That had occurred to me on the train. My ayah's voice had come back to me over the years. Once she had said: 'There are two of you; Susan and Anna. Susan . . . she is the gentle one who wants to live at peace, who will accept what is. But there is Anna. She will be the strong one. She will go and get what she wants and take nothing less.'

She was right. I had a dual personality; and now I needed all my strength, all my resilience, all the resolution which was in the stronger side of my nature.

Already Anna Pleydell seemed a different person from Susanna St Clare.

'So you will call me Miss Pleydell. You can do that easily.'

'Well, we looked after Colonel Pleydell so now it will be natural to look after his daughter, Miss Pleydell,' commented Jane.

'You two know how I loved my father . . . and my son.'

Jane bit her lip and Polly turned her head away to hide the tears in her eyes.

'I shall never forget them . . .' My voice faltered and suddenly the tears started to flow. It was the first time I had wept since the beginning of my sorrow. And then I was sobbing broken-heartedly and Jane and Polly with me.

Jane was the first to recover. She poured out a cup of tea and brought it to me.

'There,' she said. 'This won't drive the pigs to market, will it, as the farmer said when the wheel came off his cart and the horses run away.'

Polly looked at me and smiled through her tears.

'No,' I said, 'it won't. We've got to be practical. I have to work out what I am going to do. I don't know yet. Plans won't come. I just know that I'll be better here than anywhere else even though there is so much to remind me of my father.'

'He was a dear good man and so kind to us,' said Jane.

'He was one in a million,' added Polly.

'We'll look after you, Mrs – I mean Miss Pleydell. It takes a bit of getting used to, calling you that, but we'll manage it.'

'I'll put the warming pan in your bed, Miss Pleydell,' said Polly.

'You'd better,' added Jane. 'We've had some nasty damp days lately. Damp gets in everywhere.'

I felt I was right to come.

Later I went out to the stables and saw Joe. He had already heard the news.

'It's good to see you back, Miss Pleydell,' he said, with a wink to remind me that he had remembered the instructions which had already been passed on by Jane and Polly. 'Carriages is meant to be driven – not left standing. They don't like it. They've got wills of their own, carriages have. Don't I know it – doing the London to Bath run all them years.'

I could see the sympathy in his eyes; Jane and Polly would have told him all I had told them; they had all loved my father and Julian. They shared my grief as I felt no one at the Minster had.

Yes, I thought, I believe I can make a fresh start.

It wasn't easy. When I awoke in the morning the depression descended upon me. I had had vague dreams of Julian. I thought: What am I doing here? What hope is there of starting a new life? What does it matter where I live? Whether I am here or at the Minster, the loss is the same.

Jane came in with a cup of hot chocolate. And what would I like for breakfast? she asked.

'Nothing, thank you, Jane.'

She shook her head at me. 'Was the bed comfortable? Did you have a good night?'

'The bed was comfortable. When I sleep, I dream.'

'Well, drink up that chocolate. It's nourishing.'

She stood there, implying that she would not move until I had drunk it. She reminded me of my ayah in a way. I was thinking a good deal about her lately. She had known something about that Devil Doctor. I wished she had told me.

I drank the chocolate to please Jane, and then lay there asking myself what I should do when I got up. I should have to take a ride to please Joe. 'Carriages are not meant to stand idle.'

He could go and collect my luggage from the station and I should then unpack. The day would pass somehow. Why had I thought it would all be so different in London?

Slowly the days passed. I took a ride now and then through the streets of London to please Joe. I did a little desultory shopping. Jane and Polly devised meals for me at which I pecked like a bird, said Jane disgustedly.

'You're getting like a skelington,' Joe told me. 'I reckon you want to put on a bit of flesh, Miss Pleydell. Bones ain't much good without it.'

'I'm all right, Joe,' I said.

'Begging your pardon, Miss Pleydell, you ain't,' he retorted sharply.

I guessed he discussed me with Polly and Jane. They were really getting quite anxious about me.

I don't know how long I should have gone on in that state of lethargy but for the accident in Oxford Street which brought Lily Craddock into my life.

Now and then I went out shopping. I would buy little things

for the house, and I liked to find small presents for Jane and Polly to whom I was very grateful. Our relationship was not that of mistress and maids. There was a feeling of belonging to a family in that house. It had been so with my father; and it was doubly so with me, I think, because of the circumstances. They felt for me; they made my grief theirs; and I knew that they were all worried about my health. Aubrey would have said that it was their own future which concerned them, not mine, for if I were ill and died what would become of their comfortable jobs? But I was sure they really felt for me – Jane, Polly, Joe, all three of them.

Joe had taken me out on one of those little shopping expeditions, and as we were leaving the shop where I had bought some gloves and were trotting along Oxford Street in the midst of a certain amount of traffic, all of a sudden Joe pulled up with a jerk. I looked out of the window. We were stationary and people began to gather. Joe had alighted and I got out of the carriage. I stared in consternation, for lying in the road, with blood on her face, was a girl.

Joe looked at me. 'She dashed right off the pavement . . . right under the horses' feet and before I could say Jack Robinson she'd gone down. There wasn't time to pull up.'

I knelt down by the girl.

She was pretty with masses of fair curly hair; her blue eyes looked at me appealingly.

I said: 'It's all right. We'll take care of you.' I put my hand on her forehead. She closed her eyes at once and seemed comforted.

The driver of a passing carriage leaned out and shouted: 'Whatcher been up to, Joe? Better get her to the hospital . . . quick.'

I said that was a good idea.

A policeman was making his way through the crowd which had gathered. I told him that the girl had run out into the road right under our horses. 'I'd like to take her to the hospital,' I said.

The policeman thought that would be the best thing to do.

Some instinct made me take charge. 'We must be careful that she hasn't broken any bones,' I said. 'If she has, we shall need a stretcher.'

The policeman said: 'Can you stand up, Miss?'

I said: 'Let me.' I knelt beside her. She turned her eyes to my face and I was aware that she trusted me, which sent a warm glow through me. I suddenly felt capable and glad that I was there to do what I could for her.

I said: 'You have been knocked down. We want to know if you have broken anything. May I just see what I can do?'

I touched her legs. She did not wince so it occurred to me that if she could stand up there could be no fracture. I helped her up and she stood without pain. Obviously there were no bones broken.

'We'll take you to the hospital,' I said.

She looked alarmed but I whispered to her soothingly, 'It'll be all right. We'll see what they have to say.'

The policeman nodded his approval and we helped the girl into the carriage.

'St David's is not far off,' said the policeman and added that he would accompany us.

The girl sat between us. I noticed she shrank from him. I put my arm around her and she lay against me. I was very relieved because I did not think she was badly hurt.

I asked her her name, which was Lily Craddock. I gave her mine and my address, but I doubted she was in a state to take it in.

We arrived at a tall grey building.

'I think I'd better take her in, Miss,' said the policeman.

The girl looked at me appealingly and I said: 'I'll come this afternoon and see how you are.'

She gave me a piteous half-smile which seemed far too grateful for the little I had done. Joe talked about the incident all the way home.

'They just don't look where they're going. Out she darts . . . Tilburies, gigs, carts . . . and whiskies everywhere. I don't know what gets into 'em. They're going to cross that road if it costs them their lives. Different from the open road,

Miss Pleydell . . . going along at a spanking pace . . . and the horses' hoofs ringing on the road.'

'Yes, it must be. I think she will be all right. I don't think she was badly injured.'

'I thank me stars for that. I wouldn't want a corpse on me conscience. After all them years of good driving that wouldn't be nice. But it would have been the young person's own fault, though.'

'Poor girl! Perhaps she had something on her mind. She had a pleasant face.'

'You never know with them girls, Miss Pleydell. The pleasant-looking ones is often the worst.'

I found myself laughing at him and pulled myself up with a jerk. I did not laugh nowadays. There was no laughter left in life for me.

But I had to face the truth. It must be over an hour since the girl had fallen under the carriage and during that time I had not thought of Julian or my father. That poor girl's misfortune had bought me an hour of forgetfulness.

I arrived at the house and let myself in. Polly came out and told me that it was almost lunch-time.

'I know,' I said. 'I'm later than I thought. We knocked a girl down in Oxford Street and took her to the hospital.'

'My sainted aunt!' cried Polly. 'Was she hurt bad?'

'I don't think so. Very shocked, of course. They'll find out in the hospital. I'm going to see her this afternoon.'

Both girls looked at me in dismay.

'You're not going into one of them places, Miss?'

'The hospital, you mean? Yes, of course. I want to know about this girl. After all, it was my carriage which knocked her down.'

'She must have been where she shouldn't have. Joe would never have run her down if she hadn't been.'

'It was probably her fault, but that makes no difference. I shall go and see her. I feel a responsibility for her.'

'Oh Miss, you can't go into a hospital.'

'Why not?'

'They're not for the likes of you.'

I looked at them questioningly and they assumed the look which I was beginning to know well and which always amused me. It meant that I was an innocent and really did not know much about the ways of the wicked big city. They had been born and bred here; they were wiser than I; they *knew*.

'Hospitals is terrible places, Miss,' said Jane.

'Of course. People there are sick or dying.'

'I'd rather be dead than go into one of them. Don't you ever let me be took in, Poll . . . not if I'm at my last gasp.'

'I must go to visit this girl to see if she is all right.'

'Miss, only the lowest of the low is there,' said Polly. 'There was a time when Jane and me thought of taking it up . . . nursing, you know . . . a profession, like. We'd looked after Ma for years and reckoned we was good at it. But them nurses . . . They're drunk half the time . . . lowest of the low, they are.'

'I am going to see this girl. Her name is Lily Craddock. I am going this afternoon and nothing is going to stop me.'

Jane lifted her shoulders. 'There's some fish for lunch,' she said. 'It's that fresh it'll melt in your mouth.'

I sat down and they hovered over me serving me.

I was surprised that I could eat a little.

I shall never forget my visit to that hospital. As soon as I entered the place I was aware of the smell. I could not think what produced it. I only knew that it was nauseating. Later I knew it came from dirt and lack of sanitation.

I walked into a room where a large blowsy woman was sitting at a table. She looked half asleep.

I roused her and said: 'I've come to visit Lily Craddock who was brought in this morning.'

She looked at me in surprise as though there was something very unusual about me.

She jerked her thumb over her shoulder towards a door. I walked to it, pushed it open and went into a room.

How right Jane and Polly were! It was a horrible sight. The room was long with several windows, half of which were boarded up. That obnoxious smell was more apparent here than outside. There were rows of beds – about fifty or sixty of them, I calculated – and so close together that there was hardly room to pass between them. It was the people in the beds who shocked me most. They looked like corpses, some of them; at the best they were in stages of decay – yellow-white faces, dirty, straggling hair, the bedlinen discoloured, ingrained with grime and excrement. One or two of them raised themselves on their elbows to look at me; most of them were too close to death, I imagined, to take notice of anything.

I advanced into the room and said in a loud voice: 'Is there a Miss Lily Craddock here?'

I had found her. She was at the far end of the room. I passed along the line of beds and went to her.

'Miss . . . it's you!' I saw the joy in her face and I was glad. 'I never thought you'd come.'

'I said I would.' I looked at her and noticed that she was different from the others. Her face looked almost healthy in comparison.

I went on: 'You can't stay in this place. I'm going to take you away.'

She shook her head.

'Yes,' I said firmly. 'I am taking you home with me. I'm going to look after you until you have quite recovered.'

A kind of wonderment spread across her face.

A woman was approaching us. She appeared to be a person with some authority.

I said to her: 'I have come to take this young woman away.'

'Oh?' she said, eyeing me rather insolently from head to foot.

'There can be no objection, I am sure. It was my carriage which ran her over. My carriage is now waiting outside for us. Bring her clothes, will you, please?'

'Who are you, Madam?' asked the woman, and I saw with delight and amusement that I had somehow managed to over-awe her.

'I am Miss Pleydell, daughter of Colonel Pleydell of the War Office. Now, let us get this girl's clothes. If she is unfit to walk, she can be carried to the carriage. My coachman will help if necessary.'

'I . . . I can walk,' said Lily eagerly.

The woman called to another. She said: 'This young woman's leaving. We want all the beds we can get. It's something to do with the War Office.'

I was laughing to myself as, when Lily was dressed – she had been wearing her underclothes in the bed – I took her arm and helped her to the door.

Joe was waiting to get us into the carriage.

I looked at the girl anxiously as we drove along.

'How are you feeling?' I asked.

'Better, thank you, Miss.'

'You wouldn't have been better long if you had stayed in that place,' I said grimly.

And that was how Lily Craddock came into my life and it started to change from then on.

I had something to do. Every morning when I awoke the first thing I thought of was my patient. She had looked fairly healthy in that hospital but that was when she was compared with people on the point of death, and as soon as I had her under my care, I discovered that she was frail, undernourished, rather fearful of the world, desperately trying to earn enough money to keep herself alive.

The care of her filled my days. I planned her meals; I tended her; I nursed her; and my pleasure in seeing her change under my eyes was worth all my efforts.

Once she said to me: 'I reckon my good angel sent me under that carriage. I didn't know there was people like you in the world. When I think of what you've done for me . . .'

I was deeply moved and I said to myself then: I don't think it is anything much compared with what you are doing for me.

I was moving away from despair, from melancholy. I would never cease to mourn my dead, but I had been shown almost by a miracle that life was not entirely barren for me. There was something worthwhile that I could do.

Lily once said: 'I feel better when you stroke my forehead. It's something about your hands, Miss Pleydell.'

I looked at them. Long, tapering fingers – 'artist's fingers,' someone had once said. I had no skill in the arts – unless one could call nursing an art.

I was haunted by those people in the hospital and the memory of the few nurses I had seen. They were unclean, blowsy and unkempt; they smelled of gin, and I was sure they neglected the sick and vulnerable. That seemed terrible to me and I rejoiced that I had been able to take Lily away.

As for myself, I was eating more; tending Lily made me hungry. Special dishes were prepared for her, for Jane and Polly had thrown themselves wholeheartedly into the task of, as they said, 'getting her on her feet'. I would sometimes be tempted – yes, actually tempted – to share those dishes and nothing could have pleased Jane and Polly more. They were nursing *me* back to health as well as Lily Craddock.

Sometimes the gloom would descend on me and I would think of my baby crying for me when I was not there, unable to breathe and no one there to care for him . . . and finally that doctor . . . that wicked doctor who had come to experiment on him. Perhaps he knew what he gave him would not save his life but he wanted to see the effect.

Somehow the neglect of those hospital patients became linked in my thoughts with that doctor. Those nurses cared only for themselves. They were unemployable in most things so they came to the hospital. What a way to choose people for this most important of professions. Those who entered it should have dedication; they should feel they had a duty to succour the sick. They should be properly trained. Yet what those women wanted was a lazy life, food for themselves and shelter. And that doctor . . . in his way he cared nothing for life either. He wanted to prove the effect his drugs had on people and he had no compunction in using them to further his evil experiments.

I remembered hearing of the infamous Madame de Brinvilliers who had lived in the seventeenth century. She had wanted to murder people who stood in her way, and before poisoning them, she had tested her poisons on hospital patients to see the effect, and whether she could administer them without detection. The hospitals must have been something like the one I had seen. I could imagine that woman visiting, as an angel of mercy, ministering to the sick, bringing them food laced with poison. That doctor was a similar case, only being a doctor he had more opportunity of carrying out his murderous methods than she had.

I was filled with a burning desire to *do* something. I had changed. I no longer felt that I had finished with life. It was like being born again. I could see a purpose in my life. It was as though I had had a divine revelation. I was being told something about myself, and it was only now that Lily Craddock had brought it home to me so clearly that I realized what it was. My ayah had said, 'You have healing hands. It is a gift and the gods do not look kindly on those who do not use the gifts they bestow on them.'

Had I a gift? Yes, I had. It was to save lives. I had seen the suffering in those beds of pain and it had affected me deeply. I felt inadequate. What could I do about it? My own child, I believed, had been neglected. Murdered! That was a wild statement; but if they had called Dr Calliber in time he might have saved his life. Instead, Aubrey had brought his devilish familiar to my child's bedside and that man had given him a drug and killed him.

Because he had been my beloved son I might be passionately unreasonable in this case, but I believed that they might have saved his life and had failed to do so. I was going to find that doctor. I was going to confront him; I was going to prevent him from causing the death of someone else with his diabolical experiments.

I had taken a gigantic step forward.

I had a purpose in life. I would grow strong and well and in due course it would be revealed to me which road I should take.

In the meantime I was finding solace and indeed exhilaration in nursing Lily Craddock back to health.

She had been with us for two weeks and was greatly improved, then a melancholy seemed to come over her and progress slackened.

Jane and Polly discovered the reason.

'You know what, Miss Pleydell, that girl's worried.'

'She has no need to be.'

'Well, she's getting better. I reckon she's enjoyed being the invalid. What she is thinking now is: What am I going back to?'

'You think she's anxious about the future?'

'She's that all right.'

'I see,' I said. I had been thinking about Lily's future for some time.

She was a seamstress, we knew, and finding it hard to make a living. She had been a country girl until two years ago. She belonged to a big family and times were hard; she had had to leave the family circle and earn her own living. She had been in service and had not liked it. She had come to London where she thought the rich lived and that she might therefore earn a good living with her needle.

It was clear to us all that she was not going to do that with any great success.

I explained my feelings to Jane and Polly. 'I am not a rich woman,' I told them, 'but my father has left me adequately provided for if I am not extravagant. I could offer Lily a job here. She could help you . . . perhaps sew for us and do the shopping.'

'Not the shopping,' said Jane. 'She's too soft, with her country ways. She'd get done all the way round. To put her loose in the market-place with the mistress's money would be like putting one of them martyrs into the lion's den. And she's no Daniel.'

I laughed.

'You had better carry on with the shopping, then; but I could manage to pay Lily a little salary and at least she would be well fed and housed.'

'You're your father all over again, Miss,' said Polly. 'Don't worry. We were wondering about asking you if we could keep her.'

When I put the suggestion to Lily her joy was overwhelming and from that moment there was a change in her. That perpetual nervousness and apprehension slipped away from her.

I thought: I am almost happy.

I used to sit with them in the evenings and gradually learned about their lives before they came into mine. Jane and Polly had had a hard childhood, with a drunken bully of a father whose entrance into the house was a signal for terror.

'He'd knock Ma about something shocking,' said Jane. 'He'd come rolling in, and then he'd roar and it would start. Me and Poll used to hide under the stairs as long as we could . . . and once we went out and tried to stop him lamming into Ma. He turned on us. He broke your wrist once, didn't he, Poll?'

'Never been quite right since,' said Polly. 'Give us a bit of rain and it hurts like billy-o.'

'I reckon we'd have done for him one day if he hadn't fallen down the stairs and done for himself before we got old enough to do it.'

'What a terrible story,' I said. 'I'm glad that the drink and the stairs killed him so that you didn't have to.'

'I would have done,' said Jane, her eyes blazing. 'There's some as ain't fit to live in this world.'

I closed my eyes and saw the Devil Doctor, mysterious with horns and cloven feet. She was right. Such people should not be allowed to live.

'We had a right old time when he was gone,' said Polly. 'Ma used to go out cleaning steps, and when we was old enough we did all sorts of things, didn't we – running errands, doing cleaning. Sometimes we went hungry, but we didn't mind that so much because we'd got rid of him. Then Ma died and we was on our own. We nursed her, didn't we, Jane? I reckon he had done for her. She was never well. He spoilt everything for us when we was little, didn't he, Jane?'

Jane agreed that he did. 'You see,' she went on, 'you marry 'em . . . as Ma did him. He must have been all right then or she would never have been such a fool as to let herself in for that . . . and then, after the wedding, out they come in their true colours, some of them.'

Polly threw a warning look at her sister, which I intercepted. I knew what she meant. I, too, had had a disastrous marriage from which I had just escaped.

Listening to all this, Lily, feeling herself to be one of us, opened out and talked of herself.

'There was ten of us,' she said. 'I was the sixth. I used to look after the little 'uns. We used to go gleaning, harvest time. And sometimes we'd go picking fruit and lifting potatoes. We had to get out and earn and when I was twelve I went into service.'

'You didn't like it?' I asked.

'It was all right at first. And then there was this son . . . he come home, you see. He used to talk to me on the stairs, and come in the kitchen sometimes when no one was there but me. I thought he was nice at first. Then he used to ring the bell in his bedroom. And then . . . and then . . . Oh, it didn't half frighten me something shocking. I didn't know what to do. I wanted to run away but I didn't know where to run to. Then one day the mistress came in and saw us and I was sent home. Oh, it was awful. I was put out of the house with my tin box. Nobody believed it wasn't my fault.'

'Men!' said Jane. 'The bad ones causes grief all right.'

'Ought to be boiled in oil and cut into collops and served to donkeys,' added Polly.

'And then I come to London. There was a girl in our village who was mad to go. She said the streets were paved with gold and you only had to pick it up and be rich. So we ran away together. We got a lift in on a cart which was going to London. We went to an inn and they gave us a bed if we worked for them. We stayed there for three days. There was a lady there who'd torn her dress and I mended it for her and she said that was very neat. She paid me well and said I should be doing sewing for a living. So I thought I would. I found a room, which was more like a cupboard, and I went round to the tailors' shops for work. They'd give you shirts to make and men's coats and waistcoats to make the buttonholes and sew the buttons on. I liked it better than scrubbing, but you had to work all hours to get enough to live on. And the clothes was heavy. You had to take them away and bring them back. My friend . . . she'd gone off. I don't know what happened to her. She said there were easier ways of earning a living. She was very lively. Men noticed her. I think I know what she meant.'

'And what were you doing when we found you?' I asked.

'I wasn't looking where I was going. I was that upset. I'd just come from the tailor's. I'd taken in a pile of waistcoats. I'd been doing the buttonholes and buttons and I'd been up half the night because I had to get the money that day. It was a horrid little shop . . . dark and dingy. I'd seen the man before but he hadn't been the one to pay me then. I didn't like the look of him; his face was greasy and hairy and he was so fat. He said, "Hello, Goldilocks, I suppose you want some money." There was a dozen waistcoats and that's quite a lot. I said, "Yes, sir. There's a dozen there." He said, "Well, first give us a kiss." I was frightened of him. It reminded me of my first job in service. I screamed, "No," and he was very angry. He threw the waistcoats on the counter and put his thumb under the buttons and half pulled them off. "Don't," I cried. He said, "Get out. We don't pay for work like that." "But you did it," I said. "It was you." "Get out of here, you slut," he said, "or I'll have the police on you." I was so frightened, I just ran out. I was in such a state I didn't know where I was and then . . . suddenly I was under the horses.'

I felt angry as I listened. Poor child! To be treated so. No wonder she was afraid of life.

I looked at Jane and Polly who shared my emotion.

I said quietly: 'Nothing like that is ever going to happen to you again, Lily.'

She took my hand and kissed it, looking at me in a wondering kind of way. I thought then: I have to do something. I wish I knew what. But I should discover. Fate had brought her to me and through her I had regained my will to live. And I knew somehow that I had a duty to perform. It was to help people like Lily Craddock.

There were wicked people in the world. Men and women exploiting people, but mostly men exploiting women, for their own ends. I could clearly picture the young man who had attempted to seduce Lily and the evil man in the tailoring establishment. And the embodiment of them all was that doctor . . . the Devil Doctor . . . who had helped to ruin my husband and who had allowed my son to die.

My mind was made up. I was going to find that doctor. I was going to expose him to the world for what he was.

The prospect gave me a zest for living. I needed that so much.

Lily settled in with the utmost ease. She went through our wardrobes and mended everything that needed mending. She found some sheets which were going to be thrown away and she indignantly declared they could be turned. She found work for herself, being determined to make a worthwhile contribution to the household. She could not know how much she had done for me. Jane and Polly knew it, though; and they were indulgent towards her, protective, seeing her as the helpless little country girl who had not had the advantage of being brought up in the great metropolis.

She was making a dress for me of emerald green velvet. She had seen the material in a shop and prevailed upon me to buy it. 'With your reddish hair and those green eyes, Miss Pleydell, don't you see . . . it is just the thing for you. And the dress I will make . . .' She sighed in ecstasy.

So I bought it to please her. I had not yet reached the stage when I could be the least interested in clothes.

One day when I returned to the house after a brief trip to the shops, I was told that a lady and gentleman were in the drawing-room. They had come ten minutes before and Jane had told them I should not be long, so they had said they would wait. 'They said they was Mr and Mrs St Clare,' said Jane.

I was puzzled.

I went into the drawing-room and there was Amelia with a

man whom I immediately recognized. She ran to me and embraced me. She looked younger than I remembered her.

She said: 'Oh, Susanna, it is lovely to see you. I have some news for you.'

She held out her hand and Jack St Clare took it.

'You're . . . married?'

Amelia nodded.

'Oh, I am so pleased for you.'

'We have been friends for so long. It seemed foolish to wait.'

'I saw it all coming,' I told her. 'And your letters betrayed it.'

I congratulated them both and I was genuinely pleased. I was so fond of Amelia and she was the sort of woman who needed a husband. I hoped she would have children, successfully this time. But I could not bear to think of children. When I saw them in the Park my misery would overwhelm me . . . either that or my anger.

I asked if they would care for some refreshment. What about coffee, tea or some wine?

'Not now, thank you,' said Amelia. 'I just called to tell you we were in London.'

'For how long?'

'Only a week. We are staying with my parents.'

'Are they pleased about your marriage?'

'Delighted. I want to come and see you and talk. There's so much to tell you. Could I come tomorrow? Jack has some business to do.'

'But of course.'

And so it was arranged; and the next day Amelia called and took tea with me.

When we had settled down and were alone she said: 'I hope you didn't mind my coming without warning. I know you wanted to get right away entirely but I hoped you didn't include me in the things you wanted to get away from.'

'I certainly did not.'

'I know you have reverted to your maiden name. I have told Jack about that and he understands perfectly. I shall make sure I call you Miss Pleydell.'

'And Anna . . . the second part of my name. I want to be quite different.'

'I'll remember. Sometimes I blame myself for not warning you before you married him. Stephen had an idea that you would save him. He was really very fond of his brother. Stephen wanted the marriage very much after he had met you. He said he knew you'd be strong and stable. But I knew you would have to find out before long.'

'Do you think I could have done anything, as Stephen seems to have thought I could?'

She shook her head. 'Perhaps there was a remote possibility. But I see that after the child's death you couldn't stay there.'

I hesitated – for a moment too emotional to speak because she had brought back memories of my beautiful child.

'You see,' I stammered, 'I left a healthy child and came back and found him . . . gone.'

'I know. I know.' And she did because she had lost children of her own. 'You see, he started this drug-taking when he was quite a young man. He read those books . . . and he was fascinated by that man.'

'Dr Damien?'

'I told Stephen that was what started it, but Stephen wouldn't have it. The man was a friend of his and Stephen thought the world of him. He believed in all that working for mankind and so on. I never did. The nature of the man came out in his books. All that erotica . . . hinted at. You could realize that he revelled in it. Aubrey met him at the Minster. He was completely bowled over. There is a hypnotic quality about him. It was soon after that meeting that Aubrey was experimenting with drugs.'

'I am sure that man has played a diabolical role in our lives,' I said. 'But one day he will be brought to justice. Believe me.'

There was a pause and then she said: 'Susanna . . . oh no, Anna . . . I must remember that . . . what are you going to *do*?'

'Live here until some plan comes to me.'

'It must be difficult, living as an unmarried woman when you have a husband from whom you are living apart.'

'There is no reason why that should affect me. I have taken on this house. My father rented it and now I do. Almost everything he had I have inherited. I am quite comfortable here.'

'You have a pleasant staff . . . sisters, isn't it?'

'Yes. They were with my father and they are staying with me. Then there is the coachman and we have another girl now, a seamstress.'

'A seamstress! Do you mean you employ a seamstress permanently?'

'She does other things besides. She came to me in a rather special way.' I told her the story and she was most interested.

'I went into a hospital when I brought her here,' I concluded. 'It was a horrible experience and one I cannot forget. I am just haunted by the memory of all those beds close together and those poor creatures on the point of death . . . dirty . . . uncared for. I can't bear to think of it.' She nodded, and I went on vehemently: 'Something has to be done.'

'Well, at least you took the girl away and she has a good home now. By the way, my parents are having a family dinner-party . . . there will only be us. They want you to come.'

I hesitated.

'They know all about this and they sympathize. There'll be no need to say anything. You'll just be Miss Pleydell. You ought to get out now and then. I don't suppose you do often, do you?'

I shook my head. 'It is the last thing I have wanted to do. I want to be here alone. I am well looked after. Jane and Polly would do anything for me – and so would Lily Craddock and Joe the coachman.'

'It will be different coming to us. Do come.'

I still hesitated, but as she was persistent I said I would.

There was great pleasure in the household when they heard I was going to a dinner-party. I was sure that in the kitchen they had decided it would be good for me.

Lily said it would be an occasion for me to wear the green velvet dress she had made. She had added the post of lady's maid to her duties and I had to admit that she filled it well. She had natural good taste and her attitude to me was one of almost adoration which I found a little embarrassing and not really deserved.

Joe, too, was delighted as he drove me in the carriage to the residence of Sir Harry and Lady Carberry close to the Park. 'That's what carriages is for,' he commented complacently.

I was far less eager than the rest of them, even though my host and hostess would know my story and there was no fear of an embarrassing exposure; but all the same it did bring back to my memory times which I was trying to forget.

I was greeted warmly by Amelia and her husband and parents.

'We are not quite alone,' said Lady Carberry.

'Henrietta and her fiancé called this morning and Mama asked them to dinner,' said Amelia apologetically. 'I believe you have met Henrietta.'

She was coming towards me. I remembered her well. She was the vividly attractive girl I had met at the Minster before my marriage.

'The Honourable Henrietta Marlington and her fiancé, Lord Carlton,' said Lady Carberry.

I was surprised by the fiancé. He was not quite as tall as Henrietta, who was almost as tall as I was, and he must have been about twenty years older than she was. There were pouches under his eyes. I was disappointed in the vibrant Henrietta's choice.

'Miss Anna Pleydell,' said Amelia, introducing me.

'Oh . . . we've met before.' Henrietta was opening her sparkling eyes very wide. 'I thought . . .'

'Miss Pleydell lives in London now,' said Amelia firmly. 'She is in the house her father took when he came back from India. It is very convenient.'

The Honourable Henrietta looked as though she were about to pursue the subject of our meeting before and I guessed she was remembering me as Aubrey's fiancée and was wondering what had happened. It struck me that she was an impulsive person who did not pause to consider before she spoke. But somehow Amelia had managed to convey that questions were not to be asked. I knew she was thinking how unfortunate it was that Henrietta was a fellow guest.

We went into dinner and I found myself opposite Henrietta. We talked about India. Lord Carlton knew it well and he had at some time met my father there. Conversation was lively and I found myself joining in and enjoying it. There was talk of the Great Exhibition which had been opened to the public from May to October of the previous year and what a great achievement it was and what a credit to Prince Albert.

'The Queen is delighted that people appear to appreciate him at last,' said Lord Carlton.

'But not for long,' added Sir Henry. 'They will soon find something in him to complain of.'

'There is a great deal wrong with the country, I believe,' said Lady Carberry. 'It looks as though Lord Derby will resign.'

I said on impulse: 'One thing that's very wrong is the state of our hospitals.'

Everyone was looking at me and Lord Carlton said: 'Surely a young lady like you has not had experience of such places?'

'Tell them, Anna, about your little adventure,' said Amelia.

So I told them about the carriage incident and how I had taken Lily to the hospital and therefore I could speak with some authority.

'I could never have imagined such a place,' I told them. 'The smell was overpowering, sickening, and those people unwashed . . . uncared for. And they call that a hospital! It's a disgrace. How can people allow it!'

There was a silence round the table. Then Lord Carlton said: 'My dear young lady, you are vehement. You remind me of the Nightingales' daughter.'

'Oh, how is Fanny?' asked Lady Carberry. 'It's such a long time since I've seen her.'

'She worries a lot about Florence. So does poor old W.E.N.,

I think. As for her sister, Parthenope . . . she is almost frantic about what they call Florence's obsession.'

It was the first time I heard that name which was to become so important to me.

'Tell me why I remind you of Miss Nightingale, Lord Carlton,' I asked.

'She's got some notion that she has a mission . . . being called by God. And what do you think it is? She wants to be a nurse! You know the family, Henry. It's most unsuitable. No lady can become a nurse.'

'She would be turned thirty now, I suppose,' said Sir Henry. 'Time she grew out of her fancies.'

'Florence should have grown out of them years ago. It's sheer obstinacy. W.E.N. thinks the world of her, however.'

'Who is W.E.N.?' I asked.

'William Edward Nightingale, who has the misfortune to be the father of this headstrong young lady. I don't think they will ever succeed in getting her away from all this. Do you know, she has been to some place in Germany. Kaiserswerth, I think is the name.'

'I have heard of that,' said Lady Carberry. 'It's some sort of institution . . . charity, I think. They have a school for orphans, I believe . . . run by nuns or deaconesses. They have a hospital there. Flo actually went there to work. Apparently she enjoyed it.'

'Yes, and they treated her like a servant. Then she came back and declared she had enjoyed it more than anything she had ever done.'

'And when you think what W.E.N. and Fanny have done for that girl! She could have made a brilliant marriage.'

'Perhaps she did not think that a brilliant marriage was the best thing that could happen to a woman,' said Henrietta.

I was listening avidly and excitement was gripping me.

'In Germany, did you say?' I asked.

'I'm sure it was Germany.'

'I'd like to know more about it.'

'Just one of those institutions. Here today, gone tomorrow,

I should imagine. People like to do good for a while but they soon get tired of it.'

'Poor W.E.N.,' said Sir Henry, 'all he wants to do is live in peace. And all Fanny wants to do is get her girls well married. Good-looking girls too, both of them . . . and particularly Florence.'

'So she felt she had a mission,' I said slowly, and I noticed Henrietta was studying me closely.

She said: 'It must be exciting to be called . . . like the infant Samuel, wasn't it? Didn't it happen to him?'

'Well, you've been called,' said Sir Henry. 'You've been called to marriage almost as soon as you came out.'

There was general laughter and I could see that Lady Carberry thought we had had enough of Miss Nightingale's obsession, and determinedly she led the conversation to other subjects.

But a seed had been planted. I felt very excited and it seemed to me that I was being guided in some strange way. First my encounter with Lily Craddock and my introduction to the horrors of those institutions they called hospitals; then my awakening from the lethargy into which my melancholy had plunged me and facing the fact that whatever had happened to one, one must go on; and now tonight.

Ideas were forming in my mind.

Joe was talkative as he drove me back, telling me stories of his adventures on the road from London to Bath. I listened half-heartedly. My thoughts were far away. He was in a contented mood. I had no doubt that he had consulted with Jane and Polly and that they had all decided that this was a sign that I was coming out of myself.

The next day I had a visitor. I was astonished when I went into the drawing-room to receive her and was confronted by the Honourable Henrietta Marlington.

She held out her hands to me. 'I hope you don't mind my calling so soon. I had to come. I had to talk to you. I couldn't last night. It's all so secret.'

I looked at her in surprise and she went on: 'Oh, I know it seems inquisitive, but it is not really . . . or not *all* that. I do want you to help me, and I think you might. I believe you'd understand.'

'Of course, I'll help if I can.'

'I liked what you did for that girl, and you cared so much about the hospitals.'

'Anyone would care if they could be made to see them.'

'Oh, I don't think everybody would. First of all, you did marry Aubrey St Clare, didn't you? Oh, don't worry. I'll not breathe a word. Only I must know. It is important to me.'

'Why?'

'It's like an example, you see.'

'I don't understand.'

'Well, that's what I'm going to explain. May I sit down?'

'Of course. I'm sorry. I was taken by surprise. Would you like some tea?'

'That would be cosy, wouldn't it?'

I rang the bell and Jane appeared.

'We'd like some tea, please, Jane,' I said.

'Very good, Madam,' replied Jane. The manner in which she slipped into being the model parlourmaid when the occasion demanded it always amused me, for when we were alone the relationship was hardly that of mistress and maid.

'This is a pleasant house,' said Henrietta, after Jane had gone.

'Yes, my father and I found it when we returned from India.'

'I heard of your father's death. It was very sad.'

'And unexpected,' I said. 'That's always harder to bear.'

She nodded. 'The house is just about the right size for you, I imagine,' she said.

I smiled. I knew she was making trivial conversation until the tea arrived and we could be undisturbed.

After tea was brought and Jane had discreetly retired, Henrietta said: 'You must be wondering why I have burst in on you like this. It's unconventional, isn't it? But then I am unconventional and, I believe, so are you. That is why I had the courage to come.'

'What is worrying you?'

'Quite a lot.'

'And you think I can help?'

'I don't know of anyone else who can or would.'

'Tell me what it is.'

'It's getting married. You see, now I come to think of it, I don't want to.'

'But how do you think I can help . . . about that?'

'I thought you could tell me what to do.'

'I can't think what I could say except break it off, and you would know how to do that much better than I.'

'Well, let me explain. They are all so eager for this marriage.'

'I imagine Lord Carlton is.'

'Oh, not only him. It's my mother and father and the whole family. There's a big clan of Marlingtons. They are everywhere and they are all terribly poor and they all have the family name and estates and things to keep going. All my life I have heard nothing but fears about dry rot in the woodwork and death watch beetle in the roof. I just accepted that it would always be like that until I discovered they were all relying on me. "Henrietta will make a good marriage," they used to say. Really, I was brought up with that purpose in mind. Money – hard to find – was invested in me. The finest finishing school in the world, trained in all the arts of allurement. I dance, I sing, I play the pianoforte; but most important of all, I have had to learn the art of conversation . . . not serious conversation, the light-hearted, rather frivolous kind – how to coax and wheedle and assume complete adoration of the men around me, providing of course they are influential enough – and I believe that means rich enough – to warrant my attention.'

I smiled. 'I think a lot of young ladies are brought up with such aims and so-called ideals.'

'You weren't?'

'Mine was not a normal upbringing. I was in India, you see, and that made a difference; and when I was in England I went to school and spent my holidays with some relations in a country rectory – very humble compared with the society in which you obviously move.'

'Lucky Miss Pleydell! They were just waiting for me to come out. I don't know why they should leave it to me to work the miracle.'

'You are very attractive.'

She grimaced. 'I'm not really pretty, if you take a close look.'

'It's all that vitality, that gaiety. I suppose attractiveness is not so much a matter of features as of personality. They did a good job at your charm school – or perhaps they didn't have to because it was there already.'

'I'm beginning to wish I had been born with a squint and spots.'

'Please don't despise the gifts the good fairies bestowed on you. They are bound to come in useful although sometimes they lead to difficulties. But go on.'

'Well, I came out most expensively. They invested in me, sure that they would get good dividends. There was a rather nice young man. I liked him very much. Good family . . . but no money . . . so I was steered away from him. And then Tom Carlton came on the scene. He was the answer to their prayers. He is one of the richest men in the country. Made a fortune and acquired a peerage, and what should he be looking for but a wife who could supply the background. The Marlingtons could do that all right. We could trace it right back to the Conqueror, or almost. It was to be the most convenient of marriages. They say it is the perfect union of the Carlton millions and the blue blood of the Marlingtons.'

'And the one person in the family who does not see it as ideal is the prospective bride.'

She looked at me and nodded. 'At first I thought it was wonderful. You see, Tom was so pleased with me. He is so generous and it was bliss not to hear all that growling about damp and dry rot. For a week or so I really was radiantly happy. We were saved and I had saved us all.'

'And then you realized that there is more to marriage than family pride.'

'Exactly. And I have been wondering ever since what I could do about it.'

'Why do you think I can help you to make up your mind? I am a stranger. This is only the third time we have met. I know nothing except what you have told me.'

'I have been frank with you. Will you be with me? I swear that not a word of what you tell me shall be passed on by me.'

She was dramatic in her moods, changing in seconds; a little while ago she had seemed almost tragic, the sacrificial lamb on the altar of family pride; now her eyes were flashing with excitement. She was the conspirator.

I found her charming. I could understand why the astute Lord Carlton, who must have known it was his fortune which made him so desirable to the Marlingtons, had become a victim to her charm.

I said: 'I do not want my affairs talked about.'

'I will keep silent. I swear I will.'

'All right. I did marry Aubrey St Clare. The marriage wasn't successful. I had a little boy. I stayed with my husband because of him. When he died, I left.'

'You left? That was a brave thing to do.'

'There was nothing brave about it. I could not stay there, so I came away. I was fortunate. I had enough money from my father to live on – not extravagantly but with a degree of comfort – and that is what I am doing.'

'I have an income, too. The family think it is a pittance, but I dare say it is not all that small . . . only if you want to support a big house with a retinue of servants and prop up leaking roofs and fight the death watch beetle. If you were in my place, what would you do?'

I lifted my shoulders. 'How can I say? I don't know all the details. There must be a great deal more to this than you have told me.'

'I think that was a fateful evening . . . last night.'

'Oh?'

'Yes, meeting you . . . and all that talk about Florence Nightingale. I've met the Nightingales. Not Florence, but her mother and father. I didn't take much notice of them. It would have been different if Florence had been there. I am sure that would have been most exciting. Well, anyway, the talk last night made me feel that I could break out of the trap if I had the courage of people like you and Miss Nightingale.'

'Do you mean you want to break off your engagement?'

She nodded.

'If you feel like that, you should.'

'You see, at first I thought of all the rejoicing in the family and how pleased Tom was, and how nice it was to stop everyone worrying about what this and that cost . . . but then I thought of the things I should have to endure. Well, he's very nice, but sometimes the way he looks at me – to tell you frankly, Miss Pleydell, I feel a little scared, no, not a little bit, a lot. And then . . . and then . . .'

Memories were coming back; awakening in that bedroom in Venice and seeing Aubrey standing by the bed. How did one know what secret desires could take possession of people? I looked at this girl – fresh, young and so vitally attractive. What had happened to me could scar one for a lifetime . . . perhaps for ever; it could colour one's outlook on life; it could warp one's healthy and natural instincts.

I knew that Henrietta should break off her engagement because when I looked into her lovely face I could see the terror peeping out.

She was looking at me earnestly, almost pleadingly.

I said: 'It seems strange that you should come to me with your problem. You hardly know me. There must be someone else . . . someone near you.'

'Who? My parents? My parents' friends? They think it is the catch of the season. They say there is not a debutante who isn't green with envy because I have captured the prize. You know how people are. He's highly respected. He's a lord – a title he earned for himself, which should be applauded, but as you know, people think more of those who have had their titles handed down. He's a friend of important people like Lord Derby and Lord Aberdeen and Lord Palmerston. Prince Albert approves of him because he brings a lot of business to the country. I ought to be honoured and flattered, and I am. But I am scared, more scared than flattered.'

'It is a matter for you to decide.'

'I know what you'd do. You'd break it off. You're strong. I admire you. You left your husband and they would all say that was social suicide. But you don't care about that, do you?'

'I don't seek to go into society.'

'Prince Albert wouldn't receive you. He's very strait-laced.'

'I can well do without Prince Albert's company. I do not want to be received by anyone. I am comfortable here. I am quite ready to leave everything as it is until I find out what I can do.'

She looked at me with sparkling eyes. 'I thought it was wonderful the way you went into that hospital.'

'Wonderful! It was horrible.'

'I know. But to go in and get that girl out. It was magnificent. So I thought you were the one whom I should ask.'

'My dear Miss Marlington, you are the only one who can decide on that.'

'But if it were you, would you go ahead and marry him?'

I closed my eyes. Those memories persisted. This man who was so much older than herself, how did she know what he would expect of her? She was not in love with him. That much was clear; and fears had come to her. I remembered the dream I had had on the night before my wedding. Had that been a warning? I had not recognized it as such. But this girl was being more clearly warned.

I said: 'You are not in love with him. If you were, you would want to marry him.'

'So you think I should break it off?'

'How can I advise you? It is for you to decide.'

'But if you were in my place, what would you do?'

I did not answer.

'I know,' she said triumphantly. 'Thank you, Miss Pleydell.'

Her mood changed. She became very merry. She told me amusing incidents about coming out in society; how the importance of making one's mark was astonishing. Her first ball had been a nightmare before it started and turned out to be a triumph. 'I was so scared that I should be a failure and no one would ask me to dance. To be a wallflower is the haunting fear of every debutante. And if you are a success, all the mamas are a-titter and terribly jealous – except your own, of course, who is triumphant. It is an ordeal.'

'Which I am sure you came through with flying colours.'

'I had lots of partners and it was fun, and it went on being fun for a long time. Then Tom appeared, and there was all the excitement which grew and grew. I was petted and pampered, their darling, their ewe lamb, their saviour. It is a terrible responsibility.'

We had come round to the subject again.

When she left me, she took my hand and held it. 'May I call you Anna?' she asked.

'Of course.'

'And you will call me Henrietta.'

I agreed. I expected I should not see her again, but I should probably hear whether or not she had broken her engagement. It would be in the society columns of the newspapers.

I was unprepared for the sequel. Two days later a jarvie arrived at the house. I looked through the window and, to my amazement, saw Henrietta stepping out. The driver was carrying two travelling bags to the door.

Jane answered the knock.

I heard Henrietta's voice. 'Is Miss Pleydell at home?' And then to the driver. 'Just bring those bags in, will you, please? Thank you very much.'

I waited.

Jane came into the drawing-room where I had been sitting reading.

'That young lady is back, Madam,' she said in her parlour-maid's voice. 'And it looks like she's come to stay.'

Henrietta, flushed and triumphant, was ushered into the drawing-room.

'I've done it,' she said. 'I couldn't face the family so I ran away.'

'But . . .' I began.

'I thought you'd let me stay . . . just for a little while . . . just till they get used to it. There'll be such a storm.'

'Wouldn't it have been better to stay and face it?'

'Well, to tell the truth, I think they would try to persuade.'

'But if you have made up your mind . . .'

'You don't know my family. There'll be weeping and wailing and gnashing of teeth. I couldn't have stood it. I'm not strong like you. Mama would have wept and I hate to see that. I might have given way and I know I must not give way. The only thing to do was to leave. So I thought, as you'd been so kind to that girl who had gone to the hospital, you'd be kind to me, too. You won't send me away, will you?'

'Of course I wouldn't do that. But I do wonder if you have been wise.'

'I feel loads better. I really was scared of Tom Carlton. It was the way he looked at me . . . as though there were all sorts of things in his mind. He's old and he has had lots of mistresses . . . all sorts, I believe. I didn't feel I would come up to his expectations. So it is better for him really that I get out now, before we both realize what a big mistake we've made. I thought I'd stay here till the storm blows over. Tom can find someone else and my family will get over the disappointment in time. After all, those death watch beetles have been at it for hundreds of years, a few more won't make much difference, and then perhaps we'll have someone in the family who knows how to retrieve the fortune, and perhaps one of them will be able to find a benefactor and marry him. I'm babbling on, aren't I? I do, you know. But if you could understand how relieved I feel . . .'

I said: 'You may certainly stay the night. Perhaps in the morning you will have changed your mind. Have you told your parents where you are going?'

'In my note, I said to a friend. I have a number of acquaintances where I could go. And I've written to Tom trying to explain that I don't think I'm ready for marriage.'

'I will ask them to prepare a room. We have just one spare room. This is not a big house, you know.'

'I know. That's what I like about it. I'm heartily sick of baronial halls and magnificent linenfold panelling which has to be preserved at the cost of one's self-respect.'

182

'I think you should consider your future. You see, I am a woman who has left her husband. Society is not very kind to people like me.'

'Who cares for society?'

'I don't. But are you sure you don't?'

'Absolutely. I'm going to love talking to you.'

'I think you make rather hasty judgements.'

'Well, perhaps, but I'm right in some, and I'm right about us. You and I are going to be friends.'

And that was how Henrietta Marlington came to live with me.

It was not to be expected that Henrietta's family would allow her to escape lightly. For weeks there were comings and goings, entreaties and threats. I was amazed at Henrietta's resolve. I had thought her rather frivolous, and so she appeared to be in many ways, but the frivolity hid an iron resolve. I was rather disturbed to find myself in the centre of a storm, which was the last thing I wanted; and there were occasions when I wished I had not allowed myself to accept the invitation to Amelia's parents' dinner-party. Yet on the other hand I was growing increasingly fond of Henrietta. She was an enchanting creature and her presence in the house was a joy to us all. Jane, Polly and Lily were her fervent admirers; they were ready to take up arms against the whole Marlington clan and Lord Carlton himself if they persisted in their attempts to force Henrietta into taking action which was repulsive to her.

Henrietta's mother came to see me to beg me to try to persuade Henrietta to think of her future.

I said I believed that that was what so concerned her.

She replied that Henrietta was young and had always been headstrong, and she did not realize what an opportunity she was throwing away. I had great influence with her.

I explained that I had met her on only two occasions when she had come to my house. I had known nothing about her feelings. She had just asked that she might stay in my house while she made up her mind. I could not persuade her one way or another.

And then, finally, they seemed to have decided that all hope of bringing Henrietta to her senses, as they called it, was futile, and they must accept the inevitable. They wished Henrietta to return to them. Henrietta declined; and by that time she had become part of our household and we were all very pleased about it.

For more than two months Henrietta's affairs dominated our lives; and when the storm finally died down, I found I was another step away from my overwhelming grief and was beginning to take a greater interest in life.

Lily Craddock's affairs were next to demand our attention. I had noticed a change in her. She went out more frequently; she had always been an outstandingly pretty girl, but now she was radiantly so.

It was not long before Jane and Polly prised the secret from her.

Lily often called at her favourite haberdasher's where she said she found the best lace trimmings and coloured silks in London, and she was on fairly good terms with the owners – a Mr and Mrs Clift. A few weeks previously she had been in the shop when a handsome soldier had come from the parlour while Mrs Clift was serving Lily. She had said: 'Oh, William, you must meet Miss Craddock. She's one of our best customers.'

'It seemed,' said Jane, recounting this to me, 'they took to each other . . . and that was it. What you might call love at first sight.'

'So,' I said, 'this is the reason for the change in Lily.'

'Lily is, in a manner of speaking, courting,' added Polly.

We were all very excited about this turn in Lily's fortunes, particularly when it seemed that William Clift was serious in his intentions.

Lily was asked to tea in the Clift establishment and she came back in a daze of happiness. I said she must ask William to tea with her, and there was a good deal of preparation and bustle in the kitchen. Jane made a cake and Lily made new collar and cuffs for her best gown. Henrietta thought that we should all be present and that the tea-party should take place in the drawing-room. But Jane firmly put her foot down. What sort of place would the Clifts think this was with servants taking tea with the mistress in the drawing-room?

No! Jane knew how these things should be done. There should be tea in the kitchen – which was the right place for it – and then Henrietta and I should come down *after* they had all eaten and we should be introduced to William in the proper manner.

Everything went according to plan. Henrietta and I went down at the appropriate time and were formally introduced.

William was a good-looking young man and his manly bearing was enhanced by his uniform. He told me that he hoped to leave the army when he married and settle down in the shop, which was now becoming more prosperous than it had been when he enlisted. He thought he and Lily would live there with his parents when they were married.

It sounded ideal and I was delighted for Lily.

After William had left she came to me and told me rather tearfully how much she appreciated what I had done for her.

She said: 'The luckiest day of my life was when I walked under your carriage. When I think it might have been someone else's carriage I go cold with fear.'

That was one of the nicest compliments I could receive but I felt I didn't deserve it. I had really done very little. I was so much better than I had been. Involvement in the affairs of those around me had taken me away from my troubles.

Henrietta was now settled in. She was part of the household and she told me that she felt so different, so happy and alive.

'Compared with what you have been used to, this must be a very humble existence,' I said.

She did not deny it. She said thoughtfully: 'But here I have something I never had before. Freedom! Do you know, I am beginning to believe that that is the most desirable thing in the world. Here I think my own thoughts. I don't believe what has been put into my mind is gospel truth. I make my own decisions. How glad I am that I did not marry Tom Carlton. I should now be his wife. Think of that.'

'So rich. So highly cherished in society,' I reminded her.

'My birthright sold for a mess of pottage.'

I laughed at her. I understood what she meant. She talked a great deal about her childhood, her coming out, her mission in life, as she called it: 'To find a rich husband and save the family fortunes. Now I am free. I shall marry whom I like or no one at all . . . if that is what I want. I go where I want to. I do what I want to. Glorious freedom.'

I found I was confiding in her. I told her a little of my married life, which culminated in the death of my son. 'I want more than anything to forget. I want to make something else so important in my life that I do not constantly look back. I want to put the past behind me. I want to forget disappointment, disillusion and grief. Henrietta, I want to nurse the sick, bringing them back to health.'

She looked at me in horror. 'Do you mean become a nurse?'

'Yes, I think I do.' I spread my hands and looked at them. 'I think I have a talent for it. My hands have a healing touch. It's almost mystic, but it has been apparent once or twice.'

She took them and looked at them. 'They are beautifully shaped. They should be adorned with fine emeralds, diamonds and such gems.'

'No,' I said, withdrawing them, 'they should be doing useful things.'

'Anna, seriously, you could not be a nurse. You saw what they were like when you went to get Lily.'

'But I want to change all that. I want to make it different.'

'Miss Nightingale is trying to do just that. I was always hearing about her before I ran away. She, like you, is appalled by all that misery in the hospitals. Of course, they all think it is very unfeminine of her. Her people don't like it at all. They've done everything they can to stop her.' She smiled. 'But no one can stop a woman like her from doing what she has really made up her mind to.'

'I am making up my mind, Henrietta. Oh, my thoughts are jumbled and I dream a lot. And there is one figure which haunts my dreams. It is a man . . . an evil man. His name is Damien. He has lived a strange life. He has gone native in remote places of the world.'

'Did he write a book?'

'Yes.'

'The one I am thinking of is a great doctor . . . some sort of pioneer.'

'Posing as one, I believe. I want to find him. There is much I want to know about him. I believe he is responsible for my husband's deterioration . . . for my son's death.'

'How?'

'He is interested in drugs . . . opium . . . laudanum . . . and strange ones which are to be found in the East. He experiments with them. Perhaps even on himself in moderation . . . but he gets other people to take them so that he can see the effect. He ruins lives so that he can make great discoveries and enhance his reputation. Have you ever heard of Madame de Brinvilliers, the poisoner?'

'Vaguely. Didn't she try out her poisons on people in hospitals?'

'Yes. Well, I class him with her. They are of a kind.'

'But she was a wicked woman. She poisoned people for their money, I believe.'

'He is a wicked man. He poisons people in the name of science so that he can tell the world of his great discoveries. He is even worse because he is a hypocrite.'

'I should have thought she was that – going round the hospitals as a benefactress to the poor patients and testing out her poisons on them.'

'Well, they are both in the same class. Henrietta, I want to find that man. I want to come face to face with him. I want to work in secret and expose him. I want to catch him . . . redhanded at his evil work.'

She looked at me in astonishment. 'That doesn't sound like you,' she said. 'You're usually so calm . . . so reasonable.'

'And you don't think I'm being calm and reasonable now?'

'No. You're vehement. You hate this man whom you've never seen.'

'I have seen him once . . . in Venice. He brought Aubrey back to the palazzo . . . drugged.'

'Do you think he was responsible?'

'I am sure of it.'

'How exciting! How do you propose to find this man?'

'I don't know.'

'That's where it becomes so wild.'

'Plans come into my mind and they seem so impossible that I reject them. But my determination continues. I can never be at peace with myself until I find this man. There are questions I want to ask him. Only by knowing him can I discover his methods.'

'I thought you knew his methods.'

'I know in my heart that he is evil. He is doing a great deal of harm and I am going to find him, Henrietta.'

'All right, then. But how?'

'It's like fate in a way. He is a doctor.' I looked down at my hands. 'I have this desire to nurse the sick, to do something about those appalling hospitals. It seems as if it is ordained. As a nurse, I should have a chance of finding him. It is something I have a feeling for. I *know* I should be a good one. My first step will be to become a nurse.'

'How?'

'I don't know yet.'

'You couldn't go into one of those hospitals. They wouldn't have you. You wouldn't fit in among those sordid people.'

'I have heard certain things about Miss Nightingale. She is trying to change the way in which we care about our sick. I am sure she would want people like me to study nursing . . . people who are dedicated to helping the sick. Those so-called nurses in the hospital did not care in the least about the old, the sick and the poor. That must change. They are themselves derelicts of society. Miss Nightingale is going to change all that, and when she does she will want her dedicated nurses beside her. Henrietta, I want to find out how to train to be a nurse!'

She nodded. 'I think I should rather like that, too.'

'*You?*'

'Why not? I like to be doing something. I don't want to spend my life idling away. I have decided. I'm going to train to be a nurse with you.'

'Do you remember that dinner-party at the Carberrys'?'

'As if I would forget! It was when I knew you'd help me.'

'There was talk of Miss Nightingale's going to some place in Germany. Kaiserswerth, I think.'

'I remember.'

'I want to find out about it. You knew the family, didn't you?'

'Yes.'

'And you do see some of your old friends occasionally?'

She nodded again.

'Perhaps you could make a few enquiries.'

'About Kaiserswerth and whether it is possible for two aspiring nurses to go there?'

'Exactly.'

Henrietta's eyes sparkled. She looked intrigued; and I wondered whether it was the idea of tracking down the Devil Doctor which appealed to her, rather than entering into the profession of nursing.

The enthusiasms had taken root. The excitement of Lily's engagement had died down. She was now a sober young woman collecting for her bottom drawer. That was very pleasant, but Henrietta liked excitement.

The great project, as she called it, was now her main concern. She set about her mission with a skill worthy of a secret agent.

A few days later I was startled to receive a letter from Minster St Clare. My fingers trembled as I opened it. It was from Amelia.

She wrote:

My dear Anna,

You will be surprised to see me writing from the above address. As a matter of fact, Jack and I are here. We were advised to come. Aubrey is very ill indeed. It was inevitable. His condition deteriorated considerably after you left apparently, and we are informed that in such cases decline is rapid.

The doctor believes that he cannot long survive. He is allowed regular doses of laudanam – which of course contains opium – and it is his addiction to that drug which has brought him to this state. He cannot be deprived of it absolutely, say the doctors, for if he were he would probably become violent.

It gives me great pain to write to you in this way, for in spite of all that happened I know you feel something for him. He is lucid for periods and he talks continually of you. If you could come and be with him for a little while, the doctors think it would soothe him.

My dear Anna, this is a very sad letter for me to write, and if you say you cannot come, I will understand. I am writing this because the doctor suggests I should. I believe Aubrey has not long to live. Perhaps you could reassure him in some way. I think he has a deep sense of guilt and would like to make his peace with you.

My love as always, and I hope that I shall see you.

Amelia

I was stunned. I had not thought to see Aubrey and the Minster again.

My first thoughts were: No, no, I cannot go. I cannot revive old memories. It is asking far too much.

For a whole day I did not reply to the letter.

When Henrietta noticed my preoccupation she wanted to know what was wrong. I showed her the letter.

'I can't go,' I said vehemently. 'It will revive all that I am trying to put behind me. There will be memories of my little boy everywhere. With everything that has been happening, I have managed to forget a little. It would open it all up again.'

'Anna Pleydell,' said Henrietta solemnly, 'if you don't go, you will have it on your conscience all your life. I know you well, and that is how it will be. Your husband failed you. You needed to get away. You wanted freedom. I know what that meant to you. Yes, old wounds will be opened. You will suffer, but you will suffer more in all the years to come if you don't go.'

I pondered what she had said. For all her outward frivolity she was capable of flashes of wisdom; and after more consideration, I decided to go.

I was met at the station by Jack St Clare.

As we were driving to the Minster he said: 'You will see a great change in Aubrey.'

'I expected to. But it is rather sudden, isn't it?'

'It would be about a year since you last saw him, I think.'

'Yes,' I answered.

'The doctor said that when the final stages set in they would advance rapidly.'

'He is dying, isn't he?'

'I don't think he can live very long in the state in which he is. He is becoming very thin. He is nervous, irritable and scarcely eats anything. I think he suffers pain when he attempts to. The doctor says that to deprive him of the drug entirely now can produce disturbances and collapse.'

'Do you mean he could become violent?'

'If deprived altogether he would do anything to get the drug.'

'Should he be kept at home?'

'There is nowhere he could go. He has a small dose of laudanum every day. He craves for it. Really it is pitiful to see him and think what he was, and what he might still be. The doctor thought you should know of his state, and although he believes that nothing will bring about an improvement, he does think that your presence might soothe him.'

I was silent, dreading what lay before me.

Amelia greeted me very warmly. 'Somehow I knew you would come,' she said.

They took me to Aubrey's room. He was sleeping. I hardly recognized him. He looked years older than when I had last seen him. He lay on his back breathing heavily.

'Come to your room,' said Amelia. 'When he wakes he will be told that you are here. I haven't given you your old room. I thought you would rather not.'

How well she understood!

I went through the gallery so well-remembered, with the

wicked Harry looking down at me with sardonic amusement, to my room in the front of the house which overlooked the drive. As I looked out I pictured Julian running about in the grass down there. I steeled myself against all the memories which came flooding back.

Later when I saw Aubrey, I could not help being sorry for him. He was as feeble as an old man.

'Susanna,' he murmured. 'You came, then.'

I sat by his bed and he held out a hand to me. I took it and grasped it firmly.

'That,' he said, 'is pleasant. I always loved your hands, Susanna. They soothed me. God knows, I need soothing now. I'm glad you came. It is good of you. I want to say I'm sorry.'

'It's all over. It's finished. Don't let's blame anyone.'

'It could have been different.'

'I suppose everything could.'

'So easily . . .' he said. 'Remember . . .'

'I remember a great deal.'

'I meant it to be . . . the turning-point. I meant to give up the old ways.'

'I know that now.'

'If only . . .'

'Don't let's grieve over what can't be changed.'

'Forgive me, Susanna.'

'Forgive me, too.'

'Not you,' he said. 'Not you, Susanna. I've thought so much lately how different it could have been.'

'I know.'

'Stay here with me.'

'That is what I have come to do.'

'It won't be long now, you know.'

'Perhaps you will recover.'

'From what is wrong with me? No, Susanna. I saw a man once . . . just like me. The craving . . . it is terrible. You'd do anything for it . . . even kill. It's terrible.'

'I understand.'

'People should know before they start.'

'They do,' I said. 'But they go on.'

192

'Talk to me about Venice . . . the first weeks in Venice before I gave way. If only . . . I might have started then. I might have found my way back.'

So I talked of Venice, of my delight in the gondoliers, the palazzo, the Doges' Palace, the lovely bridges, and I brought back to us both some of the magic of that honeymoon.

He kept a hold on my hand. He said it soothed him; and afterwards he fell into a deep and peaceful sleep.

If only he could have remained like that.

It was later the same day when I heard him screaming and shouting in the agony of withdrawal from the drug – and need. He had a male nurse who was more like a jailer, I thought. He was a strong man, as he had to be to control Aubrey in his dangerous moods, brought on by the craving.

Jack explained to me: 'It has been a typical day with him. He has times when he is lucid and gentle, and then when it is time for his dose, this violence comes upon him. The dose is never enough, you see. He has become so addicted. Jasper knows how to handle him. We don't go near him when he is in one of his violent moods.'

After one of these seizures Aubrey would be exhausted and sleep for hours, which was a good thing, said the doctor, for he could not be given opiates as most of them contained opium, which was the enemy we were fighting against, and it would be unwise to increase the daily allowance of the drug.

I talked a great deal with Amelia and Jack. On Aubrey's death, Jack would inherit Minster St Clare, and on the advice of the lawyers had already taken over some of the work of the estate – so Minster St Clare would still be in the hands of a St Clare. I was glad for him and for Amelia.

But those were sad days for me. I was plunged right back into that period of suffering. Once I went up to the nurseries and sat there while dusk was falling and my heart cried out for my lost child.

Longing for him, my anger at his death was as fierce as it had ever been. I remembered so many things: his first tottering steps; his first smile; his first teeth; the manner in which his chubby fingers had curled round mine; the way in which his eyes lighted up when I appeared.

I mourned afresh my beloved boy.

And I said to myself: I will do it. I will find the man under whose influence Aubrey has been reduced to that wreck who is now living out the last days of his miserable life upstairs, the man whose experiments could have robbed me of my child.

Amelia found me there. She chided me. 'You must not sit here brooding,' she said. 'It is unwise. I felt that you were making a new life for yourself. And now you have Henrietta with you. Perhaps I should not have asked you to come back.'

'I'm glad I came,' I said. 'But it has changed things . . . I feel differently about Aubrey. Perhaps I could have helped him once. But I am glad I came back even though it has been painful. It had to be. I realize I have not forgotten one little part. It has just been there all the time . . .'

'My dear, you have to go on with the new life you are making.'

'Yes, I am going to. I think coming back has strengthened my resolve.'

Another day had passed. Aubrey seemed weaker. I sat by his bed and again we talked of the past, of our meeting in India, of those days on the ship journeying home, which had seemed magical to me. It seemed they had to him, too. I had not realized that in a way he had been reaching out to me then. He had seemed so worldly, so sophisticated, and I so inexperienced and innocent. Had I been older and wiser, I might have had an inkling. But I had not; and I felt I had failed him in some way. I had been unable to beguile him sufficiently to lure him away from the old habits, and my love had not been strong enough to keep me with him.

I held his hand. He liked that. He talked about my soothing hands.

When I saw that he was getting restive, I left. The change in him was frightening. I did not want to see him in those moods, restrained by the man I thought of as his keeper.

I had risen early that morning. I sat at the window looking

out over the drive and thought of how I had planned to give Julian his first pony when he was a little older. I must escape from memories which could do me no good.

I had been so helped by all those in the London house. I tried to think of them – the volatile Henrietta, my practical Jane and Polly; dear old Joe with his memories of the London to Bath run; and Lily with her romance. They had helped me through the difficult months and now that I was away from them I was slipping back into melancholy.

While I sat at the window contemplating these matters, there was a knock on my door.

Amelia came in and immediately I knew that something was very wrong.

'It's Aubrey,' she said. 'He's gone. Disappeared.'

'But where?'

She shook her head. 'He's not in the house. Jack and I have looked everywhere.'

'But where could he have gone?'

'Jasper has no idea. He took his dose last evening and appeared to go to sleep. This morning his bed was empty.'

'What can have happened to him?'

'We've no idea. He can't have gone far. His clothes are there.'

'Do you think he has done himself some harm?'

'We did think of that.'

'Do you think he found the laudanum?'

'Jasper says no. He has it locked away in his room. The cupboard had not been tampered with and the bottle had certainly not been touched since he put it away.'

'What are we going to do?'

'He can't have gone far in his night things . . . he only had on his slippers and dressing-gown. He must be somewhere in the house.'

'Has everywhere been searched?'

'Yes. They're going over it again. I thought I ought to come and tell you.'

I went downstairs with her. I saw Jack. He shook his head. 'He is simply not to be found.'

'Do you think he has left the house . . . gone into the grounds?' asked Amelia.

'We're searching them. He can't have gone far.'

I followed them out of doors and went towards the wood.

'We've searched it,' called Jack.

'I wonder . . .' I murmured, for a thought had occurred to me. I started to run through the wood. I came out on the other side. I climbed up the hillock and slid down the other side and as I did so I saw that the door of the temple was open. Some instinct told me that that was where I should find him.

I went in. A chill pervaded the atmosphere. I could smell the same smell which I knew now came from the drugs which had been smoked here.

I felt a great desire to turn back, not to penetrate that evil place. I had an uncanny feeling that if the door shut me in I should not be able to escape.

I remembered the first time I had come here. I found a stone and propped it against the door. I took a deep breath of fresh air before advancing through the passage to that open space which I now knew to be a shrine to the Devil.

Then I saw the idol and Aubrey. The great statue with the yellow eyes, the horns and the cloven feet was lying on the floor and there was something beneath it.

I knew.

It was Aubrey.

To me it was symbolic. The statue represented the man who had destroyed him. In one of his frenzies he had gone to the temple and attacked it, with the result that it had toppled over and killed him. The great fear, ever since his obsession had resulted in those violent moments, was that he would do some harm either to himself or some other. At last it had happened.

Poor doomed Aubrey.

I stayed at the Minster for the funeral. There were few people at the ceremony. In the circumstances, Amelia and Jack had thought that it should be as quiet as possible. Afterwards the will was read. It was very much as we had expected. Jack was now the master of Minster. I had been left an amount of money which would bring me in a small income, and that, added to what I had already from my father, made my future free from financial anxiety.

Amelia and Jack took an affectionate farewell, extracting a promise that I would visit them again soon.

I had let them know in London the time of my arrival so Joe was waiting at the station. When I stepped into the house Henrietta dashed out to embrace me and Jane and Polly stood at a respectful distance, waiting for their turn to greet me.

There were flowers everywhere and laurels had been hung over the pictures.

'We missed you so much!' said Henrietta.

And I felt I had really come home.

Henrietta wanted to hear all that happened; and she listened, wide-eyed, when I told her how Aubrey had met his end.

I said: 'I am sure he was trying to pull down that hideous statue. Of course, the thing was a hundred years old. It must have given way and fallen on top of him. I believe he thought it was Damien . . . the man who had destroyed him.'

'We'll find him one day,' said Henrietta, smiling secretly.

'You think it is a wild thing to attempt.'

'Most things worthwhile are. You're very sad,' she added.

'I feel remorseful about Aubrey. Perhaps I should have stayed and looked after him.'

'You did what seemed best at the time. You mustn't get a conscience about it all. How could you have lived with a man who was drugged half the time. You did what seemed right then. It's no use looking back. You have to go forward.'

'You're right. I feel I have come to the end of a phase. I'm a widow now, Henrietta.'

'Which is a more respectable thing to be than a woman who has left her husband!'

'I suppose you are right. I'm a little richer, too.'

'That's a good thing. Finances were a bit stretched, weren't they? You've taken on a seamstress. If ever you feel remorseful about Aubrey, remember what you've done for Lily. You can't

197

save all the world at the same time.'

'You're a comfort to me, Henrietta. I'm glad you came.'

'There, you see, you are glad, so that is a mark in my favour. But think of all the black marks I get for jilting Tom Carlton.'

'Are you sure you have no regrets about that?'

'Completely and utterly sure. Life has become exciting, full of possibilities. I have not been idle while you have been away.'

'What have you been doing?'

'For the moment it's a secret.'

'I hate secrets which I don't share.'

'So do I. But you will know this . . . in time. I don't want to spoil it by telling you half before it's ready.'

'I am very curious. Is it a lover?'

'How people's minds run along one track. If a girl has a secret, everyone presumes it must be a man. Even you, Anna.'

'Isn't it, then?'

'You look relieved. Is that because you thought I might be going away?'

I nodded.

'Well, that's the nicest thing. I've wondered sometimes whether I've been something of a burden. I did drag you into my affairs and didn't give you much chance to refuse involvement. It was because I knew there was something special about you. I knew we were meant to be friends. I can't thank you enough for what you've done for me. Whatever happens, we shall always be friends. My secret is something we'll be in together.'

'You've told me so much, why not tell me all?'

'In good time. Just be patient a little longer.' She turned the conversation to other things. Lily's projects for marriage were going along at great speed.

'My only regret is that he is a soldier,' I said. 'Soldiers go away and leave their wives.'

She chatted on and I listened, so happy to be home; and knowing that a painful chapter of my life was closed forever.

Kaiserwald

It was two days later when I heard of Henrietta's activities. She had been waiting for a letter and when it arrived she ran to her room with it.

A few minutes later she burst into mine. She was triumphant.

'It's happened,' she said. 'I've done it.'

'I'm longing to hear.'

'I told you that while you were away I was not idle. You knew that we were acquainted with the Nightingale family. I thought I would make good use of the connection. First of all I learned through a friend what Miss Nightingale was trying to do. Like you, she was deeply concerned about the state of the hospitals and the standards of nursing. She had been to that place in Germany – Kaiserswerth – to learn something about it. She wants to make our hospitals places where the sick can be properly attended to, and the first thing she is looking into is the nursing profession. It is no use having those drunken sluts, who call themselves nurses, sitting around in the hospitals because it seems an easy way of getting a living. She wants the nursing profession to be an honourable and respected one. She wants nurses to be trained. She is making a great stir about it in high places.'

'I did not know that was her aim.'

'I wanted to see her, to tell her about us. Of course I couldn't get to her. She has so much to do and is in constant demand. She is passionately dedicated and on friendly terms with the Palmerstons, the Herberts . . . and several influential people. But I did get an address to which I could write and I told her about us . . . you mostly, how you had that feeling for nursing and wanted to learn something about it and that I had heard there was a place called Kaiserswerth.' Her eyes were sparkling. 'I had a letter back. She did not think we could be taken into Kaiserswerth. That was an institution of which the hospital was only a small part and it was staffed by Deaconesses who had been consecrated by the Church. But some of these Deaconesses had been sent to form institutions in various parts of Germany. There is one of them which is given over almost entirely to a hospital and where young women who wished to train as nurses might be accepted. Miss Nightingale would find out if we were acceptable and let us know.' She waved the letter at me triumphantly. 'I was waiting for this. Of course I didn't know whether I should hear anything. But it came this morning. Miss Anna Pleydell's and Miss Henrietta Marlington's application to train at Kaiserwald is accepted.'

'Henrietta!' I cried.

'Say I've been clever.'

'You have been magnificent, and so secretive.'

'I wanted to burst on you with the whole of the good news. It's never so effective piecemeal.'

'It's wonderful.'

'When do we go?'

'Next month?'

'So long to wait?'

'We have to get ready. Besides, we must be here for Lily's wedding.'

'There'll be a lot to do. How long shall we be away?'

'Three months, I believe.'

'Does it take that long to train?'

'I can learn a lot in three months. So can you.'

I smiled. It was just what I needed. I wanted to get right away from my thoughts of Aubrey, and having been at the Minster my yearnings for my child had become more intense again.

On a brisk October day Lily was married.

I was pleased to see such a happy sequel to her story. She was radiant and William seemed a very pleasant young man.

Mr and Mrs Clift were obviously delighted by the marriage and already fond of Lily; so everything seemed perfect.

The bridal pair were to have a week's honeymoon in Brighton and then Lily would take up her abode in the Clift household.

Jane and Polly were a little subdued. They were going to lose not only Lily but us. It would be as it had been before I came home, they said.

'Not quite,' I replied, 'because you'll be visiting Lily and she will be coming here. She is only going to live round the corner and we shall only be away for a few months.'

'It won't be quite the same,' said Jane.

'Life never is,' added Polly lugubriously.

Joe was downcast, too. 'Carriages wasn't meant to sit in mews stables, and horses was meant to be exercised,' he commented.

I told him he must take the carriage out regularly.

'Carriages without passengers is like stew without dumplings,' said Jane.

'It's not forever. We shall be back.'

Nothing could stem our excitement and we went ahead with our preparations.

At the end of that October Jane and Polly stood at the door waving us off. Polly wiped an eye and I realized afresh how fond I was of them. Joe drove us to the station. 'I'll be there to pick you up when you come back,' he said. 'And I'm hoping that will be sooner than later.'

'We shall look for you, Joe,' I said. 'What is it that the newsboys are calling out?'

Joe cocked an ear. 'Something about Russia. There's always something about Russia.'

'Listen,' I said.

'Russia and Turkey at war,' said Henrietta. 'Well, someone is always at war.'

'War!' I said. 'I hate it. I think of William Clift. It would be awful if he had to go overseas.'

'Russia . . . Turkey . . .' said Henrietta. 'That's a long way off.'

It was true; and we forgot about the war and gave our minds to what lay before us.

When I saw Kaiserwald, I felt as though I had stepped into an enchanted land which belonged in a fairy tale. The house had been a small schloss, with towers and turrets, which had belonged to a nobleman who had given it to the Deaconesses to be used as a hospital. It was situated among mountains – wooded hills and forest. It was a perfect setting, for the bracing air of the mountains was said to be good for patients suffering from respiratory diseases; indeed, such air would be good for us all. A carriage had been waiting to bring us up to the house, and as it climbed the steep road I had felt more and more exhilarated; and when I glanced at Henrietta, I could see that she shared my feelings.

I could smell the redolent odour of pine; I could hear the water of the falls which tumbled down the mountains. Now and then we heard the tinkle of a bell which, our driver told us, meant that cows were nearby. There was a faint haziness in the air which touched everything with a misty blue. Even before I saw Kaiserwald I was entranced.

We came to a clearing in the forest and the carriage pulled up abruptly. A girl was crossing our path. Her long fair hair streamed down her back and she carried a stick; before her waddled six geese, who refused to be hurried.

Our driver called out something to her, to which she responded with a shrug of the shoulders. My German was far from perfect. I had forgotten most of what I had learned at school but I did gather that she was Gerda the Goosegirl who lived with her grandmother in a cottage nearby. He tapped his forehead. 'A little short up there,' he said, which with the help of the gesture I was able to translate.

I replied haltingly that she made a very pretty picture with her geese.

Now we were at the schloss. In front of it was a small lake – little more than a pond. Willows trailed in the water and with the mountains in the background it was a sight of breathtaking beauty.

'It's wonderful,' said Henrietta; and I agreed whole-heartedly.

We drove into a courtyard and then alighted. A young woman came out to greet us. She wore a light blue gown with a white apron over it. She was fair-skinned and fair-haired; and she spoke English. She regarded us with some curiosity, and I fancied I detected a hint of scepticism. She told us afterwards that she had heard we were two English ladies of good family who were interested in nursing, and she did not think we would stay at Kaiserwald more than a week.

We were taken to our bedroom. It was a long dormitory with whitewashed walls and divided into cubicles. In each was a bed. These were our sleeping quarters, she told us, and we should wear white aprons over our gowns and be prepared to perform any tasks which were asked of us.

There were two hundred patients in the hospital, most of them seriously ill.

'We do not take them unless they are,' we were told. 'This place is for the truly sick; and those who come here have to work. It is not often that we have visiting ladies. The Head Deaconess has accepted you to please Miss Nightingale.'

We said we understood and I explained that we were eager to be trained nurses.

'It is only years of work among the sick which can make you that,' was the answer.

'We're going to make a start,' said Henrietta with a dazzling smile.

Our guide gave her a look of disbelief; and I could understand that. Henrietta gave the impression that she was made more for gaiety. As for myself, sorrow and experience had no doubt etched a few lines on my face. My manner was more serious, so perhaps I made a better impression.

We were introduced to our fellow workers. Very few of them spoke any English. They were religious people who had come to nursing because they had an aptitude for it. Most of them came from poor homes and it was a livelihood for them, but the atmosphere here was quite different from that which I had briefly glimpsed when I had gone to Lily in the London hospital.

We were taken to the Head Deaconess, a lady of great character. She was middle-aged with iron grey hair and cool grey eyes.

She told us: 'Most of the patients here are suffering from respiratory diseases. Some will never recover. They are sent here from other places throughout Germany because the air is said to be beneficial. We have two resident doctors – Dr Bruckner and Dr Kratz.'

Her English was quite good and she went on to tell us about the aims of the hospital. 'I share the views of your own Miss Nightingale,' she said. 'Too little is done to cure the sick. We are pioneers here. Our aim is to arouse people's consciences to the need to look after the sick and heal them if possible. We have had some approval for what we are doing and are visited now and then by doctors from other countries. We have had them from your own country. They are interested in our methods. I think we are making a little progress. We are all overworked here and you will find living far from luxurious.'

'We did not expect anything else,' I said.

'Our patients demand a great deal of time. There is little leisure, and when there is we are far from towns.'

'You have the beautiful forests and the mountains.'

She nodded. 'We shall see,' she said, and I knew that she, like the Deaconess who had brought us in, did not expect us to stay.

It was not easy. I was amazed that Henrietta accepted it. With me, it was different. I wanted hard work; I wanted forgetfulness; and to find myself in unusual circumstances was of great benefit to me.

We lived like Spartans. We had expected to work hard but not quite so persistently. We were required to do whatever was needed. I was struck by the cleanliness of the ward. The bed linen had to be washed by us and we must scrub the floors. We arose at five in the morning and were often working hard until seven in the evening, until, said Henrietta, the patients were tucked up in their beds. It was a religious order and when we had finished our work we assembled for a reading from the Bible, prayers and the singing of hymns. During the first week I was so exhausted at the end of the day that I went to bed, where I sank into delicious sleep and did not wake until the rising bell. In a way it reminded me of school.

Meals were taken in a long hall with whitewashed walls and we sat at a long table where we all had our places to which we were expected to keep.

Breakfast was just before six o'clock and usually consisted of rye bread and a drink which I believed was made of ground rye. It was peasant food. We served the patients' food at eleven o'clock and assembled in the hall at twelve to have ours. There was broth, vegetables, and a little meat or fish.

We had a few hours off duty now and then, and after the first week – when we were too tired to do anything but lie on our beds and talk desultorily – we would walk down to the edge of the lake and sit there listening to the sound of the breeze in the pines; even though we were accustomed to the hard work by that time, all we wanted to do was sit and rest. I felt extraordinarily at peace.

Sometimes, as we sat there, people would pass on the way to the village which was only about a quarter of a mile away from the hospital. Most of the people had a few animals – cows mostly – and many of them did embroidery on dresses and blouses which were sold in the shops in the towns. The woodcutter would walk by with his axe over his shoulder and call a greeting to us. They all knew who we were and respected us as the nurses of Kaiserwald and they showed us the utmost courtesy.

It was a long time since I had felt so happy.

Best of all I loved the work in the ward. It was a long room with bare whitewashed walls and at each end there was a large crucifix. The beds were close together and there was a curtain across the room dividing the men's section from that of the women. The doctors worked constantly and I think they had a mild contempt for the nurses – and particularly Henrietta and myself, for they knew that we were not working for a living and that before we came to Kaiserwald we had had no experience of nursing. No doubt they thought we were ladies indulging in a light-hearted adventure to relieve the boredom of our useless lives.

This attitude irritated me far more than it did Henrietta. I was determined to show them that I was not playing at being a nurse. I knew that I had a special flair for this kind of work and I was gratified when one of the patients had an attack of hysterics and no one could calm her – not even the doctors – but myself. I think their feelings towards me changed after that and even the Head Deaconess became interested in me.

'Some are born nurses,' she told us. 'Some acquire the necessary skills. You are in the former class.' It was the biggest accolade she could bestow, and if she were anxious about a patient she would often put me in charge of that particular one. I was greatly encouraged and threw myself into the work and was happy to be there.

I often wondered about Henrietta. I think at times she felt less enchanted. But she could see I was in my element and she was glad of that.

'I feel half dead,' she said to me one day when we sat stretched out before the lake. 'But I remind myself that it is all in a good cause. It has to be endured because it is all part of the great goal. It is going to lead us to the Demon King.'

That was what she called the man I had determined to find. She would invent stories of his wickedness; she sketched how he would look. A picture emerged – dark, heavy-lidded, brooding eyes, black hair and a wicked, satanic expression.

One afternoon, when we both had a free hour, as we sat by the lake's edge, a slim figure emerged from the trees. It was Gerda the Goosegirl.

My German had improved considerably since my coming to Kaiserwald, for that language was spoken all the time apart from the occasional remarks addressed to us by the Head Deaconess and the one who had met us when we arrived; and even Henrietta, who had less than I, was able to converse, albeit rather haltingly.

I said 'Hello' to Gerda and then: 'Where are your geese?'

'All taken care of,' she replied. 'So I can be by myself now.'

She came and stood close to us, smiling to herself as though she found us rather amusing.

'You're English ladies,' she said.

'And you're a little German girl.'

'I am a lady, too.'

'I am sure you are.'

'I walk in the forest. Do you walk in the forest?'

'We don't have a great deal of time for walking. But it must be lovely in the forest, to walk under the trees.'

She stepped near to us. 'The trees come alive at night,' she said. She had a strong faraway look in her eyes as though she saw something which was hidden from us. 'There are trolls . . . They live on the hills.'

'Have you seen them?' asked Henrietta.

She nodded. 'They pull at your dress. They try to catch you. You must never look into their eyes. If you do, they will catch you.'

'You have never looked into a troll's eyes, then?' I said.

She lifted her shoulders and giggled.

'Have you seen the Devil?' she asked. She called him *Der Teufel*.

'No. Have you?'

She started to laugh and shrugged her shoulders.

I said: 'You live with your grandmother, don't you?'

She nodded.

'In a little house on the edge of the woods?'

She nodded again.

'And you look after the geese and the chickens . . . and what else have you?'

'A cow. Two goats.'

'They must keep you busy.'

She nodded. 'It was in the forest. It was the Devil.'

'Oh . . . did you meet him?'

'He liked me.'

She started to giggle again.

Henrietta yawned but I was interested in this strange girl and I wondered what went on in her hazy mind.

Henrietta had risen. 'Look at the time. We'll be late.'

I said: 'Goodbye, Gerda.'

'Goodbye,' she said and stood staring after us as we went.

'Strange girl,' I said.

'Certainly something missing in the upper storey,' said Henrietta.

'I wonder what she meant about the Devil?'

'About the trolls?'

'I suppose she hears these things and fancies a good deal. She is really very pretty – so dainty, and that beautiful hair. What a pity she is mentally deficient. Well, she can look after the geese. She's capable of that. And she seemed happy enough . . . quite proud of her encounter with the Devil. I'd like to know more about her. I'd like to meet the grandmother. Perhaps we could call on her . . . but one is never quite sure whether one is doing the right thing.'

'There is hardly time for social calls in this life here.'

'Henrietta,' I said, 'are you finding it too difficult? Would you like to go home?'

'Of course not. If you can endure it, so can I.'

'But it is different for me. I want something important to devote myself to utterly, and I fancy I've always wanted to do this without really knowing I did.'

'I'm sticking it out until the three months is up. I haven't forgotten what it's all about, you know. Gerda enjoys her encounters with the Devil. I'm determined to do the same.'

Whenever I had an hour to spare I would wander out. Once or twice I saw Gerda with her geese; she gave me that faraway smile when she saw me and when she had her charges with her she did not speak much. It was as though she could not do two things at once.

The geese would hiss at us and she would calm them. They were very unfriendly creatures.

The weather was getting wintry and it was too cold to sit about. We had to take brisk walks. There was to be a fair in the town, which was about a mile and a half away, and there was a small increase in the number of people we saw on our walks. It was a misty afternoon when we first saw Klaus the Pedlar. He had a cart and a donkey; and the cart was laden with all sorts of wares.

He called out a cheery *Guten Tag*, to which we replied in friendly fashion.

'Ladies from the Kaiserwald,' he said. 'English ladies. Them as we've heard so much about. Now I wouldn't have guessed, seeing you.' His eyes were on Henrietta. 'You don't look the part. Meet Klaus the Pedlar. Anyone will tell you who I am. Pay regular calls, I do . . . and this is Fair time. A time for good business. What have I got in my pack? Something to interest you ladies . . . combs and fairings and rings for your ears . . . lovely silks to make you a gown . . . necklets and powders to make the men love you. You want it – ask Pedlar Klaus for it. If he don't have it this time, he'll bring it to you next.'

He talked at a great rate and there were some of his words which I could not catch, but it was easy to get the gist of his conversation. He was quite handsome in a gipsy way. He was very dark, with flashing eyes, and he wore rings in his ears. He had a jaunty manner and gave the impression that he was proud and independent and cared for no one.

He regarded us with some amusement, wondering, no doubt, what had made us come to Kaiserwald. I think it was probably our youth as much as our foreignness which made us outstanding.

'Anything you want, ladies,' he went on. 'You ask old Klaus the Pedlar, and he'll bring it to you. A nice piece of silk . . . a length of velvet and some beads to match your eyes . . . blue for the one and green for the other. I can match up both of them.'

'Thank you,' said Henrietta. 'But we don't get much chance of wearing such things here.'

He wagged a finger at us. 'Always make time for your fun, ladies. Don't work all the time. It's not natural. There's fun to be had in life and them that don't take it when it's there for 'em will find it flies away and don't come back. Now a nice piece of silk for a flighty gown . . . green to show off that tawny hair of yours. That don't grow on the head of every maiden, you know. You want to do the best for it.'

I said: 'We'll think about it.'

'Don't take too long thinking or Klaus the Pedlar will be gone.'

'But he'll be back I don't doubt.'

'He'll be back. But don't forget, the sun rises, the sun sets, and that's another day gone . . . and each day brings even beautiful ladies that much nearer to old age.'

'You have reminded us of the flight of time, and we have little to spare. We must go back.'

'Quite a fascinating man,' said Henrietta as we walked away.

'He is certainly not at a loss for words,' I replied.

It was a chilly day for we were at the end of November. A blustering wind was chasing clouds across a grey sky. Henrietta and I had an hour off duty in the afternoon and on such days we liked to walk in the forest. I loved the smell of the pines and suddenly to hear the tinkle of cow bells carried to us on the wind. I had always felt that there was an enchantment about the forest. I was not surprised that Gerda had her fancies.

We passed her cottage; she was in the garden crooning to herself. We called a greeting but she did not seem to be aware of us. It was often like that with Gerda. We went on and after some ten minutes it started to rain. Through the trees I could see the black clouds. Instead of welcoming us, the forest had become dark and menacing. The trees seemed to take on odd shapes; and the wind was like moaning human voices. When I mentioned this to Henrietta she laughed at me. 'For such a sensible, practical person you have some odd fancies sometimes,' she said.

'Hurry,' I warned her. 'The rain will be pelting down in a minute. I doubt we shall get back before it does.'

We ran through the pines and by the time we came to the clearing in which was Gerda's home the rain was teeming down.

The door of the cottage opened and a woman appeared. I

had seen her once before and knew that she was Gerda's grandmother.

She called out: 'You young ladies will be soaked to the skin. Come along in. It will pass soon. It is only a shower.'

I was pleased to be invited into the cottage, for I was very interested in its occupants. Frau Leiben was, I guessed, in her late fifties, yet she was sprightly and her cottage was very clean.

'It is good of you to offer us shelter,' I said.

'It's the least I can do. Do please sit down.' We did so and she went on: 'We're all very grateful to you ladies of Kaiserwald. You do great good. And you are English . . . come to study our ways?'

I told her that we had come for three or four months and then we should go home.

She said: 'People come from time to time.'

'Where is Gerda?' I asked. 'Can she be out in the rain?'

'She'll stand up somewhere. She's got that much sense.' She shook her head sadly.

'She is a beautiful girl,' I commented. 'She looks so picturesque with her geese. If I were an artist I would paint a picture of her.'

Frau Leiben sighed. 'I worry about her. What will become of her when I am gone? I ask myself. Who will care for her? If she were like others she would marry and have a husband to look after her. Perhaps her mother will come for her.'

We were silent for a few moments, then she went on: 'She was five when my daughter and her husband left her with me. I thought they would come back but they never have. They are far away in Australia.' She looked very sad. 'Herman, my husband, was here with me when they went away. And now Herman is gone. The blessed Deaconesses did what they could for him but they could not save his life and now I am alone. For three years I am alone.'

'The people here are friendly with each other,' said Henrietta. 'It must be comforting to live in a place like this.'

She nodded. 'It's true. They were good to me when Herman died. I didn't feel the burden so much when he was here. There were two of us to share it.'

She looked at us as though she wondered whether she was talking too much. After all, we were comparative strangers. I had always had an insatiable curiosity about other people's lives; they seemed to sense this and confide in me. And suddenly the story came out. She and Herman had had a daughter, Clara. They had doted on her. She had looked like Gerda except that she was bright and intelligent. They had wanted the best for her. She had gone to stay with a cousin in Hamburg and when she was there met Fritz and married him.

'She never really came back,' said Frau Leiben. 'Just to see us . . . that was all. It wasn't her home any more. And we could see that she was happy that way. Of course, we rejoiced for her but suffered for ourselves. When Gerda was born we were so happy . . . and she turned out as she is. They didn't want her really . . . at least Fritz didn't. She wasn't a normal child and she was an encumbrance. They brought her here. They used to come now and then to see her and us. Then Fritz came out of the Navy and they went to Australia. They didn't want Gerda with them. Herman was alive then. He loved Gerda dearly. They used to go into the forest together. We had more cows then. He used to tell her stories, all the old legends about the gods and heroes . . . all the stories of dragons and trolls in the mountains. Herman had them all at his fingertips and a way of telling them. She'd listen for hours, entranced. It was easy when Herman was there, and then he died. It was his lungs. He coughed and coughed and it broke your heart to hear him. They took him into Kaiserwald, and then he died and I was alone.'

'How very sad,' said Henrietta.

'Gerda is a very happy girl,' I added.

'Oh, she lives in her dream world, living all the stories Herman used to tell her. I remember our last Christmas with Herman. We brought in the tree and dressed it with all the little bits and pieces, candles to make it bright. It will soon be time for the tree. Old Wilhelm, the woodcutter, brings one to me. I dress it. Gerda likes that. But it is a sad time without Herman.'

I noticed that the rain had stopped and that we should have to hurry back if we were not to be late.

I said: 'It has been very interesting talking to you, Frau Leiben. I hope your daughter will come to see you soon.'

'Australia is a long way to come.'

As we hurried back, I said to Henrietta: 'What a sad story! Poor Gerda. Poor Frau Leiben.'

'I don't think Gerda feels the sadness,' said Henrietta. 'It's one of the compensations of being as she is. I don't think she feels things at all. She doesn't miss her mother. She doesn't fret about being abandoned.'

'We don't know what goes on in Gerda's mind. I hope they get a nice fir tree. That's a German custom, to have a tree and dress it up. We're doing it more and more at home since Prince Albert married the Queen.'

'The Queen's mother started it before that,' said Henrietta.

'I wonder what is done at Kaiserwald?'

'Nothing, I should imagine. Just a few more hymns and prayers.'

'Something ought to be done. I think it would do the patients a lot of good. My criticism of Kaiserwald is that there is not enough jollity.'

'You'd better try telling that to H.D.,' said Henrietta. H.D. was the Head Deaconess.

'I might well do that.'

'Have a care. You'll be sent off with a flea in your ear.'

I asked for a meeting with the Head Deaconess – an audience, Henrietta called it. It was granted to me with a show of graciousness. I did detect in the lady's manner a certain respect for me which Henrietta had failed to arouse in her.

I was told to sit, which I did. She herself was seated at a desk with papers before her which from time to time she touched, as though to remind me that the time she could give me was limited.

I came straight to the point.

'It will soon be Christmas. I was wondering what arrangements there were for Christmas Day.'

'We shall sing Christmas hymns and have special prayers.'

'Will there be no celebrations?'

'I don't understand you, Miss Pleydell.'

'Well, a Christmas tree, for instance.'

She stared at me disbelievingly and I went on: 'I thought we might have two . . . one at each end of the ward, and the curtain which divides the men from the women could be drawn back so that we are all together in one big room. I thought we should have a little gift for everyone. It wouldn't be much, of course . . . just a trifle. They could be on the trees and we could distribute them.'

She had let me go on for so long because she was stunned into silence. I realized that my temerity was unheard of. No one talked like that to the Head Deaconess. No one dared to attempt to introduce new methods into the Kaiserwald.

She lifted her finger to stop me. 'Miss Pleydell, I think you have not been here long enough to know our ways. These people are sick . . . some of them very sick . . .'

'I think it would do those good who are well enough to have a little light entertainment, a little relief. Their days must seem long and they are bored, which makes them listless without any great desire to live. If they could be amused, entertained, their spirits would rise.'

'We are not here to deal with their spirits, Miss Pleydell. We are here to heal their bodies.'

'Sometimes one is dependent on the other.'

'Are you telling me that you know how to run a hospital better than I?'

'No. I am not. But I am saying that outsiders can sometimes put up useful suggestions.'

'There is no sense in this idea. We need all the money we can get. There are many *sensible* things we could do with it.'

'This *is* sensible. I believe that to lighten the spirits helps to heal the body.'

'And suppose I agreed to your preposterous suggestion?

Where should we find the money to buy these – er – trifles. There are about a hundred patients, you know.'

'I do know it. I am sure that we should be presented with the trees. The people here think highly of the hospital.'

'And how do you know that?'

'Because I have talked to them. I know some of them well enough to be sure that they would do what they could for a cause like this.'

'And the trifles?'

'I shall buy those. Miss Marlington will want to help. There is a pedlar here who could get them for us. Little things . . . handkerchiefs . . . ornaments . . . something for them to have to make it a special day.'

'It *is* a special day. It celebrates the birth of Christ. We shall sing the Christmas hymns. I shall make sure that they are reminded of the significance of Christmas.'

'But the birth of Christ should be a matter for rejoicing. It should be a happy day. I believe we should see an improvement in our patients. There would be the anticipation . . . and the day itself. I think that making people happy, making them laugh, making them enjoy life is also good for their health.'

'And I think, Miss Pleydell, that you are wasting my time and yours.'

That was dismissal.

There was nothing I could do but retire.

A few days later the Head Deaconess sent for me.

'Sit down, Miss Pleydell,' she said.

I did so, wondering whether she was going to ask me to leave. I believed my suggestion had shocked her. She was a deeply religious woman of strong and noble character but entirely without humour. I was well aware that often such people are lacking in human understanding. I think she believed that everyone should accept her own high moral code, and that did not include the sort of frivolity which I had proposed to introduce into her hospital.

Her next words astonished me. 'I have been thinking about your ideas, Miss Pleydell. You have a certain talent for nursing. I have noticed this. But you do not always adhere to our methods.'

Oh dear, I thought. It is coming.

'You have the making of a good nurse. You believe, of course, that your proposed entertainment will be good for the patients. You would be ready to uphold this with financial support. You are fortunate to be in a position to be able to do that.' A faint smile turned up the corners of her mouth. I was amazed. It was the first time I had seen her face contorted into anything like a smile. 'Your friend Miss Marlington does not have your skills in this profession, I'm afraid. But she is cheerful, and willing. I believe the patients like her. I have spoken to Dr Bruckner and Dr Kratz and they think that your proposed action would have no ill effects on the patients. Miss Pleydell, I am going to allow you to try your experiment. We shall see how many of the patients are better for your Christmas Day arrangements; and also we shall see if it affects any of them adversely.'

'I cannot believe it will do that.'

'We shall see. I shall have nothing to do with this. It will be entirely your affair. You will get the trees . . . and the trifles from your own pocket. You will set it all up and you may recruit help from the other nurses if they agree. It is entirely in your hands. It will be to your credit or blame.'

'Oh, thank you,' I cried.

She waved her hand and again I saw that contortion of her features. I fancied she looked at me with something near affection. I was elated.

I went to find Henrietta who was wildly excited by the scheme. We planned how we would do it. We would seek out the pedlar. The fair was still in progress and he had a stall there. We would go and see him the next day, and we would tell the woodcutter to get us two trees – the biggest and best he could find. He could cut them a week before Christmas so that they would be fine and fresh.

'Now,' I said, 'we have to find Klaus the Pedlar. Tomorrow we will go to the fair.'

We were amazed at the response from our fellow nurses. Most of them wanted to help and it was only a few of the older ones who thought there was something sinful about enjoyment. There were always some ready to take over our duties so that we could have a little time now and then to throw ourselves into preparations.

The patients had been told that there was to be a Christmas tree on the great day and I was elated to see that many of them were excited by the prospect and there was no doubt that they were looking forward to Christmas Day. Those who were well enough talked to each other about it; it was only the very sick who were indifferent.

I was sure that we should find the pedlar at the fair. It was to be over on November 30th so we had to find him quickly.

The fair was held in a field close to the little town. As Henrietta and I walked over there we heard the sound of fiddles. The booths with their garish blues and reds made a splash of colour against the green of the trees. As we approached we saw young girls in local costume with pointed caps and a great many petticoats under skirts which flared out and showed the frothy whiteness underneath. The men had leather breeches and three-cornered hats decorated with feathers. I thought they looked very merry. In the square a group of young people were dancing to the tune of two fiddles. I wished I could have taken them to the hospital to amuse the patients. We stood and watched for a while and threw some coins into the box which had been put on the paving stones that passers-by might express their appreciation.

We wended our way through the stalls which were laden with goods for sale; there were saddlery, articles of clothing – shoes, boots, dresses – vegetables, eggs and cheese, fairings, cloth and jewellery of all kinds.

I asked if Klaus the pedlar was here and we were directed to his stall.

There he was, perched on a wooden box, haranguing passers-by, flattering the women one moment and the next telling them how foolish they were not to recognize the outstanding value of the goods he was offering for sale.

'Chances of a lifetime!' he was shouting. 'Come on, ladies. What are you thinking of? Are you going to let an opportunity like this slip by? Now you, my pretty, a nice piece of velvet for a gown . . . soft and clinging. With a figure like yours, you owe it to it. Yes, you do, lady.'

The woman was beguiled. She was fingering the velvet. Then he caught sight of us.

'Welcome, ladies. Come a-buying! English ladies. They know a good thing when they see it.'

'See to that lady, Klaus,' I said. 'Then we want to talk.'

He sold the dress length and then he turned to us.

'I want your advice about items with which to dress Christmas trees,' I said.

'You've come to the right man, my lovely. Everything you want Klaus has got. All you have to do is take a look. Now what would you like? You whisper to me, and I'll tell you this. If Klaus hasn't got it, he'll get it.'

'It's for the hospital,' I said.

He looked at me suspiciously. 'You wanting for free?' he asked.

'No, no. We're going to pay for it. We shall want about a hundred modest little gifts.'

'A hundred!' he cried. 'That's big business. We'll talk but not in the street here. No, this is done over a table. That's how big business is done.'

He put his fingers to his nose, I presume to denote understanding between two shrewd business associates. 'Here, Jacob,' he cried. A young man, little more than a boy, came running up. 'Take charge. I'm going to talk business.'

He led us across the square to a patch of green before the inn. During the warm weather there would be tables here, but the *Biergarten* was not used in the winter. We went inside and Klaus called for beer. It was brought in tankards and he leaned his arms on the table regarding us.

I told him briefly what we planned. He suggested fancy handkerchiefs for the women, all different colours, embroidered and not all the same; strings of beads, ornaments, little bowls in pretty colours, pictures of the forest in summer and in winter with snow; little figures, jugglers with bells on their ankles, fans. For the men plain handkerchiefs . . . big ones, puzzles . . . He'd think of other things.

I said: 'I can see you have the idea. We must have them a good two weeks before Christmas.'

'There's no hardship about that,' said Klaus. 'I'll bring them next visit. I'll have them all ready for you.'

'Can we trust you to do that?' asked Henrietta.

He looked at her with the utmost reproach. 'Of course you can trust Klaus. If I say I'll bring something it's as good as there. How would I do business otherwise? I'm in this place often twice a month. I never fail. If I say I'll bring something, that something's brought.'

'I am sure we can trust you, Klaus. Particularly as you know those poor sick people in the hospital are relying on you. If you did not come with the gifts it would be a terrible disappointment. We have the trees coming. You see how important it is.'

'You have my word on it, ladies. Now, we'll do a few calculations. How many men? How many women? Let's work it out, shall we?'

So we sat there drinking our beer and laughing at Klaus, who was clearly delighted with such a large order but a little fearful about the payment, until I told him that Henrietta and I would pay.

'You ladies must forgive me mentioning such a vulgar thing as payment, but I'm a poor man with his way to make.'

'Of course we must discuss payment,' I said. 'Would you like something on account?'

'*Mein Gott!*' he cried. 'It's a pleasure to do business with such ladies. Rest assured you shall have your fairings on the dot, and if it wasn't for the fact that you're so far above me, I'd be head over heels in love with the both of you.'

We began to realize that we had spent far too long at the

fair, but we had achieved our aim; and we knew that having left a deposit with Klaus we could be sure that he would deliver the goods we needed.

When we returned to the hospital we were told that the Head Deaconess was asking for us and that we were to go to her at once.

Henrietta grimaced. 'We shall be told that we are spending too much time on this. You'll see. I am sure H.D. doesn't really like the idea and is hoping it will be a failure.'

'I don't think so. I think if she finds it really does the patients good she will be pleased.'

'Well, I wonder what she wants now.'

'We had better go and see without delay.'

She was seated behind her desk. She nodded to us as we entered and begged us to be seated.

'From time to time we have visitors to the hospital,' she began. 'They are important people, mostly doctors. Next week we shall have such a visitor – very highly thought of, as are all our visitors. It is a doctor from England. Few of us here have a command of the English language and often that has proved a barrier. I wish you two to talk with our visitor, to tell him what he wants to know, if it is in your power to do so. My English, as you know, is not without its imperfections. I shall expect you to be as helpful as you can to Dr Fenwick.'

'We shall be delighted,' I said.

Henrietta added: 'It will be a pleasure.'

'I think he will be here for a few weeks. That is usually what happens. We will have a room prepared for him. Perhaps you will supervise that. You may know what he will expect; and when he arrives perhaps you would be here to greet him.'

We repeated that we should be delighted.

We were dismissed and when we were out of hearing Henrietta looked at me. 'Well, there's a surprise,' she said. There was mischief in her eyes. 'What excitement! We are going to see an Englishman. And a highly thought of one! Fancy! A little masculine society will not be unwelcome.'

'But you have Dr Bruckner and Dr Kratz.'

Henrietta shrugged her shoulders. 'You may keep them.'

'Thanks, but I'd rather not. You are very frivolous, Henrietta. But wait and see what this Dr Fenwick is like before you start seeing him as the hero of your dreams.'

'I have a feeling that he is going to be handsome, charming and just what I need to enliven my days.'

'We shall see,' I said.

True to his word, Klaus produced what he called 'the fairings' in good time and we were delighted by the transaction.

We were busy with our tickets and numbers, and a week before Christmas the trees were put into the ward and we decorated them with candles. The gifts were laid out and there was a good deal of enthusiasm in the ward. I was sure the idea was going to be a success.

And then Dr Charles Fenwick arrived.

Henrietta's premonition proved to be correct. If he was not exactly handsome, he was good-looking and certainly charming; he must have been about thirty and there was an earnestness about him which implied that he was dedicated to his work. When Henrietta and I received him, he was delighted to find two Englishwomen installed in the place, and our common nationality meant that friendship sprang up immediately.

Henrietta said it was blissful to have someone to talk to in English, and when I raised my eyebrows she added: 'I mean of the masculine gender.'

He asked a great many questions about everything and he thought our Christmas plan was an excellent one. He spent a lot of time with Dr Bruckner and Dr Kratz, and each day went round the ward with them. He wanted to know the details of every case and the doctors compared notes; it was clear that Dr Fenwick had a great respect for the methods employed at Kaiserwald.

He did walk with us once or twice in the forest. He thought the scenery enchanting and said he was sorry his visit would not be of long duration. He might stay six weeks at the most.

He smiled at us both as though to imply that we should be

one of the reasons – perhaps the main one – for his regrets.

But I told him that we ourselves would be leaving in a month or so. We had been allowed to come for three months and that time was drawing to a close. It was only due to Henrietta's connection with Miss Nightingale that we had been given permission to come at all.

'I see,' said Dr Fenwick, 'that they would not have expected ladies like you two to be of much use. How wrong they were! But I suppose neither of you had had any experience of nursing before.'

'None at all,' I told him.

'But Anna has a feel for the work,' said Henrietta. 'Even H.D. has noticed it and given grudging approval.'

'I realized that at once.'

He talked about the appalling conditions of hospitals throughout the world – and to our shame our own country was no exception – but fortunately there were places like Kaiserswerth and its subsidiaries and attempts were being made there to improve matters. He spoke of the patients, discussing their symptoms with us as Dr Bruckner and Dr Kratz never had, and when he went on to speak of home, I could see that he was anxious about the way events were moving.

'Is Russia still at war with Turkey?' I asked. 'We heard of it just before we left England.'

'It is rather alarming,' he said. 'When that sort of thing starts, one never knows where it will spread to. For a long time Russia has coveted the riches of Constantinople and the Sultan.'

'Thank Heaven it is all happening far from home,' said Henrietta.

Dr Fenwick looked at her seriously. 'Wars have a habit of involving those who are far away.'

'You don't think *we* shall be involved in all this nonsense?'

'I wish I could say no with conviction, but we cannot allow Russia to become too powerful. Besides, we are under obligation to the Turks. The Prime Minister is against war.'

'Do you mean that we . . . in England . . . could be at war?'

'If the situation develops, yes. Palmerston is all for war, and the people are behind him. I don't really like the look of things. People glorify war. To the man in the street, safely at home, it is all flag-waving and patriotic songs. It is a little different for the poor soldier. The sights I have seen . . . wounded . . . dead . . .'

'This is a very sombre conversation with Christmas just round the corner,' said Henrietta.

'Forgive me. I get carried away.'

He laughed, and we talked about the Christmas revelries and whether I was going to make H.D. agree that I was right.

But I felt uneasy.

However, that was all far away and here we were . . . Christmas time in the heart of the forest and mountains. It would be a Christmas quite different from anything we had known before.

I woke on the day with a tingling sense of excitement. There was no time to luxuriate in bed. It was five o'clock – time to rise.

I looked across at Henrietta; she was fast asleep. I got out of bed and went to her. She looked very pretty with her curling hair in disarray – so innocent, childlike almost. A wave of tenderness swept over me when I thought of all the hardships she had endured and how different her life was now from what it would have been had she married Lord Carlton. Yet she appeared to have no regrets. She talked a great deal about freedom. I understood, of course. I myself had the same respect for it.

'Wake up,' I said. 'And happy Christmas.'

She opened her eyes slowly and looked at me. 'Oh, leave me alone,' she wailed. 'I was having such a beautiful dream. I was in the forest and a wicked old troll came running after me. A handsome knight came riding by and was just about to rescue me. Guess who?'

'Could it possibly have been Dr Charles Fenwick?'

She shook her head. 'Nothing so predictable . . . and really far more exciting. He wore a mask over his face and when he took it off, there he was black-haired, black-eyed, entirely wicked . . . our Demon Doctor. It was so maddening to be awakened just at that moment. I wanted to know what was going to happen next. You know, Anna, we have been rather forgetful of The Project all these weeks. I don't think you have given any thought to anything but that Christmas tree.'

'It has taken a certain amount of planning, and then we have our other more arduous duties.'

'Oh, why didn't you let me stay there in the forest with our Demon?'

'Come on. We'll be late for breakfast.'

What a day it was! It stands out in my memory for ever. I was amazed what a transformation those Christmas trees made to the ward. Those who were well enough talked excitedly to each other and for days there had been a buzz of anticipation.

And now . . . Christmas Day! I thought of the festive season in India when the English community there were so anxious to make what they called an English Christmas. But how could they do that? It never seemed to be right somehow. The traditional Christmases I had known had been at the rectory, with the children's party in the church hall and the carol singers coming round, standing at the gates, bearing lanterns, singing the carols we knew, out of tune perhaps, but that did not matter; and the services in church with the choir boys proclaiming in innocent, impersonal voices the glory of Christ's birth, but in a way which betrayed that their thoughts were far away, and they were all the more moving because of that. Goose . . . and Christmas pudding brought to the table in a coating of brandy flames. And Grace's homemade wine and the services in church. These were the Christmases I remembered; the Christmases at the Minster, with the knowledge that Aubrey and I were growing farther and farther apart; Christmases with Julian – the crib I had put in the nursery and the little baby Jesus who was to be slipped into it on Christmas Day, as I told myself that the next year he would understand what it was all about. But there was not to be a next year for him.

Christmas was a time for remembrance, and I had a feeling that this was going to be one which I should remember forever.

The excitement of the present-giving was all I had anticipated. Dr Fenwick picked the numbers; Henrietta picked the
names; and I found the present and took it to the patient for
whom it was intended.

It was amazing how much pleasure these little gifts gave. It
was not so much the handkerchief or the fan or the little jars
and boxes; it was the spirit of Christmas; the fact that there
was a day set apart from the others.

The presentation had taken place after the midday meal,
and we gave a little concert – if that was not too grand a name
to put to it. One of the nurses played the recorder, and Dr
Kratz gave a performance on the violin. Henrietta, who had
quite a pretty voice, sang.

I was deeply moved to watch her. She sang a variety of songs
– the old English ones which the patients could not have
understood, but they loved them. It was all spontaneous and
her choice was wide. We had *The Vicar of Bray* followed by
Annie Laurie, Come, Lasses and Lads, followed by *Early One
Morning*. She conveyed the exuberance of the country people
so vividly that although they could not understand the words,
they were aware of the sentiments expressed. With her fair
curly hair looser about her face than she normally wore it for
working the wards, she looked beautiful.

I noticed Dr Fenwick watching her as she sang and I thought:
I believe he is falling in love with her.

It seemed to me so very natural that a man should fall in
love with Henrietta.

The Christmas venture was – as no one could deny – an
outstanding success, and with the honesty of the strong, the
Head Deaconess did not attempt to do so. Others might have
carped a little. It could have been said that some of the patients
were overtired or that it had been disturbing for those who
were very ill; but it was not. The advantages had far outweighed
the disadvantages.

The Head Deaconess called Henrietta and me to her study
and said: 'It was very commendable. The doctors have nothing

but praise. You both worked very hard, and did not neglect your other duties.'

'Who could believe it!' said Henrietta as we left her. 'Do you know, I think she almost smiled. She could not quite achieve such a tremendous undertaking, but I could see it was beginning to break out.'

'At least, she did admit it was a success.'

'She had to. It was obvious, wasn't it?'

We lived in the glow of that success for several days and then it was the New Year.

'In a short time,' I reminded Henrietta, 'we shall be leaving.'

'Shall you be sorry?'

'I don't think so. It has been interesting. I feel I have learned a lot. I feel experienced . . . and it has been wonderful, but I should not want to spend my life here, would you?'

'It would be rather dull without Dr Fenwick.'

I looked at her sharply.

'Well,' she said, 'wouldn't it be?'

'Of course.'

'He's like a breath of home. It's nice to have someone who sees our jokes . . . someone one can talk to naturally. You know what I mean.'

'I do.'

'He has a great admiration for you.'

'And for you, I think.'

She shrugged her shoulders. 'He really thinks there is something special about you. He says you should not be doing the humble tasks in nursing. You should be in charge, organizing . . . Oh yes, *you* have impressed him very much.'

'I think you have, too.'

'Two Englishwomen, obviously used to a little comfort coming out to a place like this. Of course, I didn't tell him it was all part of a grand scheme and that in the guise of nurses we are sleuths on the track of a monster.'

'I'm glad you didn't. He would have thought we were mad.'

She laughed and I wondered if she reciprocated the doctor's feelings for her.

It was cold and there was snow on the mountains. We were told later that it could be heavy. Preparations were made in Kaiserwald as though for a siege. One of the nurses told me that we could wake up one morning to find the snow piled high, shutting us in. Last year, for three weeks, they had been unable to get out of the hospital. We had to be prepared for such things.

Henrietta and I were to leave in February. I knew that I should miss the place, but I did want to move on. There was no doubt in my mind that the change of scene, the sense of achieving a few steps towards my goal, had soothed my sorrow. But it was still there, ready to envelope me at any moment.

Charles Fenwick said that, if we agreed, he would arrange to travel back to England with us. Henrietta was delighted at the idea.

'Does that mean you will have to extend your stay here?' I asked.

'A little, perhaps, but I have spoken to the Head Deaconess and she is quite agreeable. She thinks you two ladies should have an escort and it would be unseemly for you to travel across Europe unattended.'

'We did come out alone.'

'Yes, but that rather shocked her. She will be pleased to allow me to remain until your departure which, I believe, is to take place at the beginning of February.'

So it was agreed.

The days took on a new quality because they were numbered. We savoured each one. I had proved without doubt that I had a talent for nursing; even the Head Deaconess recognized this and treated me with a respect she did not show to Henrietta or even to her trained nurses.

I had several talks with Dr Fenwick — in fact he seemed to talk with me more than with Henrietta. With me he discussed the patients' illnesses, how best to treat them; he told me how frustrated he felt, how ignorant of causes; and how alarming it was to have to work in the dark, so often experimenting, as it were. 'But we have to find out,' he said. 'What can we do?

227

We believe a certain method may be the cure, but how can we tell until we have tried it?'

He talked to me, also, about the political situation. 'I can only hope that this does not involve us in war. People do not realize the horrors of war . . . of soldiers in some foreign battlefield without hospitals, without medical attention, doctors . . . nurses . . .'

I said: 'I have had a glimpse into one of those hospitals in London. It was a horrifying experience.'

'Then you can imagine something a thousand times worse.'

'People everywhere must find a way of changing that.'

He looked at me with something like the admiration I had seen in his eyes when he had watched Henrietta singing *Early One Morning*.

'Something will be done. It is comforting to know that there are people like you in the world.'

'You overestimate me.'

'I don't think so,' he said.

I could not help feeling a glow of pleasure; and we were joined by Henrietta and were soon laughing.

It was the end of January; the weather was a little warmer and the snow had thawed. I put on strong boots and went for a walk in the forest. Henrietta was on duty at that time and I was alone.

I came to Frau Leiben's cottage. I wondered whether Gerda would be out on such a day. As I walked past the door opened and my name was called. I recognized Frau Leiben's voice.

'Fräulein . . . Fräulein Pleydell. Come . . . come here . . . quickly.'

Hastily I went into the cottage. She took me through to a room in which was a bed. On it lay Gerda, writhing in pain.

'Please . . . help . . .' stammered Frau Leiben.

I went to Gerda. 'Gerda,' I said, 'what is it? Where is the pain?'

She did not answer, but went on moaning.

I turned to Frau Leiben. 'Go at once to the hospital. Tell one of the doctors he must come here at once.'

She hastily put on boots and cape and was off. She was a frightened woman – and so was I when I turned to the girl, for I could see that she was very ill indeed.

I put my hand on her forehead; it was very hot.

'Gerda,' I said. 'You know me. I am here with you. I'm going to take care of you.'

That seemed to soothe her a little. I kept my hand on her forehead.

But after a few minutes she was screaming with pain.

Never had time passed so slowly. It seemed hours before Dr Fenwick arrived. He took one look at Gerda and said to me: 'Go back to the hospital, arrange some transport. I want her in the hospital quickly.'

I ran off.

And so we brought Gerda to Kaiserwald. She was given a small room – little more than a cell – but she could not have gone with the others.

Dr Bruckner was with Charles Fenwick and they sent for one of the nurses. I was a little hurt, because I was not the one. I had felt I could soothe Gerda. She knew me and I believe she trusted me. I found it difficult to go back to my work without knowing what was happening.

It was late. I could not sleep. I decided to do what I could to find out. I crept along to the room in which Gerda lay. It was very quiet and a terrible fear came to me.

The door of her room opened and Charles Fenwick came out. He stared at me. 'Miss Pleydell!' he said.

'I was anxious about Gerda,' I said.

'She's a little better.'

'Thank God.'

'She will live, though it is touch and go.'

'May I see her?'

'Better not. Wait until tomorrow. She has been very ill.'

'What was it?'

He looked at me steadily but did not answer. 'You should go to bed,' he said at length. 'You'll have to be up early in the morning.' He laid his hand on my arm. 'She will recover. She is strong and healthy. I'll talk to you in the morning. Good night, Miss Pleydell.'

There was nothing I could do but return to my bed.

The next morning I went to her room. I opened the door and looked in. She was lying in bed with her yellow hair loose about her face. She was very pale and looked as though she were dead.

One of the nurses was sitting by her bed.

I said a *Guten Morgen* and asked after the patient.

'She has had a quiet night,' was the answer.

In the afternoon Charles Fenwick came to me and asked if Henrietta and I would be going for a walk in the forest. When I said we should, he asked if he might accompany us.

As we walked under the trees I asked about Gerda. 'Has she really recovered?'

'I think it will be some weeks before she does so completely. She almost killed herself.'

'Killed herself!' I cried.

'She had an accomplice, of course.'

'What do you mean?' demanded Henrietta.

'Gerda was pregnant. She has just had an abortion.'

'What?' I cried. 'That's impossible!'

'She's too young,' said Henrietta.

'She was old enough,' said Charles.

'Gerda! No. I won't believe it.'

'That girl knows more than you would give her credit for. In the first place she becomes pregnant and then she attempts to do away with the child.'

'Which she has done, presumably,' said Henrietta.

'And nearly killed herself in the process.'

'I still can't believe it.'

'The evidence makes it clear.'

'But who . . .?'

'There must be people who would take advantage of a girl like that.'

Vague scraps of conversation came to me. What had she said about meeting the Devil in the forest? What could she have been implying? Whom could she have meant?

'The poor innocent child,' I said.

'Not so innocent,' corrected Charles. 'She knew what it was all about when she decided to be rid of the child.'

'But how could a girl like that get the means . . .?'

'No doubt she took something given to her by her lover.'

'This is terrible. Do you know who it could possibly be?'

He shook his head. 'Someone with a little knowledge of these things.'

'A little knowledge can be dangerous. Have you spoken to her?'

'No. She is too ill. I am only thankful that we brought her here in time. But for you, Miss Pleydell, calling us in so that we were able to bring her to the hospital . . . well, it could have been the end of Gerda.'

'I'm so glad I passed the cottage that day. Why didn't Frau Leiben call for help?'

'She probably knew what was wrong and thought she could manage to look after the girl.'

'You mean the grandmother may have procured that stuff?'

'One never knows. All I can tell you is that Gerda was pregnant and took something calculated to get rid of the baby . . . and it did . . . though in the process it nearly got rid of Gerda herself.'

'It's a terrible thing . . .'

'I shall warn her about taking such things. She must never do it again.'

Henrietta was thoughtful. 'Well, it worked,' she said. 'That's what Gerda will say.'

'We must impress on her that she must never do it again.'

'Her own suffering will do that more forcefully than any talking could do,' I said.

'That's true,' agreed Charles Fenwick. 'But she should never have done what she did.'

'Never have been carried away by the blandishments of a lover,' added Henrietta. 'But people are human.'

'I'd like to know how she got hold of that stuff. Some old woman, most likely. That should be discovered and stopped.'

'Well,' said Henrietta thoughtlessly, 'perhaps it has turned out for the best.'

'I should not like to have to make a decision on that,' said Charles. 'And I should very much like to know more about the case. First, who was the scoundrel who took advantage of her innocence, and who was the one who gave her that destructive potion. I want her watched for a day or so until she is back to normal.'

'You think she isn't normal now?'

'I do not. She is in a sort of daze.'

'One is never sure what Gerda knows.'

'She is sure to be in a highly emotional state. I am going to suggest that you, Miss Pleydell, are put in charge of her. I could not ask you earlier as we needed a nurse experienced in midwifery. Now I think you will be the best for her.'

'Shall I go to her right away?'

'First I will see the Head Deaconess. She has agreed that you shall look after the girl, but I will see her first . . . as soon as we return.'

I sat by her bed. How frail she was! I stroked the unruly curls back from her narrow brow, and she opened her eyes and smiled at me.

'I'm in Kaiserwald,' she said.

'That's right. You've been ill and you are getting better.'

She nodded and closed her eyes.

I continued to stroke her brow.

'That's nice,' she murmured. 'It makes me feel better.'

She slept a while and I did not wake her until I took some gruel to her.

'Am I going to stay here?' she asked.

'Until you are better.'

'I was ill, wasn't I?' Her face crumbled. 'It hurt. It hurt so much.'

'It was because of what you took, Gerda. Where did you get that medicine?'

She smiled secretively.

'Did you know what it would do?'

'It was to make me better.'

'It gave you a lot of pain.'

'It made me better.'

I said: 'You told me about the Devil. You met him in the forest. Was it the Devil who gave it to you?'

She wrinkled her brow.

'Who was it you met in the forest, Gerda?'

She was silent.

'You told me it was the Devil.'

She nodded. Her face changed and she was smiling. I could see that in her mind she was back there with whoever it was who had seduced her.

'Who?' I whispered.

She whispered back: 'It was the Devil.'

'And who gave you the medicine?'

She closed her eyes. She looked very ill and I thought I should not be questioning her. I am bringing it all back to her, I thought. I am worrying her when what she needs is peace. I must wait until she is better.

But something told me I was not going to find my answer from Gerda.

Gerda grew stronger every day. After two weeks she left Kaiserwald and went back to her grandmother. She looked very frail, daintier than ever; and she seemed quite guileless and unaware of what had happened.

I did talk to her grandmother once. The poor old lady was griefstricken. I tried to comfort her.

She said: 'That it should happen to one of mine! I never thought to see that.'

'Frau Leiben,' I said, 'have you any idea who . . .'

She shook her head. 'There aren't many young men about here. They go to the towns when they're old enough. There's

233

little for them here . . . and those who are here are decent young men. They wouldn't take advantage of Gerda.'

'I suppose one can never be sure what people will do on impulse. She talked about the Devil.'

'One of her fancies. She was always one for fancies. She talks sometimes of seeing the trolls. It's due to all those tales Herman used to tell her.'

'And that stuff she took. Did you see anything of that?'

'Nothing. I thought she was a little changed. I had no idea that she was three months gone.'

'It must have been a great shock. What has upset the doctors is that she might have killed herself. They would like to know who gave her whatever she took. If you should ever find out, I think you should let the doctors know. They are very anxious that such a thing should not occur again.'

She looked startled.

'Oh,' I said quickly, 'they weren't thinking of Gerda, but of some other girl who might find herself in a similar position.'

'If I knew I would tell,' she said.

And I believed her.

February was almost upon us. It was the month of our departure. Our minds had been so taken up with Gerda's affair that we had not realized how speedily the time was passing.

Our walks through the forest took on a new significance for me. Often I thought: I shall soon say goodbye to all this. I wonder if I shall ever see it again.

It had been a very worthwhile experiment. It had in a way put a bridge between me and my grief. There had been quite long periods when I had been so involved in what was going on around me that I had forgotten my loss. Now I could believe that I was on the way to making a new life for myself.

Charles Fenwick contrived to be free when we were and the three of us walked together in the forest. Talk now was about plans for going home.

Charles said that it was good to see what was happening in Germany, and it was very commendable, but of course there

234

was plenty of room for improvement even here, in diagnoses if not in nursing care.

'They will miss you two,' he said. 'You must have been a most useful acquisition to the nursing staff.'

'They'll miss you, too,' I replied.

'Well, Kratz and Bruckner are very efficient . . . very methodical, very conscientious.'

'Very German,' added Henrietta.

'You could say that. They have made this into an excellent establishment. I had heard good reports about it from a friend of mine who was here not long ago.'

'Another doctor, I suppose?'

'Yes, a very eminent man. Dr Adair.'

'And he was favourably impressed?'

'Very. And he would be hyper-critical. He did say there could be improvements. But he is appalled by conditions in hospitals throughout the world.'

'Perhaps he will do something about it?'

'I feel sure he will. He is the sort of man who takes up something and very soon it is done. His energy is prodigious.'

'He sounds something of a paragon,' said Henrietta.

'I don't know about that.' He laughed. 'There have been some scandals about him.'

'I am becoming more and more interested,' cried Henrietta.

'Well, there always would be about such a man. He has been out East . . . travelled very widely . . . lived among the natives as one of them. He has written books about his adventures. He believes that we should not shut our eyes to the methods of other races simply because they are alien to us. He believes that people may have drugs or methods of healing that we might well learn from.'

My heart was beating furiously. I heard myself say: 'What did you say this doctor's name was?'

'Adair.'

'I read a book once by a doctor who did just that. But it was not Adair.'

'Was it Damien?'

'Yes.'

Charles laughed. 'That is his name . . . his Christian name. He writes under the name of Damien. Apparently it would be inconvenient to use his full name. He needs some anonymity.'

I was looking at Henrietta. She opened her mouth to speak, but I silenced her with a look.

I said slowly: 'And he was here recently?'

'Oh yes. It must have been only a short time before you arrived.'

I felt dizzy. We might have met him. I pictured myself coming face to face with him.

'Do you see him . . . often?' I asked.

'Good Heavens, no! He's here, there and everywhere. He's always busy on some project. An eminent man, as I said. But I did happen to see him when he came back this time. He told me about this place and said it was well worth a visit. As a matter of fact, he arranged it for me.'

'That's very interesting,' I said. 'After having read his books . . .'

'Perhaps you will meet him one day.'

'I hope to,' I replied.

When he left us to see a patient, Henrietta said: 'At last we are on the trail.'

'Just think. We might have met him.'

'Fate must have brought us here. I wonder about him. Charles seems to think highly of him. Do you detect a little hero-worship?'

'Yes,' I said. 'It's the effect he seems to have on some people. My brother-in-law Stephen was the same.'

'He must be a fascinating man.'

'He's devilish,' I said.

'Well, that doesn't mean he isn't fascinating. That sort of person can be . . . very. What are we going to do?'

'I'm not sure. But at least we have discovered who he is. We know his name. That's a great step forward.'

'And now we are qualified nurses. But would you say we were qualified?'

'Hardly, after a few months making beds and washing linen.'

'Still, Kaiserwald has a name, and now we are in the profession, who knows, we might come across him somewhere. We've got to do all we can to make sure we do . . . and do you think Charles is going to say "Goodbye and it was nice to have met you" when we get home? Because I don't. I think we have a friend there. And don't forget *he* is a friend of our Demon Doctor. We will invite him to the house. That will please Jane and Polly. And we will say – or I will, because that sort of thing comes more naturally from me – "And do bring that fascinating friend of yours. We are so interested in the East – and as you know, Anna was once in India."'

I felt an immense excitement at the prospect.

'Which one of us will slip the hemlock into his glass?' went on Henrietta. 'It had better be your task. You have the stronger feelings. I have just a terrible fear that I might fall in love with him.'

'You are quite repulsive.'

'Yes, I know I am. But it is all rather exciting.'

'There is something which has occurred to me, Henrietta.'

'Please tell.'

'He was here. Remember he is devilish. Perhaps he saw Gerda in the forest. She said it was the Devil, didn't she? Perhaps . . .'

She stared at me aghast. 'Oh no, not our much travelled, worldly, brilliant Devil Doctor and simple little Gerda.'

'Why not? I could imagine her being very attractive to a man like that. He would experiment. Isn't he always experimenting? And where did she get the potion or whatever it was that almost killed her? Charles said it was something very effective. Somebody who knew about such things would have given it to her.'

Henrietta continued to stare at me in disbelief.

'It fits,' she said. 'It's too much of a coincidence. He was here. You can imagine him . . . probing into methods . . . harrying poor old Bruckner and Kratz, bearding H.D. in her den, demanding to know this and that. His supercilious smile, his condemnation of everything. I expect his German is fluent.

It would be, wouldn't it? And then . . . for a little light relaxation he strolls in the woods and there he comes upon the pretty little goose girl. Simple, desirable, experimental material. "Come with me, child. I will show you the delights of nature." Perhaps he thought it would be a good idea to see what sort of child this simplest of girls could produce after mating with the most brilliant of men. On the other hand, he gave her the dosage. Better perhaps to eliminate all evidence of that frolic in the woods. Perhaps after all, that was all it was . . . a little light recreation for the god on Earth.'

'All this has occurred to me. I am becoming more and more convinced that he is responsible. Who else could it be? Frau Leiben's neighbours would respect her granddaughter too much to do such a thing. They are kind people . . . neighbourly, friendly. Oh, how I wish Gerda would tell us.'

'At least,' said Henrietta, 'we now know who our quarry is. Never fear, we shall track him down in time. I feel it in my bones.'

'Yes,' I said. 'We shall.'

Storm at Sea

It was a mild February day when we arrived back in England. We had stood on the deck and watched the white cliffs getting nearer – Henrietta on one side of Charles, I on the other. We all admitted to a certain emotion at being in sight of home.

Charles insisted on taking us right to the house. From there he would go to his home in the Midlands. He was a little uncertain about what he would do. His father was in practice and he might join him. He had, however, thought of going into the army, for he believed there was a dearth of doctors in that sphere and they were greatly needed.

At the moment he was wavering between prospects. It was for that reason he had wanted to go to Kaiserwald to, as he said, 'sort the thing out'.

Joe was waiting with the carriage at the station and his pleasure at seeing us was evident. 'Them girls of yours, Miss Pleydell, have been counting the days,' he said. '"You're a fine pair," I said to them. "Living like ladies you are, and pining to have 'em back." They said it wasn't natural just being there without you two ladies to look after.'

'It's a nice welcome home,' I said.

And when we arrived Jane's and Polly's delight was obvious. They were a little shy – so unlike them – and I was deeply touched.

Then there was all the bustle. Lamb chops done with sauce, 'Miss Marlington being so fond of them. And there's some of that there cheese for you, Miss Pleydell. Jane went all over the place to find it. Ain't it a mystery how they've never got what you want when you want it.'

'A little like life,' I commented. 'This is Dr Fenwick who was with us at Kaiserwald.'

Jane and Polly dropped little curtsies. 'And he'll be here for lunch, Miss?'

'Yes.'

'Lay another place, Poll.'

It was good to be home.

I wanted to hear about Lily and they exchanged looks which were revealing.

'Really?'

'Yes, Miss . . . really.'

'When?'

'July.'

'And she's delighted?'

'My goodness, Miss, you should see them Clifts. You'd think nobody had ever had a baby before.'

My thoughts went back to poor little Gerda who must have been very frightened to take that evil medicine. How different was Lily.

Luncheon was served with great ceremony. Charles was impressed by the devotion of our servants. He kept saying how glad he was that we had met at Kaiserwald. 'It was quite the nicest thing that happened there.'

When he left in the afternoon Joe took him to the station.

'We shall meet again soon,' he said before he went. 'I shall be in London and I'll call, if I may.'

'We shall look forward to that.'

He took my hand and that of Henrietta. I thought how good he would be for her, but I did wonder whether she would be for him. I was so fond of her; but at times she seemed a little reckless, so eager to grasp at life. Compared with her, I was a sober experienced woman. Perhaps that was what suffering did for one.

In any case I hoped that we should see Charles Fenwick again.

It was difficult settling into the old life. There had been so much to do at Kaiserwald that we had snatched at our few hours of leisure. At first it seemed so luxurious to sleep in a comfortable bed, to have one's breakfast brought in to one – which Jane and Polly insisted on doing – to have a varied diet of dishes tastefully prepared. How different from thin broth and the same vegetables over and over again, a real cup of tea instead of that brewed from rye. Jane's comment was that they had starved us at that place. You could never trust foreigners and Jane and Polly were going to feed us up; they prepared delicacies which we had to eat for fear of offending them.

'You will make us into two fat ladies,' complained Henrietta. She looked wryly at her hands and I glanced at mine – no longer beautiful. Wielding a scrubbing brush and constant immersion in water had made them chapped, and the nails, which had been a problem often, were only just beginning to grow normally.

Henrietta said that our first task would be to bring them back to their pre-Kaiserwald state, for such hands as ours had become would never be accepted in London society.

'Are we going into London society?' I asked.

'We have to be ready to pursue our Devil Doctor whenever the opportunity occurs, and I have a notion that he moves in the highest circles.'

We smothered our hands in goose grease every night and went to bed in cotton gloves.

Often I thought of Gerda, and I felt a great anger against the man who had seduced her. I was sure it was he – the man who had ruined Aubrey's life and had failed to save my son's. And I hated him as much as I ever had.

On the very day of our arrival, Lily came to see us. She was radiant and already looked a little matronly.

We told her how delighted we were and she talked a great deal about the coming baby; it was clear that she was a very contented young woman.

'And I owe it all to you, Miss,' she said. 'Just think, if I hadn't been run down by your carriage . . .'

'Perhaps you owe it to the man who almost ripped off the buttons. You see, Lily, causes and effects are everywhere. They go back and back in time.'

'I suppose you're right, Miss. But I reckon I owe it all to you.'

'I'm happy to see you happy, Lily.'

'There's only one thing to worry us.'

'What's that?'

'That William might have to go away.'

'You mean into foreign service?'

'Well, that wouldn't be so bad, because I'd go with him, taking the baby. But it's all this talk of war.'

'War?'

'Oh, you've been away. The papers have been full of it. Something about Russia and Turkey and all the people saying we ought to show 'em, and calling for Lord Palmerston and all that.'

'I see.'

Some of the joy had gone out of her face. 'You see, Miss, William is a soldier.'

'Yes, of course. It's a pity. He might have been working in his father's shop.'

'That's what I'd like him to do. Of course, he looks very fine in his uniform.'

'And that's how you fell in love with him. Don't worry. Perhaps nothing will come of it. After all, the trouble is between Russia and Turkey.'

'That's what William's father says. But there's been a lot in the papers and there are people as thinks we ought to be out there fighting.'

'Well, let's hope nothing comes of it.'

But when I saw the papers and read some of the comments, I could understand why Lily was worried. I realized that in Kaiserwald we had been cut off from world affairs and that we were nearer to war than I had imagined. The great powers of Europe had attempted to intervene and bring about a peace between Russia and Turkey but Russia was determined to overcome what she called the 'Sick Man of Europe', meaning

Turkey, and would accept nothing but surrender. Negotiations were broken off and war seemed imminent.

There was tension in the streets. Everywhere one went there was talk of war. The headlines in the newspapers demanded intervention; anyone who stood against it was a traitor. We should go in, it was said, and we could settle the Russians in a week.

Battles are so easily fought and won at the dinner table or in the clubs or any place where people congregate; and the war was the main topic. Lord Palmerston should come back. He would show the Russians the might of Britain. Something had to be done. Russia was not only threatening Turkey, but us. Aberdeen's policy of peace at any price was the reason for Russia's intransigence, said some. Had Britain stood up and showed her intention to save Turkey, it would never have gone so far.

'Call back Palmerston,' screamed the press.

They blamed the Queen who was known to be against war, but most of all they blamed her husband.

It could not go on.

A few weeks passed. It was March of that memorable year. The paper boys were running through the streets shouting the news and people were dashing out of their houses to buy papers.

'France declares war on Russia.'

Now how could Britain stand aside?

The very next day it came. We were drawn into the conflict. The disastrous Crimean War had begun.

Poor Lily! Her joy was tempered with anxiety. William had his marching orders. Lily said twenty times a day: 'They say it won't last more than a week or two once our boys get out there.'

And we pretended to agree with her.

On the day William left we were all in the streets. The Queen watched the parade from the balcony at Buckingham Palace, proudly smiling down on all her fine soldiers. It was a splendid and deeply moving sight. The shouts were deafening and the people cheered the magnificent guards with the little drummer boys marching ahead on their way to embarkation at the docks. The triumphant sound of the bands rang out:

Some talk of Alexander, and some of Hercules
Of Hector and Lysander, and such great names as these.
But of all the world's great heroes, there's none that can compare
With a tow row row row row row for the British Grenadier.

I watched with the music ringing in my ears and looked at Lily who was soon to be a mother, and I prayed that William would come safely home to her.

Polly and Jane thought the soldiers were lovely and they were determined, as they said, 'to jolly Lily out of herself', so we all went back to the house and talked about the baby and we showed Lily the clothes we had collected for the layette; and Lily's spirits were lifted to some degree.

The next day we had a visitor. It was Charles Fenwick.

'I am in London for two days,' he said, 'so I had to come and see you. I am going to the Crimea.'

'When?' I asked.

'Immediately. The war has made up my mind. They are going to need doctors badly at the front. I applied to go and was accepted at once – and I am on my way.'

'I wish you all the luck.'

He smiled at me and then at Henrietta.

'When I come back,' he said, 'we must all meet again. May I call?'

'We shall be most put out if you do not,' said Henrietta.

Our leavetaking was a little brusque. I think we were all trying to hide our emotions.

People could talk of hardly anything but war. I think they had expected miracles of the army and they were impatient because there was no news of victory.

Promptly on time Lily's baby appeared and there was great rejoicing in both the Clift household and our own. Little Willie made even the war recede a little. He was a healthy, lusty boy and the pride of Lily's heart. We discussed him endlessly; as for Jane and Polly, they were overcome with delight in the child.

The diversion was welcome, for the euphoria of the people was beginning to evaporate.

What was happening out there? The summer was almost over when we heard of the victory of the British and French at the Alma. The war would soon be over now, everyone was saying. Our soldiers were out there and that spoke for itself. But disturbing accounts were appearing in *The Times*, whose war correspondent, William Howard Russell, was sending home some very alarming despatches.

There was a cholera epidemic which had smitten the army and men were dying, not of battle wounds but of disease. The hospital equipment was pitiful. The organization was non-existent and it was the lack of medical supplies and attention which was defeating our men. The enemy was disease and mismanagement – not the Russians.

The people were restive, looking for scapegoats; in vain did the army attempt to suppress these despatches; the hideous stories kept coming through.

Something had to be done.

One day there was a paragraph in the papers which startled us.

ADAIR FOR THE CRIMEA, it announced.

I read it aloud to Henrietta.

Dr Damien Adair is to go to the Crimea. He says that he is deeply shocked by what is happening out there. He wants to look into what is going on. He says it seems like an example of crass mismanagement. Dr Adair is that doctor whose Eastern travels have interested so many. He is an expert on the use of drugs in medicine. He left today and should shortly be on the spot.

I dropped the paper and looked at Henrietta.

'How I wish,' I said, 'that I could be there.'

'What harm do you think he will do?'

I shook my head. 'Wherever he is, disaster follows.'

'It seems it has come to the Crimea without him.'

'I wonder . . .'

'So do I.'

'Wouldn't it be exciting . . . if we could go?'

'We should never be allowed to.'

'I've always told myself that nothing is impossible.'

Henrietta shrugged her shoulders. 'He'll soon be back. Perhaps he'll be in London with Charles. Then we can ask them both to dinner.'

I kept thinking of him with his demon face and those poor men lying at his mercy in some ill-equipped hospital.

The Russell articles could not be ignored. Something had to be done – and it was.

The next item of news was that Miss Florence Nightingale had been asked to get together a group of nurses to take out to the Crimea. That was all we needed.

Henrietta, through her connections, had soon acquired the information as to how the nurses would be selected. We were to present ourselves at the home of the Herberts, who had lent it to Miss Nightingale for this purpose. It was in Belgrave Square and when we arrived we had to face four ladies, one of whom was known to Henrietta. I was not sure that this was an advantage, for she would have known of Henrietta's breaking off her engagement to Lord Carlton, which would be considered a feckless action, particularly as she had gone off and escaped from her social circle, disappearing into near obscurity.

We were studied with some amazement.

'Do you realize that this is going to be very hard work?' we were asked. 'It is not for young ladies like you.'

I retorted rather warmly: 'We have been for just over three months at Kaiserwald. There we worked very hard indeed and learned something about tending the sick. I think that I have an aptitude for the work and indeed this could be confirmed by the Head Deaconess of Kaiserwald. It is my firm desire to join the party of nurses. I hope you will consider us.'

'We have no doubt,' was the answer, 'that you are the sort of person Miss Nightingale would want, but I am warning you. The majority whom we have seen have been working girls without employment . . . girls who have to earn a living.'

'We want to come,' I said earnestly.

'Miss Marlington?' said our inquisitor, looking at Henrietta.

'I was at Kaiserwald. I worked hard and I want to go very much.'

'I will put your names before Miss Nightingale and I will tell her what impression you have made.'

We left – not exactly elated.

'I think,' said Henrietta sombrely, 'that I may have spoilt it for us both. They know of me and they regard me as feckless and frivolous. I'm sorry, Anna. You should have gone alone. They would have seized you, but I fancy you are a little contaminated by your proximity to one who has proved herself no asset to society.'

'Nonsense,' I said. 'We'll go and we'll go together.'

A little to my amazement, I was proved right.

A few days later we both had a note to say that we were accepted.

During the weeks which followed there was no time to think of anything but our impending departure. The journey to Kaiserwald had seemed an exciting adventure but it was nothing to this.

Jane and Polly were wide-eyed with amazement when they heard what we were going to do.

'Lord 'a mercy,' said Polly, 'I never heard the likes of what you two ladies get up to. I should have thought young men was what Miss Henrietta ought to be thinking of . . . As for you, Miss Pleydell, a little of that wouldn't do you a bucketful of harm.'

'We have made up our minds that we are going out to nurse the wounded soldiers.'

Lily said: 'If it wasn't for young Willie, I'd come with you. Look out for William, won't you, Miss.'

I said I would.

Joe shook his head in disbelief. 'And who's going to be riding in the carriage when you're out there?' he demanded. 'Carriages isn't meant to stand in Mews. They want to be out and about, rolling along the road.'

'It can wait until we come back.'

'You be careful,' said Joe. 'Wars is dangerous things.'

When we brought home our uniforms Jane and Polly were too shocked for speech. We had been told that the nurses would be dressed all alike. There were no concessions for ladies. We would all eat together, share duties and wear the same uniform. Miss Nightingale planned it so to create a new professionalism.

I must admit to a certain horror when I saw what we were to wear.

'Why,' demanded Henrietta, 'do we have to be ugly to be efficient?'

'Perhaps they are meant to imply: "Keep off, you gallant gentlemen. We are bent on duty."'

'I don't think any gentleman will feel very gallant when he sees us in these. Yours is too small. Mine is too big.'

It was true. The uniforms were not made to measure. There were sizes and we were given the nearest to what would fit us. We had what was called a wrapper, which was a tweed dress in an ugly shade of grey; a jacket of worsted in the same dull colour; a woollen cloak and a white cap.

When Lily saw them she held up her hands in dismay.

'Wherever did they find such things?' she demanded.

'They are designed especially to show that we are not to be regarded as objects of admiration,' I explained. Then I said to Henrietta: 'You don't look too bad in yours.'

'Which is more than I can say for you. You look as if you've robbed a scarecrow.'

Lily commented: 'They wouldn't look quite so awful if they fitted.'

'Perhaps you can shorten Henrietta's and turn up the sleeves,' I suggested.

Lily examined the garment. 'Yes, I can do that.'

'But I think mine is a hopeless case.'

She was kneeling at my feet. 'There's a tidy hem here . . . and as you're like a beanpole you don't take up much in the body. I could lengthen the sleeves, too.'

She got to work immediately, eager to do something for us. She was more sombre than the others. I think Jane and Polly thought our going to the Crimea was something of a joke. Lily did not take it quite like that. But I think she was secretly glad we were going. She had such a high opinion of me and believed I could look after William, for it seemed to her that I should be sure to find him, since we were going to the same place.

There was a slight improvement in our uniforms when they fitted better; and Lily, with her needle, was a miracle worker.

Feverishly we prepared for our departure, and on a bright October Saturday morning, we set out for London Bridge on our journey to the Crimea.

All the nurses were travelling together and I had my first glimpse of Miss Nightingale. She was an extremely handsome woman, which surprised me. I had heard, through Henrietta, that she could have made a brilliant marriage and been a star of society; instead she was absorbed by her mission, which was to nurse the sick and to give England hospitals of which she could be proud. She was noble. She was admirable. In fact I thought then – and this was confirmed later – that she was the most remarkable woman I had ever met. She was aloof, yet at the same time obviously watchful of everything which was going on. She had a rare dignity and distinction; and I thought her wonderful.

We were to go to Boulogne, where we would disembark and travel immediately to Paris, where we would spend one night; from there, we would go down to Marseilles, staying there for four days to enable supplies to be collected before we boarded the ship which was to take us to Scutari.

I was very eager to discover what our fellow nurses would be like. There were forty of them. 'All sorts and conditions,' said Henrietta to me. And indeed they were so. There were about half a dozen very like ourselves; as for the rest, they baffled me. Some of them had ravaged faces and were not very young. I wondered why they had been chosen, and I learned afterwards that they had been accepted in desperation because it had not been easy to recruit nurses for such an undertaking.

On the ship going to Boulogne, I had the opportunity of meeting some of them. Henrietta and I were on deck when one of the nurses, seeing Henrietta, called out: 'Henrietta! How wonderful to see you! So you are in this, are you? I think it is going to be interesting.'

She was a tall woman of about thirty with haughty patrician features. Henrietta introduced her: 'Lady Mary Sims. Miss Pleydell.'

We shook hands.

'Dorothy Jarvis-Lee is here, too,' said Lady Mary. 'We came together. When we heard about it, we were simply wild to come. Isn't Florence marvellous? Do you know, I don't think she wanted to take us. She wouldn't at first. It was only when they found it so hard . . . She thought we shouldn't care about mixing with *hoi polloi*. Oh, there is Dot. Dot, I've found Henrietta Marlington.'

Mrs Dorothy Jarvis-Lee came over. She was angular with a rather weather-beaten face, which suggested life in the country.

'Henrietta. So nice to see you.'

'And this is Miss Pleydell.'

We shook hands.

'I know you are a great friend of Henrietta. You went with her, didn't you, to that place in Germany?'

'Yes, Kaiserwald,' I said.

'It is supposed to be one of those pioneer places. When I heard about this, I felt I had to come. After all, it is a way of serving one's country.'

While we were talking I had noticed two women watching us. One was large and the other small and very pale. The larger one seemed to be bursting out of her uniform and the small one to hang in hers.

They were watching us intently and I saw a smile curve the lips of the big one. It was not very pleasant.

Then, turning to her companion, she said in a loud drawling voice which was obviously meant to be an imitation of that of Mrs Jarvis-Lee: 'Oh, 'ello, Ethel, what are you doing 'ere? Me . . . I've come to serve me country. I told Florence I'd come. I met 'er the other night at Lord Lummy's castle and he said to me, "'Ere, Eliza, why don't you go and 'elp Florence with the soldiers? Mind what company you keep 'cos you'll get some funny old birds going out with you. I don't suppose they've ever made a bed in their lives. Never mind, it'll be nice for you to mix in such company."'

There was silence while Mrs Jarvis-Lee and Eliza looked at each other. The contempt on one side, and the hostility could be felt.

Eliza said: 'Come on, Ethel. I reckon we ought to be careful what company we keep. We don't want to pick up with the likes of some.'

The smaller woman looked at us nervously, and big Eliza held her firmly by the arm as they walked off, Eliza swaying in a manner which she clearly thought was the affected manner of the rich.

'Well,' said Mrs Jarvis-Lee, 'if that is the sort we have to live with there is going to be trouble. She was deliberately insolent. I shall refuse to eat at the same table with people like that. I think there should be some way of seeing that ladies are kept separate from them.'

'I believe the rules are that we shall all be together and that there shall be no distinctions,' I said.

'I can see how impossible that will be,' was the response. And I felt that there would indeed be difficulties ahead.

I was amazed by the welcome which was given us when we embarked at Boulogne. Of course, the French were our allies; and I had no doubt that they also heard something of the conditions in Scutari and that we were going out to nurse the sick – not only our men but theirs, also.

They took our baggage and carried it to the hotel where we were to eat; there we were given a good meal, free of charge – so grateful were these good people, and so much did they admire what we were going to do.

It was about ten o'clock that night when we arrived at the Gare du Nord, to be fêted again. We were all very tired and after eating we went to the beds provided for us. Lady Mary Sims and Mrs Jarvis-Lee had collected three or four women rather like themselves and came with us.

Early next morning we were heading for Marseilles.

Our party kept together and we did a little sightseeing in Marseilles, making a few purchases of things we thought we should need. The resentment between Us and Them – as Mrs Jarvis-Lee put it – was growing, and I wondered how much good we were going to do if there was bickering among ourselves. In vain did I look for someone who felt as I did about nursing. I knew Miss Nightingale did, but what of the others? I was certain that Lady Mary and Dorothy Jarvis-Lee looked upon this as an adventure to enliven the monotony of the days and at the same time serve the country in a spectacular way. Several of the 'ladies' felt that, I was sure. On the other hand there were those who had worked now and then in hospitals and had some experience, but who were with us not because of a dedication to the nursing profession but because they needed to earn a living, and they thought that this might be an easy way of doing so.

Some of them smuggled bottles of gin into their luggage and it soon became obvious that there were several who indulged in tippling whenever they had the opportunity.

I thought of the strict discipline at Kaiserwald and the Deaconesses who had scarcely gone outside the hospital; and I trembled to think of how we should manage at Scutari.

My first sight of the *Vectis* was not very inspiring. She was an old ship, very battered, and even to a person who knew so little of such things it was obvious that she was scarcely in mint condition.

We boarded her at Marseilles for the trip to the Bosphorus and as soon as we settled in I knew that my fears were well grounded. Cockroaches scuttled across the decks . . . quick, silent, horrible. I don't know why they filled me with such revulsion; they were harmless, I supposed. I think it must have been because they were the outward sign of uncleanliness. It was impossible to walk without treading on them.

There was little comfort on board that ship. Even in calm seas its creaks and shudders alarmed me. We were eight in a cabin, and Dorothy Jarvis-Lee, who was adept in such matters, had marshalled eight of us to share.

'We want none of *them* near us,' she declared. 'I hope we are not going to spend very long on this dreadful ship.'

We had not been a day at sea when we ran into a violent gale, and our poor unseaworthy vessel was tossed about unmercifully by the cruel waves. Almost everyone was smitten with appalling seasickness and only wanted to stay in their bunks. I was relieved when we reached Malta, but quite a number of the nurses were too ill to go ashore. Miss Nightingale herself was laid low; and the ship had sustained some damage in the storm.

Henrietta and I went sightseeing with some of the nurses, in the charge of a soldier who was stationed at Malta headquarters. He herded us all together like sheep and it was not much fun. I was glad to return to the ship and to resume our journey, for I felt that the sooner we arrived at our destination and could leave the rickety *Vectis* the better.

Then we were on our way. The weather had not improved. The wind was howling round us and it was impossible to stand up.

I could not endure the fetid cabin with so many of my fellow travellers – including Henrietta – very sick, so I staggered out on to the open deck. The wind was fierce and the ship groaned and creaked so continuously that I felt that at any moment it was going to be torn apart, and I wondered what chances I should have in that turbulent water.

I almost crawled my way to a bench and sat down. I clung to the sides of it for I felt that at any moment I should be picked up and flung against the rail. So violent was the storm, so frail the vessel, that I began to believe that we should all be drowned. How strange that I should have come to such a point only to have reached the end.

I realized then how much I wanted to live. When Julian had died I had at times thought rather longingly of going with him. But now that death seemed very close, I knew how much I wanted to survive. The thought surprised me. Desperately I wanted to live, to do something with my life – to save life, to nurse the sick to health. It did not seem a world-shattering ambition. To be a nurse! It was not like being a great scientist or a doctor.

My thoughts switched to Dr Damien Adair. What was his purpose? I thought I knew. Honour for himself. Kudos. To strut upon the stage with the great, to be Dr Adair who had made amazing discoveries, who had lived a wildly adventurous life, who used people for his experiments and had not cared what became of them. If they died, it was all in a cause – the cause of the aggrandisement of the scientific discoveries of the great Dr Adair.

He had experimented with Aubrey. A terrible sadness came upon me when I thought of Aubrey. I think it was guilt. I kept remembering those first weeks of our honeymoon when everything had been perfect. And it could have been but for his addiction, which had ruined our marriage. And it was due to that man. I knew Aubrey was weak and should not have allowed himself to be led. But men like Damien Adair preyed on the weakness of others. They cared nothing for the ruins they left behind. All that mattered to Damien Adair was the acquisition of knowledge which he would use for his own glory. He had ruined my husband; then he had experimented on my son. He had destroyed them both.

Oh, how much I wanted to live! I wanted to come face to face with him. I wanted to stop him using other people as he had used my husband and my son.

I clung to the bench on which I sat. 'I am going to find him,' I said, 'and I am going to nurse the sick. I am going to heal them . . . and I am going to find him.'

I was then aware of a frail figure stumbling along the deck. It was Ethel, the girl I had noticed before – pale, thin, half-nourished. She was often with the blowsy and bellicose Eliza – and incongruous companions they were.

I was sure the forceful Eliza was aware of the divisions between Them and Us which were already building up, and she resented them deeply.

But this was frail Ethel.

I watched her staggering along. At times I thought she would be thrown over. She was so light. She clung to the rail and leaned over; she stood very still for a while, the wind tearing at her hair and shrieking around her like a thousand banshees . . . looking down into the swirling waters. She moved . . . lifting herself. I knew instantly what she intended to do.

I dashed from my bench. The wind impeded me and the rolling of the ship made progress difficult, but I struggled towards her with all my strength.

'No!' I shrieked, but my voice was caught on the wind and she must have thought it part of the storm.

I reached her just as she was going over. I seized her and pulled her to safety.

She turned and looked at me. I saw the despair in her little face. I cried: 'No . . . no. You must not. That's not the way.'

She continued to stare at me and I took her arm. I dragged her to the bench. She sat beside me, my arm in hers holding her tightly.

'I saw . . . in time,' I said.

She nodded. 'I wanted to. It was best, really.'

'No. You just feel like that now. You'll feel differently later. I know.'

'He's gone,' she said blankly as though talking to herself. 'I won't never hold him again. He was so pretty. He was all I had, and now he's gone.'

'Perhaps he'll come back.'

'He's dead,' she cried. 'Dead . . . dead . . . my little baby's dead.'

I felt an immediate kinship with this girl.

I heard myself say: 'I know . . . I know.'

'You can't. Nobody can. My little baby was all I had. He was everything. There was nothing else. If I hadn't have gone out . . . I had to, though. I had to get money somehow. He was my little baby and when I came back he was gone. I wanted to get things for him . . . good broth and milk and it was all for him. And I came in . . . he was lying there . . . cold . . . stone cold . . . and his little face like wax.'

I kept saying: 'I know. I understand. Nobody could understand better than I.'

The depth of my emotion seemed to convey itself to her. She turned to me and saw the anguish in my face. Oddly enough, it did not surprise her; and I realized that in that moment, a bond had been forged between us.

'Do you want to talk?' I asked. 'If you don't, it doesn't matter. Just sit with me.'

She was silent for a while, then she said: 'I knew it was wrong. There wasn't enough . . . not in sewing.'

Sewing! So she was in the same profession as Lily had been. I supposed there were many of them in attics stitching away for dear life.

> Stitch, stitch, stitch
> In poverty, hunger and dirt,
> Sewing at once with a double thread
> A shroud as well as a shirt.

'I had to earn some money . . . for him.'

'Yes,' I said, 'I understand.'

'I didn't want him, but when he came . . . oh, he was all the world to me, my little Billy was. And then to come in like that and find him . . . I should never have left him.'

'You had to. You did your best.'

She nodded. 'You shouldn't have stopped me.'

'Yes, I should. You'll see that one day. You'll be glad.'

'You couldn't know.'

'I could. I lost a child . . . a little boy.'

'You!'

'My husband is dead, too. I don't tell people about it. I prefer to be thought . . . unmarried. It's a secret.'

'I won't tell.'

'Thank you. But you see why I understand. My little boy was everything to me.'

'He wouldn't have gone hungry.'

'No. But I have lost him, all the same. I'm telling you this so that you know I understand.'

And then I was living it all again. I felt my cheeks wet, and not with spray.

She looked at me in wonderment and I saw that she was weeping too.

I don't know how long we sat there, buffeted by the wind, not speaking. I was thinking of Julian and she of her child. We were as one – two sad, bereaved women, silently sharing grief while the storm raged round us.

Someone had come on deck. It was Eliza. She made her staggering way towards us.

'Gawd a'mighty,' she cried. 'What are you doing here, Ethel?'

She sat down on one side of Ethel and stared at us. She must have thought we were an incongruous sight sitting there – representatives of the opposing camps, silently weeping.

Ethel said: 'I was going to end it, Liza.'

'You never was.'

'She . . . she stopped me.'

Eliza regarded me with hostility.

'She told me about herself. She was good . . . and she stopped me.'

'You should never have come up here on your own.'

'I had to, Liza. I couldn't stand it no more.'

Eliza shook her head and I noticed how tenderly she spoke. 'What did you tell her?' she asked.

'About the boy.'

I said: 'I understand. I lost a boy myself.'

Eliza stared ahead. She said: 'We'll all be overboard if this goes on. I never knew it was going to be like this or you would never have got me on this lark.' She turned to me, her expression softening: 'She needs looking after,' she added.

'Yes,' I agreed.

257

'She's had bad luck. Cruel bad luck. She ain't meant for all this. Wants looking after. How was it?'

'I was sitting here. She came out and I saw her . . . I saw what she was going to do. I brought her here and we talked. We found we had had a similar experience.'

'You! Not you!'

'Yes. I was married. I lost my husband and my little boy.'

'Thought you was a Miss.'

Ethel spoke for the first time. 'It's a secret. You mustn't tell, Eliza. I've promised.'

'I prefer to be known as a single woman,' I said. 'It's a way of forgetting.'

Ethel nodded vigorously as a gigantic wave almost lifted the ship out of the sea. In that moment we all thought we were going to be flung overboard.

'Do you think we are going to get there?' asked Ethel.

'God knows,' said Eliza.

As for myself, I wondered too. The crashing and pounding of the waves and the violent creaking of the timbers were unnerving. I was sure that in that moment we all thought the ship was about to break up and we should all be flung into that turbulent sea. I felt that it did not really matter if they knew my secret. It helped Ethel to think of me as a bereaved mother, as she herself was. It occurred to me that it was a strange commentary on human nature that sorrow was easier to bear when other people suffered, too.

'Funny . . . to come all this way for this,' said Eliza.

'It is something I have never considered until now,' I answered.

'Well, there we are.' She paused. 'I worry about her,' she added.

'I know you do, Liza,' said Ethel. 'You shouldn't. All I done was of my own free will.'

'I dunno. Times like this sets you thinking. You see, Miss – er . . .'

'Pleydell,' said Ethel. 'You mustn't never mention she was a Mrs Somebody.'

'Do all them stuck-up friends of yours know?'

'Only Miss Marlington.'

'The pretty one? She's your special friend. She don't look so bad.'

'She is very nice. You would like her.'

'Can't stand them others. Noses in the air. They look at you like you was stinking fish.'

'We are all here together and Miss Nightingale said there should be no distinction.'

'Oh, Miss Nightingale's a real lady, she is.' She added a little hesitantly, 'Like yourself.'

'Thank you,' I said.

'I wonder what it feels like to drown.'

'It would be quick in a sea like this,' I said comfortingly.

'The three of us would go down together,' said Ethel.

'I'm not sure it is as bad as that,' I said. 'Perhaps it seems so because we are unused to the sea.'

'Funny,' went on Eliza, 'I never thought about dying . . . not yet anyway. That's why I'm worried about her. You see, I was the one who started her off. It was all right for me. I thought it would be all right for her.'

'What happened?'

'You don't mind if I tell her, do you, Eth? I'd like to get it off my chest. She couldn't make a go of it. She was sewing half the night and still there wasn't enough to keep her going. I said to her, "Look here, girl, there's an easier way." So I took her out with me. You get used to it. I did. I thought she would. Then she goes and falls in love with this chap. Silly girl.' She gave Ethel an affectionate push. 'And he's all lovey-dovey and things look good for Ethel. He's going to marry her and settle down. Then she's going to have this child and he's off. That's about all. But you see, if I hadn't brought her into it she would have been stitching away with just herself to keep – and who knows, she might have got by.'

'You did what you could to help,' I said.

'That's true. But it didn't, did it? And then she went back to it all . . . for the sake of the kid. And one day while she leaves him there, while she's out on the game . . . she comes back and finds him gone.'

'It is so very sad.'

'She's never got over losing him.'

'I know. One doesn't.'

'Then I thought: Well, this is it. We'll go to the war. We'll be nurses. We both once did a spot of work in the hospitals. Horrible it was . . . washing dirty floors and not much for it. Anyway, it gave us what they call experience. But you see I've always felt I had to look after her.'

'I can see how she relies on you.'

'And then she creeps out and tries to do this. Just think. If you hadn't been there, she would be down there now.'

'But I was here, and she has promised not to do it again. When she wants to talk about things she'll come to me. We'll talk about our little boys together.'

'I'm glad,' said Eliza. 'I'm glad you was there.'

We sat in silence, holding on to each other because of the pitching and tossing of the ship which threatened to dislodge us; and I think we all drew comfort from each other. I know I did from them.

The storm continued, abating for a while and then increasing. We spoke now and then, speculating as to what it would be like when we reached Scutari, speaking of ourselves. I told them about my visit to Kaiserwald, and I described the Deaconess and the magic of the forest.

They listened and sometimes I had almost to shout to make myself heard above the raging of the storm. Then I told them about my childhood in India and how my father had died.

I learned something of them both. Eliza had had a hard life. She had not known her own father but had a stepfather. When she was ten years old he had tried to 'interfere with her'. She had hated him and left home, so she had learned to fend for herself at an early age. She had a great contempt for the opposite sex, so I guessed she had suffered a good deal at their hands. But she was strong and determined. I doubted anyone would get the better of Eliza nowadays. Ethel – like Lily – had come from the country to make her fortune in the big city.

Sad stories, both of them – and I now felt that I knew them well. The truculence of Eliza was due to the fact that she had

had to fight her way in the world; the timidity of Ethel was the manifestation of the knowledge that she was unable to.

We grew very close to each other on that night. We were very self-revealing probably because, in our minds, we thought that the *Vectis* might not survive the storm; and we found comfort in baring our souls.

It must have been for several hours that we sat, huddled together; and when the storm did abate and we found ourselves alive, a strong bond of friendship had been formed between us.

In the Streets
of Constantinople

❧

On a bleak November day we sailed into the Bosphorus, that narrow strait which separates Europe from Asia. The wind was shrieking, for the storm had stayed with us and it buffeted us as we stood on the deck. It was a wonderful sight in spite of the rain. Promontories rose on either side of the bays and gulfs, and cypress and laurel grew along the shores. Picturesque boats, like gondolas – which we learned were called *caïques* – made their way up and down the waters. One of the gulfs formed the harbour of Constantinople and opposite that was Scutari, which was to be our destination. About a third of a mile separated the two towns.

In the semi-darkness of early morning, the scene was romantically beautiful, but as it became light it was less so.

We could then see the muddy shores, and the vast Barrack Hospital which had looked like a Caliph's palace rising out of the gloom was now seen to be dirty, crumbling and in a state of decay. Tents, booths and huts had been set up about it, presided over by an array of nationalities. I saw two soldiers, one limping and one with a dirty bandage round his head, making unsteady progress among the booths.

Soon we were disembarking, which meant being lowered into the *caïques* with our carpet bags – and then taken ashore.

And so we arrived at the hospital at Scutari.

There was no real road – only a rough and muddy path; and to reach the plateau on which the hospital was situated it was necessary to climb up this path.

My first impression of that hospital was so depressing that I almost wished I could get back to the *Vectis* and ask to be taken home. Hopelessness seemed to permeate the air. I sensed that even Henrietta's spirits were quelled. I was not sure what we had expected, but it was not this.

We were breathless when we had climbed up to the plateau and the nearer we came to the hospital, the more our misgivings increased. Now we could see the stalls and booths clearly. Most of them sold drink. I saw a woman in a spotted velvet gown clutching a bottle under her arm, and making her way to the hospital.

'Camp followers,' I whispered to Henrietta.

'I can't believe that.'

'I've read about them.'

'Not in the hospital, surely.'

'We'll see.'

And we did.

The hospital was truly enormous. At least, I thought, we shall have plenty of room. This was not the case. Most of the space was taken up with the wards. When I saw how many sick and suffering lay there, I was astounded; and later I learned that they were not suffering from the effects of war but of disease. There had been a cholera epidemic which had killed thousands.

Damp ran down the hospital walls, and the once grand tiles of the floors were broken in many places; the courtyard was littered with decaying refuse which must have been left there for some time. Disorder and decay, with the inevitable disease, seemed to be the chief characteristic of the place.

How could an army fight a war from such a background?

I felt angry with those at home who had sent out men – like Lily's William – to suffer the hardships they would inevitably endure. Better to die in combat, I thought, than to be brought to such a hospital.

People like Lady Mary Sims and Mrs Jarvis-Lee were becoming more and more disenchanted, and their desire to do good for their country was rapidly waning.

Miss Nightingale was in despair, but she was not one to give way to such emotion; and I could see that she was immediately formulating plans to remedy the situation and was beginning to grapple with the unexpected setbacks which awaited us.

Six rooms had been allotted to us; one of these was a kitchen and the other so small that it would be impossible to get more than two people in it.

'Well,' she said, 'we must for the time being accept what is here.' She hoped there would be improvements later.

When we saw the rooms our hearts sank even lower, although we were now prepared for discomforts. There were divans round the walls, Turkish fashion, and we were expected to sleep on these. They were damp and dirty.

Miss Nightingale said: 'The first thing we must do is clean them and then divide ourselves up as to how we shall fit ourselves in. Let us remember that we are not here to be comfortable but to heal the sick.'

We immediately set about cleaning the rooms. Eliza kept with us for, since that encounter on the deck, we had become good friends. I had told Henrietta about the episode; she had been very sympathetic and with her natural charm she had managed to convey that she wished to be friends. We often found that Eliza was beside us and that was good for us. Eliza was a natural protector. She was big, domineering and bellicose, and most of the others were a little afraid of her. Her attitude to Ethel had shown a softness in her, a natural kindliness which she would try to hide; and although she showed she had a mild contempt for the manner in which we spoke, behaved, and were unaccustomed to the harshness of life, she was our friend.

'This will be our corner,' she said to me with a wink. 'We'll claim it and once we have, it's ours. Look,' she went on, pointing to a heap of dirt. 'Rats! They've been here. What can you expect with all that rubbish about? I reckon the rats live like lords. I'm beginning to itch. Wouldn't surprise me if there wasn't a few hoppers around here.'

I was very glad of their companionship; and I think Henrietta was too. I had a notion that she was beginning to think that marriage with Lord Carlton might have been preferable to the situation she now found herself in. Henrietta was not a dedicated nurse, but she had beauty and charm which had showed itself at Kaiserwald and made her very popular with the patients. It was different with me. I would rather do nursing than anything else; and if I had to do it in Scutari instead of the dream-hospital I had imagined at home, then so be it.

When I think back to that arrival in Scutari, the images are confused. What I remember most vividly is those poor men lying in their beds without adequate clothes and bedcovering – nothing but dirty sheets against the cold. I think of floors with rats scuttling across them; of the horrible smell of disease and corruption. I knew that Miss Nightingale turned with fierce indignation against those ministers snug in their London comforts who had sent these men out to fight the country's wars with inadequate medical supplies. How foolish they were! How shortsighted! Everyone at home thought the British army invincible. But it took more than might and power to fight disease. At once it was apparent to me that disease – cholera and dysentery – were a greater enemy than the Russians.

The first thing we did was to scrub and wash. We had to bring some cleanliness into this hospital. Dirt – hand in hand with disease – was the curse of this war.

There were no candles. Miss Nightingale had discovered that there was a dearth of them and said they must be saved for necessary purposes. So we went to bed in the dark and stretched out on our divans; Ethel and Eliza on one side, Henrietta next to me.

'This is a fine caper,' said Eliza. 'Who would have thought we should end up like this?'

And as we lay there listening to the rats scurrying across the floor, we were so exhausted that we were soon asleep.

During the next day I saw Charles Fenwick. He looked thinner and tired. We were busy cleaning our quarters, for the more we saw of the Barrack Hospital, the less desirable it seemed. Of course, Miss Nightingale had been right in ordering that before we could do anything we must clean up the place as best we could. It was an almost superhuman task and should have been done by degrees, but at least we could make a good start.

Charles had heard that we had arrived and came to see us. He took my hands and we looked at each other.

'So you are here?' he said. 'And Henrietta?'

'She is with me.'

'But you must be horribly shocked.'

I admitted that we were. We had not expected anything luxurious, but this . . .

'It has that effect on us all. But you look well, Anna.'

'I am well, thank you.'

'Oh yes. There is so much to do. It was the cholera epidemic which made it as you see it now. We could have managed the casualties, although supplies are grossly inadequate. It makes one feel quite helpless.'

'Something will be done now Miss Nightingale is here. She is determined that this state of affairs shall not continue.'

He smiled. 'There is prejudice against her. Oh, we are bedevilled by the authorities, Anna. People who know nothing of conditions here . . . people at home in Whitehall are giving the orders. It won't do.' He looked anxiously at me. 'Anna, are you going to be able to endure this?'

'We have come to do a job and we shall do it.'

'You and Henrietta will. I wonder about the others. It was spartan at Kaiserwald, I know, but nothing like this. That was minor discomfort. This is real hardship. And the winter will be coming on.'

'Oh dear, this is not a very happy welcome, is it?'

'I do not like to think of you and Henrietta here, seeing the sights you will see.'

'Charles, we have come here to nurse the sick and we shall do it.'

'And Henrietta . . . she will never be able to endure it. She is not as strong as you are, Anna. Not so determined.'

'She will stay here, I believe,' I said. 'I must find her. You will want to see her.'

I brought her to him.

He took her hands and gazed at her as he had at me. I smiled

266

at them fondly. I believed he was attracted by her and that seemed inevitable to me. Everyone must be attracted by Henrietta.

'Charles!' she cried. 'How wonderful to see you! This is like old times. I could expect the H.D. to come bustling in at any moment and give me one of those withering looks of hers.'

'It is very different from Kaiserwald, Henrietta,' I said.

'I can see that already. There is work to be done here.'

'I was saying to Anna that it is going to be hard for you. Women should not be here.'

'We get very cross with men who say things like that, don't we, Anna?'

'Very,' I agreed.

He said: 'God bless you both. But I am truly concerned for you.'

'What about all the men out here? We haven't seen the wards properly yet, but . . .'

'It will distress you,' said Charles.

'Then it is time we came to help,' I replied briskly.

'We . . . heard that Dr Adair was here,' said Henrietta. 'You know . . . the one who has written those books.'

'Oh yes,' said Charles, 'he's here. He's mostly in the General Hospital.'

'Where is that?' asked Henrietta eagerly.

'It's all part of the same place, really. It's about a quarter of a mile away in fact.'

'Perhaps we shall meet the famous gentleman one day,' said Henrietta.

'I dare say you'll see him about. He's here quite often. Usually he's in a rage about the lack of vital supplies . . . as we all are.'

The mention of his name affected me emotionally although he had never been far from my mind.

I said: 'Miss Nightingale will do something, I am sure. She will be sending despatches to London. Something will be done now she is here.'

'It's like getting blood out of a stone. These senseless people at home! I mustn't go on about them but they do make me angry.'

'I can well understand that,' I said. 'Now we shall have to be getting on with our work. We shall see you later, I hope.'

'Often, I hope,' said Charles. 'If you are in any difficulties come to me. I'll see what I can do.'

'Isn't that a comfort?' cried Henrietta, giving him one of her languishing smiles.

He said: 'It's wrong of me . . . but I *am* glad you are here.'

'Wrong?' queried Henrietta. 'Why wrong?'

'Because of what you will go through.'

'You forget we chose it,' I reminded him. 'It is what we want.'

He smiled at me. 'I know,' he said. 'I think you are wonderful.'

We went back to our scrubbing.

Henrietta said: 'I have a feeling that soon we are coming face to face with the demonic doctor.'

She was right.

I knew that Charles would be coming out of the ward at a certain time and if he were in the vicinity he liked to have a word with us. We had not been allowed to do any nursing yet. There was some conspiracy among the medical staff to keep us out, as incompetents. But, as Miss Nightingale said, no nursing could be of any use without fundamental cleanliness so there was plenty for us to do meanwhile until we could prove ourselves worthy of professional trust.

There was a small room close to the entrance of the ward and I expected Charles to be there. As I approached I was aware of the sound of voices. I hesitated and then I heard a man speaking in deep resonant tones which made him very audible: 'I want supplies . . . not a parcel of these Nightingale women. What good are *they* going to be? None at all! Just a damned hindrance. We shall have them fainting all over the place . . . having the vapours . . . going into hysterics . . .

demanding feather beds. I want supplies and they send me these foolish women.'

I was so enraged that I stood there stunned.

Then I heard Charles's voice: 'You are wrong. There are some very good girls among them. You will have to change your opinion.'

'I doubt it. Oh, I know some of these women like the idea of *playing* nurse. The reality will be quite another matter. You know what's wrong. The Army is being decimated. Not by the Russians but by disease and neglect. Because there is nothing here . . . nothing with which to cure them. Nothing, nothing . . . and they send us a parcel of . . . Nightingales. Shortly we shall be getting the wounded in from Balaclava and what have we got? Medicines? Dressings? No! A gaggle of useless women.'

I acted on impulse. I opened the door and went in. My eyes were blazing, my cheeks scarlet.

'Anna!' cried Charles.

'I overheard,' I said.

I was looking straight at him and I knew at once who he was. He was tall – rather leaner than I had imagined; his hair was black; his eyes were such a dark brown that they looked black also; they were deeply set and luminous. His high cheeks gave a lean look to his face; his nose was long and straight; his mouth was curved into a smile which I think meant he was amused. His appearance had not disappointed me. He was almost exactly as I had imagined him.

'Ah,' he said. 'A Nightingale herself. Well, they do say that listeners never hear any good of themselves.'

'This is Dr Adair, Anna,' said Charles. 'Adair, Miss Pleydell.'

He bowed almost ironically.

I said: 'I have read some of your books.'

'How gracious of you to mention it.'

He was waiting for eulogies and got a cool silence.

'I'm sorry you have such a poor opinion of us,' I said. 'I do not think we are going to be a hindrance.'

'Miss Pleydell was at Kaiserwald,' said Charles. 'I believe she made quite an impression there. They thought she was an excellent nurse. Miss Marlington was with her. I am sure you will change your opinion . . . at least of these two.'

I was trembling. Here he was standing before me. In my imagination I had put horns on his head and given him cloven feet. I pictured him in Aubrey's Temple of Sin. I was trying to calm myself, but my emotion was overwhelming me. After all, this meeting was what I had been working for; it was the thought of revenge which had sustained me during my months of mourning. And here I was. I had tracked down my quarry. Who would have believed it would be in a hospital in Scutari?

I realized at once that he was formidable.

I heard Henrietta's voice. 'Anna, are you there? Is Charles there?'

She came into the room.

I said: 'Henrietta, this is Dr Adair.'

'Oh!' Her eyes were wide and for a moment I was afraid she would say something impetuously.

'This is Miss Marlington who was with Miss Pleydell in Kaiserwald,' said Charles.

He bowed coolly.

'How do you do?' said Henrietta, the colour coming into her cheeks and her eyes dancing with excitement.

'Dr Adair has just been expressing his contempt for us,' I said. 'He thinks we are going to have vapours and demand feather beds.'

'Any bed would be preferable to our flea-ridden divans,' said Henrietta. 'I should not be particular about the feathers.'

'I think you will find more to complain of than your divans,' said Dr Adair.

'And *I* think it is brave of them to come out here,' said Charles. 'I have the utmost admiration for them all.'

'Let us hope that everyone will share your feelings.' And with a rather imperious movement of the head, Dr Adair indicated that the meeting was over.

Charles said: 'I must get on, too. I hope all is well with you.'

'As well as can be expected,' replied Henrietta.

Dr Adair gave us a nod and was gone.

'So that is Dr Adair,' said Henrietta.

'You mustn't take to heart what he said, Anna,' Charles told me.

'What did he say exactly?' asked Henrietta.

'That we were a feckless, useless lot of women – a parcel he called us – and we're going to be an encumbrance rather than a help.'

'He was just expressing his fury about not having the supplies he needs. He is very angry about that. We all are.'

'He wasn't talking about supplies, but us,' I insisted. 'He has made up his mind about us before he knows us. He is arrogant, conceited, impossible. I do not think I am going to like your Dr Adair.'

'Why do you call him mine?' asked Charles.

'Because I can see you think he is something of a hero.'

'He works very hard here.'

'And so do you. So do we all.'

'There is something special about Dr Adair.'

'Yes. An aura of self-satisfaction. "I am the great man. Whatever I do is wonderful!"'

'How vehement you are, Anna. He has upset you with those careless remarks.'

'Not only the remarks,' I said tersely.

I wanted to get away. I was beginning to show my feelings, and that was not wise. My hatred for this man was too strong for me to hide it; the meeting – although I had expected it – was in a way too sudden.

'We must go,' I said to Henrietta.

'I'll see you later,' said Charles.

'Well,' said Henrietta when we were alone, 'so that is the man. Impressive, isn't he?'

'He is just as I imagined him to be. Now that I've seen him I hate him more than ever . . . if that is possible.'

'H'm,' said Henrietta. 'I did think he was rather fascinating.'

I looked at her impatiently and she laughed at me.

'Do you know,' she said, 'I think this is all going to be worth while just to meet him.'

*

All thought of anything else was wiped from my mind on that terrible day when they brought in the wounded from the battle of Balaclava to Scutari. The suffering of those men was beyond description. There was no way of bringing them to the hospital except by carrying the stretchers up the incline to the plateau and it was heartrending to watch those poor wounded men groaning in agony as the Turkish bearers brought them clumsily up the slope.

We had not enough beds for them all and many had to lie on the floor. There was a pathetic dearth of blankets and not enough bandages. But what we lacked chiefly was medical supplies.

The doctors were in despair. How were they going to deal with so many casualties? The terrible truth was that many who could have been saved had we been properly equipped were going to die. Miss Nightingale decided that ten of us should be sent to the General Hospital, which was really an extension of the Barrack; the remainder of our party was to stay at the Barrack. I was one of those chosen to go to the General with Henrietta, and we were delighted that Eliza and Ethel were with us. It had been noticed that we got on well together and it was probably thought a good plan to mix the two sides – the ladies, as they said, and the others, between whom a certain hostility had been noticed.

My first thought was that we were going to work where *he* was, and I did not know whether to be glad or sorry. I wanted to know more about him, of course; but on the other hand I was sure that I should be in conflict with him. He had already shown me that he despised us. That was not a very good relationship between doctor and nurse.

During those terrible days we were too busy to think of anything but tending the sick. The suffering I saw so disturbed me that I tried to purge my mind of it and I did succeed in some measure in eliminating it from my thoughts. But it came back to me in odd moments and filled me with melancholy and I knew in my heart that it was something one could never forget. Looking back, there is a blurred picture of blood and horror – sights I never thought to witness and fervently hoped

I never would again. Never could the horrors of war have been brought home more clearly than they were in that hospital in Scutari; and the stupidity and callousness of the men who planned it for others to perform filled me with an indignation which inspired me to carry out tasks which I should otherwise not have had the strength to do.

Days moved into night. I was there constantly without relief, hurrying from bed to bed. I took only a few hours' sleep here and there and I saw pain and suffering which I should remember all my life. I was touched beyond belief by the hope in those poor, pain-crazed eyes of cruelly wounded men, and Miss Nightingale came quietly through the wards, holding her lamp high, pausing by the beds of those most afflicted, whispering a few words of encouragement, telling us what should be done. I had never thought to see such horror, to live through such terrible human suffering, and yet I was uplifted. I knew this was my mission and what I was born for. Moreover, I felt I was doing some good. I had the power to soothe and there were occasions when the touch of my hands on a fevered brow seemed to have a miraculous effect.

Henrietta did well. She lacked my strength and tired easily, but I noticed that her feminine presence brought solace to many. She was so pretty, like a flower among all that horror; nothing could rob her of her exquisite daintiness, not even exhaustion and our far from becoming uniforms. Ethel was gentle; she was too easily moved, but the patients saw this and loved her for it; as for Eliza, she had great strength and could lift a man with ease. So the four of us in our different ways did not give such a bad account of ourselves.

During the days when there was nothing to do but work, and in the desire to perform well-nigh impossible tasks, I forgot everything but the work on hand. I did not even remember that I had wanted to come here for a personal purpose and that was to find the man who, I believed, had ruined my husband and by his neglect killed my child – and to expose him in all his villainy. He was nearby, working indefatigably like the rest of us. I saw him now and then, his white coat often crimson with blood, his mouth stern, his eyes blazing in fury; and he affected me deeply. Sometimes he would bark out orders to us in a way which showed he did not expect much from us and wondered why we were cluttering his hospital.

I had a notion that he was aware of me, although he often passed me as though we had not been introduced by Charles, though sometimes he would nod briefly and give a command. 'Go and wash that patient. Be careful. He's a very sick man.'

I wanted to shout at him sometimes, but I never did. I always meekly obeyed. He had a way of subduing those about him and was treated with great awe throughout the hospital.

There was a terrible morning when the wounded were being brought in and among them was one man with his right leg smashed.

I was trying to make him comfortable when Dr Adair came up with one of the other doctors, whose name was Legge. I stood back while they examined the man, who lay back looking as though he were on the point of death.

The doctor moved away and Dr Adair said: 'Gangrene. It's got to come off.'

'The shock will kill him,' replied Dr Legge.

'The gangrene will kill him in any case. I'm going to take the risk and the sooner the better.'

'He'll never stand up to it.'

'I shall do it,' said Dr Adair. Then he noticed me. 'You can be in attendance,' he added.

Dr Legge was looking at him in horror.

'But . . .' he began.

'She's come here as a nurse,' said Dr Adair. 'If women undertake to be professionals, they'll have to get used to these things.' He looked at me sardonically. 'We've got to make use of what we've got. God knows, it's poor enough.' His glance raked me like a scalpel.

I was not sure whether he was referring to me or to the equipment – both, I supposed.

'I'll perform the surgery at once.'

'He can't stand it.'

'There's just a chance and I'm going to take it.'

It was like something out of a hideous nightmare. The operation had to be performed in the ward. There was nowhere else. The patient was put on a board supported by trestles.

'This will be gruesome, Miss – er – Nightingale,' said Dr Adair to me with a twist of his lips. 'I hope you won't faint. It doesn't help and you will be ignored if you do. We shan't be leaving the patient to administer sal volatile.'

'I didn't expect you would and I shall not faint.'

'Don't be too sure. You will soothe the patient. Hold his hand. Let him grip you. Do your best.'

'I will.'

And I did. I used all my strength. I was praying earnestly all the time. 'Dear God,' I kept saying. 'Dear God.' And that poor man was saying with me. 'Dear God.'

I did not look at what was happening. I knew that I could not do that. I just held his hand and he clung to mine, gripping it so fiercely that it felt numb . . . and I went on praying aloud with him.

Mercifully he dropped into unconsciousness.

'There's nothing more you can do,' said Dr Adair.

I turned away. I felt I had come through the most taxing ordeal of my life and not too badly. I saw Dr Adair next day and he was ungracious enough to say nothing of my part in it.

Later that day the man died.

I learned it from Dr Adair himself. I was outside the ward when I saw him.

'Our operation was not successful,' he said.

'It seemed . . . unnecessary,' I said.

'Unnecessary! Do you know what gangrene is? It's the death of the tissues. It's the result of the interruption of the blood supply.'

'I know. He would have died, but it seems unnecessary to have inflicted extra pain.'

'Are you advising me, Miss – er – Nightingale?'

'Certainly not. I am just saying that it seems sad that this man, who was doomed in any case, had to suffer the amputation unnecessarily.'

'Our job is to save life, Miss Pleydell. If there is a chance we must take that chance. At best we have saved a life; at worst we have gained a little experience.'

'So the patient, having already been used by those who wish to make war, still has his uses. He may help renowned doctors to become even more so.'

'There,' he said, 'you have got to the root of the matter.'

He bowed ironically and passed on.

I was very shaken by the experience, but there was no time to brood. Men were still arriving from Balaclava – surely the most futile battle ever fought. Oh, it was magnificent, the Charge of the Light Brigade. Glorious, some called it – those who had not seen the wretched survivors. The fortunate were those who died in that wild, foolhardy charge.

Soon afterwards Lady Mary Sims and Mrs Jarvis-Lee went home. They said they thought they could serve their country better in England. Perhaps they could, for they were useless as nurses but would be very efficient organizing charity balls and bazaars for the support of the hospitals.

People talked a great deal about the brilliant Dr Adair. We were so fortunate to have him in the hospital, they said. I believed he was all that I had thought him to be – a clever doctor, no doubt, but without sympathy or sensitivity. I was sure he looked upon his patients as material for his experiments. I told myself that all along he had known he could not save that man's life by amputating his leg; but he had wanted to do so in the hope of learning something. Suffering did not touch him. What mattered to him was his quest for knowledge and, of course, the aggrandisement of Dr Damien Adair.

When the terrible aftermath had begun to die down a little and the dead had been buried and the survivors were teetering on the brink of life and death, I did not see Dr Adair for two days. I was very aware of that, for the days seemed oddly empty. I missed the flaring of resentment, the anger against him which had become so much a part of my existence; and my determination to bring him to his just desserts – in some way as yet not clear to me – was stronger than ever.

Then I heard that he was no longer in the hospital.

Although Charles was in the Barrack Hospital, as it was so near we did meet now and then; and when I saw him I asked what had happened to Dr Adair.

'He has just gone off . . . for a few weeks, I believe.'

'Surely not on holiday!'

'Maybe he wanted a little respite.'

'A respite? When all this is going on?'

'He has worked very hard.'

'So have we all. I should have thought his place was here.'

Charles said: 'He was working day and night.'

'But we all were.' I wondered why everyone wanted to defend him.

And that was all I knew.

Life went on grimly. After the Battle of Inkerman was won by the British and French, we had thought Sebastopol would fall into our hands and that, we guessed, would be the turning-point of the war. Alas, the powers that be had made another misjudgement. Sebastopol was under siege and that was how it was going to remain for some time to come. There would be no easy victory.

The winter was approaching fast and casualties were arriving constantly. We had very little time off duty but I think it was realized that we needed some respite and that if we did not have it, we ourselves should be ill.

We needed to get away from the hospital for a few hours and we were told that a party of us might take one of the *caïques* and visit Constantinople for an hour or so.

We set out in a group of six. We should not have been allowed to go in pairs. Some of us were to pick up stores which were needed.

We felt quite excited to get away from the gloom of the hospital and the perpetual presence of pain; and we all had a feeling of determination that for this short space of time we must stop thinking about the horrors through which we had all lived for so long and which would be waiting for us on our return.

The *caïque* carried us across to the opposite side of the Bosphorus and Constantinople lay before us. The very name had a romantic ring, and how magnificent it looked with its domes and minarets. There was the old castle of the Seven Towers with its gloomy history, since so many sultans had been put to death there by rebellious soldiery, and where many other prisoners had been incarcerated for years and submitted to hideous torture. I wanted to see the Topkapi Palace, home of sultans, with their fabulous wealth and harems.

Often I had looked across the narrow strip of water and felt there was a world unknown to me, a world strangely different from Victorian England – perhaps a little like that of India which I had known in my youth, for that had seemed different before I had seen it through adult eyes and it had lost so much of its romance.

We had been warned that we must be careful. We knew that there were really two cities – one was called Christian Constantinople and that other, which was often called Stamboul, was the Turkish quarter and lay on the south side of the Golden Horn. There were bridges connecting the two and we were told on no account to venture into Stamboul.

It was so exciting to be among all that Saracenic and Byzantine architecture and I was longing to explore.

I suppose we were conspicuous in our uniforms with our holland scarves on which was embroidered *Scutari Hospital* in red. I noticed how people glanced at us and stood aside to let us pass.

It was the bazaars and little alleys which attracted most of the nurses. These were crowded and it was difficult to keep together. Henrietta slipped her arm through mine. 'Don't lose me,' she whispered. 'I'd be a bit scared if you did.'

The streets grew narrower; the shops were like dark caves in which all sorts of merchandise was displayed . . . brass, ornaments, jewellery, silks. Here and there one of the owners sat at his door smoking a hubble-bubble pipe; strange music came from somewhere; barefooted boys ran through the crowds, pushing against us, reminding us that we must take care of what little money we had.

We stopped at a stall to look at some earrings. There were various colours in enamel and they were very pretty.

'Hardly suitable for ward duty,' I commented.

'My dear girl, we are not going to be here forever. You wait. Sebastopol will fall, and it will be home for us.'

'I hope you are right.'

'I am going to buy some. These blue ones. You should have the green.'

The old man set aside his hubble-bubble pipe, scenting business, and the transaction took a little time. We were expected to bargain but did not know how, and I think we disappointed our salesman, who would rather have had a lower price and a little entertainment.

And when we had paid for our earrings we discovered that we were no longer with the party.

'Never mind,' said Henrietta. 'We'll find our way back.'

'And I think we should set about doing it immediately,' I replied.

We attempted to retrace our steps but instead of coming out of the maze of bazaars we found ourselves getting deeper into it.

I noticed a dark man watching us, and it seemed to me that he might be following us.

We came to an alley.

'Let's try this,' said Henrietta. 'It's less crowded. Perhaps we could find someone who speaks English and could direct us.'

We had not gone far when, to our dismay we realized that the alley was a cul-de-sac, and as we attempted to retrace our steps, several boys – they must have been in their early teens – came towards us. Two slipped behind us and the others barred our way.

I took Henrietta's arm and attempted to push past them; but they had surrounded us. One of them seized my cloak; the others had Henrietta by the sleeve.

I said: 'We want to get to the *caïques*. We have to get back to the hospital.'

One of them came closer and held out his hand. 'Money,' he said. 'You give poor boy.'

Henrietta looked at me. 'We're poor nurses,' she said. 'We have no money.'

It was clear that they did not understand a word. They were glaring at us menacingly.

I don't know what would have happened then but the dark man whom I had seen in the bazaar came into the alley.

He made straight for us and let out a stream of words which must have been abuse at the boys; and it was effective for it sent them scurrying away.

He turned to us. He had only a few words of English, which made communication difficult, but I imagined he was asking us if he could help.

I said: 'We want to go to the *caïques*. We must get back to the hospital.'

'Hospital,' he said, nodding and pointing to our scarves. I looked at Henrietta with relief. This seemed like a stroke of good fortune.

'Follow,' said our rescuer.

We did and he led us out of the cul-de-sac to a spot where two or three horse-drawn carriages were waiting, evidently for hire.

I said: 'We do not need a carriage. We cannot be far from the waterfront.'

But he was already handing Henrietta into one of them. I got in beside her, protesting, and while I was trying to get Henrietta out, the carriage started and our rescuer was giving the driver instructions.

It was not long before I noticed that we were not going in the direction of the waterfront.

'This is not the way,' I muttered to Henrietta.

Her eyes were wide with alarm. 'Oh . . . Anna, what do you think it means?'

I shook my head. I dared not imagine what this man's intentions were when, to my horror, I realized we were crossing one of the bridges which spanned the Golden Horn and so were being taken out of Christian Constantinople to that other part of the city into which we had been warned not to enter.

The horse increased its pace and I thought that any moment we should overturn; this did not happen, though I feared that those children and old people in our path would be ridden down; somehow they always managed to escape. We had come to a street of several tall houses; they looked dark and mysterious because there were few windows.

Then our carriage turned into a gateway and we were in a courtyard.

'Out,' said the man.

I looked at Henrietta, wondering whether we should refuse to get out. It was not, however, our choice. Our captor had made it clear that we must obey. He pulled first Henrietta and then me out of the carriage; and gripping our arms, he led us through a doorway to a dark passage. Before us was a flight of stairs.

'Up,' said our captor.

I turned to him. 'Listen,' I said loudly. 'Where is this? I demand to know. We are nurses. English nurses. You implied that you were taking us to the waterfront. Where is this? I will not go a step further.'

His answer was to take my arm and push me up the stairs. I heard Henrietta gasp. 'Anna . . .'

'We have to get away,' I said.

'How . . .?'

A man appeared at the top of the stairs. Our captor spoke to him and he stood aside. They talked together excitedly for a few seconds; then the man who had brought us here took our arms and forced us into a corridor.

We were pushed into a small dark room, heavily curtained, with divans along the walls; and the door shut on us.

I ran to it and tried to open it. I could not do so, for it was locked.

'It's no use,' said Henrietta. 'We're prisoners.'

We stared at each other, each trying to pretend that we were only half as frightened as we felt.

'What does it mean?' asked Henrietta.

I shook my head.

'We were idiots. Why did we get lost? These wretched earrings . . .'

'I thought the others were with us.'

'What is going to happen to us?'

I saw the thoughts forming in her mind. She said: 'I've heard of this sort of thing. There have been many cases of women . . . taken . . . made into slaves . . . in harems.'

'Oh no!'

'Why not? That's how the sultans live, isn't it? They have women in all those harems. They take them captive during wars and they become slaves.'

'These are our allies. Don't forget we are fighting *their* war.'

'Would they mind that? That man was following us. Perhaps it was all arranged . . . those boys to surround us and he came along and rescued us . . . to bring us here. Do you think this is a sultan's palace?'

'It's certainly not Topkapi.'

'Oh, Anna, I hope they don't separate us. I've been longing for something to happen all through these dreary days. I was so sick of the smell of blood and disease and all the horror. I prayed for something to happen . . . anything, I said, to get me out of this place . . . and now this. I wonder what it is like in a harem?'

'Somehow I don't think that is the answer. Just look at us. We're hardly objects of desire. These uniforms . . . Look at my hair. Somehow I can never wash it properly here. We both look pale and tired. Scarcely prizes for a sultan's seraglio.'

'We'd seem different, though. There might be an allure about us because we are foreign; and when we've been bathed in asses' milk and decked out in jewels we could be very fascinating.'

She laughed but I could hear the note of hysteria in her voice.

'Stop it, Henrietta,' I said. 'We're going to need all our wits. We have got to look for a way of escape. Watch out.'

She gripped my arm. 'We've got to stay together. Because you're here I'm not afraid . . . at least not so much afraid as I should be if I were alone.'

'Whatever happens we'll try to keep together.'

'What will they be thinking back at the hospital?'

'That we disobeyed orders and left the party.'

'It was the party which left us! Do you think they will send someone to look for us?'

'Of course not. They're all needed for more important things.'

'Anna, what will become of us?'

'We have to wait and see. Be ready. We've got to get out of this place.'

'How? And if we do, where are we?'

'We could find our way to the waterfront. That's all we have to do. There are *caïques* all over the place. Listen.'

The door opened. We sprang towards it. It was our dark captor.

'Come,' he said.

'Where are you taking us?' I demanded.

He did not answer.

Henrietta and I looked at each other. We were waiting for that opportunity. When it came we must be ready. Holding us firmly, he took us up a flight of stairs. Only then did he release Henrietta that he might scratch on the door with his fingers. A voice from within said something and our captor opened the door and pushed us in.

The heavy curtains were drawn. I saw a table and on it was an ornate lamp which gave a glimmer of light to the room. A man was reclining on the divan; he wore a turban and there was something immediately familiar about him.

I thought: It can't be, and yet . . . And when he spoke I knew.

'A pair of nightingales,' he said.

'Dr Adair!' stammered Henrietta.

'I knew there would be trouble bringing out a parcel of women.'

'What does all this mean?' I demanded. The fear of the last hour was rapidly vanishing and in its place was an exultation and a tremendous excitement. 'We have been insulted . . . brought here against our will. We have been led to believe . . .'

I looked at Henrietta. Her mood had also changed. I saw the sparkling excitement in her eyes.

'The meaning is simple,' he said. 'Two foolish women allowed themselves to wander round the bazaars, were about to be robbed, were rescued and brought here. Thank your good fortune that you were in uniform. Those scarves you are wearing are your talismans. Scutari Hospital. Everyone knows where it is and that you come from it. It was for that reason that you were brought here.'

'To you?' I said.

'I have friends in this city. My connection with the hospital is known. So when two nightingales leave the nest and are discovered fluttering about in the sleazy quarters of the city they are snared and brought to me.'

'I can't believe it,' I said.

'How else could it have been?' asked Henrietta.

'How else indeed? I am surprised that you were allowed to walk in the city.'

'We came with a party,' said Henrietta.

'And you mislaid the others?'

'They mislaid us. We stopped to buy something and then they weren't there.'

'But what is this place?' I cried. 'What are you doing here? It's not a hospital.'

'I do have a life outside hospitals,' he said. 'Why I am here is my own affair.'

'And dressed like a sultan!' said Henrietta with a little giggle. Poor girl, she had been truly frightened and I could see that hysteria still hovered.

'I am sure that you are both two well-brought-up young ladies and that your nannies told you many times that in the best society one does not ask impertinent questions.'

'I didn't think it was impertinent,' began Henrietta.

I interrupted her: 'Will you please tell us what is taking place?'

'Certainly. You were discovered in the streets by a friend of mine. He saw that you could easily walk into danger. He watched you for a while and followed you to a spot where you were about to be robbed . . . possibly harmed. He rescued you and because it was clear from where you came, he brought you to me. You have been very fortunate today. First in wearing your uniform and secondly that I happened to be here at the time. I dare say you will be reprimanded for your tardy return to the hospital and I hope you are severely dealt with. This should be a lesson to you. Never, *never* venture into these streets alone. This is not Bath or Cheltenham, and well-brought-up young ladies would not be allowed to wander alone even there. This is a foreign land alien to your home. Ideas are different here . . . manners, customs, everything. Remember it. I shall give you coffee now, for we are waiting for a friend of mine who will take you back to the hospital.'

'And you . . .?' I began.

He raised his eyebrows.

I stammered: 'I . . . I thought perhaps you might be returning. The casualties are mounting. It seems . . .' I looked round the room and at him in his turban, which made almost a stranger of him. He looked darker, his eyes more luminous.

'You are reproaching me for my self-indulgence, I see,' he said.

'You *are* needed at the hospital.'

He was smiling at me oddly – a smile which I could not understand in the least.

At that moment there was a scratching at the door and a man came in carrying a brass tray on which were coffee and cakes. Dr Adair said something to him which I could not understand and he set the tray down on a table.

'You will need a little refreshment,' he said to us. 'This is how they drink coffee here. I hope you will like it.'

We were seated on the divan beside him and he served us with the thick sweet coffee and the little spiced cakes.

He looked at us solemnly and said: 'I have no doubt that your adventure to the Crimea is becoming a little wearisome. That is the way of these adventures. They are never quite what one thinks they will be when one sets out on them. I dare say you had pictures of yourselves in crisp white aprons and becoming gowns playing angels of mercy to grateful men. It is a little different, eh?'

'We did not expect it to be quite like that,' I said. 'We knew there would be hardship and suffering.'

'But such hardship? Such suffering?'

'We did see something of the sick at Kaiserwald,' said Henrietta. 'But I'll admit you're right. I never expected anything like we found.'

'And if you had you would not have come.'

'No,' said Henrietta, 'I wouldn't. Anna would, though. Wouldn't you, Anna?'

'Yes,' I said. 'I would.'

He looked at me with some scepticism.

'You are a young woman who would never admit she was in the wrong.'

'That is not true. I am often in the wrong.'

'About trivia, yes. But the big undertakings?'

'Not true again. I have undertaken important things and failed, and I have not deluded myself into thinking they were anything but my own failures.'

'Anna is a very unusual person,' said Henrietta. 'A rare person. I knew that as soon as I saw her. That was why I went to her when I decided to change my way of life.'

He looked from one of us to the other, nodding slowly. 'And you intend to stay the course?'

'If you mean until we are no longer needed, yes,' I answered.

'But I hope the war will soon be over,' added Henrietta. 'They are saying Sebastopol can't hold out and that it is the key to victory. Once it has fallen the war will be over.'

'"They" often delude themselves. Optimism is a good thing and a great help – but perhaps realism is more so.'

'Do you mean you think it will not fall quickly?' I asked.

'I think the Russians are fully aware of its importance and that they are as determined to keep it as the British and the French are to take it.'

'I don't think I could bear years and years of this sort of thing,' said Henrietta.

'Then I should go home. I believe some of your people have.'

'Those who did not understand what nursing is, have left,' I said. 'But I believe that is nothing for us to regret.'

Again there was a scratching on the door. Dr Adair called out something – in Turkish, I presumed, and the man who had brought the coffee looked in and with him was another man. He was tall, brown-haired and brown-eyed, but he looked quite fair compared with the darkness of our host.

'Philippe!' said Dr Adair. 'Good of you to come so promptly. Let me introduce you. Monsieur Philippe Lablanche, Miss Pleydell, Miss Marlington.'

Philippe Lablanche bowed.

'They have had the misfortune to lose themselves in the city,' said Dr Adair. 'Will you take them back to Scutari?'

'It will be my pleasure,' said the gallant Frenchman, his eyes shining with admiration which I thought must be for Henrietta, who looked very pretty in spite of her uniform.

'I won't offer you coffee,' went on Dr Adair, 'because they should be getting back without delay.' He turned to us: 'Monsieur Lablanche is one of our inestimable allies. He will take good care of you.'

'I shall do my best.'

'There is a conveyance in the courtyard. It will get you to the shore.'

'We must depart then, ladies,' said Monsieur Lablanche.

We rose and I said to Dr Adair: 'We have to thank you.'

He bowed his head in acknowledgement.

'What we should have done without you . . .' began Henrietta with a shiver.

'It's worthy of a little contemplation,' he replied. 'Look on it as a worthwhile experience and it will make you less rash in future.'

'I really had imagined our being drugged and taken off to someone's harem,' she told him.

'I hope the disappointment was not too great.'

Henrietta burst out laughing. 'Well, it all ended most satisfactorily. Thank you, Dr Adair. Thank you a thousand times.'

'Once will be enough,' he said.

And we left.

As he said, there was a conveyance waiting in the courtyard. As we got in I could not help feeling exhilarated and not a little puzzled by the adventure. What was he doing there dressed like that, living like a Turkish pasha? What could it all mean? What a man of mystery he was! He became more and more intriguing the more I knew of him.

Philippe Lablanche proved to be charming. He was very gracious and seemed especially so when compared with Dr Adair. He pointed out the landmarks of the old city as we passed through it. It was dusk and from the minarets the faithful were being called to prayer. The city, beautiful and mysterious, seemed alluring yet sinister in the dim light. I looked at Henrietta. She was wide-eyed and excitement brought colour to her cheeks. She looked as though she were entranced.

Philippe Lablanche told us that he was attached to the French army and that Dr Adair was a great friend of his.

'A wonderful man,' he said. 'I know of no one quite like him. He is . . . what it is you say when a man is . . .'

'Unique?' I suggested.

'What is unique?'

'How one is if there is no one on earth like one.'

'That,' he said, 'is Dr Damien Adair.'

'Have you read his books?' I asked.

'But of course. They have been translated into French. So I read them. But perhaps that is not so good. One day I read them just as Dr Adair wrote them.'

'He is a man who likes adventure.'

'It is the breath of life to him.'

'You, too, must have an adventurous time, Monsieur Lablanche.'

'Yes, yes. But that is so with war.'

'I suppose,' went on Henrietta, 'we should not ask questions about what you do?'

'How understanding you are.'

'Then,' went on Henrietta, 'we will not ask. We will let our

288

imaginations work in secret and we shall never be sure.'

'That is kind of you . . . to think so much of me.'

'It is you who are kind. You are taking us back to safety.'

'Dr Adair is right, you know. It is unwise for ladies to walk alone.'

'We imagined that we were being taken to some sultan's harem,' said Henrietta with a laugh.

'Oh . . . it is not an impossibility. Such things have been known to happen. Some ladies have been carried off. You see, these people do not feel as we do.'

'I know,' I said. 'Women are of no great importance in some countries, existing merely to serve the men.'

'That is so, Mademoiselle. So you see, in strange places we must be prepared for strange customs.'

'We shall never forget this day, shall we, Anna?' said Henrietta. 'First a few hours' freedom. What bliss! Then to be lost . . . and all the terror of being driven through the streets not knowing where we were going. If only he had told us! But he couldn't, poor man, not understanding the language. And to find ourselves face to face with Dr Adair looking like a sultan himself . . . Wonderful!'

She was looking at Philippe Lablanche almost wheedlingly. She was implying: Tell us what you know about the strange habits of our fascinating doctor.

But charming as he was – and he really seemed eager to please – he was not telling us, that was if he knew anything to tell.

We were crossing the Bosphorus now.

'Leaving Europe for Asia,' said Henrietta. 'That sounds very adventurous . . . but it is just a little channel of water. What a fascinating place this is! I wish we could see more of it. Odd, isn't it, to be in this place and all we see is rows of hospital beds.'

'I think you are wonderful,' said Philippe Lablanche. 'I know you are a great comfort to those wounded men.'

'It is more than Dr Adair thinks we are,' I said.

'Oh no. He thinks you are doing good work. Nobody could

disagree with that. We have heard so much of you and the good lady Nightingale. She is regarded as a heroine . . . more than that. A saint. And you, her helpers, are angels . . . angels of mercy. You will never be forgotten.'

'We don't feel much like angels, do we, Anna?' asked Henrietta. 'Not in the hospital. Though some of the men like to see us, I believe. But the powers that be . . . half the time think we are a nuisance.'

'It is not true. It is just that there is no time to say how good you are. There is so much to do.'

We had reached the shore. 'I shall come with you to the hospital,' said Philippe Lablanche.

'Oh, there is no need to,' I told him. 'We shall be all right now.'

'I should not consider my mission complete if I did not. And I will tell you this: I have business in the hospital. Many of our men are there. There are duties. I come now and then.'

'Then we may see you again,' said Henrietta.

'I shall hope so. In fact, I shall make sure that we meet again.'

We climbed the slope. The hospital lay before us, looking almost romantic in the darkness without the pitiless sun showing us its crumbling decay. Now it could well be the sultan's palace.

'We are so grateful to you,' said Henrietta. 'You have been so gracious and kind . . . not making us feel that we are a pair of fools. Hasn't he, Anna?'

'Indeed he has. Thank you, Monsieur Lablanche.'

'It has been my great pleasure to escort you.'

He was holding my hand and smiling at me. Then he took Henrietta's hand. She gave him one of her dazzling smiles.

'Thank you. Thank you,' she said.

He was still holding her hand.

'Goodbye,' she said.

'No . . . not goodbye. I come here often. I shall seek you out. It is *au revoir*. That is a much nicer way of saying farewell . . . for the moment.'

'Indeed it is,' replied Henrietta.

'Come along,' I said. 'Let's hope we have not caused too much trouble by being late.'

We went into the hospital. In a few minutes we should be on duty. And that, I thought, is the end of that little adventure. But I could not stop thinking of Dr Adair and wondering about him.

I glanced at Henrietta. I was sure she was doing the same.

Last Days in Scutari

We talked about it afterwards as, side by side, we washed sheets in the enormous tub, sleeves rolled up, arms plunged deep in the greying water.

'Do you know,' said Henrietta, 'I believe he has a harem in that place. I believe he lives like a sultan. When we went into that room I was waiting for him to clap his hands and say: "Take them away; bathe them in asses' milk; encircle their anklets with jewels; perfume them with the scents of Araby and send them to my couch."'

'I believe he is capable of anything.'

'I am sure he is. But, Anna, isn't he the most fascinating creature you ever met?'

'He is the strangest. I detest him.'

'I wonder about him. He just walks out of the hospital when he has had enough of it – and goes to his harem. Who else would think of such a thing? I'd like to see them, wouldn't you?'

'Who?'

'The harem women, of course. I imagine them . . . black-eyed and luscious. That black stuff they put round their eyes makes them very enticing. There is something about those women in yashmaks. Imagine withholding yourself from the world because your lord and master commands you to. You can see there is one aim in their lives: to be attractive to men. Wouldn't it have been amusing if we had been dragged to *his* harem and to confront him there and say, "Dr Adair, I presume."'

'Your imagination always runs away with your common sense. I don't suppose there was a harem. I believe people gather in places like that to take drugs. You can imagine them all lying about on divans smoking hookahs.'

'You're worse than I am! I much prefer the harem. But what an interesting man. I never met a more fascinating one.'

She talked of him continually.

Winter was with us. Icy winds blew across the land and it was impossible to keep the patients warm. Always we were in need. Since we had arrived, Miss Nightingale's organization, persistence and common sense had made a great deal of difference, but there was still not enough.

Eliza was now working in what was called the invalids' kitchen, which had been installed by Miss Nightingale. She herself had brought with her and paid for herself arrowroot and meat essences, which she wanted for the very sick. Eliza's strength was useful in lifting the heavy pans; and I think the work was more suited to her than actual nursing.

Ethel had changed. She looked happier. I discovered the reason why one day when I saw her tending one of the wounded. It was something in the manner in which she smoothed his sheets, the smile about her lips; and I saw in his response that there was some understanding between them.

She was gentle, quiet, some might think ineffectual, but that frailty and helplessness had an allure, even to a man lying on a sickbed who must be feeling rather helpless himself.

One day when I was in the kitchen helping to prepare food for one of the very sick men, Eliza said to me: 'Have you noticed Ethel?'

'Yes,' I answered, 'I have.'

'She's in love.'

'With that man.'

'That's it. I wish this war was over. Only hope he don't get cured enough to be sent out again. Not a chance in 'ell of him coming back if he goes out there again.'

'What's wrong with him?'

'Usual. Bullet in the chest. They thought he was a goner when he was brought in, like so many of them, poor devils. But he's come through? If you ask me it's love what's carrying him along.'

'So he is in love with Ethel?'

'They was both smitten at the same time. Cupid, ain't he? Well, he got a direct hit on them two.'

'It's charming. She looks so different . . . so pretty.'

'True. She does. Wonderful what a bit of love can do. Do you know, since Cupid struck, he's been getting better. So has she. She worried me at times. Remember that time on deck? I bet you do. Something we would none of us forget in a hurry. She would have done it, you know. They've got a lot of guts, them little 'uns. She'd have gone right over if you hadn't stopped her.'

'I felt that, too.'

'Well, she didn't. Do you know, I reckon if she comes out of this all right and she's got him to look after, I reckon that would just about be a bit of all right for Ethel.'

'Do you think he would marry her?'

'It's what he's said. He's got a little farm out in the country somewhere. Shares it with his brother. Brother's keeping it nice and warm till he gets back. Just the ticket for our Eth. Gawd 'elp us. I pray that poor fellow don't get well enough to be sent out again . . . just well enough when the right time comes to be sent home . . . and back to that little old farm with our Ethel.'

'Eliza,' I said, 'you are a very good woman.'

'What! You going stark raving mad or something? It's what this place does to you.'

'I'll tell you what this place does to you. It makes you see things and people more clearly.'

'I'd be pleased to see little Ethel settled. It's what she wants. The idea of her going back to that pigsty of a room, stitching away. It gives me the creeps. She wouldn't be there more than two years.'

'We wouldn't let her do that.'

'Who do you mean – we?'

'You. Me.'

'What's it got to do with you?'

'As much as it has with you.'

She looked at me through narrowed eyes and laughed.

'You know what you said about me a little while ago?'

'Yes.'

'Well, I'll return the compliment.'

'Thanks.'

As I was about to move away she said: 'And I'll tell you another whose got it as bad as Ethel.'

'Got what?'

'Love.'

'Oh?'

'Henrietta.'

'Henrietta? But with whom?'

'I dunno. You tell me. Someone. You can see it in her face. And let me tell you something else. It was when you came back from that late night out . . . when you got lost.'

I nodded.

'I saw her face. It was all a-shine. I've seen that look before and I know what it means. I wouldn't mind betting that Henrietta has got as badly hit as our Ethel.'

'You're mistaken. There isn't anyone.'

'I reckon there is,' she said. 'You can't fool old Eliza.'

'I'll find out. I know her well.'

'You do . . . and you'll see I'm right.'

After that I thought a great deal about Henrietta.

There was little time for anything but work. Although the casualties had decreased slightly, men were coming in from around Sebastopol almost frozen to death without adequate clothing, and starving. We were working for days with scarcely a break, snatching a few hours' rest on our divans when we could.

I did talk to Henrietta now and then and I saw what Eliza meant about her. There was a certain radiance. I was very disturbed because she talked a great deal about Dr Adair.

'I wonder if he will come back. Isn't it different without him? It seems so dull. What a man! Imagine him . . . sporting with his harem while we are here.'

'I think he is absolutely despicable. He is a good doctor and we need good doctors. And he just walks off and leaves us . . . in pursuit of pleasure.'

'One would never really *know* a man like that.'

'Perhaps it would be better not to know him.'

'I should love to find out everything about him.'

The shine in her eyes, the lilt in her voice. Oh no, I thought, Henrietta could not be so foolish as to fall in love with him. Or could she? But he had gone and we might never see him again. Then I fell to thinking of my project to show the world what he really was, to prevent his using people as he had used Aubrey, to prevent his carelessly experimenting with lives as he had with my son's. No, that was not fair. He had not exactly taken Julian's life; he had simply not saved it because he wanted to experiment, in the same way as he had submitted that soldier to pain in order to gain some experience.

He was callous; he was hard and cruel; I hated him, and because of the intensity of my hatred the hospital seemed a dreary place without him. It must be so, of course, because that was what it was; but when he was there, the prospect of meeting him suddenly, of feeling the hatred and resentment flare up within me, gave me some lifting of spirits and a meaning to the days.

One day when I was on my way to the wards I encountered Philippe Lablanche. He expressed great pleasure at the sight of me and told me that he was on one of his periodic visits to the hospital. He trusted I was none the worse for my adventure and I told him that I certainly was not and that it had all ended very pleasantly.

'No more trips into Constantinople?'

I shook my head. 'That was a very rare occasion. We are so busy here. There is little time for junketing.'

'Soon Sebastopol must fall and then perhaps you will have a little time to look around that amazingly interesting city.'

'I shall before we go home.'

'Not just at first, though. You will have to stay a little while to look after your patients, I dare say. Then perhaps . . .'

He was smiling at me in a friendly fashion. Then he said: 'And your friend?'

I told him where he would find her and he left me.

Later I saw Henrietta and asked if he had found her. 'Yes,' she said. 'The gallant Frenchman. He's rather a pet, isn't he?'

'I think he is very charming.'

'He says that he does come to the hospital quite often. He would very much like to take us on a tour of Constantinople.'

'Unfortunately we are not here as sightseers.'

'A pity. Still, I must say I could enjoy another little encounter with our fascinating friend. I only wish . . .' I looked at her questioningly and she went on: 'I believe you miss him as much as I do.'

'Who?'

'The demonic one.'

I forced a laugh, but I felt a tremor of uneasiness. I could not get Eliza's words out of my mind.

'I wish he would get tired of that harem and come back to us.'

'I suppose we should not expect such a man to put duty before pleasure.'

She laughed at me.

'Oh, Anna, I can't help it. You look so stern. You always do when you talk of him. And all the time I think you find him as fascinating as I do. Are you still bent on your quest?'

'If you mean do I still want to find some way of showing him up for what he is, yes.'

'But what is he? That's what we don't know. That's what makes him the most exciting thing in our lives. I'm sure he'd get the better of us anyway . . . whatever we tried to do to him.'

She was laughing secretly to herself and I thought: She is obsessed with him.

I believed that I might be, too. But that was different. *I* knew he was a danger to those about him. I had seen the disintegration of my husband and I blamed him for that. I had read his books and I knew a great deal about him through them. His pagan spirit had looked out at me and I knew it was there.

I continued to be anxious about Henrietta. I knew how impulsive she could be. If he returned, if he had any notion of her feelings for him, what would he do? Would he attempt to exploit them? I feared he might.

I hope he will never come back, I said to myself.

But in my heart I longed for his return.

There was a small room close to the wards where we kept a few supplies and I was in there one day when Charles Fenwick came in. He looked very tired. Like all the doctors, he worked constantly and always under the shadow of frustration because of the lack of equipment.

'Oh, Anna,' he said. 'I'm glad I found you alone. I wanted to have a word with you.'

'It seems so long since we have spoken together,' I said.

'The two hospitals are really one and yet it is amazing how little one sees of one's friends.'

'How is everything going?'

'Not very well. This wretched siege! If only they could break through. We haven't the heavy casualties now but the weather is killing our troops. Cholera . . . dysentery. These have always been a greater enemy than the Russians. It's got to end. They can't hang out indefinitely.'

'They are a very determined people and they know how to suffer. Think what happened to Napoleon when he marched on Moscow.'

'This is different. Sebastopol has to fall. It is amazing that it has held out as long, but it can't indefinitely and then the war will be virtually over. But it isn't that I want to talk about with you. It's us.'

'You mean . . . the doctors?'

'No. You, Anna . . . and myself.'

I looked at him questioningly and he laid a hand on my arm. 'I'm thinking ahead to when this is over and we go home. Have you thought about that?'

'A little.'

'Will you go back to that house of yours?'

'There's nowhere else. Miss Nightingale is going to reform the hospitals at home. I should like to be involved in that.'

'Have you thought about marriage?'

'Why . . . no.'

'I have,' he said. 'I feel I want to purge myself of all this horror. I want to forget it . . . these smells which have become part of daily life . . . the pain and suffering all around us.'

'Isn't that part of the lives of doctors and nurses?'

'Not unnecessary pain and suffering like this, not these ghastly diseases which are brought about by insanitary conditions, starvation and festering wounds which can't be properly treated. I can only get through these days by thinking of the future.'

'I think we all feel like that.'

'I want a future to look forward to – a quiet practice somewhere . . . perhaps in the country. Or if you would prefer, London.'

'I?'

'I want you to share it with me, Anna.'

'Am I hearing you correctly?'

'I think so.'

'Then this is a proposal of marriage?'

'It is just that.'

'But Charles . . . I thought . . .'

'What did you think?'

'I knew you liked me, but I thought it was Henrietta in whom you were interested . . . I mean in that way.'

'Of course I like Henrietta, but it is you whom I love.'

'I am just astonished.'

'My dearest Anna, of course I love *you*. I love your strength and your seriousness, your dedication. I love everything about you. If you promised to marry me as soon as we are free of all this, it would give me a great deal to look forward to, to plan . . .'

He had taken my hands and was looking earnestly into my eyes.

'Oh Charles,' I said, 'I am so sorry. I was so . . . unprepared for this. I know that sounds like the cry of the bashful maiden, but I really am. I had no idea. I was certain that it was Henrietta.'

'Well, now you know it is not, what do you say?'

I was silent. I thought of the country practice, a new life, a new home, the village green, the ancient church with the yews which would have stood there for hundreds of years, dew on the grass, the lovely smell of damp earth, the gentle rain, daisies and buttercups – and I felt a great yearning for it all.

He was watching me eagerly.

'Charles,' I said, 'there is a great deal you don't know about me.'

'It's going to be exciting learning about each other.'

'We are here . . . in this place,' I reminded him, 'and things are not natural here. You might make decisions which you regret afterwards.'

'I don't think I shall regret this.'

'As I said, you don't know me.'

'I know you well. Didn't I see you at Kaiserwald? And here? I know your sterling character, your honesty, your goodness, your compassion. I have seen you give yourself wholeheartedly to the sick.'

'You have seen a nurse, that's all. I'm a good one, yes. It would be false modesty to deny it. But that is one part of me. I can't think about marriage. I am not ready.'

'I understand that I have sprung this on you. Think about it. I love you, Anna. We could make a good thing of it. Our interests are so closely woven together.'

'There is something I must tell you, Charles. I've been married before.'

'Anna!'

'And I had a child.'

'Where is your husband?'

'He is dead.'

'I see. And the child?'

'He died, too. It became an unhappy marriage. My husband was addicted to drugs which in the end killed him. My child died when he was not quite two years old.'

The tears pricked my eyes. He saw them and put his arm about me. 'My poor Anna,' he said.

'I have not yet grown away from it,' I told him.

'I understand.'

'I took my maiden name and started out again as a single woman. I felt that was best. I could not bear to talk of my marriage and the death of my child, but I tell you because it will help you understand why I cannot think of marrying anyone.'

'You will . . . in time.'

'I don't know. It seems so recent. I don't think I shall ever recover from the death of my child.'

'There is one way to recover from such a tragedy,' he said, 'and that is to have another child.'

I was silent.

'Anna,' he went on, 'don't say no yet. Just think about it. Think what it would mean. It would be something for us to plan for when we get out of this . . . hell. It can't last, I know. The end is in sight. You and I, and the children we shall have. This is the best way to lay the ghost of the past. You can't go on grieving.'

He kissed my hands and I felt a great affection for him. I knew he was a good man and he would make me see a way out of my unhappiness. It was a different way from that of revenge which I had followed so far. I saw myself on that country lawn, the doctor's wife, with her family growing up around her, her children who might look a little like Julian . . . children whom I would love and cherish . . . children who would soothe that aching void which had never left me since I had lost him.

I was suddenly aware of the passing of time. One always felt guilty when one snatched moments from hours of duty.

'I must go,' I said.

'Think about it,' Charles insisted.

I shook my head, but I knew I should.

He kissed me gently.

'Anna,' he said. 'I love you.'

*

I did not tell Henrietta of Charles's proposal. I could not bring myself to speak of it. I felt she would urge me to accept him. She liked him very much and she had said she thought he was a good doctor and a good man. There were times when I thought marriage to him would be the best thing for me. Was I going to spend the whole of my life as a lonely woman? True, I wished to nurse in one of the new hospitals which Miss Nightingale would attempt to set up in England on our return, but was that enough for me? I had experienced motherhood, and my overwhelming love for my child had taught me that I should feel my life was wasted if I did not have children.

Like so many people, I had an admiration for Florence Nightingale which was near idolatry. There was something about her indomitable spirit, her single-minded dedication, her quiet, almost ruthless efficiency which had impressed even those men who had in the beginning been most sceptical about her endeavours. She had turned her back on marriage and motherhood for a cause; but she had never experienced the joy of holding her child in her arms. I had; and that had convinced me that nothing else could ever take the place of that joy with me.

Here was a new path for me. I could marry Charles. I could be a wife and mother. I could turn my back on the past. I could forget those futile longings for revenge. The new prospect opening for me made me see them for what they really were. Childish anger. Little children tried to soothe their hurt by turning on some inanimate object. Aubrey had been weak; he had been easily led; a strong man would never have succumbed to drugs as he had. I had blamed Dr Adair for his downfall – and he was in part responsible – but people's fate was in their own hands.

And while I thought of my Eden in England – the country practice, the children round me, I saw the Demon, as I had always called him in my thoughts, laughing at me.

I would forget him, I told myself.

But somehow I knew I never would. He had some devilish quality. He could put a spell on one. I believed he had on Henrietta. Had he on me?'

He had travelled through the East as a native. He had discovered all manner of strange secrets and customs. Perhaps mysterious ones . . . the occult, even. He was not like other men. One could not judge him by the same standards. What had he been doing in that house in Constantinople dressed in that fashion? What did it mean?

I brought my thoughts back to Charles and his proposal, but I could not get the demon doctor out of my mind.

And one day I came face to face with him.

He was walking the wards in his white coat as though he had never been away. He gave me a curt nod which implied there was nothing unusual in his sudden appearance.

But he was soon making his presence felt. He found signs of inefficiency in the wards. He blamed the nurses. Patients had been neglected, he said. As if he did not know that the poor girls were worn out after hours without rest. And this from the man who would absent himself for a few weeks' respite when he felt like it!

My anger against him was fierce and I felt more alive than when I had last seen him.

He thought that nurses should not be too long in one place and he wanted some of them sent to the Barrack Hospital and others brought in from there to replace them.

Henrietta and Ethel were among those chosen to go to the Barrack. We were dismayed, although we were not so far apart, but one did not see nurses so often if they were in a different hospital.

Henrietta was resigned. Not so Ethel. She was in great distress.

'You see,' she explained to Eliza and me, 'I won't be seeing Tom. We'll never see each other.'

'You'll be able to come here and see him,' I comforted her.

'It's not the same. I look after him. I haven't told him. It'll kill him.'

'What's all this potty idea about moving people?' demanded Eliza.

'It's that Dr Adair,' said Ethel. 'He says we've been neglecting our duties. I was with Tom when he come through the ward the other day. He must have noticed.'

I said angrily: 'It's so stupid. The nurses are overworked. Of course they are going to forget things now and then. He's just trying to make trouble.'

Ethel was in despair.

Eliza sought me out afterwards. 'This isn't half going to upset young Ethel. I reckon it could blight the budding romance. Do you think you could do something about it?'

'How?'

'Speak to him . . . the almighty one.'

'Do you think he would listen to *me*?'

She looked at me shrewdly. 'He just might . . . to you.'

'He despises us all. And I haven't done anything to make myself especially acceptable in his eyes.'

'I think he *knows* you. What I mean is . . . the rest of us is just bits of furniture to him, not useful pieces either.'

'Oh, even he must see what the nurses are doing here.'

'Perhaps he does but he won't let himself see. He is the high and mighty doctor and nurses is just skivvies to go here and come there at his command.'

'And *you* think *I* could change him?'

Eliza nodded. 'It would be worth a try.'

I couldn't help laughing at the prospect, but in that moment I decided to make the attempt.

The opportunity occurred that very afternoon. I saw him go into that room where Charles had proposed to me and I followed him.

'Dr Adair.'

He swung round and as he looked at me, I felt all the anger and resentment I had harboured against him flare up.

'Miss – er –'

'I know you are thinking I have great temerity in daring to address you . . .' I paused and he did not deny it. 'But there is something I have to say to you. I believe it is your idea to move some nurses from the General to the Barrack and vice versa.'

'Am I expected to discuss my plans with you?' he asked almost pleasantly.

'I am asking you to discuss this particular plan with me.'

'May I know why?'

'Yes. You are moving nurses willy-nilly without considering what work they may be doing.'

'I know what work they are doing.'

'And despise those menial tasks. But Dr Adair, I assure you they have to be done and doctors should be grateful to Miss Nightingale for all she has achieved.'

'Thank you, Miss – er – for reminding me of my duty.'

'There is one nurse, Ethel Carter. She is being moved. She must not be.'

He raised his eyebrows and those dark luminous eyes surveyed me. I could not fathom what they expressed. Cynical amusement, perhaps.

'Let me explain,' I said.

'I must beg you to.'

'She has formed an attachment with a young soldier. His condition has improved greatly and she herself is much better. They cannot be separated.'

'This is a hospital, not a marriage bureau, Miss – er –'

'As you seem to have such difficulty with my name, let me tell you it is Pleydell.'

'Ah . . . Miss Pleydell.'

'And I do not think this place is a marriage bureau. I have been here long enough to know what it is. It is a place of great suffering.' I was furious with myself because my voice broke. I had to fight hard not to show my emotion. 'If a soldier can be made happier isn't that part of his recovery? Of course, I suppose that is something you do not believe in.'

'How do you know what I believe? You take a great deal upon yourself, Miss Pleydell.'

'Is it a great deal to ask? Just that this nurse should not be moved?'

'If her name is on the list for the Barrack she should go.'

'And what about this soldier who would have given his life for his country and perhaps has . . . what of him? Is he to have no consideration because some demi-god has made out a list?'

His lips curled faintly. I think he rather liked the idea of being called a demi-god, seeing himself supreme, no doubt.

'Listen to me,' I went on, growing more and more angry every moment. I had my enemy before me, the man I had planned to destroy, and how I wanted to! I hated his supercilious smile. He was taunting me, amused by my passion, urging me to hurl more and more abuse at him, which he believed I would regret later.

'I can hardly do anything else,' he reminded me, 'short of leaving you, which might be considered somewhat impolite.'

I went on: 'The soldier was brought in from Sebastopol. He was almost frozen to death. It was believed he could not last more than a few days. Ethel Carter looked after him and a special relationship grew up between them. Since then he has started to recover. I can tell you that she has had an unhappy life. She lost a child.' My voice faltered again. 'They are planning to make a life together. They are helping each other. They cannot be separated. Oh, I know you don't understand this. You are far too clever to understand the simple things in life. When you are tired of it you just go off . . . you leave others to carry on while you indulge yourself in fancy costumes in some . . .'

'Yes?' he said. 'Do go on. Where do I indulge myself?'

'You know very well. I, fortunately, am ignorant of these places and wish to remain so.'

'Ignorance is not something the wise desire.'

'It is a joke to you. But there are other means of healing than those you practise. There is happiness . . . contentment, hope for the future. They are as effective as medicines. Oh, I know it is foolish to appeal to you, and over something which you would consider of no importance. You are hard and ruthless and human suffering means nothing to you.'

'I did not know we were so well acquainted,' he said.

'I don't understand you.'

'And yet you have given a detailed account of my character.'

I felt numb with dismay, horror and frustration. What had I done? Just succeeded in making a fool of myself.

I turned and went from the room.

I returned to my duties, my cheeks burning and my eyes blazing. I was near to tears.

Why had I said all that? All the hatred had come tumbling out and he had stood there laughing at me. He was wicked. He was cruel. He cared nothing for people's feelings. They were objects to be used; their bodies were to be experimented on so that he could acquire experience and astonish the world with his knowledge. If only I could bring him crashing from his pedestal. If only I could show the world what he really was!

It was the next day when I saw Eliza in the kitchens.

She said: 'The swap's been made. Our lot's gone to Barrack and the Barrack lot are now in the General.' She gave me a nudge. 'Ethel's still here. She ain't half glad about that. 'Er and Tom is having a special cuddle.' She winked at me. 'Spoke to him, didn't you?'

I nodded.

She started to laugh. 'There! I told you you could do it.'

'It might not have been that. He didn't say he would help. In fact he implied quite the opposite.'

'Men!' said Eliza with a reminiscent grin. 'Some of them is like that. High and mighty and all that. Still, what's it matter? You done it.' She looked at me solemnly for a moment. 'Gawd bless you, Anna. I 'ope it comes right for you. You wants some little 'uns, that's what you want . . . like Ethel. There's some as does and some as don't – and you two are ones that does.'

That was a terrible winter. I hope never to see another like it.

I thought constantly of those poor men on the plateau outside Sebastopol – longing for the surrender which must come; but they would reflect that those inside the city – although doom was inevitable – did not suffer the hardships of the besiegers.

A sickness which some called Asiatic Cholera and others simply Gaol Fever struck the army. I used to see the men arrive in *arabas*, which were a kind of Turkish tumbril. Many of the men were dead when they were brought in. It was heartbreaking to see the Turkish workmen digging graves – great holes into which the bodies were thrown.

Some of the nurses caught the fever. It raged through the hospital and we were all living in fear of imminent death.

It was a wonderful sight to see Miss Nightingale take her nightly walk through the wards. She looked beautiful and serene in her black woollen dress with the white linen collar and cuffs and apron, and white cap under a black silk handkerchief, holding her lamp high, stopping at a bed here and there to touch a fevered brow, to utter a word of comfort, to smile and somehow bring a message of hope. She was regarded as a being from another world, an angel. Those men were very much aware of what she had done for their comfort. It was amusing to see how those who had hardly uttered a sentence in their lives which did not contain some obscenity, moderated their language when Miss Nightingale was near. She was indomitable; she had a presence and grace and beauty; plainly clad as she was, that was obvious. She commanded instant respect and adoration.

I shall always feel privileged to have worked close to her.

Even that terrible winter had to pass and with the coming of the spring fewer casualties were arriving at the hospital.

There was fresh hope in the air.

They cannot hold out much longer, everyone said.

I saw less of Henrietta. During those dark winter months we were working every hour of the day and well into the night and when we snatched a little rest we sank into an exhausted sleep.

Philippe Lablanche was a frequent visitor to the hospital. He often came to look for me and exchanged a few words; and I knew he did the same with Henrietta. Charles made a point of coming into the General to see me when he could, but like all doctors, he was even more busy than we were.

Sometimes he would say: 'Still thinking?' and I would answer: 'Yes.'

And there were times when I thought I was foolish to hesitate. I had the chance to share the life of a good man. I could even be of use to him in his work. I was no longer a wide-eyed girl. I knew something of marriage. I wasn't looking for a knight in shining armour to carry me off on his steed. I had the opportunity to share a life which would be interesting and rewarding. But I continued to hesitate.

The coming of the Crimean spring was a tonic to us all. It gave us hope to see crocuses and hyacinths growing on the plateau.

News of conditions at the front and in the hospitals had been sent home by war correspondents and there had been an outcry in the press. One of the good things which came out of this was that Monsieur Alexis Soyer, the renowned chef of the Reform Club, came out to supervise the kitchens. How we blessed Monsieur Soyer! He was dedicated to his art; he chose soldiers who he thought had some talent for cooking and took them into his kitchens; he trained them to produce excellent and nourishing stews. He would go through the wards with his men carrying big soup tureens and he was cheered by the invalids as it was ladled out. He made good bread, and he invented a teapot which held enough to serve fifty men, and the beverage was as hot for the fiftieth as it was for the first. Monsieur Soyer made a great difference to our lives.

We had a little free time now and then but my periods of freedom did not always coincide with those of Henrietta. We were almost light-hearted during those spring days. We had come through the winter and Sebastopol could not possibly survive another. We told ourselves that this time next year we should all be home.

An amusing incident happened at this time. A very pompous gentleman arrived at the hospital with two grand servants in gold braid, wide trousers and gold-coloured cummerbunds.

He was very excited and we could not understand what he was talking about until someone thought of calling Dr Adair.

I was hoping that he would not understand the language 'for,' as I remarked to Henrietta, 'we have only his word for it that he is master of all these Eastern tongues.'

He did understand and he and the pompous gentleman entered into a serious conversation.

Several of the nurses had gathered to see what the outcome would be – myself, Henrietta and Eliza among them.

At length Dr Adair turned to us and said: 'I think I should see Miss Nightingale immediately. This gentleman – on behalf of his very rich and distinguished master – is offering a good deal of money for one of the nurses who would be added to the distinguished gentleman's harem.'

We stared at him in astonishment.

'I wonder which one it is,' he added. 'It will be interesting to know.'

We did not have to wait long for the gentleman, smiling broadly, stepped towards us. He approached Henrietta and bowed to her. Then he turned and addressed himself to Dr Adair.

'So you are the elect,' said Dr Adair to Henrietta. I saw the speculation in his eyes as though he was wondering what special qualities Henrietta had to appeal to the oriental taste. She must have been seen somewhere. I did know that she had dined out with Philippe Lablanche.

Henrietta was most amused.

She said: 'What will you tell him?'

'That you are not for sale.'

'Won't that offend him?'

'I will explain tactfully. Perhaps that you are already spoken for.'

Henrietta giggled. 'I've often wondered what it would be like to find myself in a sultan's harem.'

'You might not enjoy it as much as you think. Now it would be polite if you retired and left me to deal with the matter. I shall need great tact. He must not be slighted in any way.'

We left. I noticed that people glanced at Henrietta. It did not surprise me in the least that she was the chosen one. She was far prettier than any of us; and she was more vivacious too; it was obvious that she would attract attention.

'You will have to be careful,' I told her. 'He might decide to kidnap you.'

*

About a week after that there was evidently more activity at Sebastopol and the wounded were coming in in large numbers.

When we saw the *arabas* approaching the hospital we nurses went out with the men who carried the stretchers to try to make the wounded as comfortable as possible while they were being carried in.

This was always a heartrending job. I dreaded it; but I was accustomed to horrific sights now and although they affected me as deeply as ever, I was at least prepared for them.

As I watched one poor man being lifted, groaning, on to a stretcher I thought he had a familiar look. Dirty and unkempt, his jacket bloodstained, he looked like so many of these poor men; and yet there was something about him.

Then I knew, and my heart leaped and then sank in horror, for this young man was Lily's husband, William Clift.

'Oh God,' I prayed, 'don't let him die.'

I thought of Lily and her delight in her baby; I could imagine her at home waiting for news. It must not be news of her husband's death. She had had such hopes of happiness. I remembered the change in her, the day when she had told us that she was going to marry William; and then the coming of the baby.

'Please don't let the baby be an orphan,' I prayed. 'Don't let Lily be a widow.'

But how many widows and orphans must there be because of this stupid, senseless war!

'But not Lily,' I continued to pray. 'Not Lily.'

I went into the ward and looked for him. It took me a long time but at last I found him.

I knelt by his bed. I said: 'William, do you know who I am?'

It seemed as though he was listening but his eyes did not focus on me. I feared he might be half dead already.

'William,' I went on, 'it's Anna Pleydell . . . Lily's friend.'

'Lily,' he murmured and I think he was trying to smile.

'Don't die,' I muttered to myself. 'You mustn't die. You've got to get well. There are Lily and the baby.'

But I was terribly afraid.

I went into the small room which I used as a sort of refuge.

It seemed to have a special significance since Charles had asked me to marry him there. And it was there that I had talked to Dr Adair and persuaded him not to part Ethel from her Tom. Some instinct led me there. I knew I had to find Damien Adair, for ironically enough I had the idea that he alone could help.

I was not surprised to see him there. He had taken some bottles from a shelf and was frowning at them.

'Dr Adair.'

He swung round. 'Miss – er –'

'Pleydell,' I said.

'Oh yes, of course.'

I said: 'There is a man out there. I know him. I know his wife. She has a baby.'

'There are a lot of men out there. I dare say many of them have wives and babies. What is there special about your man?'

'He must not die. He must be saved.'

'It is our duty to save them all if that is possible.'

I went to him and, seizing his arm, shook it. He looked surprised and faintly amused.

'Please,' I said. 'Look at him . . . now. Tell me that he can be saved. You *must* save his life.'

'Where is he?'

'I will take you to him.'

He followed me to the ward and I took him to the bed in which William Clift lay. He examined him, which took a little time. I stood watching his deft fingers probing.

Finally he pulled the blanket up over William. He walked towards the little room and I followed him. There he turned and looked at me.

'There are two bullets in his thigh,' he said. 'They are festering. He might have a chance if they were taken out at once.'

'Give him that chance, please, I beg of you.'

He looked at me steadily. Then he said: 'Very well. I will operate at once. You know him. You'd better be there. You may be of help.'

'Yes,' I said eagerly. 'Oh yes.'

'Let him be prepared. Get a screen put up round the bed. I'll have to do it there. There's nowhere else.'

'I will at once.'

I felt suddenly grateful to him. I knew he was the only one who could do it, even though he had cost me my own son with his experiments.

That was the strangest experience I had lived through so far. William lay on his bed. He was not sufficiently conscious to know what was about to happen to him. I was glad of that.

I kept whispering to him: 'You're going to be all right, William. You're going home to Lily and the baby . . . such a bonny baby. Lily's so proud of him and so will you be. Home, William, that's where you're going.'

I did not know whether he understood what I was saying, but he seemed to be comforted.

When Dr Adair came to us he looked at me steadily. He said: 'I'd rather you did not talk about what you are about to see. I want you to be here. I think the patient needs you. But this is between us . . . the doctor, the nurse and the patient.'

He took a phial from his pocket.

'Give me a cup,' he said.

He took it and poured a liquid into it.

'Lift the patient's head.'

I did so and held it while he drank the liquid.

'What's his name?'

'William Clift.'

He nodded and leaned over William. He said: 'William Clift. Look at me. Look into my eyes. Look. Look. What do you see? You see into my mind. I am going to take two bullets out of your thigh. You will feel nothing . . . nothing . . . nothing at all. Your friend is here with you, your friend from home.'

He went on looking into William's face, saying: 'You will feel nothing of this . . . nothing . . . nothing . . .'

William closed his eyes and appeared to sleep.

'We will act quickly,' said Damien Adair to me, 'while the effect stays with him.'

I was trembling. I felt I was in the presence of some mystic being whose wildly unorthodox methods were different from anything I had ever known.

'You can talk to him,' he said. 'Talk of his wife, his child and home . . .'

So I did. I said: 'We'll go home, William. Lily is waiting. The baby will have grown. He'll want to see his father. Lily is so happy, waiting for you . . . waiting . . . in the shop you know . . . and you'll go back and there'll be no more blood, no more slaughter . . . just home . . . home . . . You'll take the baby into the park. The park is lovely now, and the band plays there on Sundays.'

I went on and on saying the first things which came into my mind. I turned and saw the deft fingers at work. He held up one bullet; he was smiling in a triumphant way which seemed to me to be almost inhuman. What amazed me was that William had not moved while the operation was being performed.

'Go on talking,' he commanded; and I did.

Then I heard him give a sigh. I turned. He was holding the second bullet in his hand.

'The deed is done,' he said. 'He will feel the pain presently . . . not yet though. He is all right for a while. When he wakes, just sit with him quietly. If he tries to talk, answer him. In an hour or so he'll be in pain. I am going to give him something to stop it. Come to me at once if you see any sign of pain. I shall be about the ward. Keep the screens round the bed until you are told to move them.'

I sat there beside William. I felt strangely exalted. It was like witnessing a miracle. That man had strange powers. What was it Philippe had said about him? Unique. That was true. And there was a secret between us. I was to tell no one what I had seen.

My emotions were in turmoil. I sat there for almost an hour; then I saw that William's face was contorted in pain. I hurried away to find Dr Adair. He was, as he had said he would be, in the ward.

'I will come,' he said.

He came to William's bedside and put drops from his phial into a spoon which he gave to William.

'That will give him a few more hours' oblivion,' he said.

'And then?' I asked.

'The pain will come back, but the longer we ward it off, the more chance his body has to recover. You can leave him now. I don't doubt you have plenty to do.'

I said: 'Thank you, Dr Adair.'

I don't know how I got through my work that day. My thoughts were in a whirl. I kept thinking of that scene behind the screens – himself, myself and the man who might be dying in his bed.

There were moments when I thought: He is experimenting with his strange skills. What right had he to experiment on human beings . . . using them as guinea pigs? And yet . . . if he had saved William's life . . .

I could not stop thinking of him. But then I had been doing that since I had met him . . . and before.

There was no one to whom I could talk of what had happened. He had implied that it was between us two.

So I lay sleepless and the first thing I did in the morning was visit William Clift.

He looked pale and very ill.

But he was still alive.

During the evening of the next day I believe he sought me out. I was in the ward and he went to William Clift's bedside and examined him. As he left the bedside I went into the little room. I wondered whether he would come in or pass by.

He stood at the door. He was smiling at me triumphantly.

'Well,' he said, 'I think we are going to keep our patient.'

Waves of relief swept over me. I forgot my animosity towards him in that moment.

'Are you sure?'

He looked impatient. 'No one can ever be sure. At the moment I can say he is as well as can be expected, no better. And that is progress.'

He studied me intently. 'He will need careful nursing,' he went on.

'Of course.'

'You should look after him. Keep him regaled with stories of his wife and baby.'

My voice was shaky. 'I'll do that.'

He nodded and went out.

I was with William a great deal. I dressed his wounds. I talked to him of home. I saw the listlessness drop from him. I saw the hope in his eyes.

A week after the incident Dr Adair passed me in the ward. He said: 'I think we are going to send our patient home hale and hearty to his wife and baby.'

I don't think I had felt so happy since Julian had died.

During the long summer months fewer casualties were brought into the hospital and, as always, most of those who came were suffering more from disease than from wounds. William Clift was recovering satisfactorily, which meant not too fast, for I feared if he were fully recovered he would be sent out to fight again. He was very weak but he was no longer in danger – and that was how I wanted it.

Ethel was officially engaged and radiant. She talked continually about the farm in the country. She was so grateful to Tom because when she had told him about herself, he understood. She planned to have lots of children and live happily ever after.

Eliza was delighted with the way life had turned out for Ethel. I had discovered that she was a woman who liked to have someone to look after; and now that Tom was looking after Ethel, she turned her attentions to me. She was one of the few people who knew about my past, since I had told her during that stormy night on deck; she never betrayed the confidence, but it had changed her attitude towards me. She wanted me to find a husband as Ethel had done. She was aware of Dr Fenwick's feelings for me and she thought that ideal. It was rather amusing to discover the soft side of her nature. She looked so formidable, so ready to fight for what she considered her rights. Quite a number of nurses were afraid of her – so were the patients, and they obeyed her without question. They called her Big Eliza. I had grown very fond of her.

Henrietta was in good spirits. She had been flattered to be the chosen of the unknown pasha or sultan who wanted her for his harem and laughed a great deal about the incident. She talked of the mysteries of the East and what fun it would be to explore them. She said she could understand Dr Adair's absorption with the subject. She seemed often to bring the conversation round to him.

'I saw him today,' she would say. 'He really is magnificent. He has that air of authority. None would dare disobey his orders. You have the impression that he is a superior being. Do you feel that, Anna, now that you know him a little?'

'No,' I retorted. 'He is a doctor who likes to experiment. I think he enjoys taking risks.'

'He saved Lily's husband's life.'

'Sometimes risks are successful, but I think he was showing how clever he was.'

'You are unfair to him, Anna. I think he is wonderful. I often laugh about our project. Do you remember how we used to talk about him? How we set out on our quest to find him with the object of exposing him as a fraud . . . a conceited mountebank?'

I was silent.

'It was all a bit of a game, wasn't it? We never really meant it seriously. How could we? And when you see him here . . . He makes the others seem very insignificant. Oh, I don't mean that . . . quite. Charles is such a *good* man, but . . .'

'You prefer the sinner to the saint.'

'I don't think the terms apply. Charles isn't a saint, is he? And Dr Adair . . . well, perhaps . . . Anyway, I think he is the most attractive man I have ever met.'

She folded her hands across her breast and raised her eyes to the ceiling. Henrietta's gestures, like her talk, were often exaggerated.

I did not say anything more. I felt I could not discuss him with Henrietta.

But Eliza talked of Henrietta to me.

317

She said: 'I'm worried about her. There could be trouble. I don't think it's good for a young woman to feel like she does about that Dr Adair. It's what got poor Eth. And look at that. The swine goes off and leaves her with a child.'

'What has that got to do with Henrietta and Dr Adair?'

'She's got that feeling for him. She'll be wax in his hands.'

'Oh, Eliza, you are too melodramatic.'

'I know men. In the trade you had to. All that adoring is just what they want. They can't have enough of it at first. Then when they're tired of a girl they don't want it no more . . . not from her. But at first it's right up their street. I don't reckon Dr High and Mighty's any different from the others. And she's going round making no secret of the fact that she's there for the taking.'

'No, Eliza, that's not true. It is just that we've always been rather interested in him.'

She looked at me sharply. 'Not you! You'd have more sense, wouldn't you?'

'Enough sense for what?'

'To keep away from the likes of him.'

'Yes, Eliza, I'd have that much good sense.'

'The other doctor is a very nice gentleman. He's sweet on you and you could do worse.'

'It's good of you, Eliza,' I said with feeling. 'I believe you really do care.'

''Course I care. I don't want to see you or Henrietta make fools of yourself over *men*.'

'We won't.'

She shook her head as though to imply she was not so sure.

We were through August, and September was with us. We were all feeling a little uneasy. The thought of having to go through another winter was very depressing.

The Russians were getting desperate. So were the French and English. Then we heard that a terrific battle was raging before Sebastopol and in trepidation we waited for the result.

We did not have to wait long. A messenger arrived, and we all rushed to meet him to hear the latest news.

The French had stormed and taken Malakoff Fort.

'Thank God,' the cry went up, for we all knew that the Fort was the key to Sebastopol.

'The Russians are fleeing from the city, but they have set what is left of it on fire. It is nothing but a mass of flames.'

Then suddenly we were all embracing each other.

For nearly twelve months we had been waiting for Sebastopol to fall; and now it had happened. There was not a doubt among us that the war was over.

We were right, although there were a few pockets of resistance to overcome. The bulk of our work was over. Everyone was talking of home. But, of course, the hospital was full of patients, some of them too ill to be moved. We could not all go and leave them. It was decided that we should go in relays and some of us would have to remain until there was nothing left to be done.

In view of the exceptional circumstances, Ethel was one of the first to leave. Although Tom was well enough to go, he still needed attention and Ethel was to go with him to give it to him.

I stood with Henrietta and Eliza watching them embark. How different she was from the girl who had come here. I fell to thinking that there appeared to be good even to come out of evil, for the war had taken Ethel out of a wretched life which could not have been of long duration and had given her a future which promised to be good.

She stood at the rail watching us, and we waited there until the ship was out of sight. Then we went back to the hospital, too moved for speech.

I had written a letter to Lily which Ethel promised to deliver. I wanted her to know that William was really well and under my care. I knew nothing could give her more comfort except the return of William himself.

The hospital was different now. Each day some of the men would be sent home. Only the worst cases remained. Some would die, of course; but it was hoped that in a few months the others would be well enough to go home.

Charles was to go with a batch of the wounded.

He came to me and told me of his orders.

'I wish, Anna,' he said, 'that you could come with me.'

'I shall be home soon. I am looking after William Clift, and although he is doing well, he is not yet quite ready to be moved. So . . . I am needed here.'

'You would always put duty first, of course.'

I was not sure that he was right. I did not want to go yet. I had the feeling that I had come here for a purpose and that purpose was not completed. I had to be near Damien Adair for a while – though I was not sure what I wanted to do.

Charles kissed me tenderly.

'As soon as you're back, I'll come to you. I think by then you will have made up your mind.'

'Yes, Charles,' I said, 'that will be best.'

'Everything will be different at home when we get back to normality.'

I agreed with him. 'It can't be long now,' I said.

Then he talked about what we would do in the country. He would see what was going. He would choose his practice carefully and would take nothing until he had consulted me. I could see that he would be a considerate husband and that I was fortunate to have such a man love me.

I watched him sail away and when he had gone I missed him. It is so comforting to be loved even if one is not sure that one can return that love.

Our duties were comparatively light now and there were frequent occasions when we had a few hours to ourselves. Parties of us would take the *caïques* and go across to Constantinople. The town was so different now. It was no longer under enemy threat. The shops were suddenly brighter. There seemed always to be music in the streets. There were many restaurants where we could have a meal or sit merely drinking wine or thick Turkish coffee.

We were known by our uniforms and respected. We had earned a reputation for doing good work, and although in the beginning many had been sceptical of us, that was not the case now.

Henrietta was in even higher spirits than usual. She seemed almost feverishly merry. She said to me once: 'I don't know how I shall settle in England after this. I would love to go farther East. There is so much I want to know.'

Philippe Lablanche was still in Constantinople and he took us out once or twice; he often called at the hospital and I thought he was attracted by Henrietta. She was rather flirtatious towards him and he seemed to find that enchanting. She had had a great deal of attention in her life and seemed to expect it and to revel in it.

She constantly asked Philippe questions about the customs of the people, and when he talked about his travels she was spellbound – imagining herself, I guessed, riding through the desert, pitching her tent at some oasis – all very romantic. I had an idea that Dr Adair was rarely out of her thoughts.

Once she came back from Constantinople with a costume she had bought. It was of silk with swathings of material hanging loosely over trousers which billowed out and were caught in at the ankles.

'What on earth have you bought that for?' I asked.

'Because I liked it.'

'You couldn't wear it.'

'Why not? I'll put it on and show you how it suits me.'

In a few moments she was standing before me, radiant in the costume.

I said: 'You look like the queen of the harem. But you are too fair to fit the part.'

'Some of them *are* fair. Some are slaves from distant lands.'

'Henrietta,' I said, 'you are quite absurd.'

'I know. But it is fun being absurd.'

'Mind you, you could wear it as a fancy dress costume at home. It would be quite suitable for that.'

Her expression changed. It was a little uneasy.

'It will be strange to be home,' she said slowly. 'Just imagine . . . after all this. Rather mundane, don't you think?'

I stared at her in amazement. I had thought that, like most of us, she was longing for home.

'Don't tell me you are going to regret leaving the hospital, the wards, the suffering men . . . all the horrors of it, the impossibility of keeping it clean . . . the anguish, the blood, the terrible exhaustion, the conditions we have been living in. Don't tell me that you haven't longed to be home.'

'It is more comfortable, of course.'

I laughed at her. 'Is that all?'

'There is a possibility here of something fantastic happening. At home . . . what is there? Balls, parties, coming out, meeting the right people. There is something romantic here.'

'Henrietta, you amaze me! I thought you couldn't wait to get home.'

'Things change,' she said, and she was smiling into space.

A few days later Philippe called at the hospital and invited us to dine with him that evening. He would call for us at six and we would take the *caïque* across to Constantinople as usual.

I was wearing a pale green dress which I had brought with me. It was very simple and had been easy to slip into my carpet bag. It was the one dress I had, apart from my uniform. I had not worn it very much because our uniform was a protection if we should find ourselves in a difficult position – as Henrietta and I had learned during that adventure we had had in the streets of the city.

But on that evening we should be with Philippe and he was well accustomed to the ways of Constantinople.

Henrietta wore a long cloak and I was amazed to see that under it was her Turkish outfit. She looked very beautiful. There was an infectious gaiety about her which was very attractive. One felt one must enjoy an occasion because she did so thoroughly.

As we were about to step into the *caïque* we met Dr Adair.

'Are you dining in Constantinople?' he asked.

Philippe said that we were.

'Two ladies and one man! That doesn't seem right. How would it be if I invited myself to join the party?'

We were all taken aback. Henrietta's eyes were sparkling.

'But that would be delightful!' she cried.

'Thank you,' said Dr Adair. 'Then that's settled.'

The *caïque* was crowded as usual and Dr Adair said: 'Everyone wants to take advantage of the last weeks here. Very soon everyone will be free to go.'

'There are some patients who can't be moved yet,' I reminded him.

'A matter of time,' he said. 'I dare say *you* are counting the days.'

I replied that we were delighted that the war was over and there was a possibility of getting back to normal again.

'Normal is always so enticing . . . at least to look back on and forward to.'

The journey across the Bosphorus was very brief and soon we were alighting. Several *caïques* had arrived at the same time and there was quite a crowd on the shore. Dr Adair took my arm, Philippe took Henrietta's.

'Just a moment,' said Dr Adair to me quietly. 'Take a look back . . . across the bank. Doesn't it look romantic? Not much like the hospital we know. In this light it looks like a caliph's palace, don't you think?'

He was smiling at me half ironically. He looked secretive, I thought. But then he always did.

'It looks quite different, I admit.'

'You will also admit that it is something you will never forget.'

I turned away. Henrietta and Philippe were no longer in sight.

He looked around him. 'It is so easy to lose people in the crowds. We'll find them.'

But we did not find them.

We made our way along the waterfront. Dr Adair looked at me in what I fancy was mock dismay.

'Never mind,' he said. 'I think I know where Lablanche was planning to go.'

'Did he tell you? I didn't hear him.'

'Oh . . . I know his favourite haunt. Come, we'll go there. Leave it to me.'

He led me to one of the carriages which was waiting to be hired. They were drawn by two horses and we sat side by side, as we began our drive through the city. It was most romantic, especially by night. I was still getting over the shock of finding myself alone with him. He talked rather nonchalantly but knowledgeably about the architecture, in which subject he appeared to be well-informed – comparing the mosque built by Sulyman the Great with that of Sultan Ahmed the First. We had by this time crossed one of the bridges to the Turkish part of the city.

'Here I think we may find our friends,' he said. 'If not . . . we must make do with each other.'

I said: 'If you would prefer it, Dr Adair, I can go back to Scutari.'

'Whatever for? I thought you were bent on dining out.'

'I had accepted Monsieur Lablanche's invitation but as I have lost him . . .'

'Never mind. You have another protector.'

'Perhaps you had other plans.'

'Only to dine out. Come. Let us go in. It may well be that the others have forestalled us.'

We alighted and he led me into the restaurant. It was darkish and there were lighted candles on the tables. A man in very splendid livery of blue and gold with a gold-coloured cummerbund came towards us. I did not understand the conversation between them but the liveried man – presumably a head waiter – was most obsequious.

Dr Adair turned to me. 'Our friends have not yet arrived. I have asked them to find a table for two, and there we will wait for them. When they do he will tell them at once that we are here. If they do not, I am afraid, Miss Pleydell, you will be obliged to make do with me.'

We were taken to a table in an alcove, somewhat secluded from the rest of the room.

'A little seclusion is so much better if one wants to indulge in conversation,' he said.

I was feeling uneasy and yet at the same time exhilarated. I had come a long and devious way to find this man and here I was actually seated opposite him. It was success indeed.

'I hope you are ready to experiment with Turkish food, Miss Pleydell. It is rather different from what you have at home

. . . or hospital fare. But one has to be adventurous, don't you agree?'

'Yes, of course.'

'You don't seem very sure. Are you adventurous?'

'Surely one must be to come out to the Crimea, to war?'

'Up to a point, I agree. But you are a dedicated nurse and would doubtless go to the ends of the earth if your profession called you there. Would you like caviar? Otherwise there is a very tasty dish of meat stuffed with peppers which have been treated in all sorts of sauces.'

'For fear of being judged unadventurous, I might try that,' I said.

'Good, and after that I suggest this Circassian chicken. It's cooked in a sauce of walnuts.'

'Don't you think we should wait for the others?'

'Oh no . . .'

'But I was supposed to be Monsieur Lablanche's guest.'

'He has the ebullient Henrietta to entertain.'

'Do you really think they will come here?'

'There is a possibility. I am not sure of the number of these eating places in Constantinople, but at least this is one of them, and a renowned one . . . so there is a possibility that they might come here.'

'I thought you were sure they would come, that it was a favourite place of Monsieur Lablanche.'

'He is a man of discrimination so he will certainly know of this place.'

'You are not very direct. You gave me quite a different impression a little while ago.'

'We make our own impressions, Miss Pleydell, but why bother ourselves with such a trivial matter? Here we are – dining *à deux*. It is a good opportunity for us to talk.'

'Do you think we have anything to talk about?'

'My dear Miss Pleydell, it would be two very dull people who had nothing to talk about just for one brief evening. We have worked together . . . You have formed your impressions of me . . .'

'And you of me. That is, if you have ever noticed me.'

'I am an observant man. I miss little, you know.'

'But surely some things are too insignificant for your notice.'

'Certainly not, Miss Pleydell.'

The liveried man in the cummerbund was approaching our table with a waiter slightly less splendidly clad than himself, and the order was given. Dr Adair chose a wine and in a very short time the first course was brought to us.

He lifted his glass. 'To you . . . and all the nightingales who left home to come across the sea to nurse our soldiers.'

I lifted mine. 'And to the doctors who came, too.'

'Your first protégé will now be on his way home,' he said.

'Oh, you mean Tom. Yes, he is on the way home with Ethel. They are going to be married.'

'And live happily ever after?'

'That is what is hoped for. There is a farm and Ethel is a country girl.'

'And your second?'

'You mean William Clift who is recovering slowly.'

'That was a near thing.' He looked at me steadily.

The Circassian chicken arrived at that moment and there was silence while it was served.

'I am sure you will find it delicious,' said Dr Adair. He filled my glass. 'Yes,' he went on, 'I wanted to talk to you about William Clift.'

I raised my eyebrows.

'You look surprised.'

'I *am* surprised that you should think me worthy to discuss a patient with you. I fancied you thought nurses should remain in their places and should merely run hither and thither at the doctors' command and be consigned to the menial tasks.'

'Well, should they not? That does not mean that I should not want to discuss William Clift with you. His wounds are healing. He was brought close to death, but he survived . . . and in due course he will be quite fit and probably live to a ripe age. He could so easily have been dead, you know.'

'Yes, I do know that.'

'Those bullets were deeply embedded. They had started to fester. It was touch and go.'

I looked at him. I thought: I was right about him. He wants praise. All the time he wants glory for Dr Adair.

'You will remember I used unorthodox methods. It was fortunate that I did. If I had not, Miss Pleydell, William Clift would not be alive today.'

'You gave him something to drink . . .'

'More than that. I put him under hypnosis. That method is not always approved of by medical opinion at home. But, Miss Pleydell, my methods do not always fit in with conventional ones and therefore I am not a conventional doctor.'

'I know that.'

'I believe that pain retards recovery. A patient must be freed from pain whenever possible. When the body suffers pain, restoration is delayed. I would use any method to eliminate pain.'

'That seems to me very laudable.'

'But there are some people in the medical profession who do not agree. Did I say some? I mean many. They believe that pain is bestowed by God – or someone on High – as just retribution. "Let there be pain and there was pain!" I am very much against that. I have been in the East and I do not disdain methods which are different from ours. We have advanced a long way in some directions, but there are other ways in which we are behind a people who, by some standards, would be called primitive in comparison with us. Am I boring you, Miss Pleydell?'

'Indeed not. I am most interested.'

'You were present. You saw what happened with William Clift. I saved his life. But for me he would be dead and your Lily would be a widow, her child an orphan.'

Why must he boast? I thought. He is right, of course. He did a marvellous thing. But why must he detract from his action by this continual boasting?

'I put him to sleep so that I could perform the operation without his body resisting me. It is a method learned in Arabia. It is not to be used lightly. I only bring it into my work when it is absolutely necessary. You, Miss Pleydell, were so insistent that I should save this man's life. I had to show you that I could do it. And I did.'

'I cannot understand why you had to show *me* . . . just a nurse . . . just one of the adjuncts which can be useful at times but are on the whole a liability.'

'You are too modest, and I think that modesty is not really a part of your nature. I have come to the conclusion that this is false modesty. Do you like the chicken?'

'Thank you, yes. I am not modest, but you have made your opinion of us very clear.'

'Then why do I bother to tell you this?'

'Perhaps you like everyone to know how clever you are?'

'True. But I have no need to stress the point with you. You already know.'

I laughed suddenly and he laughed with me.

'Let us get to the point,' he went on. 'I believe you once had a very poor opinion of me. You believed I had deserted my post to go away and revel in riotous behaviour. You were brought to me and there I was in native costume. What did you think?'

'That you were taking a respite from the hard work of the hospital.'

'I knew it. That is why I have to explain. Tell me, did you think I had a harem tucked away somewhere, that I was living a sybarite existence, indulging in all kinds of vices?'

'I had read your books, you know.'

'That was kind of you.'

'Not kind at all. They were given to me and I was fascinated by your adventures and I could see the sort of man you were. It came out in your books.'

'It was careless of me to have betrayed myself. I have lived among natives, as I described. It is only when you become one of them that you really know them. I have learned much from them. When you were brought to me, I was just about to set off on a mission. You know there was an appalling lack of matériel at the hospital. Do you remember the man with the amputated leg? Can you imagine the shock to that man's system, with nothing to deaden the pain? What were his chances of recovery? Very poor. And yet not to have amputated would be certain death. There was just a faint hope. With certain medicines there would have been a fair chance. That was how I was expected to perform operations. So . . . I went off to find means of putting people to sleep. I knew where I could get these things. Drugs. Drugs to sedate our patients, my dear Miss Pleydell; and not the drugs which are commonly used in hospitals. These drugs would only be given to one of their own kind. So I had to be one of them. It is more than a matter of dress and of speech . . . it is outlook. They know me as they know themselves. They trust me. If I had not gone on that little expedition – when you believed me to have deserted my post and gone to revel in the delights of the harem – I could not have saved the life of your William Clift.'

'Then I am sorry I misjudged you.'

'Thank you. You are forgiven. It is so easy to draw the wrong conclusions, to blame in ignorance.'

'I do realize this.'

'And you have changed your opinion of me?'

I hesitated and he looked shocked.

I said: 'It is not for me to form opinions. I could only do so from ignorance, as you have pointed out.'

A waiter came to take the plates away and bring a rich cake of pastry filled with nuts and honey called baklava; a tray of sweetmeats was also laid before us.

'This is a most delicious meal,' I said.

'I agree. But I prefer to talk of ourselves rather than food.'

He leaned his elbows on the table and looked steadily at me.

'Dr Adair,' I said, 'you are not trying to hypnotize me, are you?'

'You would not be a very easy subject, I fear. You would resist. Poor William Clift was in no position to do so. But you sitting there – looking remarkably well, if I may say so, in spite of your sojourn in the hospital – you would set your mind against me.'

'If I submitted, what would you do?'

'I would try to lure you from your conventional ways.'

'Conventional! I think I am far from that.'

'I would discover the secret of the nightingale.'

'What do you mean by that?'

'Just what I say. I always think of you as the nightingale. That is not surprising, I suppose.'

'What amazes me is that you think of me at all.'

'No, Miss Pleydell, my dear little nightingale, you know better than that.'

'Indeed, I don't. I have noticed that you did not seem to be aware of the nurses.'

'I was aware of them all and you in particular.'

'Indeed!'

'You interested me. You are hiding something. I should like to know what it is. You ask what I should do if I could control your mind. I would say: Tell me everything . . . tell me what it is that has happened to you and which has made you as you are.'

'What do you think happened to me?'

'That is the secret. Something has . . . something very important to you . . . something tragic . . . something for which you blame someone. I should like to know.'

I felt my lips trembling. So it was obvious. Memories of going to the Minster and finding Julian dead swept over me. And the knowledge that this man had been there . . .

Indeed I had a secret, and it was to take my revenge. And now here he was sitting opposite me, and I was his guest, and I did not know why it was all so different from what I had imagined it would be. I was dreadfully unsure of him . . . and myself.

'If you would talk it might help,' he was saying.

I shook my head.

'What do you think of the baklava?' he asked.

'It's rather sweet.'

'They like sweet things, the Turks. Try one of these sweet-meats. There again, they are sweet. It is all sweetness.'

I thought: He knows too much. How could he possibly have discovered that there was tragedy in my past? Had I betrayed it? Only Eliza and Henrietta knew. Eliza had never had any contact with him – nor would she betray a confidence. Henrietta? I felt a twinge of uneasiness. I thought of Henrietta who talked of him continually. Only this night, when he had suggested joining us, how delighted she had been.

I felt I had to change the subject quickly and I started talking about his books.

'Did someone introduce you to them?' he asked.

'Yes, it was someone who was friendly with you in England . . . oh, a long time ago. Stephen St Clare.'

'Stephen, yes. He was a great friend of mine. Pleasant place they had in the country. Did you ever go there?'

'Oh yes.'

'He's dead now, poor Stephen . . . and the brother too. That was a sad case.'

'The brother?' I echoed weakly.

'Yes. He died. As you knew the family, you probably knew too that Aubrey was addicted to drugs. He took it too far. Very sad. He had an unfortunate marriage.'

'Oh?'

'Yes . . . a flighty sort of girl who was no good to him. He met her in India, I think.'

'Did you . . . know her?'

'No. I heard the story, though. Poor fellow. He was weak. He got caught up in the wrong set. A good steady wife might have changed him.'

'Oh?' I was beginning to feel indignant, but I must keep a close guard on my feelings. I had been mistaken about his indifference. There was little he missed.

'You would have thought that a wife married to a man like that would have done all she could to help him. Instead, she left him . . . went off. He went down and down after that, and you can't go on indulging in that sort of thing. It caught up with him in time. There was a child, too, who died.'

I gripped the table. I must keep calm. My impulse was to shout at him: Listen to my side of the story.

'As a matter of fact,' he went on, 'I happened to be there at the time. There was an inadequate nurse. The wife had left them to go to London. The child was neglected. That gin-sodden nurse ought not to have been left in charge of the child. A doctor should have been called in.'

'But you were called in . . .'

'Too late. The child was already dead when I saw him.'

I stared at him in disbelief.

'Why are you so interested?' he asked.

'So he died,' I said. 'And the child died, too. What happened to the wife?'

'She left . . . lived in London, I believe. No doubt she liked the social life.'

I wanted to strike him. I wanted to hit the table in my grief and anger. It was devastating to have it all brought back so vividly, to hear myself blamed. But most of all to discover that my darling Julian was already dead when the demonic doctor arrived, if he was telling the truth.

He had represented me as a frivolous uncaring woman who had left her child for the sake of a trip to London and had failed to give her husband the support which might have saved him. How many believed that? How could I talk to him of those terrible orgies in the cave, the hideous rites, the shock of discovering the kind of man I had married and the reason I had gone to London and how everything had worked against me?

How dared he interpret the case so casually, so cruelly?

'Is anything wrong, Miss Pleydell?'

'No . . . no, of course not.'

'These heart-shaped ones are rather delicious. Do have one.'

'No, thank you.'

'Ah, here is the coffee.'

It was served on a brass tray in gold-coloured cups. I tried to steady myself as it was poured out. My emotions were in a turmoil. To be with him, talking in this intimate way, was most disturbing; and when he had discussed his version of what had happened at the Minster, he had completely unnerved me.

He was watching me steadily.

'Tell me,' he said. 'Why did you have an ambition to become a nurse?'

'I felt it was something I had to do.' I wanted to shout at him: What do you know about what happened at the Minster? How could I have stayed? It would not have been possible to save Aubrey. He was too far gone. I could not have helped him by staying. I had to get away. I could not bear the grief of losing my child. How dare you speak of me as though I were light, uncaring! I forced myself to go on: 'I felt I had something within me. I suppose you would call it absurd. But when I touched people there was some response. I seemed to have some healing quality.'

He stretched his hand across the table and took mine. 'These hands,' he said. 'They are beautifully shaped hands. Pale hands . . . yet capable . . . magic hands.'

'You are laughing at me.'

He continued to hold my hand and looked into my eyes. I was afraid of those eyes. Those deep, dark eyes. I had seen their power. I had a moment of panic when I thought he was going to draw my secret from me.

'Oh no, I am not,' he said. 'I have told you that I have seen the mysticism of the East. I believe certain people are blessed with strange powers. I have seen you in the hospital. Yes, you have the healing touch. Was it that which made you want to become a nurse?'

'I think it must have been. I wanted to do something with my life.'

'Because of what happened?'

'What do you mean?'

'The secret, little Nightingale.'

I tried to laugh. 'You are building up something which is not there.'

'That is not true. It is there. Tell me. Perhaps I could be of use.'

'There is nothing I wish to tell.'

'There might be something which it would be helpful to tell.'

'Helpful to whom?'

'To you? To me?'

I shook my head and withdrew my hand which he was still holding.

'You are very aloof,' he said.

'In what way?'

'I believe you are suspicious of me.'

I laughed and shrugged my shoulders.

'You don't want me to know what you are trying to hide from me.'

'From you? Why should I hide anything from you?'

'That is what I want you to tell me. Dear Nightingale, we are not in the wards now. We are free . . . for one night, here we are.'

'What does that mean?'

'That there are no duties calling us from this most enjoyable encounter. I am glad we missed the others. Are you?'

'I – er . . .'

'Oh come, tell the truth.'

'It has been very interesting. I dare say it would have been pleasant with the others.'

'Two is so much more comfortable than four. Two can talk so much more intimately. With four there are often two conversations going on at the same time. No, I prefer this, and I am glad it happened the way it did. I believe in time I could persuade you to unfreeze.'

'I am not frozen.'

'Yes, you are. You are frozen in that secret from the past. You are letting it rule your life. You are trying to sublimate your natural impulses by becoming a nurse. What shall you do when you go back? Will you join Miss Florence Nightingale? I hear she is doing great things in London. Or will you marry Charles Fenwick? That is what you plan to do, perhaps.'

'How do you know so much about my affairs?'

'I told you I keep my eyes open, and as Charles was a doctor in the hospital, naturally I know a little about him. Are you going to marry him?'

'I don't know. I am not sure. Here everything is so different from at home. I think I should wait before making a decision . . . until I am back home among the familiar things, the familiar way of life. I will always want to use my gift for nursing in some way.'

'What a cautious lady you are! Do you never act on impulse?'

'I think I do frequently.'

His eyes held mine. 'I am glad of that.'

'Why?'

'Because it is often very stimulating. So you will marry Dr Fenwick. He will have a nice little practice in the country . . . not too big to take him away from his wife and family. The life of a doctor in the country in England can be very pleasant.'

'How could you know?'

'From observation. I don't think you would become addicted to the cosy life somehow. There is that in you which reaches out for something more . . . new experiences, adventure . . . Of course, you might settle down in your pleasant country house in your pleasant country town with your pleasant family – and never know anything of other things. There is a saying that what you never have you never miss. But you, Miss Pleydell . . . Oh, I wonder. You see, there was that something in the past which has made you not quite the conventional young lady you are striving to be.'

'Is there? Is this the result of your acute observations? I should rather call it a lurid imagination. But I am flattered that you have given so much thought to my affairs.'

'You would be even more flattered if you knew how much thought I give to them.'

I raised my eyebrows. 'You are not surprised really,' he said. 'You know, do you not, that I have a very special interest in you.'

'I imagine you are indulging in what is called polite dinner-time conversation with a companion who does not warrant serious discourse.'

'Surely that is not the impression I have given you this evening?'

I was silent.

He went on: 'Soon we shall leave this place. It has been a most pleasant evening for me. I do not want it to end.'

'It has been kind of you to give me dinner. I had no idea that you were to be my host.'

'Would you have refused the invitation if you had known?'

'Having already accepted Monsieur Lablanche's . . .'

'That's not what I meant. Are you afraid of me?'

'Afraid of you! Why should I be?'

'For a reason . . . perhaps.'

'Now *you* are being mysterious.'

'Dear Nightingale, am I not always mysterious? But not so much now because I believe you know what is in my mind. I believe that you and I should get to know each other better. After all, we have worked together in the hospital.'

'Together! You flatter me. I have just been there obeying commands.'

'Still . . . together.' He put his hand across the table. 'Don't shut yourself in with that secret past. Bring it out. Let's talk about it. Let me prove to you that you are not meant merely to be a nurse. You are a woman as well . . . and an attractive one.'

I felt the colour rush into my cheeks.

'What are you suggesting?'

'That you look at life as it is, that you do not deny yourself what should be yours.'

'I have been unaware of any self-denial.'

'Let me tell you this: I know you well. You are a woman like other women, and in this Victorian age of restrictions and repressions, so many women do not allow themselves to be themselves. They try to become some cold-blooded ideal which has been set up for them. Do you not see that it suits the community of men to have such women in society . . . as long as there is another kind of woman to whom they look for their satisfaction? Such women are expected to suppress what is natural to them – their emotions and the gratification of their senses, which I assure you should bring no shame. I have watched you. You are a normal, healthy, full-blooded woman, capable, I know, of deep emotions. You are suppressing them in this vocation for nursing. I have seen you working as though there is nothing else in life. You are fighting something, holding it at bay. If you would tell me that secret, if we could discuss it together, if you and I could become . . . true friends . . .'

I looked at him steadily. 'True friends!' I repeated.

'The truest of friends . . . the best of friends . . . between whom there are no barriers. We will go from here. You will come with me . . .'

I knew what he was suggesting and the colour flooded into my cheeks. He saw my embarrassment and was amused by it.

He was thinking I was repressed. This was a most unexpected turn of events.

He was evil. Of course he was evil. I had allowed myself to forget because he had saved William Clift's life. And why had he done that? Not for humanity's sake, but to show himself as omnipotent.

I half-rose from my chair. 'Dr Adair,' I said, 'I wish to go back to the hospital.'

He lifted his shoulders and looked at me quizzically.

'I was indeed right,' he said. 'But I did not realize how strongly you had built that prison round yourself.'

'Your metaphor is somewhat obscure. I am perfectly free and in command of my own life, and I know that I do not want to continue with this conversation. Thank you for the dinner. And now, please, if you will show me how to get back, I will say goodbye.'

'You cannot be out alone in the streets of Constantinople at this hour of the night.'

'I shall be safer . . .'

'Than with me? I think not. I would not force my company upon you. I might coerce but that is a different matter. Come, we will go, for I see you are becoming agitated. You have marked me as the villain, the seducer, have you not? I have always sensed the antagonism you have felt for me. It intrigues me. I have tried to change it . . . clumsily. I have such regard for you, Miss Pleydell, but now I have failed . . . for tonight. The first battle is lost, but first battles do not decide the outcome.'

'You talk as though there is a war between us.'

'It is really quite an apt description. But you will find I am a benign conqueror and the peace terms will be agreeable to you.'

'This is nonsense.'

He looked at me steadily and I knew I had not misjudged his intentions.

I wanted to get away, to be alone, to think of all that had been said at the table, to discover the meaning behind it.

He rose with me, and the gorgeously liveried man bowed us out of the restaurant. Soon we were crossing the bridge into Christian Constantinople.

'If you will take me to the *caïques* that will be enough,' I said.

'Indeed it will not. I shall take you right back to the hospital.'

'It is unnecessary.'

'I shall do it.'

I said nothing, but I was aware of his eyes on me. There was amusement in them, something sardonic. I felt uneasy, unclean in a way. I was very disturbed. I could not believe that I had interpreted his meaning correctly. But he was such an evil man that I was sure I was right.

We came up the slope to the hospital. There I thanked him again for his hospitality as formally as I could.

'The ending to an evening which could have been so different,' he said. 'A conventional evening which must be expected with one as conventional as yourself.'

'There could be only one possible ending,' I said. 'Thank you.'

He held my hand firmly. 'Not the only possible ending, Miss Pleydell.'

'The only possible as far as I am concerned.'

'Never mind,' he said. 'This is a beginning.'

I turned and left him.

I hurried to the bedroom. I regretted that it was not possible to be alone. We were much depleted now and there was considerably more room, but still privacy was impossible.

Eliza was already on her divan. She opened her eyes as I came in.

'Where's Henrietta? I saw you go off together.'

'Hasn't she returned yet?'

'No.'

'We were split up. Dr Adair joined us and we lost Henrietta and Philippe Lablanche.'

She lifted her head and, leaning on her elbow, stared at me. 'So you were alone . . . with Dr Adair.'

I nodded. 'I'm so tired, Eliza.'

'H'm,' she grunted, and lay down. She said nothing more and as we lay there I knew she was not sleeping.

I kept thinking of the evening, what he had said about my deserting Aubrey. It was so unfair. Who had given him that impression? And his veiled suggestion . . .! I supposed that was how he was with all women. He regarded us all as slaves. Hadn't he lived in the East? Hadn't he learned their ways? I had seen the women, their bodies covered by long robes, their faces hidden – to be seen only by their masters. He had lived as they had. He shared their views of women. We were here on Earth to pander to the wishes of men and especially men like Damien Adair. By chance he and I had been thrown together. But was it chance or had he arranged to lose the others? He had thought I would be easy. Repressed! Sublimating my natural physical desires by nursing. What impudence! And he had hinted at some sort of relationship between us. If I had hated him before, I did so doubly now.

I felt bruised and shaken. He had wounded me deeply by what he had said about my marriage.

Henrietta came in much later.

She bent over me to see if I was asleep. I pretended I was. I knew she would ask questions about the evening and I wanted to have a greater command of my thoughts before I answered her.

I could not escape the barrage of questions next day. Henrietta was avid for information

'What happened? You were there one minute and gone the next.'

'I don't know how it happened. We just found you were gone.'

'Philippe was getting me through the crowd. I thought you were following.'

'We did stop to look back, I remember.'

'That must have been it. Oh, Anna, what happened?'

'Well, Dr Adair thought you might have gone to a certain place. He said it was a favourite place of Philippe's . . . or something like that. So we went there and dined alone.'

'Alone with Dr Adair! Oh, Anna, how exciting!'

I was silent.

'He is so fascinating. Of course Philippe is very nice, but . . . What happened?'

I said: 'We just dined, talked and came home. I was in well before you were.'

'Yes. You were fast asleep. What on earth did you talk about?'

'Oh . . . about the hospital.'

'I should have thought you would have been glad to get away from all that.'

'Well, he's a doctor and it is very important to him.'

'It must have been wonderful for you.'

Silence again.

She said: 'If I had been the one I should have been most thrilled. I mean . . . all those adventures of his . . . living in a harem and all that. I should have had so much to talk to him about.'

'You always have so much to talk to everyone about.'

She laughed. 'Well, especially him. I think he is the most amazing man . . .'

I could not bear to hear her rhapsodizing over him, so I said I really must go to the wards.

It was about a week later when we heard we were to go home. Most of the wounded were to be taken back to England, and very few would remain.

As the departure grew nearer, I noticed Henrietta's abstraction. I again had a feeling that she did not want to go.

Eliza noticed and commented on it to me.

I think she was anxious about me. She was convinced that I must marry Dr Fenwick because that would be best for me.

'I've said many times,' she said, 'that you are one of them women that want a family. You want children, and that's how you'll get 'em. Oh, I know you don't see Dr Fenwick as some dashing chap who's going to be worth going to hell for. It's not like that. Life's not like that, believe me. I know. And when a girl sees a good thing, she ought to take it and not go dithering about too long, in case it's snatched away. Chances like that don't grow on trees.'

I never minded her interfering in my affairs. I liked to feel that big Eliza had taken me under her wing.

I did wonder what she would do when she returned to England, and I asked her.

She shrugged her shoulders. 'I might get into one of these hospitals they talk about. I reckon I could say I'd had enough experience now. That or the old game. Who knows? It's a toss-up.'

'But where will you live when you get back?'

'I'll find a room somewhere. Rooms is always going.'

'Eliza, come back with Henrietta and me. I've got room to spare in the house I rent.'

'What! Stay in your house! You must be stark raving mad. You can't have the likes of me in your house!'

'My dear Eliza, I choose my guests and I have the likes of whom I like.'

She laughed at me. 'No. It'll be different when you get home, you see. Friends here won't be friends there. Here, we're all the same. We're all together. But it will be different when we get home.'

'It will be what we make it, Eliza, and I want you to come and stay until you decide what you want to do. We might go into one of the hospitals together.'

'You don't want to be doing that sort of work. You're going to marry that nice Dr Fenwick.'

'Eliza, please say you'll come with us. We'll go and see Ethel in the country.'

'That would be nice.'

'It's settled, then.'

'You are a one,' she said. Her forehead wrinkled. 'I hope it will be all right with you and Dr Fenwick.'

'These things take their course.'

'There was one time when I was afraid you was getting something for that Dr Adair . . . like Henrietta.'

'For him! Oh no! He's very remote.'

'That don't make no difference. I'd say he was a bad 'un. He's out for Number One and that is Dr Adair.'

'I expect you're right.'

'But he's got something – I'll say that for him. I reckon the women fall for him like ninepins. It's that way of his . . . all them dark good looks and that mystery about the East and all that. I reckon he's lived a life . . . and somehow you know it.'

'He seems to have made an impression on *you*.'

'He'd make an impression in a stone wall, that one would. It's Henrietta I'm worried about. You've got sense. Things have happened to you. You've been married once and you know it ain't all beer and skittles. But Henrietta, she's a baby, really. She's an innocent . . . rather like Ethel but in a different way, if you get my meaning.'

'I think Henrietta can take care of herself. She seems so light-hearted and a little frivolous, but she is shrewd really.'

'I dunno. Girls can get funny about men, and with that sort of man, you can never be sure.'

'But you don't think Dr Adair and Henrietta . . .'

'I wouldn't put nothing past him. If he lifted his finger, she'd be off. You've noticed how she is when he's about . . . when he's mentioned, even. He'd only have to say the word and she'd be off with him – and that ain't going to do her no good.'

'Eliza, you're wrong. She is seeing a great deal of Monsieur Lablanche.'

'A nice fellow, that one . . . like Dr Fenwick, but it ain't always the nice ones people seem to want if they ain't got much sense, and most women haven't. I know what I'm talking about.'

Did she? I wondered.

As the day for our departure grew nearer, Henrietta became more pensive. She lapsed into silences – so rare with her. I asked if anything was wrong and she assured me that nothing was. But I knew she had something on her mind.

It was the night before we were due to sail. We were not sure exactly what time we should be leaving Scutari; but we had been warned that we must be ready to embark when the order was given.

I saw Dr Adair that day. I knew that he had been looking for me. We went into the little room next to the now depleted ward.

'So,' he said, 'you are leaving tomorrow.'

'Yes.'

'You don't want to go?'

I hesitated. He was right in a way. I felt deflated. I had come out here determined to show him for what he was; and what had I done? Nothing. He had outwitted me at every turn; all I had succeeded in doing was making myself dependent on him. It was the first time I had admitted that. Now I saw clearly that when I was with him, when I exchanged words with him, I felt alive. I fed on my hatred; I had lived for it – and the plain fact was that life would be blank without it. There was emptiness everywhere.

'So I am right,' he said triumphantly. 'You don't want to go.' He came close to me and laid a hand on my arm, holding it firmly. 'Don't go,' he said.

'How could I stay? We have been told we are to leave the hospital.'

'There are places other than the hospital. You know how interested you are in the city. I could show you some fascinating parts.'

'That is absurd. Where should I live?'

'I will arrange that.'

'Are you really suggesting . . .'

He looked at me smiling, nodding. 'Come, Miss Pleydell. Miss Caged Nightingale. Do what you want to do even if it is against the rules society has laid down for you. Stay here. I will see that everything is arranged for you.'

'Of course I know you are not serious.'

'I am in earnest.'

'Why?'

'Because I should miss you if you went away.'

'Surely not.'

'Please, Miss Pleydell. I know my own feelings.'

'Well, goodbye, Dr Adair.'

'I shall not say goodbye. If you are determined to leave tomorrow, I will say au revoir. Because we shall meet again, you know.'

He took my hand and held it, compelling me to look into his eyes. I felt emotion taking possession of my common sense. I was very sad, not because I was leaving the hospital, not because the war was over – how could I be? These were matters over which I should rejoice. But if I had to admit the truth, it was because I should not be seeing him. He had obsessed me for so long – even before I saw him. I had lived for my revenge, and now that we had come face to face that had eluded me.

I wanted to go on battling with him. I wanted more of these dinner-time *têtes-à-têtes* when he sat opposite me making oblique suggestions that there might be some relationship between us – which I, to my shame, was excited to contemplate.

I was going to feel depressed when we left. I wondered what I should do in London. I should be wishing myself back in the horrors of the Scutari hospital – working constantly, witnessing sights which sickened me and filled me with pity, dropping on to my divan at night too exhausted for anything but the brief sleep I could enjoy until morning came. But all the time there had been the possibility of seeing him, of even exchanging a few words with him, of discovering something which I could tell myself was a part of his conceit and villainy.

I should miss him. That was a mild way of expressing what I should feel. My life would be empty without him.

'Goodbye, Dr Adair,' I repeated.

He kept my hand in his.

'Don't go,' he said quietly.

'Goodbye.'

344

'You are adamant.'

'Naturally. I am going home.'

'We shall meet again.'

'Perhaps . . .'

'Not perhaps. I shall make sure that we do. You're going to regret leaving, you know.'

I just smiled, withdrew my hand and walked away.

It was later that day when Henrietta came to me.

'Anna,' she said, 'I'm not going.'

'What do you mean . . . not going?'

'I'm not going home.'

'You can't stay at the hospital.'

'I know. I'm not planning to do that.'

'But . . . you can't . . .'

'I can . . . when we leave here. We are discharged already. I can go where I like. I'm going to stay here.'

'Where?'

'In Constantinople.'

'Alone?'

'Well . . . I shall be all right. I have to make a decision.'

'What decision?'

'It's Philippe. He's asked me to marry him.'

'Have you agreed?'

She shook her head. 'I'm not sure. I want time.'

'But you could always come out again.'

'I don't want to do that. I'm going to stay here.'

'But you can't.'

'One or two are staying. Grace Curry and Betty Green and some others.'

'They're different. They can take care of themselves. They're not young girls.'

'I'll have people to take care of me. I have to stay, Anna. Nothing is going to make me change my mind.'

'Oh, Henrietta,' I said. 'We came out together. We've been together all this time.'

'I know. Ours is a wonderful friendship, but this is more

important to me than anything. You go home. You'll have Eliza with you. She's better than I am . . .'

'Don't stay here, Henrietta.'

'I must.'

'You haven't told me everything.'

She was silent. 'There are some things one can't talk of. One can't explain one's feelings. This is something I have to do on my own.'

'Have you seriously thought of what you are doing?'

'I've thought of nothing else for ages. I'm not waiting until tomorrow. I'm going tonight.'

'I can't believe this. I feel completely shattered.'

'I put off telling you. I should have done so before. But you know me. If I don't like doing something, I pretend it doesn't exist. I've always been like that.'

'Perhaps I had better stay with you.'

She looked at me in alarm. 'No, no. You must go home. Eliza's going with you. Oh, Anna, won't Jane and Polly be pleased. And Lily too. They'll kill the fatted calf.'

'Henrietta, is there something you want to tell me?'

She shook her head. 'No . . . no. I must do this, Anna. Please try to understand and one day . . . soon perhaps . . . I'll come and see you. Then I'll tell you everything. Then you'll understand.'

She embraced me, holding me tightly in silence, for we were both too emotional for words.

I found Eliza and told her what Henrietta had told me.

She said: 'I saw it coming. I knew it. Poor Henrietta, she doesn't know what she's letting herself in for.'

'I've talked to her. I've tried to beg her to come with us. I've even said I'd stay.'

'You mustn't. You must get home. You must live like you was meant to live. Dr Fenwick will come and when you are married to him, you'll wonder why you ever put it off so long.'

We said a tense goodbye to Henrietta. A few other women had decided to stay and those who were doing so left that night.

I could not believe that I was losing her. For so long we had been together. I was hurt and bewildered that she could go thus. She knew my feelings and wanted to explain, but she obviously could not bring herself to.

'It's love, that's what it is,' said Eliza. 'That gets stronger than friendship. Every other thing's forgotten when a man beckons to his mate.'

We went with Henrietta out of the hospital. We watched her make her way down the incline to the shore. We saw her getting into the *caïque*. Then I stared, for Dr Adair had joined her and was standing beside her.

Eliza turned to me.

'I told you so. I knew it.'

'What?' I said, although I knew.

'She's gone off with him. All he had to do was raise his finger and she's off, forsaking her friends . . . everyone. Well, that's the way of the world.'

'She is going to Philippe Lablanche.'

'That's a likely tale.'

'It was what she told me.'

'She didn't want you to know the truth. She was under his spell. I saw that plain as plum duff without the plums. She's gone off with him. Oh, the little fool. And we'll not be here when he throws her off. He's took her . . . I reckon he was after you as well. I know his sort. Gawd help our little Henrietta.'

'I don't believe it. She would have told me. She distinctly said Philippe.'

'He was waiting for her, wasn't he? 'Course she'll tell you it's Philippe. She wouldn't want you to know the truth. I've seen it coming. I know life, I do. She's gone off for a few weeks . . . a few days . . . perhaps a few hours with our mysterious gentleman, and she thinks that worth while!'

'Surely neither of them would do such a thing.'

'What do you mean – neither of them? He's a rogue and she's a fool. He's out for everything he can get and she's been working up to this for weeks.'

'Perhaps I should try to find her, bring her back.'

'How? Where? She'll be right in the heart of the city before you could get near her. His mistress . . . that's what she'll be. She won't last long with him neither. There's nothing we can do.'

I did not sleep all through my last night in Scutari. I lay tossing from side to side.

What were they doing now? They were together. Damien – I called him Damien in my thoughts – would be making love to her. He would be expert at that and poor Henrietta was innocent, inexperienced, a dreamy-eyed schoolgirl, really. She would believe it would go on forever, and for him she would be one of those lights-o'-love to be taken up for a brief spell and then discarded when he tired of them – like the women in the harem. Perhaps he had a harem in that place in Constantinople? I imagined them . . . women in their beautiful silks, Turkish garb . . . those sheer baggy gauze trousers caught in at the ankles . . . waiting to be summoned to their lord.

To think that Henrietta had become one of those . . . a slave, no less. And he had tried to make me one of his band! I expect he would have liked us both to be there together.

I must stop thinking of them. Henrietta had made her choice. She must abide by it. What had she done? She had cast aside her independence, a civilized way of life, to become a slave.

Lurid pictures flashed in and out of my mind. I imagined him, talking to her across the table as he had to me. I imagined their making love; and in my imagination it was not Henrietta who shared in those erotic posturings, but I. I was fighting a battle with myself. I wanted to be there. What a shameful admission! It was not true. I wanted never to see him again. I wanted to forget I had ever heard of him. But how could I? He had been part of my life for so long. I had fed my grief with titbits of revenge. I had lived through the blankness of my life in the hope of revenging myself on him. I had endowed him with all sorts of villainies. He had been the Demon Doctor

– not quite human. He had taken possession of me as surely as if he had done so physically. He was evil and yet life was so empty without him.

I thought fleetingly of Charles Fenwick. I had not felt this emptiness when I had watched him sail for home. Yet Charles was a good honest man. He was offering me a great deal, and I had turned from it. I had to be reasonable; I had to be sensible. I had to get the Demon Doctor out of my mind.

I must try to sleep, or I should be so tired in the morning and there would be a great deal to do. I forced myself to think of my homecoming. As soon as I had known, I had written to Jane and Polly telling them the date of my arrival; but I was not sure when they would receive the letter.

I should be sure of a welcome. They would kill the fatted calf, as Henrietta had said. What talk there would be. Jane, Polly, Lily, they would all want to know so much. I should have to explain about Henrietta and introduce Eliza to them.

William Clift would be travelling with us. I was to take him home. A present for Lily. What a present! I must be thankful for what I was able to do.

And it was Damien who had saved his life, and there I was back with him. It was useless to try to get him out of my mind.

I went over every detail of that day when, behind the screen, he had saved William's life with his strange methods. No one else could have done it. No one else would have dared to do what he had done. I must not forget that – nor must I forget that we had misjudged him. When we had found him wearing that turban – looking magnificent – he had not been indulging in erotic adventures; he had been procuring drugs which he had administered to William and others and so saved their lives.

He was satanic in some ways, but he was a good doctor. He had done many things which would be judged disreputable, but how many lives had he saved? And how many lost? Doctors could not save life all the time. It was the very nature of their work that they must experiment.

And here he was, dominating my thoughts, keeping sleep at bay, filling me with a wretched feeling of loss.

No sleep was possible that night.

The next day we boarded the ship which was to take us to Marseilles. It was almost as battered as the *Vectis* and appeared to be only just seaworthy; but I was hardly aware of that. My thoughts were in Constantinople.

Those soldiers who were well enough to travel came with us, William among them. At least I found comfort in the fact that I was taking him home to Lily.

I felt very emotional as we sailed down the Bosphorus, looking back at those shores, at the minarets and towers of Constantinople and the hospital at Scutari. Eliza and I stood side by side watching.

'Lots of water flowed under the bridge since we first came,' she commented.

'I remember it well . . . the four of us. We had become good friends by then. How glad I am that we did.'

'Same here,' said Eliza; she was always brief when her emotions were involved.

'At least Ethel came out all right,' she went on. 'Who'd have thought it? Little Ethel! One of life's victims. Just shows you, you can never be sure. She's had a real starry romance. I wonder how she is? Won't it be good to see her?'

'It will,' I agreed.

Then we went inside to our squalid and cramped quarters.

In a way it was like history repeating itself. It was not long before we were in the storm. Eliza and I went on deck and sat side by side, the waves crashing against the side of our frail craft, wondering, as we did on that other occasion, whether we would survive.

'It's just like that other time, only now there are only two of us,' said Eliza. 'Now Ethel's safe at home. It only goes to show you should never give up, don't it?'

'It does indeed,' I said.

'Just think. If you hadn't stopped her going over she'd never have met Tom, never have had that life in the country. Don't it make you feel sort of powerful, to have had that effect on someone's life?'

'Don't we all have effects on each other's lives?'

'I reckon you've got something there. But to have saved a life, that's really something.'

I thought of him at that screened-off bedside, holding the bullet in his hand. I thought of his methods . . . willing William to feel no pain, the administration of a drug which would no doubt have been unacceptable in our hospitals at home. He had saved other lives . . . and lost a few. How did it feel?

Eliza said: 'You're brooding still.'

'Well, there is a lot to think about. So much has happened to us since we came out. We must be different people. We have seen sights which have shocked us beyond measure . . . horrors we shall never forget. People at home hear of the triumphs of war and they imagine our gallant soldiers galloping to victory . . . and it is all magnificent and romantic. But it is not like that at all. That is something you and I will never forget, Eliza.'

'True enough.'

We were silent thinking of those long exhausting days, of the times when the *arabas* had come in with the wounded, the continual fight against the lack of beds, equipment . . . everything we needed.

She said suddenly: 'You've got a choice to make. Are you going to work in one of those hospitals Miss Nightingale is going to set up . . . or are you going to marry Dr Fenwick?'

'It's difficult to plan ahead, Eliza.'

'That means you are not sure, don't it?'

'I suppose it does. And you, Eliza?'

'I'll never have no devoted lover wanting me. I'm one of them that's got to look after themselves. It might be the hospital for me. I dunno. I never plan far ahead. Things happen to you whether you plan or not. You and me sitting here and you wanting me to go back with you. Who would have thought when we first come out?'

'You were a little suspicious of us.'

'I thought you was one of them ladies that was playing at it, and I knew it wasn't going to be no playground.'

'We got to know each other and that was a good thing. I shall always cherish your friendship, Eliza.'

'I know this sounds a bit soft, but I've got fond of you, and I was real frightened that you was going to do something silly. That man! What was it about him? He wasn't like other men, was he?'

'You mean Dr Adair.'

'That's right. Them eyes of his seemed to go right through you. He was good-looking, too. Sort of face you don't see about much. What I mean is, there's some people . . . you see them and five minutes after you can't remember what they looked like. Him . . . once seen, never forgotten.'

'Yes, I think you are right.'

'He was sort of fascinating. Even I felt it. You had the feeling he could make you do just what he wanted.'

I nodded.

'I could see how you felt about him.'

'I . . . knew of him before I met him. He's written books, you know, about his adventures in the East. He is interested in medicines used in countries remote from us. He believes we in the Western world shut our ears and eyes to Eastern methods. He thinks we should explore every avenue, leave nothing to chance.'

'I can see how he's got through to you. You sort of glow when you talk of him.'

'Glow?'

'Well, I'm not much good with words. But your eyes shine and there's something in your voice. I can see he got through to you like he did to Henrietta.'

'It was because of what I'd heard of him. I wanted to find out if it was all true.'

'I reckon he was a good doctor all right. Not the sort Dr Fenwick is. Now he's a good *man*, and that other, he's not what you'd call a good man. He wouldn't only be finding out about medicines, but customs and things.'

'He lived among them. It was the only way he could get to know them, the only way he could make his discoveries.'

'And we know what some of their ways are. He's all man, that's what I'd say of him. He's got a real opinion of himself. He thinks we're all here for him to make use of. I could see what he was doing to Henrietta.'

'I can't believe she would lie to me. If she were going to him she would have said so.'

Eliza shook her head. 'No,' she said emphatically. 'She knew how you felt about him.'

'I never mentioned my feelings about him.'

'You didn't have to. She knew because she felt it all herself, and when she went off with him, she didn't want you to know because she thought it would hurt you. So she made up this tale about marrying the Frenchman.'

'I don't believe it.'

'That's what she'd do. She turned away from what was painful. She wouldn't have hurt you for the world. She didn't want you to know she'd got the prize . . . 'Cos that's how she'd see it. She's gone to him. Gawd help her. It won't last. She's not the sort to keep him content. He had his eyes on you. You were more serious. I could see he was watching you. Then I suppose she was easier. She was ready to drop into his arms. I know men; I know women. You be thankful for what you've got. You've got a choice. Dr Fenwick and a good life with little 'uns, which is what you want to lay that other little 'un to rest, which you won't really do until you've got another. You're the kind of woman that wants 'em, as I've told you before. If you've got any sense – and I do think you've got some – you'll take Dr Fenwick. And you thank your lucky stars that he's there for you.'

'Oh Eliza,' I said, 'it's good to talk to you.'

We were silent for a while, then I said: 'Do you think this ship will make it to Marseilles?'

'She will. Though you wouldn't think it to see the battering she's taking.'

'Storms seem to invite confidences.'

'It's because you're reckless. At the back of your mind is

the thought you might not survive, so you say what you really think.'

'I didn't realize I had betrayed my interest in Dr Adair.'

'Oh, my good girl, it shone out of you. You sparkled when he came through. I've seen you come out of that room, you remember, the little one near the wards. I've seen you come out of that room with him there, all a-glowing.'

'Like Henrietta?' I asked.

'Yes, just like that. But you expect it with her. Not with you, though. So it means more.'

'Well, I shan't see him again.'

'Don't keep Dr Fenwick waiting too long. Men gets impatient, even the best of them.'

We were silent again.

Then I said: 'The storm is less fierce now.'

'There's a lull.'

'How strange it will be,' I said, 'to be home after all this time.'

Return to Kaiserwald

Somewhat battered and the worse for the voyage, we reached Marseilles. Then there was the journey to Paris, where we stayed a night in the same hotel in which we had stayed on the way out.

Then to Calais and the ship which was to take us across the Channel.

We had plenty to do looking after the soldiers we had with us, even though none of them was seriously ill.

As the white cliffs came nearer, my emotions were in a turmoil. Home seemed so cosy and comfortable, and yet I felt that so much of me had been left behind. I was disconcerted to learn that I had betrayed my feelings to such an extent. Eliza had made me realize the strength of them. Had I really looked as Eliza said I had? Transported! Glowing, was her exact word. Was it so obvious? And had he noticed?

How foolish I was! I had set out to destroy him and it seemed as though he had destroyed me.

I would have to face the truth now. I wanted to be with him. More than anything I wanted that. He was the most fascinating person I had ever met. He was complex. There was so much to learn about him . . . more than one could learn in a lifetime. Had he destroyed my child indirectly? No, Julian was already dead when he came. But he had influenced Aubrey, I believed. My encounters with him had been brief; the knowledge that he was near had exhilarated me; and what I had thought was burning anger had turned into something else.

And he had taken Henrietta!

I felt that he wanted me to know that. He had been angry because I had turned away from his advances. There was no doubt in my mind what those suggestions of his had meant. He had wanted to have me with him . . . his willing mistress and slave. There had been no hint of marriage. Would a man like that want to marry? A wife, a normal family, would impede his freedom. He would want to pursue his adventures whenever the mood took him. He was arrogant and immoral; he was accustomed to stride through life taking what he wanted and leaving it as soon as he no longer wanted it; and he would not change for any woman.

He was unique. That was why he felt he was entitled to act as he did.

And I had been foolish enough to allow myself to be caught up with him. How amused he must have been! To see me, shining with joy just because he had spoken to me! Eliza saw it, so he must have seen it, too. He would believe that I had turned away from his suggestion because I was afraid of him, afraid of stepping out of the conventional mould.

And so . . . he had beckoned instead to Henrietta and she had readily gone to him.

What a mess I had made of everything! First my marriage. Should I have stayed and tried to make a different man of Aubrey? Should I have helped him fight that terrible addiction? When it was happening I had believed there was nothing I could do about it but leave him. But had I been wrong . . . callous, indifferent? I had broken those vows I had made to love and cherish in sickness and in health. And then my senseless notion of revenge had kept me afloat in the sea of misery in which I had been drowning when I lost my baby.

I had been foolish. I should have faced up to life. I should have looked it squarely in the face and not deceived myself.

Well, now I had to start again.

Could I marry Charles? Would it be fair to him when my feelings were so strongly engaged towards someone else . . . and such a man! There could never have been anyone like him. If I saw him again, how strong could I be? So . . . how could I marry Charles?

I was thankful that Eliza was with me. Perhaps we could go

to one of the hospitals together. After all, we were trained for the work.

The cliffs were so near now. We were almost home.

It was a moment of great joy when we arrived at Victoria Station for my letter had arrived in time to warn them of my coming and Joe was waiting there with the carriage. Lily was with him. I shall never forget the sight of her when she ran into William's arms.

For some moments they clung together. She looked at him, searching his face to see if he was the same . . . her William.

Then she turned to me. 'Oh, Miss Anna . . . you saved him. You brought him home to me.'

'It was not I who saved him, Lily. It was the doctor . . . Dr Adair.'

'May God bless him. I wish I could thank him for what he has done.'

And there was Joe. He just stood looking at me.

'Home, then . . .' he said. 'Them there is like cats on hot bricks. Been in that state ever since they knew.'

'And where is Miss Henrietta?' asked Lily.

'She's staying out there . . . for a while.'

'Oh . . . I thought you was both coming home.'

'This is Eliza, Miss Flynn. She was nursing with me and she is going to stay with us for a while.'

'Well, fancy that,' said Lily. 'What a time you must have had. I'm so glad you was there, Miss Anna. I can't tell you how I felt when I heard from you that William was safe.'

'Better be getting on,' said Joe. 'Them horses is impatient. Don't like standing too long.'

And there we were in the carriage trotting through the streets.

As the carriage drew up Jane and Polly were at the door. I ran to them and they embraced me.

'Well, well,' said Polly. 'This is a day, and all. We've been counting the days, ain't we, Jane?'

Jane said they had and wasn't it wonderful to see me and where was Miss Henrietta?

I told them that she was staying behind for a while, and that

I had brought Miss Eliza to stay with us. She had nursed with me.

In the hall they had fixed up a banner on which was painted 'Welcome Home'. It was very touching. I stared at it with emotion and thought how lucky I was to have such people who cared for me.

'Well, there's roast beef,' said Polly. 'We thought you'd like that after all the nasty foreign stuff you must have been eating.'

'You think of everything,' I told her.

Eliza was a little subdued but Jane and Polly were warm and friendly towards her.

'I'm putting you in Miss Henrietta's bed because that's all aired and warmed,' said Jane. 'How long before Miss Henrietta comes home, Miss Pleydell?'

'We're not sure. I think it's a good idea to give Miss Flynn her room.'

How strange it seemed to sit at a table with spotless napery and to eat the perfectly cooked meal which Jane set before us. Lily and William stayed to eat with us and I insisted on Jane and Polly sitting down with us too. ''T'aint right and proper,' said Jane; but they were pleased none the less.

Afterwards Lily and William left; and Joe drove them to the Clift shop where I had no doubt a great welcome awaited them.

It was stranger still to lie in a comfortable bed in a room of one's own. How cool the sheets seemed and they smelt of the lavender sachets which Polly put in the linen.

And yet I felt restless and sad and as if I should never know contentment again. I was foolish and the truth was becoming clearer to me. I had fallen in love with a myth.

The days seemed long. There was not enough to do. I shopped a little, though I seemed to have so many clothes. It was something to do.

Eliza fitted in well and was soon on friendly terms with Jane and Polly. They accepted her; and the verdict was that she was one of them.

'Lord love a duck,' said Polly admiringly, 'that one's got

the strength of a man.' That was when Eliza had shifted a piece of furniture in one of the rooms. She was so eager to make herself useful and insisted on helping with the housework.

We were making enquiries about a suitable hospital where we might work. I read in the papers that Miss Nightingale was raising funds to train a superior order of nurses at St Thomas's and King's College hospitals. We wondered whether we should be eligible to join. While we were pondering on this, Charles Fenwick arrived in London.

His coming was treated with obvious approval, not only by Eliza, who had often made her feelings known to me, but by Jane and Polly.

They excelled themselves with the lunch they provided.

After the meal Charles and I went for a walk in Kensington Gardens, where he told me of his plans.

'I did say that I would wait before getting involved in a practice, that I might consult you. But this came up and it seemed ideal. I had to make a quick decision.'

'I'm glad you did. It's for you to decide, Charles.'

'You know that I hope it will be your life, too.'

'I don't want you to consider me, Charles. You see, I may not . . .'

'I understand. You're unsure. All that has happened is so unsettling. I don't think anyone who was out there and saw what we saw and lived through it will ever be quite the same again.'

'You are so good and understanding that it seems churlish of me . . .'

'Oh, nonsense! I want you to be happy. I want you to be sure that you are doing what is best for *you*.'

'I know I'm being foolish. It is just that I am so undecided.'

We sat near the Round Pond and watched the children playing with their boats.

I tried to explain. 'I'm not a young and inexperienced girl. I have been married. It all seems so wonderful at first and then it changes and you see what a mistake you have made.'

'It would make one wary,' he agreed.

'I shouldn't be . . . of you. I know how kind you are . . .

how good. It is you who should be wary of me. I left my husband. Had I been a good wife I should have stayed, no matter how hard it was. Perhaps I am not the sort of person who makes a good wife.'

'With the right marriage, you would. I'll tell you what we'll do. We'll go down to Meriton. That's the name of the place. It's rather pleasant, isn't it? It's in Gloucestershire. I love the Cotswold country. The practice is a partnership. There's a Dr Silkin. He's not exactly old but middle-aged, mid-fifties – and he wants to ease off a bit. He wants a partner with a view to taking over the whole practice in due course. It's an excellent opportunity. I took a fancy to him and the place.'

'It sounds ideal for you . . . just what you were looking for.'

'I've found a pleasant little house which would suit us nicely at first. It's almost exactly next door to the doctor's house. There's a charming garden with two apple trees and one cherry tree. It would be ideal for us to start off with. I'm longing for you to see it.'

'I'm so afraid . . .'

'You mustn't be afraid of anything. I want you to know that I understand perfectly. You're not sure yet. Well then, the wise thing is not to rush into anything. But come down to see it. No obligations. Just come and tell me what you think of it.'

'As long as you understand . . .'

'I do. I assure you I do. When will you come? Come on Saturday. Bring Eliza with you. Then you won't be travelling alone. I'll meet you at the station.'

'Yes, I'll come,' I said.

We came through the Flower Walk where the nannies were sitting while their charges ran round them. I thought how charming the children were and I felt that pang of sadness they always aroused with their memories of Julian.

Then we went back to the house where Jane was toasting muffins for tea and Polly was preening herself about the cake which, as she said, 'she had duffed up in a jiffy' because we had company.

Everyone seemed in a euphoric mood and I guessed by the

looks they exchanged that they all believed that this was, as they would say, 'my intended'.

As arranged, Charles met us at the station in the brougham which he used for his rounds. He greeted us with delight and Eliza and I sat inside while he drove up front.

The countryside was beautiful. Perhaps it seemed more so because it was so long since we had seen leafy lanes and green fields where buttercups and daisies grew. Everything seemed fresh and peaceful.

Then we came to Meriton, an ancient market town. Everywhere was the grey Cotswold stone. Aubretia and arabis grew out of the walls in front of the houses, behind which were gardens ablaze with flowers.

Eliza said: 'What a lovely place. I never knew there was such places.'

'It is rather lovely,' said Charles proudly.

'It's so peaceful.'

'Yes, that's what one thinks of . . . peace.'

We went first to Charles's house. He had already acquired a housekeeper – a comfortable, middle-aged woman who clearly, after the fashion of her kind, was determined to 'mother' him. The house with its creeper-covered grey stone walls was charming, the garden well-tended. 'A man comes twice a week. I inherited him from the previous owners.'

'You manage very well,' I said. 'I can see you are already part of Meriton.'

'We are having luncheon with my partner. He insisted when he knew you were coming. He has a bigger establishment and he said it was easier for you to go there. As a matter of fact, I am invited to lunch with them every Sunday. It's a very pleasant arrangement.'

I understood what he meant. Dr Silkin, fresh-faced, grey-haired, was a very pleasant man. He greeted us warmly and it was quite clear to me that he was immensely satisfied with the arrangements he had made. Charles, I was sure, was a trustworthy partner and it seemed to me that Dr Silkin was still congratulating himself on finding someone eminently suitable.

'You must meet my daughter,' he said. 'Dorothy,' he called. 'Where are you? Our guests are here.'

I was not expecting anyone so young. I guessed her age to be about twenty-one or -two. She had rather lovely brown eyes and smooth brown hair drawn down on either side of her face with a knot at the nape of her neck. It was a gentle face, beautiful in a way, without being regular featured but with an expression of kindliness. She was the sort of person one liked immediately because there was about her an inner goodness which I have sometimes seen in older faces, rarely in one so young.

She smiled at us and said: 'Welcome to Meriton. Charles has told us about you and the wonderful things you have been doing in the Crimea.'

'Dorothy is avidly curious about all that went on,' said Charles, looking at the girl with a kind of tender indulgence. 'She thinks Miss Florence Nightingale is a saint.'

'She is probably not far wrong,' I said.

'Did you actually see her?' asked Dorothy.

'Oh yes.'

'And she spoke to you?'

'Anna worked for her, so there,' said Charles. 'Anna, you are receiving a very warm welcome here because you have worked in the same hospital as Miss Nightingale.'

'Oh come! Not only that,' protested Dr Silkin.

It was a beautiful house and Dorothy was an expert house-keeper. In the dining-room there was an oil painting hanging over the fireplace. It portrayed a woman so like Dorothy that I guessed it must be her mother.

Later this was confirmed. She had been dead for four years, and since then Dorothy had looked after her father.

'She's an excellent housekeeper,' said Dr Silkin, looking fondly at his daughter. 'Moreover, she helps me in my work. She has a wonderful way with patients.'

'Keeping the difficult ones at bay,' said Charles with a smile, 'while offering the right touch of sympathy to those who need it.'

They talked of life in the little town: the friendly gatherings, the church functions, the musical evenings, the little dinner-parties. I could see that Charles was enamoured of it and he had obviously become on terms of great friendship with the Silkins. It certainly was an ideal arrangement.

Could I see myself part of it? Why not? It was a pleasant comfortable lifestyle. I could be of use. My knowledge of nursing would be an asset. I imagined myself in that little house with its stone walls and Virginia creeper. But should I feel enclosed, shut in? Yet I might have children . . . little ones to take away the pain I still felt at the loss of Julian.

It was a pleasant day.

In the late afternoon Charles drove us to the station. He looked at me wistfully as he said goodbye.

'Perhaps you'll come again soon,' he said. 'Just let me know. I am sure the Silkins liked you.'

'I liked them, too. I think you chose wisely, Charles.'

'So you liked it . . . and them. That's the first step.'

Eliza was thoughtful in the train.

She said: 'He's a good man. It would be a good life. You're lucky, you know.'

'If only I could make up my mind.'

'Anyone in her right senses would, unless, of course –' she looked at me obliquely – 'unless she's got plans somewhere else.'

'I haven't got any plans. I just feel it's so cosy . . . too cosy . . . stifling. Like being in a soft feather bed, sinking right down, being caught in it . . . in a cosy, comfortable sort of way.'

'You don't half have some fancies. Besides, what's wrong with a feather bed?'

She looked at me shrewdly and we were silent for a while. I sat back listening to the chugging of the train and thinking of myself in that little house. And then another figure intruded into my reverie . . . cynically smiling, holding me with those eyes. Not for you, he was saying. You want to be free to discover the world. You want to wipe away the conventions. Stop thinking what you ought to; start thinking of what you like. Discover for yourself . . . I could show you . . .

But he was gone. I should probably never see him again. And if I did, what then? Oh, I was indeed, as Eliza said, not in my right senses.

Eliza was speaking. 'What did you think of Miss Dorothy?'

'Charming,' I said.

'Yes . . . and the doctor's daughter. She'd make a good wife . . . to a doctor.'

'I dare say.'

'And I reckon she might . . . some day. It would be all very neat, wouldn't it?'

'Do you mean Charles?'

'Well, there it is, all cut and dried as you might say, and ready for the market.'

'You use some odd expressions.'

'Never mind, as long as I make my meaning clear.'

'Your meaning is clear, Eliza. You are saying that if I delay and refuse Dr Fenwick, Dorothy might very well become his wife.'

'Well, you could say it was working out that way, couldn't you? I think she thought a lot of him, working in the Crimea with Miss Nightingale . . . well, that for one thing has set him up as a hero in her eyes.'

'Those doctors were heroic.'

'And Dr Fenwick is a good man as well as a hero.'

'You have certainly always spoken up for him.'

'Sometimes when you lose something you appreciate it all the more.'

'Are you telling me that if I don't snap up Dr Fenwick very soon I shall lose him to Dorothy Silkin?'

'Just that,' she said.

'Do you know, Eliza, I am rather glad there is a Dorothy Silkin. I think she will be an ideal wife for Charles. He deserves the best and she would be better for him than I.'

'You'd be better for him . . . and he'd be good for you.'

'I just wonder how I would settle in a place like that. What happened to me has had its effect. I have told you a little about Minster St Clare, but not all. It was a strange experience. I lost my husband. I lost my child. That sort of thing cannot be shrugged aside. And then . . . Scutari. Could I settle into the cosy country life? Eliza, seeing it today, I don't think I could. And hurting Charles is something I can't bear to think of. So meeting that girl today, seeing them together . . . You understand what I mean?'

'Yes,' said Eliza. 'It would be a solution. It would put your mind at rest, wouldn't it?'

I nodded.

I closed my eyes and listened to the rhythm of the train.

Two days later two letters arrived. One was from Henrietta. I recognized her handwriting at once and tore it open.

My dear Anna [she wrote],

I expect you have been wondering about me. It really was rather an awful thing to do, wasn't it? I mean . . . to decide not to go right at the last minute. I should have told you before. But I was in such a state of uncertainty. First I was going to and then I wasn't. You know me.

The fact is I am now a married woman. Philippe and I are married. He had been asking me for some time and I was a bit cautious . . . strange for me . . . but I had that experience with Carlton, you remember. Look how I got myself into that and how hard it was to extricate myself. I didn't want to make another *faux pas*. So I hesitated and then said Yes and then No. And then the time came for departure and I thought: If I go now I won't see him again. You don't sometimes when long distances separate you. So I just had to stay and wrestle with myself.

Dr Adair was very kind. He advised me about a good many things. He knows the language and the customs and all that. What a man! I still think he is the most fascinating creature I ever saw. I don't tell Philippe this but I think he knows it. He has the most enormous admiration for Dr Adair, as a lot have. He is just someone apart. If you know what I mean.

Well, the fact is, I finally decided I could not leave Philippe – and so we were married. We're in Constantinople now until Philippe clears up his job here. It is all very important and secret, working for the French authorities and all that, and he'll have to be here for a while. Peace treaties and such like. Philippe is really quite an important man. Then we shall live in Paris. Won't that be fun? You will come and stay with us. We'll have a lovely time.

Have you see Dr Fenwick yet? I hope all goes well in that direction.

Anna, my dearest friend, do forgive me for being such a beastly little deserter, but it had to be, and I'm very happy now. I know it was right for me to marry Philippe. As soon as we leave here I shall let you know. Perhaps we shall come to England for a visit, and you will, of course, come to Paris.

I do miss having you to talk to and tell things to.

I may be pregnant. It's too soon to say yet. Won't that be glorious? You shall be the first one to know.

My love to you, my dear, dear friend.

Henrietta.

I smiled. How typical of her! She must be happy. I felt as though a great burden had dropped from me. She was not with Damien Adair; she was with Philippe. She had never gone away with him. It was all so understandable, so natural. He had seen her on the *caïque* and had crossed with her. Philippe must have been waiting for her on the other side.

And he had been helpful. He knew the language and the customs . . . I should never have listened to Eliza. What grief we bring ourselves by listening to the ignorant, however well-meaning.

I felt a great sense of relief and a deep pleasure.

In the excitement of hearing from Henrietta I had forgotten the other letter. It was from Germany. I opened it and read it.

To my amazement it was from Kaiserwald. The Head Deaconess was asking me in her rather stilted English if I would consider coming to Kaiserwald for a brief visit. She knew of my stay in Scutari and she remembered well the excellent work I had done in Kaiserwald. She begged me to come and bring my friend Miss Marlington with me. I could be sure of a warm welcome. Of all the nurses who had spent short spells at her hospital, she had the greatest respect for me.

I read it through and through again.

I felt I needed something to lift me out of this emptiness, this feeling of living in limbo, this quiet uneventful way of life which had followed on those horrifying days at Scutari.

I knew that I should go to Kaiserwald.

I talked to Eliza about it – but first I told her about Henrietta.

'You see,' I said, 'it was Philippe after all. How wrong we were about Dr Adair.'

'Well, she's married this Philippe now.'

'You still think . . .'

'That she went to him first . . . Yes, I do. I think she went to him, and then got frightened and that Philippe came along and she took him as a way out.'

'Oh, Eliza, no! She would have told me.'

'Told you? When she knew the way you was about him?'

'What do you mean . . . how I was?'

'Well, it's as plain as a pikestaff . . . to me.'

'You sometimes read something that's not there, Eliza.'

'Not me. You wasn't exactly indifferent to him, was you?'

'Nobody could be indifferent to him. Look at you. You're not.'

'Oh, I see right through him, I do.'

'Don't you think, Eliza, that sometimes you see something that isn't there? You've taken a violent dislike to him.'

'I hate all men who do what he does to women, that's what, I've seen too much of it. Some of them think we're just there for their convenience. He's one of them. I hate the lot of 'em.'

'Well, let me tell you my piece of news. I've had an invitation to go to Germany.'

She was startled and I told her of the letter from the Head Deaconess.

'Well,' she said, 'she must have thought something of you. Will you go?'

'It's rather a pressing invitation.'

'You want to go, don't you?'

'I'm getting restive here. Nothing happens. I thought we should go into nursing, but everything is so slow.'

'I feel the same.'

'Oh, Eliza, you've no idea how beautiful it is in the forest. There's a strangeness about it. You can feel that the trolls and the giants and the people from the fairy stories are not far off. I've never known a place like it. Would you like to come with me?'

'I'm not asked.'

'The Head Deaconess doesn't know you're with me, that's why. Henrietta went with me before. I don't see why you shouldn't come. You're a nurse. You'd make yourself useful. It's very hard work. She would be expecting Henrietta and you would come instead.'

'I'm used to the hard work.'

'It's not as hard as Scutari, of course.'

'Do you think I could come?'

'Why not? Henrietta is invited. Why shouldn't you come in her place. Oh, Eliza, I am going to take you to Germany with me.'

Within a few days Eliza and I were on our way. I had had some difficulty in persuading her that she would be welcome there.

'After all,' I said, 'the Head Deaconess is expecting me to take Henrietta and she would not want me to travel all that way alone. Strictly between ourselves, you are a better nurse than Henrietta and that will interest them at Kaiserwald.'

In spite of her apprehension she was excited by the project.

The carriage was waiting for us when we reached the little

station and I was immediately aware of the redolent smell of the pines as the mystic aura of the forest closed round me. I glanced at Eliza and saw that she was entranced and that the forest was beginning to cast its spell on her, too.

And there was Kaiserwald itself, and as the turrets and towers rose up before me memories came flooding back: Gerda the goosegirl; Klaus the pedlar; Frau Leiben. Poor Gerda, how ill she had been. But she had recovered and no doubt she was wiser now. All that had happened before I had met Damien Adair and my suspicions had rested on him.

How foolish that seemed now! But was it?

I must forget my Demon Doctor. I could not really be at peace until he was right out of my mind. But that was easier said than done. I must be sensible. The chances were that I should never see him again.

We were met by the same Deaconess who had greeted us when I had arrived with Henrietta – the one who spoke a little English. She looked at Eliza with faint surprise and I told her that Miss Marlington was now married and that Eliza had come in her place. She nodded, and said that the Head Deaconess was awaiting my arrival and that I was requested to go to her as soon as I came.

We were taken at once to her room and she came to greet me with arms outstretched.

'Miss Pleydell, how delighted I am that you have come. It was good of you to give me such a quick response.'

'I was indeed honoured to be asked,' I replied. 'Miss Marlington is now married and not in England. This is Miss Eliza Flynn, who was nursing with me in the Crimea. I trust you do not mind.'

'Mind? I am delighted. Welcome, Miss Flynn. It is a pleasure to meet anyone who did such good work. We shall have much to talk of.'

She bade us sit down and went on: 'You will have had so many experiences. There is going to be a change in hospitals and the care of the sick throughout the world. It seems that attention is at last being given to this important work . . . thanks to Miss Nightingale.'

'I believe that to be so,' I said. 'There are training schemes afoot.'

'And what are you doing now?'

'We are waiting, Eliza and I, to see what there will be for us.'

The Head Deaconess smiled from me to Eliza.

'You have worked together,' she said.

'Oh yes, and we hope to continue to do so. Eliza – Miss Flynn – is dedicated to nursing.'

'Yes,' said Eliza. 'I know it is what I want to do.'

'That is the spirit we need. And the nurse who came with you on your last visit, Miss Pleydell, is now married?'

'She is in Constantinople. She married a Frenchman connected with the French Legation out there.'

'Ah yes . . . our allies. A very pleasant personality but I do not think a dedicated nurse. It's a hard profession, as you have had reason to know.'

'It is and all,' Eliza agreed.

'And we have to be devoted enough to accept hardships. I have arranged for you to have a room to yourselves. I dare say you would like to go to it now. We will talk more later.'

'Thank you,' I said; and the Deaconess who had received us when we arrived was summoned and showed us to the room.

It was very small – resembling a cell. There were two beds in it, a chair and a cupboard and a small table. The walls were bare except for a crucifix.

'What a woman,' Eliza said, 'and she runs this place!'

I nodded. 'Eliza, you don't understand how honoured we are. A room to ourselves! Henrietta and I slept in a sort of dormitory, divided into cubicles. This is luxury.'

'It's lovely,' said Eliza. 'Fancy running a place like this! I want to see the wards. I want to see how it's done. And with that forest all round you and the trees and all that . . .'

'I'm glad you like it, Eliza. I'm glad you've come. She might have something to offer us. If she did . . . oh, but it's early days yet. Let's wait and see.'

Later we talked again with the Head Deaconess. She questioned us at length about the methods used at Scutari. We told her of the horrendous lack of equipment, the diseases with which we had had to cope, and which had proved to be more disastrous than the wounds received in battle. She admitted that she was very concerned with sanitation and she believed that if it were not adequate it could be the major cause of death.

It was very interesting to talk to her and I was immensely flattered by the manner in which she took me into her confidence. I was also grateful for her acceptance of Eliza, for she included her in the talk, and listened attentively when she expressed an opinion.

I had rarely seen Eliza so greatly pleased; she was obviously enjoying the visit.

That night I lay in my bed, with Eliza in the other one – and I was so glad she was with me. I was so fond of her, and I did want life to be happy for her. She was such a good woman in spite of her attempts to prove otherwise.

Dear Eliza, I really was as capable of taking care of myself as she was of herself. Yet was I? I had, in spite of myself, become involved with someone who could never bring me happiness. I lay there thinking of my previous visit here. That was in the days before I had met Dr Adair. It was strange how my life seemed divided into sections; the time before I had been aware of his existence, followed by those years when he had been a shadowy figure of menace; and then the actual confrontation.

At length I slept and dreamed of him. I was in the forest and Gerda the goosegirl was there. It was all muddled and I was glad to awake from it.

Eliza was in high spirits.

'What lovely air!' she cried. 'Oh, I love the smell of them trees. It's peaceful here. I'm glad I came. It'll be good to work here for a bit.'

I smiled at her. It was so wonderful to see her happy.

How well I remembered the long wooden table at which we sat down to oatmeal and rye bread, and the drink of ground rye. The Deaconesses remembered me and showed their pleasure in seeing me again. They were welcoming to Eliza. So much had happened since I had been here; but in some ways it felt as though I had never left.

After breakfast we were taken round the wards. After that we went to the Head Deaconess's sanctum for more talks.

I was delighted that Eliza was able to contribute in a way which showed her ability. She said she would like to work in the wards while she was here, for she had seen that there was room for more nursing.

So it was agreed that we should start on the next day.

'Take a little rest this afternoon,' said the Head Deaconess. 'You've had a long journey and you need to recover from it. I know how you used to like to walk in the forest, Miss Pleydell.'

So in the afternoon I took Eliza for a walk, just as Henrietta and I used to when she was here.

Eliza loved the place. She said: 'I've never seen anything like this. What's them bells you hear in the distance every now and then?'

I explained that the bells were worn by the cows who could easily get lost in the forest. 'The bells, of course, indicate where they are.'

She was enchanted.

We passed the cottage where Gerda's grandmother had lived. There was no sign of anyone there. When we came to a clearing I suggested we sit down for a while.

Eliza said: 'I'd like to work here. There's a peace about it. You see . . . I dunno how to say it . . . it's as though some things don't matter at all. Everyone is important and yet not important, if you know what I mean.'

'I think I do, Eliza.'

'When you get married . . .'

'Oh, but I'm not sure.'

'You're going to marry Dr Fenwick if you've got any sense.'

'Perhaps I haven't.'

'Yes, you have. Your head's screwed on the right way. It's just you're dazzled, that's all. And you can't see straight for a bit. You're going to marry him because he's right for you . . . and you're going to be all right. But what about me?'

'Eliza, you'll always be my friend and welcome wherever I am.'

'I know that. It's not easy for me to say this. I think the world of you. You're a fine woman, Anna. You're one of the best. I'm never going to forget what you done for Ethel . . . and for me, too.'

'You exaggerate. It was Dr Adair who saved Tom for Ethel.'

'Him! Oh, showing off, that's all. It was you what done it.'

'That's ridiculous, Eliza.'

'I'm getting silly in my old age. I was just saying that I want you to get what you deserve. I reckon you'll have a lot of kids and you'll be happy ever after, for that Dr Fenwick's a good man and good men don't grow on trees. From what I know of them they're as rare as snow in July.'

'You're an old cynic, Eliza. Don't let's talk about me. What would you like to happen to you? If you could have a wish, what would it be?'

'I'd like to be that Head Deaconess in a place like this with a hospital all my own. I'd do it my way. I'd have the best little hospital in the world. Funny . . . when we got to Scutari I wanted to come straight back. I wondered what I'd let myself in for. And then . . . after seeing what we did . . . I was just glad I was there. I knew I wanted to nurse the sick. There's nothing I want to do more than that.'

'I know how you feel.'

We sat on the grass, our backs against a tree and she told me of her dreams. She had loved this place immediately. She wanted to have a hospital of her own where she could make the rules, where she could dedicate herself to the sick.

We talked for a long time and Eliza had never been so self-revealing.

I loved her very much and I prayed that one day her dreams might be realized, for hers was a noble ambition.

Someone was tapping at the door. It was one of the younger Deaconesses. The Head Deaconess was asking me to go at once to her sanctum.

We had just returned from our walk and Eliza still looked bemused, still in the dream of being in charge of a hospital like Kaiserwald.

I said: 'I'd better go at once.'

I knocked at the door of the sanctum.

'Come in,' called the Head Deaconess and I entered.

A man was standing with his back to the window.

'Oh, there you are,' said the Head Deaconess. 'I am so glad you have come in. You two know each other well, I believe.'

I stared at him disbelievingly. He had been so consistently in my thoughts that for a moment I thought I had conjured up this image of him. I heard myself stammering: 'Dr Adair . . .'

'The same,' he said. 'How pleasant to find you here.'

He had come forward to take my hand.

'I have heard some account of Scutari from Miss Pleydell,' said the Head Deaconess. 'I feel honoured to have you both here . . . and Miss Flynn, too. You have shared a terrible but wonderful experience.'

'We only did what was expected of us. Isn't that so, Miss Pleydell?'

'Yes, of course. We just worked hard and did the best we could.'

'It must have been very different from Kaiserwald,' said the Head Deaconess.

'Completely different,' he said.

'Do sit down . . . both of you. Did you enjoy your walk in the forest, Miss Pleydell? Miss Pleydell is enamoured of our forest, Dr Adair.'

'I can understand that. It's an enchanting place. Romantic, eh, Miss Pleydell?'

'Yes, I find it so.'

He brought a chair and held it while I sat down. I looked over my shoulder and thanked him. He was smiling slightly sardonically and I could not interpret the meaning of that smile.

'Pray be seated yourself, Dr Adair. Miss Pleydell, Dr Adair has been discussing some project with me and he thinks you may well be involved in it . . . for I told him you were here.'

I turned to look at him. I thought I detected a mischievous look in his eyes.

'Yes, Miss Pleydell. I was delighted when I heard that you had arrived in Kaiserwald. This project concerns Rosenwald . . . a place not unlike Kaiserwald – not so large, nor so well ordered.' He smiled gallantly at the Head Deaconess, who bowed her head well pleased and murmured: 'We were not always as we are now, Dr Adair. It takes time to develop a place.'

'But you do agree that in time . . . with the right Head . . . Rosenwald could become a Kaiserwald?'

'I certainly believe it could with the right persons working together . . . dedicated people who are ready to make sacrifices.'

'We all have the highest respect for your abilities, Miss Pleydell.'

'I'm glad to hear it.'

'The fact is, I am going out to inspect the place. The Head Deaconess cannot of course make the journey with me. We have discussed the matter together and have come to the conclusion that as you are here so fortuitously –' he gave me that smile again – 'well, my idea is that *you* should visit Rosenwald with me and give me your opinion of its possibilities.'

'With some object in view?'

'I don't know what your plans are.'

'You mean that I might work at this place?'

'I want your opinion of it. You have proved yourself to be a good nurse. You may discover a great enthusiasm to build up this place . . .'

'That would mean giving up my home . . . everything . . .'

'You are looking too far ahead. Come with me tomorrow. We shall inspect the place together and you will tell me what you think of its possibilities. I am leaving for Rosenwald tomorrow morning early . . . on horseback. You do ride, don't you, Miss Pleydell?'

'Yes, I ride. But I have no habit with me.'

'Could we fit her out?' he asked.

The Head Deaconess thought it might be possible. No one in the hospital rode, of course, but there was Fräulein Kleber who was a great horsewoman and would be ready to lend what was needed.

'If that could be arranged today we could leave tomorrow morning. It will take us the whole morning to get there. But we could be back before nightfall. If there were any difficulties we could stay at Rosenwald.'

The Head Deaconess was looking rather concerned. I imagined she thought we should have a chaperon. I thought she was going to suggest that one of the Deaconesses should accompany us but I dismissed that thought as I knew none of them could ride.

I said: 'Eliza Flynn is here with me, Dr Adair. You may remember her.'

He frowned in concentration.

'She was rather big . . . a very efficient nurse.'

'Ah yes,' he said. 'Big Eliza. I don't think she should be a member of the party. But does she ride well?'

'I'm almost certain that she does not.'

'I have planned that you and I should go alone, Miss Pleydell. We don't want a crowd. It is just to look over, to assess possibilities and so on . . .'

I could not help it, but my spirits were rising. I was going to spend a whole day in his company. I did not think for one moment that I should want to work at Rosenwald. All I cared about was that he had come back and that I was going to be with him alone . . . for a whole day.

I really did not think beyond that.

Eliza was dumbfounded.

'That man . . . here!'

'Don't be surprised. It's only natural that he should be here. He's a famous doctor. He's interested in places like this. Germany has been the centre of some of Europe's best hospitals and it is only natural that now all this reform is going to take place, people should come here.'

'I believe he's arranged all this. He got you here . . .'

'Oh, Eliza, don't be absurd! Why should he?'

'Because he's interested in you. He's finished with Henrietta and now it's your turn.'

'I tell you it's a hospital we're going to see. There's nothing romantic or mysterious about that.'

'Just you and him . . . alone! I'll come with you.'

'We have to go on horseback and you can't ride. Oh Eliza, it's nothing . . .'

'Well, you're looking pretty pleased about it.'

'I'm interested in this place . . . Rosenwald. Perhaps we could both go there for a while.'

She brightened a little at the prospect and I said hastily: 'I have to go and see Fräulein Kleber, who lives nearby. The H.D. says she will lend me a riding habit. She has several and she is about my size.'

'Do you mean the H.D. is going to allow this? You going off with him alone?'

'You are making a lot out of nothing. Come on. I'm going to Fräulein Kleber. Do come with me.'

Almost reluctantly, she came.

Fräulein Kleber lived in a very pleasant house not far from Frau Leiben's cottage.

We found it easily, and as we approached the house we heard the sound of a shot. We were startled and looked at each other in dismay, and as we did so another shot rang out and another and another.

'Something's happening,' said Eliza.

We hurried to the house. There was no sign of anyone. As we walked through a beautifully kept garden to some stables, we heard another shot. The sound was coming from the other side of the stables.

Then we saw what it was. A target had been set up against a tree and a woman was firing at it. She heard our approach and turned to us.

'Oh, forgive me,' she cried, 'I'm getting a little practice for the *Schützenfest*. It's less than a month away and I'm a little rusty.'

She was middle-aged and greying, slim and tall and about my size.

I said: 'Have we come at an inconvenient time?'

'Oh no, no. You're from Kaiserwald, aren't you? I knew you were coming and of course I'm delighted to fit you up.'

I introduced Eliza, but as she had no German she could not join in the conversation.

'It is kind of you,' I said. 'I haven't brought a habit with me. I did not think there would be an opportunity to ride.'

She nodded. 'I had forgotten when you were actually coming. I've been so caught up with the *Schützenfest*. We have it every year. I always join in these things and I've been caught up with this. I look forward to the *Vögelschiessen* – that's the popinjay shooting. I always hope I shall be *Schützen-König*. That's the best shot selected every year. Of course, there has never been a woman who has achieved that yet.'

'I wish you luck,' I said.

'Come into the house. But first excuse me while I put my rifle away.'

We had come to a barn which had been converted into a sort of gun-room.

'My father was a great shot. He was *König* almost every year. These are his guns. I inherited them. But not quite his skill, alas.'

She put the rifle in a case and turned to us. She studied me closely. 'Well, we are about the same size so that should offer no difficulties.'

We went into the house and up to her bedroom. She had four riding habits, all of which would fit me. She asked me to take which I liked and I chose a pale grey skirt and jacket with a grey hat.

I tried them on. 'Might have been made for you,' she said. 'Got a good mount?'

'That is being provided for me.'

'From Herr Brandt's stables, I expect. He'll see you're all right. He has some very fine horses.'

'I am very grateful to you, Fräulein Kleber.'

'I'm always happy to do anything for Kaiserwald. Everyone

round here is. We're proud of it . . . and it has been of great benefit to us all. So . . . I'm delighted to fit you up.'

'Very interesting woman,' I said as we walked away. 'A pity you couldn't understand her.'

'I did catch a word or two,' said Eliza. 'I think I'd pick up the language quickly if I was here long.'

'I'm sure you would.'

'That get-up suits you.' She looked at me closely. 'You look . . . different.'

I did not comment further.

I lived the rest of that day in a kind of daze. It was like a dream. I had come to Kaiserwald and he was there. It was like a miracle. I had been thinking of him so constantly that it was as though the intensity of my thoughts had conjured him up. And I was to spend a day with him . . . alone. Eliza, I knew, was very disapproving. I did not want to discuss the matter with her. When we went to bed that night I pretended to fall asleep immediately. I was sure she was fully awake.

I was up early next morning. I donned Fräulein Kleber's riding habit. I knew it suited me, for I had always looked well in riding clothes. I felt exhilarated.

Dr Adair had provided the horses, I learned, from Herr Brandt's stables. He had a fine black one; mine was a chestnut mare. He rode magnificently, as I had expected he would. Seated on a horse, he looked like some figure from Greek mythology. I hoped my mood of exhilaration was not too obvious.

As we rode away from Kaiserwald, I glanced back. I saw a movement at a window. So Eliza was there. I could imagine the expression on her face. She was so very much against this enterprise; and she was a person who, when she had once made up her mind, adhered to it. It would take a great deal to change her opinions of Dr Adair. She insisted that he had taken Henrietta and melodramatically cast her off to Philippe Lablanche – and nothing was going to change her. But what she feared most was what he would do to me.

'How do you like your mount?' he asked.

'She seems . . . amenable.'

'Good. Horses can be temperamental and it will be a long day. I hope you are as proficient on a horse as you are in a ward.'

'I rode in India and in the country. I am no expert, of course, but I think I can manage a horse reasonably well.'

'Well, I shall be with you to take care of you.'

'That,' I said, 'is a comforting thought. How long did you stay in Scutari?'

'No longer than was necessary. There was a certain amount to be cleared up. I came to England as soon as possible.'

'Did you see any more of Henrietta?'

'Oh yes. I saw her with Lablanche. They seemed to be very content with each other.'

'In her letter Henrietta mentioned that you were very helpful.'

'I did what I could. The rest was up to them.'

'I hope it works out well.'

'That, again, is up to them.'

'These matters do not always . . . even though people expect them to in the beginning.'

'All we can do about that is wish them well.'

'How strange that you should be in Kaiserwald at the same time as I am.'

'It is not so strange, really.'

'Don't you think so?'

'I arranged it. In other words I asked the Head Deaconess to invite you to come. And when I knew you had arrived I came, too.'

'But . . . why?'

'I have a project.'

'You mean this Rosenwald? Are you suggesting that I might take up this post . . . whatever it is?'

'I thought it might be a good idea to take you out to see the place.'

'So you planned all this?'

'I admit it. So you see it is not so fortuitous as you at first thought.'

'It is kind of you to plan my future.'

'You are a good nurse, and your talents should not be wasted. You know the plight of hospitals all over the world. You are a disciple of Miss Nightingale and you know what she is proposing to do.'

'Yes,' I said.

I felt deflated. When he had said that he arranged this meeting, for a moment I had thought he had wanted to see *me*.

'I shall be very interested to see this place,' I said coolly.

'I knew you would be. I can assure you I am looking forward to the outcome.'

We rode in silence for some time, then he asked me what my plans were. I told him that I was really waiting to see what happened. I knew there were going to be reforms in hospitals but I was not sure where I should fit in.

'And Big Eliza?'

'We plan to be together.'

'You have become good friends, it seems.'

'She is a very good and reliable person.'

He was silent.

I said at length: 'What of you? What are your plans? Are you going off to some wild country to live as a native and discover secrets of the East?'

'Like you, I am waiting on events.'

'So you have nothing planned?'

'I have much planned, but there are circumstances to be considered. I sometimes feel it is tempting fate to make too many plans in advance.'

'You mean that Man proposes and God disposes.'

'God or someone.'

We were riding through a village street and I had to fall in behind him. I noticed that people glanced at him as he rode by and I was not surprised. So distinguished did he appear.

When we were in the country again he talked a little about Rosenwald. The nurses would not be Deaconesses and this would not be a religious institution, merely a hospital. It was in its infancy at the moment. There were few patients, not more than thirty, he believed. The nurses were country girls from the surrounding districts – simple girls with no real training.

'You seem to have a very special interest in it.'

'My interest is in finding the right person to run it. The Head Deaconess is a very capable woman. Kaiserwald would not be what it is without her.'

'I agree.'

'Ah . . . we are not far off now. It wasn't too long in the saddle for you, I hope.'

'No. It has been easy going.'

'And the little mare has behaved impeccably. Look. You can see the towers from here. Pleasant setting, isn't it?'

I looked ahead. It was a small schloss in the heart of the forest, not unlike Kaiserwald.

We rode into a courtyard. A man came out to take our horses and Dr Adair gave orders that they should be fed and watered.

We were received by one who, I supposed, was the head of the nurses. She was clearly overawed by Dr Adair.

'I dare say you need some refreshment,' she said. 'It is quite a distance from Kaiserwald.'

He said we should like something and could we take it together out of doors. We had certain things to discuss.

We sat at a table in front of the schloss, looking down on a valley. The mountains in the distance made a fine background and the forest was beautiful.

I felt happier than I had for a long time. Why? I wondered. Because he was going to offer me a post. I could come here and bring Eliza with me. Perhaps occasionally he would call, if he could find the time between his visits to exotic places; and if he thought of me at all, he would think: Oh yes, Anna Pleydell, the woman I put in to Rosenwald.

'This is pleasant,' he said. 'Do you agree?'

'Yes, it is very pleasant.'

'A good place to work?'

'It's very beautiful.'

'Life would go on much the same every day. Patients coming and going. How does that appeal to you?'

'I don't know that I want peace . . . and nothing more.'

He laughed. 'No. I did not expect that. But it is a pleasant place . . . for the right person. One would have to be dedicated to the job. This could be a little kingdom with the one in control as the powerful head . . . ruling this little world, but of course having very little connection with what is beyond. This beer is good, isn't it? And *Sauer-braten* and the inevitable sauerkraut. Well, we are after all in Germany . . . and the forest is a wonderful setting, don't you agree?'

I said I did.

'When we have finished we will make our tour of inspection, for we must not be too late in leaving.'

But he did not seem in any hurry and we sat for some time over the beer and meat. It was so peaceful, the weather so fine. There was a faint mist in the air which gave a blue tinge to the mountains. I felt very happy just to sit there, now and then looking up to find his eyes on me. There was an air of unreality about the scene and I could almost convince myself that I had dreamed the whole thing.

Later we went through the ward together. There were, as he had said, about thirty patients. He looked at them all and asked the nurses a good many questions, not only about their patients but their duties. We inspected the kitchens and the sleeping quarters. They were very similar to those at Kaiserwald. The long dormitory was divided into cubicles; it was all very neat and clean.

It was about four o'clock when he suggested that we leave. I was surprised that he had allowed it to be so late. I very much doubted that we could get back before dark; but he probably knew that; he did not seem to be perturbed.

We said goodbye to the nurses and left.

'That is over,' he said, 'a very necessary part of the proceedings.'

'The whole purpose of the expedition,' I reminded him.

He smiled at me and I noticed his manner had changed.

He said nothing for a mile or so and then he brought his

horse close to mine. 'I am afraid we have left it rather late for getting back to Kaiserwald.'

'Why did we not leave earlier?'

'Having come so far, we had to see everything. We could, of course, go to an inn.'

'I did not notice a great many on the journey here.'

'Nevertheless, there are a few. On the other hand, a friend of mine has a hunting lodge not far from here. I think it would be an excellent idea if we threw ourselves on his hospitality for the night.'

'The Head Deaconess is expecting us back.'

'She will think we have stayed the night at Rosenwald. I did suggest that was a possibility.'

We rode on for about fifteen minutes. The sun was low in the sky; it would soon disappear altogether.

We were deep in the forest now. 'Very soon we shall come to the lodge,' he said. 'It's a delightful place.'

'Your friend will be surprised. He might have guests.'

'I have an open invitation to use the place whenever I wish to. He doesn't actually live there. It is, after all, merely a hunting lodge.'

'It might well be shut up.'

'There are always servants in residence.'

We had come to a clearing and before us was the lodge. It was bigger than I imagined – a miniature schloss with a tower and turrets. Close to it was a cottage and to this he led me. As we approached a man appeared at the door. When he saw us he gave an exclamation of pleasure and recognition.

'Herr Doktor!' he cried.

'We've come for a night's lodging, Hans,' said Dr Adair. 'I suppose the Herr Graf is not here.'

'No, Herr Doktor. I will open up the lodge.'

'Do, please, Hans. We have come a long way. We are tired and hungry.'

I said: 'Surely we should go to an inn. Your friend is not here . . .'

'No . . . no. It is an arrangement we have. If the Graf thought we had come here and gone away he would be most put out. Moreover, he might come. If he is out hunting he might well stay the night here. The fires will be laid, the beds ready for airing and there is always food.'

'It seems extraordinary . . .'

'It's the general practice in fact.' He smiled at me. 'I believe you are having misgivings.'

'Everything seems to have changed suddenly.'

'How? Tell me.'

'When we set out to see the hospital and while we were there inspecting it, everything seemed normal . . . reasonable.'

'And now you find it unreasonable?'

A young man had come out of the cottage to take our horses.

'Good evening, Franz,' said Dr Adair. 'Is Frieda well?'

'Yes, Herr Doktor.'

'And the little one?'

'Very well.'

'We are staying the night. Your father is opening up for us. Has your mother something for our dinner?'

'But yes. As you know we are always prepared.'

'Good.'

'The Herr Graf was here a month ago.'

'So I heard. It is so good of him and you all to make us so welcome.'

'The Herr Graf would be angry if you did not make use of the lodge when you are hereabouts.'

'So I have been telling my companion.'

I said: 'This is a most interesting place.'

'And comfortable, thanks to the good family Schwartz,' said Dr Adair. 'Let me take you in. I'll guess the fires are already lighted.'

He took my arm and drew me towards the hunting lodge.

'There,' he said. 'Are you satisfied? We are not gate-crashing. And I am not playing some trick. This is indeed the hunting lodge of Graf von Spiegal, and it is a fact that he is a friend of mine and would take it as an insult if we were here and in need of lodging and went to an inn.'

'You are fortunate to have such friends.'

'You are right. I am.'

We went into a large hall. The fire was already alight and beginning to burn up. 'The bedrooms are ready. All they need is the application of the warming pans.'

'Is that what you call German efficiency?'

'It is certainly efficiency, and as we are now in Germany you may be right.'

A woman came into the hall; she was middle-aged, and rather plump, with rosy cheeks and a mass of flaxen hair.

'Ah, here is Else,' said Dr Adair. 'Else, this is Miss Pleydell. You have come to look after us, I know.'

'We have hot soup and cold venison. Will that do, Herr Doktor?'

'It sounds just what we need.'

'And the rooms? The Oak and the . . .?' She hesitated and looked from him to me. I felt myself flush at the implication. Was she to prepare one room or two?

He was aware of my embarrassment and seemed amused.

He said: 'The Oak Room . . . and the one next to it, please, Else. I think that would do very nicely. It is very good to be here. What an excellent idea of mine to remember this hunting lodge was so near. This is much more comfortable than some wayside inn.' He went on: 'Sit down. The food will be some little time, I dare say.'

'Half an hour, Herr Doktor,' said Else.

'Excellent. Perhaps in the meantime we could wash off the stains of the journey. Might we have some hot water?'

'I will get Frieda to bring it.'

'And Frieda is well?'

Else put her hands on her hips and looked sly.

'Expecting another,' said Dr Adair. 'How old is young Fritz? Not more than two, I know.'

'Frieda is pleased.'

'And all goes well?'

'All is well, Herr Doktor.'

'Come and sit by the fire,' he said to me.

'You seem to know them very well.'

'I do. I have stayed here several times. The Graf is a most hospitable man.'

He was watching me closely. 'I fancy,' he said, 'that you are a little uneasy. Let me guess. You are thinking that you are going to be alone with a man whose reputation you consider shady. Is that it?'

I said quickly: 'Should I be thinking that?'

'Perhaps.'

'You are not the same as you were when we set out,' I said. 'You were cool . . . aloof almost.'

'And now I am warmer and a little intimate. Is that it?'

'Tell me why you have brought me here.'

'To give you a night's shelter. It would not have been comfortable sleeping in the forest; and some of the inns hereabouts can be rather indifferent.'

'Did you know that we were coming here . . . I mean, when we set out?'

'I thought it a possibility. I had better make the situation clear. The servants will be in their cottage. We shall have the lodge to ourselves.' He was watching me closely. 'How do you feel about that?'

'I hardly think it is what the Head Deaconess expected.'

'Well, it is not her concern, is it? It is you and I who have to satisfy ourselves. How do *you* feel about it? There is no need to ask. You have a very expressive face. You always had. I remember well seeing the hatred and contempt in your eyes . . . on occasions. Here are the facts: you and I will be in this place tonight . . . alone. It is a very romantic spot. A hunting lodge in the heart of the forest. You think I am not to be trusted. I am some monster in whose company no respectable woman should be alone. Perhaps you are right. But let me set your mind at rest. If you wish it, I will tell Hans and the rest of them that we are not staying here after all. We will go on and find an inn, or if that goes beyond the bounds of propriety we will ride through the night back to Kaiserwald. There. The decision is yours.'

'How could we go now? They are preparing everything for us.'

'We could say we had made a change of plans. They are

good servants who never question the eccentric behaviour of those in command.'

Frieda appeared with two cans of hot water. He talked to her for a few moments about her children – the one she had and the one she was expecting. I thought how charming he could be at times.

Then we went up the staircase.

'The Oak Room is the best room,' he said, 'so I will leave that to you.'

It was certainly delightful, with the fire now crackling away and the leaping flames throwing shadows round the room. Candles had been lighted. There was a big fourposter bed and in an alcove was a ewer and basin.

I washed in the hot water and tidied my hair.

After a while there was a knock on my door. I called 'Come in' and he came in. He had discarded his jacket, which showed his white silk shirt and full bishop sleeves. It was open at the neck.

'Ah,' he said, 'you are ready. You must be hungry. I believe the food is waiting for us. We will eat downstairs. They are very unobtrusive. Quite the best servants to have.'

Downstairs in that hall with its high ceiling and trophies on the walls – guns and spears which had presumably been used throughout the ages – a table was laid, and on it stood a tureen of soup from which the steam was rising.

There was wine on the table.

Else was standing there. She ladled out the soup and served us. Then she poured out the wine.

'It is the Graf's . . . from his own vineyards,' said Dr Adair. 'He would never allow any but the best to be served to his guests. He says his grapes have a special quality.'

Else remarked that everything except the soup was cold. She had brought in the venison and bread; and there was apple pie to follow, and as that was cold she would leave us to our meal.

'Just leave when you have finished,' she said. 'I will clear all away . . . later . . . so as not to disturb.'

'How thoughtful of you. Good night, Else.'

I said goodnight, too.

I was beginning to feel slightly intoxicated by the turn of events. He had planned this. I knew it and I could not help myself but I was elated. I felt alive, as I had not done, I realized now, since I had last seen him. It was no use my pretending. I wanted to be with him. I did not want to be practical, as Eliza wished me to be. I wanted to live every moment and not concern myself with common sense and the future and what was best for me. This was what I wanted and no one could excite me as he did. Life had been dull and serene for too long. I wanted to live no matter what the consequences were.

He held the chair while I sat down; then he took his place opposite me. He lifted his glass. 'To us . . . and this night.'

I drank with him.

'Let us try the soup. I am sure it is excellent. Else is a very good cook. I have so much to say to you but first we should eat.'

'I am eager to hear what it is you have to say.'

He looked at me across the table. 'Candlelight is charming, do you not agree? How silent it is. Sometimes during the night one hears the sounds of the forest . . . the birds, the animals of the night. It can be fascinating.'

I scarcely tasted the soup. I was too excited to pay attention to food. I was asking myself what his intentions were . . . and in my heart, I knew.

He stood up and took my plate.

'You are playing the servant. What an unusual role for you.'

'This,' he replied, 'is an unusual night. The venison would come from the forest. I am sure you will enjoy it.'

'Thank you. Do you hunt when you are here?'

'I am not a hunter . . . of animals. It is not an occupation which appeals to me. You know something of my interests. They do not include hunting.'

'You hunt . . . for information. You search for knowledge.'

'Well, I am a doctor. I am very interested, as you know, in the methods used around the world. You could say that is my hunting-ground.'

'I know.'

'There is a good deal of prejudice in our profession. I am a man who does not like to run along on the lines laid down for me. It has brought me criticism . . . not only from the members of my profession.'

'You mean your unorthodox methods have not always been approved of.'

He nodded and filled my glass.

'The Graf will want to know if we appreciated his wine. He would be displeased if we did not do justice to it.'

'I do not care to drink a great deal.'

'Nor I. It dulls the senses. And that I should not want. Tonight I want to savour every moment.'

'What were you going to say to me?'

'Something which I think you know already. I have made a discovery.'

'Oh? What is that?'

He looked at me steadily. 'That my life is very dull without you.'

I stared at him.

'You are not really surprised,' he said. 'You knew.'

I shook my head. 'You have just shown me that hospital, and you have hinted that I might be in charge of it. I thought that the reason for your interest.'

'Certainly *that* is not my intention.'

'But you have behaved . . .'

'I was setting the stage. I wanted to bring you here . . . right into the heart of the forest where we could be alone . . . quite alone.'

I rose to my feet and he came to stand beside me. He put his arms about me.

'You must know how it is with us.'

Then he held me to him and kissed me . . . not once but many times. I felt dizzy with excitement. I thought: I don't care. Even if it is just for tonight, I want to be here. I want to stay with him . . . If there is no more . . . I must be with him tonight.

He released me and I heard him laugh quietly. It was a laugh of triumph.

'You see how it is,' he said.

I looked at him helplessly.

'We were meant for each other,' he went on. 'We always knew it. You fought against it. You were determined to hate me. You couldn't hate me so much . . . unless you loved me.'

I heard myself say: 'I don't know. I feel bewildered.'

'But in your heart you know. I love the red in your hair. It glows in candlelight, and your eyes are green . . . very green when you are happy. They are very green now.'

'Please,' I said. 'Shall we sit down?'

'And finish the meal? An excellent idea. There is the apple pie. We must not offend Else.'

I felt calmer. He was seated opposite, his eyes gleaming. They seemed dark and deep. I remembered how he had hypnotized William, and I felt I wanted to lose myself in those dark eyes. A voice within me was telling me to take care. He was a practised seducer. There would have been many occasions like this in his life. No doubt this was the way in which he always treated women with whom he wished to amuse himself for a little while. But I would not listen to that voice again. I had been lonely and sad too long.

I did not want to look beyond this night. I was surprised at myself. This was the enemy, the man whom I had sworn to destroy, and now here I was, his willing victim.

I think he knew what I was feeling; he knew that he had the power to overcome any resistance I felt I had to make.

He said: 'You were very prejudiced against me before you met me. I know why.'

For a moment I was startled. But he went on: 'You had read what I had written. I had stepped out of line, hadn't I? What could a well-brought-up young lady think of a man who had lived as an Arab in a tent, who had for some time become an Arab . . . an Indian . . . a Turk . . .'

'You must have had a most exciting time.'

'Life should be exciting, don't you think?'

'Alas, it is not so for everyone.'

'Then if it is not, people should find out *why* and make it so.'

'I can see you would be adept at that.'

'I think you might be, too. You have your secrets. Oh, don't look alarmed. I shall not attempt to prise them from you. You have made up your mind that life is not to be enjoyed. It is my task – my duty – to prove you are wrong.'

'And how will you do this?'

'By showing you how good it can be.'

'Do you think that is possible?'

He nodded, smiling at me. 'When I realized how much I wanted you in my life I did something about it.'

'I am not the simple creature you may believe me to be. I am not to be beguiled with protestations and sweet words.'

'Indeed you are not. And it is not words I think of, but deeds.'

He threw aside his napkin and stood up. He held out his hands, taking mine and drawing me up to stand beside him.

'My dear Nightingale,' he said, 'this is inevitable.'

I tried to speak but my heart was beating so fast that it was impossible. He held me against him and I just stayed there.

'It is early yet,' he said. 'There is a balcony at the window of the Oak Room. Let us go and look out at the forest.'

'And all this –' I indicated the table.

'They will creep in discreetly and remove it when we have retired. Isn't this the most romantic of spots? How different from that little room in the General at Scutari – do you remember? – where some of our little skirmishes took place?'

I said: 'I remember.'

He put an arm round me and we went upstairs to the Oak Room, where the burning logs threw a flickering light over the oak walls. He led me to the window and for a few moments we stood on the balcony looking out into the dark forest. The smell of the pines was intoxicating. A dark shape flew past the window and I heard an owl hoot.

'The bats are flying low tonight,' he said, and kissed me.

He went on: 'How I have wanted this . . . for a long time. I am so happy tonight.'

'I am so surprised, so . . .'

'Happy,' he said.

I was silent and he went on: 'Speak the truth, Nightingale. You are not going to turn away from me.'

'I am alone here,' I began.

'But you came of your own free will. Much as I need you, I would not have it otherwise. If you do not wish me to remain with you, you may send me away.'

I put up my hand and touched his face; and he took it and kissed it swiftly.

'I don't understand myself,' I said.

'I understand, my dearest. You have been lonely, struggling with grief, hating when you should have been loving, refusing to see how *good* life could be. And tonight, because I am with you here, because we are in the heart of the forest, because there is magic in the air, you will forget all the barriers which you set up for yourself. You are going to stop grieving and live.'

A lassitude had come over me. I did not want to resist. I wanted to open my arms to him. Tomorrow I would face my folly; but tonight it was irresistible. I let him lead me to the fourposter bed and we sat down side by side.

He kissed me and said: 'At last. Let us forget everything except that we are here together . . . that I mean to you what you mean to me, and when that happens to two people, there is only one outcome.'

I turned to him. He kissed my throat and my lips; and as he went on kissing me I felt myself slipping into such bliss as I had not thought possible.

The dawn was just beginning to appear. I had awakened and I lay there thinking of what had happened. I had never known such passion, nor such joy. I thought of Aubrey and those first days of our marriage. He had been a tender lover and our relationship had seemed idyllic then. Then there had come the awakening in Venice and the slow realization that it was not Aubrey I had cared for; it was being in love, being admired, adored . . . loving and taking pleasure.

This was not like that. This had been a tremendous adventure with a man to whom I was irrevocably drawn and yet who was a mystery to me.

I was completely fascinated. I could think of nothing but him. What I had felt for Aubrey was quite different. It was like comparing pale moonlight with the rays of the sun.

I felt again that glorious lassitude. I thought: I shall never forget this night. It will stay with me for the rest of my life. If he goes, I shall remember. I might have known there could never be anyone like him.

I had been a fool, perhaps. I had succumbed so willingly – hardly succumbed; my eagerness had matched his. I had discovered a new person in myself – a sensuous, demanding woman. I had never known that I could be like this. He had awakened me to myself.

My hands were lying limply by my side and suddenly I felt him take one of them.

'Awake, Nightingale?' he asked.

'Yes. It will soon be morning.'

'And then we shall go from here. You have no regrets . . . Susanna?'

'No,' I replied. 'None.' Then I was startled for I realized he had used my real name. He had called me Susanna and I had always been Nightingale or Miss Pleydell to him.

'Why did you call me that?' I asked.

'Why not? It is your name. Susanna St Clare, a charming name. Anna was never quite you. Susanna, that is different. You are a Susanna.'

'You knew that I . . .'

'The closely guarded Secret of the Nightingale,' he said. 'It was never a secret to me.'

'Why did you not say?'

'Was it for me to mention something which you were so determined to put behind you?'

'When did you discover?'

'Right from the beginning. I saw you in Venice.'

'Oh. I saw you, too. That night . . . you brought Aubrey home.'

'So you knew who brought him home. The wicked Dr

Damien who, you believed, had encouraged him in his folly.'

'Yes. I was sure of that.'

'I knew it.'

'And you said I was a flighty, frivolous wife and that it was unfortunate that he had married me, that I might have saved him.'

'Well, mightn't you have saved him?'

'How could I? It was horrible. That cave place . . .'

'Aubrey was absurd and melodramatic. When he heard about Francis Dashwood at Medmenham, he had to do the same. He was a boy, really.'

'You encouraged him in his drug-taking.'

'That's not true!' He was vehement in his denial. 'I was interested to see the effect of it. I had to, because I could see there was medicinal value in what was being taken recklessly and purely for sensationalism. I had to find out.'

'So you found out through these people. You let them take their drugs so that you might see the effect.'

'Not at all. I have tested them on myself. They took their own drugs.'

'You could have become an addict, too.'

'Not I. I knew what must be done.'

'You were there . . . in that cave.'

'Yes. It was an amazing revelation.'

'You were in India when it all started.'

'There was a little group there. I forget the people's names. A silly woman who found life boring and started this little club. I did spend time with them. I had to learn.'

'Why didn't *you* try to save Aubrey?'

'I *was* concerned about him, and I tried to do precisely that. His brother was a great friend of mine. I thought he might be turned away from the habit, but when he started that cave it was clearly hopeless, and when you left him, even more. He quickly went downhill then.'

I said shakily: 'And that night . . . when my baby died . . . you were there. You gave him one of your drugs. You experimented on him . . . and he died.'

'That is not true, either. I told you he was dead when I came to him. I was there, yes. I was in the cave. I was observing the dangerous antics of these people under the influence of the drugs they had taken. It taught me a good deal. We returned to the house. One of the girls was in hysterics about the child. The old nanny was drunk. I went up to find the child was already dead. He died of congestion of the lungs.'

'If you had been called earlier . . .'

'Who knows, perhaps . . .'

'If I had not been away . . .'

'Ah, if you had not been away.'

'You seem to draw certain conclusions. My father was dying. I had to go to him. My child was well when I left him.'

'I am sorry,' he said. 'I know how you have suffered.'

I felt the tears on my cheeks. I was living it all again . . . that terrible moment when I had gone into the house and found my baby dead.

He took a strand of my hair and wound it round his finger.

He said gently: 'All that is past. There is a future ahead of you. You have to forget. Susanna, my love, there is a new life for you. You have to stop grieving. You have to live again.' I did not answer and he went on: 'Susanna St Clare. It is such a pleasant name. There is a symmetry about it. But I think Susanna Adair would be better.'

I was silent as the significance of his words swept over me.

I said haltingly: 'Are you suggesting . . . that I marry you?'

'I know of no other way in which you could acquire my name. What do you think of it? It is pleasant, isn't it?'

I turned to him and he put his arms about me and held me close.

'You must say you agree with me,' he said, 'for, as I told you, I find my life dull without you. And one thing I cannot bear is dullness. Please marry me at once, Nightingale.'

'You are hasty.'

'Never. I have had this in mind for a long time.'

'You didn't give me any indication.'

'I had to knock down that wall of resistance.'

'You have certainly done that now.'

'Have I . . . completely? You still see me as something of an ogre, I believe.'

I laughed. 'If I do . . . I don't care.'

'That's what I like. You have taken me with all my sins upon me. And they are legion, I fear. Much of which you accused me is true, you know.'

'I know of the wild nomadic life, the conquests . . . the wanderings in paths not frequented by English gentlemen.'

'True, but it is due to these wanderings that I am able to recognize the worth of my true love.'

'You turn everything to advantage.'

'That is the way I live, Susanna. I am going to show you how it is done. Will you come with me to those wild far-flung corners of the world?'

'Yes,' I said.

'At a moment's notice? That is how it is with me.'

'If we marry . . .' I began.

'*When* we marry,' he corrected me.

'There could be children.'

'That is a possibility.'

'If ever I had another child, I should never leave that child to the care of nurses. Never. Whatever the temptation.'

'Well?'

'You would want to go off on your wanderings . . . your wild adventures. What then?'

'If there were a child,' he said, 'that would make a difference to us both. I have no doubt it would change me as well as you. But sometimes I may leave you, for a refreshing scene. I promise you my absence will be brief.'

'I cannot see you settling down, carrying on a professional life like –'

'Like a normal doctor. My dear Susanna, I am a man of many parts. When the time is ripe for me to leave my adventuring life I shall settle down with my family. I shall find means of adding to my knowledge of medicine and of life. I think I shall be an ideal father.'

I closed my eyes. I thought: Absolute happiness is early

morning in a hunting lodge in the heart of a forest with the man I love beside me.

The forest was beautiful in the early morning.

We had risen with the dawn and were on our way. Everything seemed perfect: the early morning sun glinting through the trees; the awakening of the birds; the gentle breeze ruffling the fir trees; and that unforgettable smell permeating the air.

I had not known there could be such contentment.

He said: 'We must leave within the next few days. When we arrive in England we will marry as soon as possible. I see no reason for delay, do you?'

'No,' I said.

He smiled at me. I was in a mood of exaltation. I had never felt thus in the whole of my life. For so long I had carried my grief round with me and had tried to soothe it with thoughts of revenge; but how much sweeter were the thoughts of love.

Life is going to be wonderful, I thought. Nothing will be commonplace with him. I shall follow him in his adventures and if I have a child . . . life will be wonderfully complete. I shall never forget Julian, of course. Could any mother forget a child she had borne? But I shall see Julian in my child and this child would be Damien's. I should be contented for evermore. I thanked God for bringing me out of my wretchedness to this perfect happiness; and I fell to thinking that the present could not be so wonderful if I had not suffered in the past.

In this mood I came to Kaiserwald.

We were greeted by the Head Deaconess. I could see she had some misgivings because of our night's absence.

'We were so enthralled by Rosenwald,' Damien told her, 'that we delayed leaving. After all, there was no point in our going if we were not going to see it all. However, we stayed the night at Graf von Spiegal's hunting lodge.'

She looked relieved. 'And how is the Herr Graf?'

'Oh, very well.'

That satisfied her. He looked at me mischievously.

It was not so easy with Eliza. I could see she was shaken.

I thought it would be better to tell her immediately. I said: 'I am going to marry Dr Adair.'

'Oh! That's a sudden decision.'

I nodded.

'You look different,' she said.

'I feel different.'

That was all. She changed the subject and asked about Rosenwald, but I saw her lips pressed together in disapproval. I talked enthusiastically of the possibilities of the place. 'At the moment they have untrained nurses. It would be a great challenge to someone who wanted to make a Kaiserwald of it.'

'I thought you were going to do that.'

'I thought so at first. I thought he was showing me the place for that purpose.'

'But he had another purpose. You haven't thought much about this, have you?'

'I . . . I didn't have to think, Eliza. I knew. It is like that sometimes.'

'I reckon you're making a mistake. If you marry him you'll sup sorry with a long spoon, as they say.'

'I think I'll sup a lot of joy with an even longer spoon,' I said.

'You're pretty far gone, ain't you?'

'Yes, Eliza. I am very far gone.'

'He's that sort of man. He only has to lift his finger and beckon. That's enough. You follow.'

'My dear Eliza, there are many things we cannot know about each other. This is right for me. This is what I want more than anything. I am happy as I never thought to be. I can put my sadness behind me. He makes me feel alive . . .'

'For how long?'

'For the rest of our lives, Eliza. I am going to see that that is so.'

She sighed. 'Tell me more about this Rosenwald,' she said.

I would not allow Eliza's implications of doom to depress me. I gave myself up to happiness. He had told the Head Deaconess that we should be leaving within the next few days, and that we were going to be married.

Her first thoughts were for Rosenwald. 'I had thought that perhaps Miss Pleydell . . . It would have been a challenge for her.'

'Indeed yes,' he said with a smile, 'but she is taking up an even greater challenge.'

Eliza came with me when I took the riding habit back to Fräulein Kleber. As soon as we approached the house we heard sounds of shooting. She was still practising. I went round to the back of the barn. Several people were there.

'Oh, here you are, Fräulein Pleydell,' she said. 'And you've brought the habit back. Was it comfortable?'

'It was excellent. How can I thank you for being so kind?'

'By wishing me luck in the *Schützenfest*.'

'Oh, I do, most heartily.'

'These are people from the neighbourhood. They'll all be there for the *Fest*. I am lending them guns.'

'You seem to be the benefactress round here, lending people your possessions.'

'It is foolish in the case of the guns because these people will be my rivals.'

'I am sure you will excel them all.'

'If I don't it won't be for want of practice. You'd be surprised at the number of them who come to me, to practise. Well, I have my father's guns and they might as well be put to some use. Come into the house and have a glass of wine.'

I thanked her and said I would not interrupt the practice; and in any case we had to get back to Kaiserwald. We were leaving in two days' time.

'Well, I'm glad to have been of use.'

'Thank you so much, and may you hit the target every time.'

'What a friendly woman,' I said as we left; and Eliza agreed.

In my thoughts I had called him Dr Damien the Demon Doctor. I told him that and he said: 'Now I shall be Damien, the perfect husband.'

'We have to wait and see whether you earn that title. Now I shall just call you Damien.'

'I like the way you say it. You make it sound godlike.'

He complained that we could not be alone in the hospital. There was always someone to interrupt.

'That friend of yours, Big Eliza, clings like a leech. She breathes fire on me every time she sees me.'

'You are mixing similes and metaphors. Dragons breathe fire, not leeches.'

'She's a very capable woman. She can make the transition from leech to dragon at the batting of an eyelid. Let's go for a walk in the forest. There we can make plans. Do you realize there is a lot to be settled yet?'

'Yes, I do.'

'We'll go separately, otherwise we shall have Eliza trailing us. I'll meet you in the clearing . . . say ten minutes.'

I agreed.

I shall never forget that afternoon. I had known disaster before but never anything so sudden. I had never before been plunged from the heights of ecstasy to the depths of despair.

I left the hospital, light-hearted, engulfed in happiness. It had never occurred to me that anything could change so quickly.

I came to the clearing. He was already there. He saw me and as he started to hurry towards me, the shot rang out. I heard the loud report. I saw him, standing there for half a second, and then he slowly fell to the ground.

I dashed to him. There was blood everywhere. He was lying on the grass. I stared at him in horror. I heard myself murmur: 'Damien . . . dead.'

I knelt beside him. 'Damien,' I whispered. His eyes were closed and there was a terrible stillness about him.

I knew that I must take immediate action. I thought the bullet had entered his back. What we needed was a doctor . . . without delay.

I ran with all the speed I could muster, back to the hospital.

*

I was thankful for Dr Kratz and Dr Bruckner. They acted speedily and efficiently. A stretcher was brought out and Damien was carried to the hospital. It was a blessing that medical help was so near.

They were with him for a long time and I knew that he was seriously hurt.

I prayed: 'Oh God, don't let him die . . . not now . . . when we have just found each other. I could not bear that. I will do anything – anything – but don't let him die.'

It was the incoherent prayer of a frightened woman flung from the pinnacle of happiness to the very nadir of despair.

I waited for the doctors to emerge. They had a certain respect for me and I knew they would tell me the truth.

'We have extracted the bullet,' they told me.

'He will recover?'

They were silent.

'Tell me. Tell me,' I cried.

'We do not know. It was his spine. It's early days yet.'

'I shall nurse him,' I said.

'Yes . . . yes.'

'May I go to him?'

'He is not conscious.'

'Just to sit by him.'

They looked at each other and nodded.

So I went in and sat there. How different he looked! He was so pale; his deepset eyes were closed and his chiselled features looked more prominent. I had always seen him so vital . . . so much more alive than anyone I had known and now he looked . . . dead.

The Head Deaconess came in. She laid a hand on my shoulder. She said: 'It is better to leave him. He needs rest, and you need care, my child.' I turned to her with the misery in my eyes and she said: 'We must pray that he will recover. He is a very strong man. He would always get his way and he very much wants to live now that you and he have made plans together.'

I let her lead me from the room. She took me to mine and made me lie on my bed.

Eliza came in.

She said to her: 'Look after Miss Pleydell. She needs you.'

Eliza nodded.

How long the days seemed! How long the nights! I lay sleepless.

Eliza did not sleep either.

'Perhaps it was all for the best,' she said.

'Eliza,' I said, 'if he dies I shall never be happy again. I have been so wretched, so immersed in my tragedy, I have brooded on the cruelty of life and I can now see that I magnified my troubles. I've grown away from that. He showed me how foolish I was. With him I could have become my true self again. If he does not recover, I have lost that chance. When he asked me to marry him I knew complete happiness. I want to be with him all the time. Do you understand that, Eliza?'

'I think I begin to.'

'He *must* get well. You and I will nurse him back to health. You will help me, Eliza?'

'Yes,' she said. 'I will help you.'

'Oh, thank you.'

'I thought you would have been happy in that house with Dr Fenwick,' she said, 'but I see now that this is the one you want . . . no matter what he is.'

'I'm glad you see that now, Eliza.'

In the morning I had an interview with the doctors. The news was heartening.

'We think there is a good chance of his recovery.'

I was overwhelmed with joy. Then I saw the glances pass between them.

'What is it?' I asked fearfully.

'We don't know how it will be with him . . . if he recovers.'

'I see.'

'Yes, Miss Pleydell. There is only one thing we can do and that is wait and see.'

★

My concern for him had made me pay little attention to the mystery which occupied everyone's mind.

Who had fired the shot which had obviously been intended to kill him? He had been there in the clearing alone, exposed to view. Someone must have taken a shot at him from the shelter of the trees.

There had been a great deal of activity in the neighbourhood recently because of the *Schützenfest* which was shortly to be held and the sound of shots could be continually heard. People were shooting everywhere. Could it have been a stray bullet which had hit Dr Adair, maybe from some young man or woman who was not accustomed to using a gun?

The bullet was examined. It was common enough and there was little to be learned from it. Who would have wanted to kill Dr Adair? He was not an inhabitant of the place. He was not even a resident doctor – only a visiting one.

Fräulein Kleber's practice range had not been far off. Could it really have been that someone who had been trying to hit that had missed so widely?

It seemed the most likely explanation.

Enquiries continued but no one came forward with a solution to the mystery. Investigations found nothing suggesting that anyone had tried to murder Dr Adair.

A week passed – a week when my hopes had risen only to be dashed and to rise again. He was still alive. Dr Kratz said he clung to life with a tenacity which was amazing. He was aware of me and I knew he drew great comfort from my presence. When I was not with him, Eliza took over. I was amazed at the care with which she did this. She was fiercely protective of him; she, who had hated him so intensely, was determined that he should recover.

At first we had feared that he would be paralysed. I tried to visualize what his life would be – he, the most active of men, to be confined to his bed. I vowed that I would look after him and dedicate my whole life to him.

But his fierce determination had its effect. Within a week he could move his legs; and within three he was walking with the aid of a stick.

Meanwhile enquiries were proceeding. No one admitted to having fired that shot. But was it possible that someone could have done it without being aware of it?

I took brief walks in the forest – Eliza and the Head Deaconess insisted that I should for my health's sake. I wanted to spend every minute at his bedside; but I did realize the wisdom of what they said.

My walks invariably took me to the clearing; and one day my thoughts turned to Gerda and what had happened to her. She said she had met a devil in the woods; she had been seduced and nearly lost her life when she had taken the potion to get rid of her child.

I remembered talking to her grandmother. I had not seen Frau Leiben since I had returned to Kaiserwald. The door of her cottage had always been shut. I began to wonder then. I had thought Damien might have been that devil in the woods. Was that possible? Just suppose it was? Just suppose Frau Leiben knew? Suppose she had fired that shot . . . for revenge?

No. The man I knew would never have taken advantage of a simple girl. But would he? I was not sure. The miracle was that if I were it would make no difference.

The idea haunted me and each day when I took my walk I went to the clearing.

I thought of Frau Leiben, devoted to the granddaughter who was not like other girls . . . the simple girl dreaming as she walked with her geese.

How Frau Leiben would have hated the one who had betrayed her granddaughter! I could well imagine her vowing revenge. Had I not sworn revenge on the man I believed had cost my child his life? Yes, I could understand Frau Leiben's emotions.

The cottage was actually in the clearing. She could have shot him from one of her windows. It would have been easy for her.

One day when I was passing, the door was open. I went over and called: 'Frau Leiben.'

She came to the door. She stared at me for a moment, then

recognition dawned. 'Why . . . if it isn't Fräulein Pleydell. So you are back with us, then.'

'I have been here for only a short while. I haven't seen you before.'

'I've been away. I'm only just back. I've been visiting. There's been an accident here . . . while I've been away.'

'Yes. Dr Adair was shot.'

'Who shot him?'

'It's a mystery.' I looked at her steadily. 'Someone had a gun and . . .'

'There's always shooting going on at this time of year. But we've never had accidents before.'

'It seems rather far-fetched to imagine a stray bullet could do that.'

She showed admirable self-control if she were guilty. She said: 'I couldn't believe it when I heard.'

'How long have you been away, Frau Leiben?'

'A month . . . perhaps a little more. I'm only just back.'

I pictured her returning to the cottage. Did she keep a gun in the house? Most of them did. They shot the pigeons which they ate. There were foxes who raided the fowl houses and it was necessary to shoot them. She could have looked from her window and seen him. I could imagine her in an access of fury taking her gun and shooting him. It could so easily have been done. Then she could have lain low. Who would know when she had come back? She had a perfect alibi.

'It's a shocking thing,' she was saying. 'And Dr Adair. I heard that he was recovering.'

'Yes,' I said. 'He is.'

'Did he have any idea who . . .?'

I shook my head.

'Come in for a moment, will you?'

I entered the cottage. The first thing I noticed was the crib with the baby in it.

'I brought him back with me.' Frau Leiben's face was creased in tenderness. 'Isn't he a little angel?'

I went over and looked at the child. 'Whose baby is he?'

'Gerda's.'

'Gerda! Where is Gerda?'

'She's travelling round with her husband. They don't settle long, though. They've got a nice little cottage about forty kilometres from here. That's where I've been. They're not there much. It's the wandering life for them.'

'So . . . she married.'

'Oh yes. I never thought it would happen.'

'Her husband . . .?'

'You might remember him. He's Klaus, the Pedlar. He was always fond of Gerda and she of him. He was always one to go his own way and always will be. Gerda suits him. She asks no questions. Neither of them is like other people. She seems more sensible with him and he seems softer . . . more gentle. He looks after her. He's bright. He'll do well. He *is* doing well. Gerda's happy. She's with him all the time . . . travelling the roads. Gerda's contented. She has someone to care for her. I did my best. You see, her parents went off. They didn't want her. That can do something to a child. She couldn't make any headway with her lessons like the other children did. She was always dreaming. And then there was that time . . . Dear me, just to think of it frightens me. There she was to have a child . . . my little Gerda.'

'Does Klaus know about that?'

'He knows a good deal about it. He was the one. It was his child. He never denied that.'

Floods of relief swept over me. I had been so sure that I should find the solution here . . . but I had dreaded doing so.

I said: 'But she talked about meeting the Devil in the forest, I remember. We thought it was someone she did not know.'

'It wasn't like that. She knew she shouldn't have done what she did. I was always warning her. I expect I didn't do it properly. I told her it was sinful and that the Devil tempted girls. She thought it was the Devil in Klaus tempting her. You can't imagine how muddled Gerda gets. She could never work anything out for herself. In her mind it was the Devil coming to her through Klaus, you see. That was what was on her mind.'

'I see. But she tried to get rid of the child.'

'That was Klaus again. He hadn't thought of settling down with a wife then . . . and what could he do with a child? He had given her the stuff to take within the first two months . . . if she should be with child. Poor Gerda, as if she could work that out! Well, she left it too late and it would have done for her . . . but for you good people at Kaiserwald. Klaus said the stuff he gave her would have been quite all right if she hadn't left it so late. He'd sold it to many girls who had used it with the required result.'

The baby started to cry.

'Excuse me,' she said. She picked him up and brought him to show me.

'A bright little fellow . . . takes after Klaus. That's who he is. Little Klaus.'

'You are happy to have him with you.'

She smiled. 'It seems like old times when Gerda was left to me. I feel young again . . . with something to live for. This one's a bright little fellow . . . as sharp as a monkey. Not like my poor Gerda. Even when she was his age we could see she was not as other children. He's different. He's his father all over again.'

'I am so glad everything worked out well for Gerda and that she is happy.'

'Yes, she's happy. Never seen her so happy. She loves the travelling life and Klaus is there to look after her. They'll be here sometimes . . . on their rounds. How long will you be with us this time?'

'I am not sure.'

'Well, I hope you'll be with us some time yet. I'll never forget what you good people at Kaiserwald did for Gerda.'

I told her I must go; and thoughtfully I walked back through the forest.

I reproached myself. I had blamed him for Gerda. How could I? I had deliberately built up the case against him to soothe my wounds. I had used hatred as the soothing balm.

How could I ever make up to him for what I had done?

★

Each day his condition improved. He could now take short walks up and down to the lake. We would sit there and talk of the future.

I was very happy.

He said one day: 'It might well have been that I was unable to walk.'

'I know. I planned to spend my life looking after you.'

'That would have been no life for a strong young woman.'

'It was what I chose.'

'I believe you would have married me. You would have been my nurse.'

'I should have been that . . . happily.'

'You would have tired of it . . . in time.'

I shook my head vehemently.

'I intended to go to Egypt as soon as we were married. A fascinating country. You would have enjoyed it.'

'We are going to my house in London and we shall stay there until you are fit to travel.'

'And who will decide that?'

'I shall.'

'I see I am marrying a very forceful woman.'

'It is as well that you recognize it.'

'Over the last few days I have been thinking that I am the most fortunate of men. I get a bullet which might have injured my spine permanently, but by some stroke of good fortune it just missed a vital spot. That in itself is something of a miracle. And in addition to that I have my Susanna to minister to me, to cherish and protect me for the rest of my life.'

'And I am the most fortunate of women because I have found the only one whom I would want to be my companion for the rest of my life – and the miracle is that in spite of his various adventures he should want me.'

'It is indeed a wonderful realization. We are not two young people setting out starry-eyed on the adventure of life. We know the pitfalls, don't we? I have lived, as you know, precariously, in odd places. I have done many things which would not be acceptable in polite society. In other words, I have lived a full life. And you, my dearest, have learned what suffering

409

is. Let us be grateful for what we have learned because that is going to enrich our lives. In the first place it has made us grateful for Now.'

'You are right, of course.'

I confessed to him that I had suspected him of being Gerda's seducer. He had been unware of Gerda's existence.

He laughed.

'It is a great advantage not to have to live up to an ideal. All I have to do is show you that I am not as bad as you thought me to be.'

And so my happiness returned. He was recovering fast. Soon he would be well.

He was eager to get home, but I said we should wait for another week so that he might be really strong. We should return to my home which I intended to keep on. It would be our pied-à-terre in London – the house to which we would return after our travels.

'Jane and Polly are there,' I told him, 'and there is old Joe, the coachman. It is their home. They are part of the family, as it were. They must always be there.'

He thought it was an excellent idea. And as soon as we arrived home we should be married.

One day when we sat by the lake Eliza came and joined us.

She said: 'There is something I have to tell you. I don't know what you'll do. I've been wondering whether to say nothing . . . but somehow I have to tell you. I can't go on like this. Sometimes I've thought of drowning myself in that there lake.'

'Eliza, what are you talking about?'

'I was the one. I did it. I don't know what they do to you here. At home it would be murder . . . attempted murder or something like that. Do they hang you?'

'Oh Eliza,' I said. 'So . . . it was you.'

She nodded.

'It came to me all of a sudden. I heard him say he would meet you there. Something came over me. It wasn't oniy him

. . . It was my stepfather and some of the men I'd had to work for. It was all the lot of them. It was *men*. I just wanted to avenge myself and all women . . . But most of all, there was you. I'd always told myself I'd never care for anyone, not really care . . . so that they was more important to me than myself. And I thought of you and all you'd done for Lily and for me, and what a great day it was when we got to know you. I've often thought of that night in the storm. And I wanted you to have all that was good . . . all that was right . . . all you ought to have. And there was that Dr Fenwick and I thought of you there in that lovely place with all the little children you'd have. And there was him . . . stopping it all.'

'So you took a pot shot at me,' said Damien with a smile. 'Not a bad shot, really. Though it didn't quite find the bull's eye.'

'Thank God I didn't. I can see now what a mess I'd made . . . trying to take things into my own hands. I might have killed you. I'd have had that on my mind for the rest of my life . . . and I see now I wouldn't have done anything for her.'

'Was it the first time you'd handled a gun?' asked Damien curiously.

She nodded. 'But I'd watched them. I knew how it was done. The barn door was open. They'd forgotten to lock it . . . Fräulen Kleber's barn, you know. There were all those guns in there. I just took one. It was loaded. I saw to that. And then I went out and waited among the trees. And when you came, I shot you. Then I put the gun back and got away. Once or twice I've thought of going back to that barn and getting a gun and shooting myself. Because I saw what I'd done. I see now you can't tell people what they ought to do. Anna wasn't going to marry Dr Fenwick no matter what. I thought I knew better than she did . . . and it was all for her. Then when she thought you was dead, and I saw in her face what you meant to her, I just wanted to die. I knew I'd done wrong . . . a terrible wrong . . . because whatever you are, you're what she wants and she would never get over it if you was a goner. I just wanted to get out of the world. I didn't think there was no place for me in it . . . after what I'd done.'

'Oh, Eliza,' I said, 'you did all that for me.'

'Yes. It was for you. It seems I get funny about people. I was about Ethel. I just had to look after her because she couldn't look after herself. Nor, I thought, could you. I had told Ethel she could earn more money my way . . . and look what happened. She got that baby and it died. Poor Ethel, she was well nigh frantic. I just had to look after her because she didn't know nothing about life and the wickedness of men. Then she found that Tom. He seemed all right and she's happy now. And then there was you. I took to you that night in the storm. I could see there was something special about you. You made me feel different about things . . . about people. Then there was that Dr Fenwick and he was a rare good man. But you had set your eyes on *him* . . .'

'And so,' said Damien, 'you decided to remove me and make the way clear.'

'I thought she'd come to see it in time. She'd see which side her bread was buttered. Once you'd gone, she'd get over it . . .'

'It is all very logical,' he said.

'Now I've told you. It's a load off my mind. What are you going to do about it? You'll give me up, I reckon. He will . . . anyway. I'm finished. Well, it wasn't much of a life. Funny . . . the best part was that awful hospital in Scutari, working with Ethel and you, and seeing Dr Fenwick and feeling there was some good in the world after all.'

'Oh, Eliza,' I said, and I went to her and put my arms round her.

'Well, that's me,' she said. 'I'm a murderess, ain't I? Or as good as makes no difference. I tried and I failed, but I might have done it.'

'I understand, Eliza. I know how you suffered. Your stepfather . . . and all those men . . . the humiliation, the degradation. I understand it all. And the doctor is well. He is recovering fast . . . Oh, Eliza, I'll do everything I can to help.'

'I know . . . I know . . . even though if I had done it would have been all over for you. But it ain't for you to say, is it? It's him. He's the one I tried to kill.'

Damien was watching her intently. 'Why didn't you finish me off when you were looking after me? That wouldn't have been so difficult, would it?'

'But I knew then . . . Perhaps I knew as soon as I'd fired that shot. And when I saw her . . . later on . . . and all that misery in her face . . . I just wanted to go away and die. I would have done anything to go back to that morning and not have taken that gun, and just let things go on the way they was drifting. Then I did everything I could to put things right. I was going to do all I could to nurse you back to health.'

'You did nurse me very well. You're a really good nurse . . . one of the best. But it wasn't very logical. To take that shot and then nurse me as you did.'

'I told you . . . I'd seen then . . . the way it was with her . . .'

'You did all that for her,' he said. 'It was a great deal. I've just made a decision as to what I'll do about this.'

We looked at him fearfully. He smiled from one to the other of us tantalizingly.

'I'm going to suggest that Eliza goes to Rosenwald.'

'To Rosenwald . . . what for?' I stammered.

'To run the place, of course. She's a strong-minded woman . . . not afraid to take firm action when she thinks fit. Just the person we are looking for. There, Eliza, you can expiate your sin; and when you have saved your first life you can say: "Now I have wiped out the deed."'

'You mean . . . you are not going to give me up . . . prosecute or whatever they call it?'

'No. I think this is a better plan.'

'How would you trust me? I was ready to kill you. How do you know I won't do something like that again?'

'Once is enough for that sort of thing. You'd never try that again.'

'And you would put me in charge of . . . people?'

'It was my life you were going to take . . . in your opinion it was worthless . . . a menace to someone you cared for. It was logical thinking and I am a great upholder of logic.'

'But it was wicked of me to do what I did . . .'

'Indeed yes. But your motives were not for personal gain. You took such action for someone else. That shows a great capacity for affection. You care very deeply for someone I care for. That shows we have a great deal in common. Your assessment of my character is not entirely at fault. I am a most unworthy person. You have great potential for running a hospital. How fortunate you are that your bullet landed where it did. If you had killed me I should not have been able to offer you Rosenwald.'

'You are treating this . . . flippantly,' I said.

'Not at all. Eliza gave vent to her feelings. She will never attempt to kill again because she knows now that she cannot condemn completely and no one ever can, because all the circumstances must be known before judgement is passed. She knows now that no one is entirely wicked . . . even I; no one entirely a saint – not even the good Dr Fenwick. Eliza is wiser than she was. She knows that we all have to go our own way in life and it is not for any of us to arrange that way for others. She will do good at Rosenwald. What a waste of time useless trivia and accusations would be! It is a matter between ourselves. I killed a man once. He came to my tent with a knife. I strangled him and buried his body in the sand. It was either him or me. It bothered me for some time; and when I saved a patient's life I felt the score was even. That is how it will be with Eliza.' He turned to her with a smile. 'I think you should go down and have a look at Rosenwald soon.'

I could see that Eliza was overcome with emotion. She looked as though a great weight had been taken from her shoulders.

She stood up and said: 'I don't know what to say except I'm glad you know. I didn't think it would be like this. It's been a dead weight on me ever since it happened. I didn't think I could take any more.' She looked at the lake. 'It seemed peaceful,' she went on. 'I thought one night when it was quiet . . .'

'Oh, Eliza, I'm glad you told us instead.'

'And him . . .' she said. 'To offer me this way out . . . well,

I dunno . . . I really dunno how anyone could be like that about someone who'd tried to murder 'em.'

'Well,' said Damien, 'it is easier for a sinner to understand people's little foibles than it is for a saint. And when you understand, you forgive. You've got strength, Eliza. You've got courage to do what you think is right. You're capable of loving . . . wholeheartedly, and believe me, that's not a very common attribute. You know how to put a loved one's interests before your own. I admire that. You'll have Rosenwald outstripping Kaiserwald in no time.'

She looked at me and her smile expressed relief and above all hope. She was looking into a future which she had believed was lost to her forever.

She nodded towards Damien. 'I never knew anyone like him,' she said.

'No,' I replied. 'Nor did I.'

Fontana Paperbacks: Fiction

Fontana is a leading paperback publisher of both non-fiction, popular and academic, and fiction. Below are some recent fiction titles.

- ☐ THE ROSE STONE Teresa Crane £2.95
- ☐ THE DANCING MEN Duncan Kyle £2.50
- ☐ AN EXCESS OF LOVE Cathy Cash Spellman £3.50
- ☐ THE ANVIL CHORUS Shane Stevens £2.95
- ☐ A SONG TWICE OVER Brenda Jagger £3.50
- ☐ SHELL GAME Douglas Terman £2.95
- ☐ FAMILY TRUTHS Syrell Leahy £2.95
- ☐ ROUGH JUSTICE Jerry Oster £2.50
- ☐ ANOTHER DOOR OPENS Lee Mackenzie £2.25
- ☐ THE MONEY STONES Ian St James £2.95
- ☐ THE BAD AND THE BEAUTIFUL Vera Cowie £2.95
- ☐ RAMAGE'S CHALLENGE Dudley Pope £2.95
- ☐ THE ROAD TO UNDERFALL Mike Jefferies £2.95

You can buy Fontana paperbacks at your local bookshop or newsagent. Or you can order them from Fontana Paperbacks, Cash Sales Department, Box 29, Douglas, Isle of Man. Please send a cheque, postal or money order (not currency) worth the purchase price plus 22p per book for postage (maximum postage required is £3.00 for orders within the UK).

NAME (Block letters) _____

ADDRESS _____

_____

_____

While every effort is made to keep prices low, it is sometimes necessary to increase them at short notice. Fontana Paperbacks reserve the right to show new retail prices on covers which may differ from those previously advertised in the text or elsewhere.